TARAN MATHARU

SUMMNER

— THE NOVICE —

h

Hodder
Children's
Books

To my mother, for always being there for me

To Alice, the rock against which this story was written

And to my Wattpad readers, without whom
none of this would be possible

HODDER CHILDREN'S BOOKS

First published in Great Britain in hardback in 2015
First published in Great Britain in paperback in 2016
This edition published in 2020

1

A CIP catalogue record for this book is available from the British Library.

ISBN: 978 1 444 95825 6

Typeset in Garamond by Avon DataSet Ltd, Bidford-on-Avon, Warwickshire

Printed and bound by Clays Ltd, Elcograf S.p.A.

The paper and board used in this book are made from wood from responsible sources.

Hodder Children's Books
An imprint of Hachette Children's Group
Part of Hodder and Stoughton
Carmelite House
50 Victoria Embankment
London EC4Y 0DZ

An Hachette UK Company

www.hachette.co.uk

SUMM✪NER

'Brilliant and colourful … This superb story, with strong characters and a narrative which both flows with its sweeping backdrop and draws brilliant details, now deserves all the success that will come its way'
The School Librarian

'A dramatic escapade of adventure, magic and brutal mayhem … A great solid Young Adult fantasy'
Mr Ripleys Enchanted Books

'This book doesn't just survive the hype; it deserves it'
The Bookbag

'Matharu's tale grabbed me from page one with its Middle Earth Harry Potter vibe. Toss in magical creatures from the cute to the downright ugly, add a few Elves, Dwarfs, Demons and Humans, and you have the makings of a cool fantasy'
Caffeinated Book Reviewer

Also by Taran Matharu

SUMMONER
The Novice
The Inquisition
The Battlemage
The Outcast

The Summoner's Handbook

CONTENDER
The Chosen

The Novice: Character List

Fletcher Wulf – orphan and summoner, student at Vocans Academy

Pelt Villagers

Didric Cavell – guardsperson
Jakov – guardsperson
Berdon Wulf – blacksmith, Fletcher's mentor and father figure
Janet – trader and leatherworker
Caspar Cavell – moneylender, Didric's father
Calista – guardsperson

Others

The Pinkertons – lawmakers from the city
Rotherham 'Rotter' – soldier, Fletcher's friend
James Baker – battlemage, owner of the summoner book
Grindle – servant to the Forsyths

The Nobles

Old King Alfric – former king of Hominum, founder of the Inquisition, leader of the Pinkertons, overseer of Judges
King Harold – King of the Hominum Empire
Lord Edmund Raleigh – former noble of the Southern frontiers, master of Sir Caulder
Lord Henry Faversham – noble, owner of the Beartooth lands
Lady Ophelia Faversham – the old King's cousin (King Alfric), Lord Faversham's wife
Lord Zacharias Forsyth – noble

The Dwarves

Athol – dwarf, Uhtred the blacksmith's apprentice

Thaissa Thorsager – Othello's sister
Atilla Thorsager – Othello's twin brother
Briss Thorsager – Othello's mother
Uhtred Thorsager – Othello's father
Hakon – dwarf
Ulfr – dwarf

Vocans Academy

Mayweather – cook
Jeffrey – servant

Students

Rory Cooper – first year, student, commoner
Genevieve Leatherby – first year, student, commoner
Sylva Arkenia – first year, student (elf)
Seraph – first year, student, commoner
Atlas – first year, student, commoner
Othello Thorsager – first year, student (dwarf)
Tarquin Forsyth – first year, noble and brother of Isadora
Isadora Forsyth – first year, noble and sister of Tarquin
Malik Saladin – first year, noble
Penelope Colt – first year, noble
Rufus Cavendish – first year, noble
Amber – second year, noble

Teachers

Provost Scipio – teacher, battlemage, noble
Major Goodwin – demonology teacher, noble
Captain Arcturus – officer, battlemage, spellcraft teacher, commoner

Captain Elaine Lovett – summoning teacher, noble
Inquisitor Damian Rook – summoning teacher, Lovett's substitute, noble
Sir Caulder – weapons master, commoner, non-summoner

Demons

Ignatius – Fletcher's demon (Salamander)
Sacharissa – Arcturus's demon (Canid)
Sariel – Sylva's demon (Canid)
Malachi – Rory's demon (Mite)
Azura – Genevieve's demon (Mite)
Solomon – Othello's demon (Golem)
Silver – Seraph's demon (Barkling)
Barbarous – Atlas's demon (Lutra)
Trebius – Tarquin's demon (Hydra)
Tamil – Isadora's demon (Felid)
Eve – Penelope's demon (Vulpid)
Anoup – Malik's demon (Anubid)
Vuko – Major Goodwin's demon (Lycan)
Ransom – Rufus's demon (Lutra)
Valens – Captain Lovett's demon (Mite)
Lysander – Captain Lovett's demon (Griffin)
Caliban – Rook's demon (Minotaur)
Anzu – Amber's demon (Shrike)

1

It was now or never. If Fletcher didn't make this kill, he would go hungry tonight. Dusk was fast approaching and he was already running late. He needed to make his way back to the village soon, or the gates would close. If that happened, he would either have to bribe the guards with money he didn't have or take his chances in the woods overnight.

The young elk had just finished rubbing its antlers against a tall pine, scraping the soft velvet that coated them to leave the sharp tines beneath. From its small size and stature, Fletcher could tell it was a juvenile, sporting its first set of antlers. It was a fine specimen, with glossy fur and bright, intelligent eyes.

Fletcher felt almost ashamed to hunt such a majestic creature, yet he was already adding up its value in his head. The thick coat would do well when the fur traders came by, especially as it was now winter. It would probably make at least five shillings. The antlers were in good condition, if a little small, they might fetch four shillings if he was lucky. It was the meat he craved the most, gamy red venison that would drip sizzling fat into his cooking fire.

A thick mist hung heavy in the air, coating Fletcher in a thin layer of dew. The forest was unusually still. Normally the wind rattled the branches, allowing him to stalk through the undergrowth unheard. Now he barely allowed himself to breathe.

He unslung his bow and nocked an arrow to it. It was his best arrow, the shaft straight and true, the fletching from good goose feathers rather than the cheap turkey feathers he bought in the market. He took a shallow breath and drew back on the bowstring. It was slippery on his fingers; he had coated it in goose-fat to protect it from the moisture in the air.

The point swam in and out of focus as he centred it on the elk. Fletcher was crouched a good hundred feet away, hidden in the tall grass. A difficult shot, but the lack of wind brought its own rewards. No gust to jar the arrow in its flight.

He breathed and shot in one fluid motion, embracing the moment of stillness in body and mind that he had learned from bitter and hungry experience. He heard the dull thrum of the bowstring jarring and then a thud as the arrow hit home.

It was a beautiful shot, taking the elk through the chest, into the lungs and heart. The animal collapsed and convulsed, thrashing on the ground, its hooves drumming a tattoo on the earth in its death throes.

He sprinted towards his prey and drew a skinning knife from the slim scabbard at his thigh, but the stag was dead before he got to it. A good clean kill, that's what Berdon would have said. But killing was always messy. The bloody froth bubbling from the elk's mouth was testament to that.

He removed the arrow carefully and was happy to see the

shaft had not snapped, nor had the flint point chipped on the elk's ribs. Although he was Fletcher by name, the amount of time he spent binding his arrows frustrated him. He preferred the work Berdon would occasionally give him, hammering and shaping iron in the forge. Perhaps it was the heat, or the way his muscles ached deliciously after a hard day's work. Or maybe it was the coin that weighed down his pockets when he was paid afterwards.

The young elk was heavy, but he was not far from the village. The antlers made for good handholds, and the carcass slipped easily enough over the wet grass. His only concern would be the wolves or even the wildcats now. It was not unknown for them to steal a hunter's meal, if not his life, as he brought his prize back home.

He was hunting on the ridge of the Beartooth Mountains, so called for their distinctive twin peaks that looked like two canines. The village lay on the jagged ridge between them, the only path up to it on a steep and rocky trail in clear view from the gates. A thick wooden palisade surrounded the village, with small watchtowers at intervals along the top. The village had not been attacked for a long time, only once in Fletcher's fifteen years in fact. Even then, it had been a small band of thieves rather than an orc raid, unlikely as that was this far north of the jungles. Despite this, the village council took security very seriously, and getting in after the ninth bell was always a nightmare for latecomers.

Fletcher manoeuvred the animal's carcass on to the thick grass that grew beside the rocky path. He didn't want to damage the coat; it was the most valuable part of the elk. Furs were

3

one of the few resources the village had to trade, earning it its name: Pelt.

It was heavy going and the path was treacherous underfoot, even more so in the dark. The sun had already disappeared behind the ridge, and Fletcher knew the bell would be sounding any minute. He gritted his teeth and hurried, stumbling and cursing as he grazed his knees on the gravel.

His heart sank when he reached the front gates. They were closed, the lanterns above lit for their nightlong vigil. The lazy guards had closed up early, eager for a drink in the village tavern.

'You lazy sods! The ninth bell hasn't even rung yet.' Fletcher cursed and let the elk's antlers fall to the ground. 'Let me in! I'm not sleeping out here just because you can't wait to drink yourselves stupid.' He slammed his boot into the door.

'Now, now, Fletcher, keep it down. There's good people sleeping in here,' came a voice from above. It was Didric. He leaned out over the parapet above Fletcher, his large moonish face grinning nastily.

Fletcher grimaced. Of all the guards who could have been on duty tonight, it had to be Didric Cavell, the worst of the bunch. He was fifteen, the same age as Fletcher, but he fancied himself a full-grown man. Fletcher did not like Didric. The guardsman was a bully, always looking for an excuse to exercise his authority.

'I sent the day-watch off early tonight. You see, I take my duties very seriously. Can't be too careful with the traders arriving tomorrow. You never know what kind of riffraff will be sneaking about outside.' He chuckled at his jibe.

'Let me in, Didric. You and I both know that the gates should

4

be open until the ninth bell,' said Fletcher. Even as he spoke he heard the bell begin its sonorous knell, echoing dully in valleys below.

'What was that? I can't hear you,' yelled Didric, holding a hand up to his ear theatrically.

'I said let me in, you dolt. This is illegal! I'll have to report you if you don't open the gates this minute!' he shouted, flaring up at the pale face above the palisade.

'Well you could do that, and I certainly wouldn't begrudge you your right to. In all likelihood we would both be punished, and that wouldn't do anyone any good. So why don't we cut a deal here. You leave me that elk, and I save you the trouble of sleeping in the forest tonight.'

'Shove it up your arse,' Fletcher spat in disbelief. This was blatant blackmail.

'Come now, Fletcher, be reasonable. The wolves and the wildcats will come prowling, and even a bright campfire won't keep them away in the winter. You can either leg it when they arrive, or stay and be an appetiser. Either way, even if you do last until morning, you'll be walking through these gates empty-handed. Let me help you out.' Didric's voice was almost friendly, as if he was doing Fletcher a favour.

Fletcher's face burned red. This was beyond anything he had experienced before. Unfairness was common in Pelt, and Fletcher had long ago accepted that in a world of haves and have-nots, he was definitely the latter. But now this spoiled brat, a son to one of the richest men in the village no less, was stealing from him.

'Is that it then?' Fletcher asked, his voice low and angry. 'You think you're very clever, don't you?'

5

'It's just the logical conclusion to a situation in which I happen to be the beneficiary,' Didric said, flicking his blond fringe from his eyes. It was well known that Didric was privately tutored, flaunting his education with flowery speech. It was his father's hope that he would one day be a judge, eventually going to a lawhouse in one of the larger cities in Hominum.

'You forgot one thing,' Fletcher growled. 'I would much rather sleep out in the woods than watch you take my kill.'

'Hah! I think I'll call your bluff. I've a long night ahead of me. It will be fun to watch you try and fend off the wolves,' Didric laughed.

Fletcher knew Didric was baiting him, but it didn't stop his blood boiling. He gulped the anger down, but it still simmered at the back of his mind.

'I won't give you the elk. There's five shillings in the fur alone, and the meat will be worth another three. Just let me in, and I'll forget about reporting you. We can put this whole thing behind us,' Fletcher suggested, swallowing his pride with difficulty.

'I'll tell you what. I can't come away completely empty-handed – that wouldn't do now would it? But since I'm feeling generous, if you give me those antlers you neglected to mention, I'll call it a night, and we can both get what we want.'

Fletcher stiffened at the nerve of the suggestion. He struggled for a moment and then let it go. Four shillings were worth a night in his own bed, and to Didric it was nothing but pocket change. He groaned and took out his skinning knife. It was razor sharp, but it was not designed for cutting through antlers. He hated to mutilate the elk, but he would have to take its head.

A minute later and with some sawing at the vertebrae, the head was in his hands, dripping blood all over his moccasins. He grimaced and held it up for Didric to see.

'All right, Didric, come and get it,' Fletcher said, brandishing the grisly trophy.

'Throw it up here,' said Didric. 'I don't trust you to hand it over.'

'What?' cried Fletcher in disbelief.

'Throw it up now or the deal is off. I can't be bothered to wrestle it from you and get blood all over my uniform,' Didric threatened. Fletcher groaned and hurled it up, spattering his own tunic with blood as he did so. It flew over Didric's head and clattered on the parapet. He made no move to get it.

'Nice doing business with you, Fletcher. I'll see you tomorrow. Have fun camping in the woods,' he said cheerily.

'Wait!' shouted Fletcher. 'What about our deal?'

'I held up my end of the bargain, Fletcher. I said I'd call it a night, and we'd both get what we want. And you said earlier you would rather sleep in the woods than give me your elk. So there you go, you get what you want, and I get what I want. You really should pay attention to the wording in any agreement, Fletcher. It's the first lesson a judge learns.' His face began to withdraw from the parapet.

'That wasn't the deal! Let me in, you little worm!' Fletcher roared, kicking at the door.

'No, no, my bed is waiting for me back at home. I can't say the same for you, though,' Didric laughed as he turned away.

'You're on watch tonight. You can't go home!' yelled Fletcher. If Didric left his watch, Fletcher could get his revenge by reporting him. He had never considered himself a snitch, but for Didric he would make an exception.

'Oh, it's not my watch,' Didric's voice shouted faintly as he descended the palisade steps. 'I never said it was. I told Jakov I'd keep an eye out while he used the privy. He should be back any minute.'

Fletcher clenched his fists, almost unable to comprehend the extent of Didric's deceit. He looked at the headless carcass by his ruined shoes. As the fury rose up like bile in his throat, he had only one thought in his mind. This was not the end of it. Not by a long shot.

2

'Get out of bed, Fletcher. This is the only time of year I actually need you up on time. I can't mind the market stall and shoe the packhorses at the same time.' Berdon's ruddy face swam into view as Fletcher opened his eyes.

Fletcher groaned and pulled his furs over his head. It had been a long night. Jakov had made him wait outside for an hour before he let him in, on the condition that Fletcher bought him a drink next time they were in the tavern.

Before Fletcher had a chance to bed down, he had to gut and skin the elk, as well as trim the meat and hang it by the hearth to dry. He only allowed himself one juicy slice, half cooked on the fire before he lost patience and crammed it into his mouth. In the winter it was always best to preserve the meat for later; Fletcher didn't know when his next meal was coming at the best of times.

'Now, Fletcher! And clean yourself up. You stink like a pig. I don't want you driving customers away. Nobody wants to buy from a vagrant.' Berdon yanked his furs away and strode out of

Fletcher's tiny room at the back of his forge.

Fletcher winced at the loss of his covers and sat up. His room was warmer than he had expected. Berdon must have been at the hot forge all night, preparing for trading day. Fletcher had long ago learned to sleep through the clanging of metal, the roar of the bellows and the sizzle as the red-hot weapons were doused.

He trudged through the forge room to the small well outside, where Berdon drew his dousing water. He hauled up the bucket and, with only a moment's hesitation, poured the freezing water over his head. His tunic and trousers were soaked as well, but since they were still covered in blood from the night before, it would probably do them some good. Several more bucketfuls and a brisk scrub with a pumice stone later, Fletcher was back in the forge room, shivering and clutching his arms to his chest.

'Come on then. Let's have a look at you.' Berdon stood in the doorway to his own room, the light from the hearth illuminating his long red hair. He was by far the largest man in the village, long hours of beating metal in his forge giving him broad shoulders and a barrel-like chest. He dwarfed Fletcher, who was small and wiry for his age.

'Just as I thought. You need a shave. My aunt Gerla had a thicker moustache than that. Get rid of that wispy fuzz until you can grow a real one, like mine.' Berdon's eyes twinkled as he twirled the red handlebar that bristled above his grizzled beard. Fletcher knew he was right. Today the traders were coming, and they would often bring their city-born daughters with their long pleated skirts and ringleted hair. Though he knew from bitter experience that they would turn their noses up at him, it wouldn't hurt to be at least presentable today.

'Off you go. I'll lay out the clothes you're going to wear whilst you shave. And no complaints! The more professional you look, the better our merchandise does.'

Fletcher trudged back outside into the freezing cold. The forge lay right by the village gates, with the wooden palisade edge just a few feet from the back wall of Fletcher's room. A mirror and small washbasin lay discarded nearby. Fletcher removed his skinning knife and trimmed away the fledgling black whiskers, before scrutinising his face in the mirror.

He was pale, which was not surprising this far north in Hominum. The summers were short in Pelt, with a brief but happy few weeks spent with the other boys in the forest, tickling trout in the streams and roasting hazelnuts by the fire. It was the one time when Fletcher did not feel like an outsider.

His face was harsh, with sharp cheekbones and dark brown eyes that were slightly sunken. His hair was a thick, shaggy mess of black, which Berdon would literally shear when it got too wild. Fletcher knew he was not ugly, but nor was he handsome compared to the rich, well-fed boys with ruddy cheeks and blond hair who populated the village. Dark hair was unusual in the northern settlements, yet since he had been abandoned in front of the gates as a baby, Fletcher was not surprised he looked nothing like the others; just another thing to set him apart from the rest.

When he returned, Fletcher saw Berdon had laid out a pale blue tunic and bright green trousers on his bed. He blanched at the colours but swallowed his comments when he saw Berdon's

11

remonstrative stare. The clothes would not look unusual on trading day. Traders were well known for their flamboyant garb.

'I'll let you get dressed,' said Berdon with a chuckle, ducking out of the room.

Fletcher knew that Berdon's teasing was his way of being affectionate, so he didn't let it get to him. He had never been the talkative type, preferring his own company and thoughts. Berdon had always been respectful of his privacy, ever since he had been first able to speak. It was a strange relationship, the gruff, good-natured bachelor and his introvert apprentice, yet they made it work somehow. Fletcher would always be grateful that Berdon took him in, when nobody else would.

He had been abandoned with nothing, not even a basket or swaddling. Just a naked baby in the snow, screaming at the top of its lungs outside the gates. The snobby rich folk wouldn't take him in, nor could the poor afford to. It had been the hardest winter Pelt ever endured, and food was scarce. In the end, Berdon offered to keep him, since he had been the one who had found him in the first place. He was not wealthy, but he had no mouths to feed and he did not rely on the seasons to work, so in many ways he was ideal.

Fletcher harboured deep hatred for his mother, even if he had no idea who she was. What kind of person would leave her naked baby to die in the snow? He had always wondered if it had been a girl from Pelt itself, unable or unwilling to raise him. He would often look searchingly into the faces of the women around him, comparing their features to his own. He didn't know why he bothered. None of them looked anything like him.

Fletcher's stall, now laden with shining swords and daggers, was already set up by the main road that ran from the gate to the back of the town. His was not the only one. Along the way there were more stalls, heavy with meats and furs. Other wares were on display: furniture hewn from the tall pines that grew on Beartooth and silver-petalled mountain flowers in pots for the gardens of the rich city housewives.

Leather was another of Pelt's famous wares, their jackets and jerkins prized above all others for their fine craftsmanship and stitching. Fletcher had his eye on one jacket in particular. He'd sold most of his furs throughout the year to other hunters, and had managed to save over three hundred shillings for this one purchase. He could see it hanging further down, although Janet – the trader who had spent several weeks making it – had told him he could only buy it for three hundred shillings, if nobody made a better offer by the end of the day.

The jacket was perfect. The inside was lined with downy mountain-hare fur, soft and grey with a peppering of hazel. The leather itself was a deep mahogany colour, hardy and unblemished. It was waterproof and would not easily stain, nor would it be torn as he chased his prey through the forest brambles. It was closed by simple wooden toggles and came with a deep peaked hood. Fletcher could already picture himself in it; crouched in the rain, warm and hidden with an arrow nocked to his bow.

Berdon was seated behind him outside the forge, beside an anvil and a pile of horseshoes. Although his weapons and armour were of high quality, he had found that there was plenty of money to be made in reshoeing the packhorses for the weary traders, whose long journey to the remote villages along Beartooth had only just begun.

13

The last year the traders had stopped by, Fletcher was kept busy the entire day, even sharpening their swords after the stall had been emptied. It had been a good year for selling weapons. The Hominum Empire had declared war on a new front on the northern side of the Beartooth Mountains. The elven clans had refused to pay their yearly tax, money that the Hominum Empire demanded in exchange for their protection from the orc tribes of the southern jungles, all the way on the other side of Hominum. The empire had declared war to extract their dues and the traders had feared elven raiding parties. In the end, it became a war of principle with a few skirmishes but nothing more, and ended in a gentlemen's agreement not to escalate. There was one thing that both Hominum and the elven clans agreed on implicitly; the orcs were the true enemy.

'Will I have time to look around this year?' Fletcher asked.

'I should think so. Not much call for new weaponry at the moment. Beartooth's new military may be old men and cripples, but I think the traders believe the presence of troops will dissuade brigands from roaming around here and attacking their convoys. The worst part is, they're probably right – can't see them having to defend themselves much this year. We won't get a lot of business from *them*. But at least we know there's still demand for my services from the military, after your visit to the front line last month.'

Fletcher shuddered at the memory of his journey over the mountain to the nearest fort. The front line was a grim affair, full of dead-eyed men, waiting for release from their military contracts. The elven front was the dumping ground for the men the military didn't want. The empty bellies who could no longer fight.

Chaffing. That was what the soldiers had called it. Some considered it a blessing, away from the horrors of the jungle trenches. Men died in their thousands on the orcish front, their heads taken as trophies and left on spikes at the jungle's border. The orcs were a savage, mindless race, dark creatures with merciless and sadistic intent.

Yet it was a different kind of horror on the elven border. A steady degradation. A slow starvation from half-rations. Endless drills from tired sergeants who knew nothing else to do. Uninspired generals who would stay in their warm offices, whilst the men shivered in their cots.

The quartermaster had been reluctant to buy anything, but his quota needed to be filled and the supply lines over Beartooth had long been reduced to a trickle as the demand on the orc front increased. The bundle of swords Fletcher had been carrying on his back since that morning were sold for far more than they were worth, leaving him with a heavy, but considerably lighter load of a bag of silver shillings. If he had brought muskets he would have been paid in gold sovereigns. Berdon was hoping that the traders might trade firearms for swords. If that happened, he could upsell the muskets to the quartermaster next season.

As Fletcher lay in his borrowed bunk in the barracks that night, waiting for the morning so he could return to Pelt in the light of day, he resolved that should he ever join the military, he would never allow himself to end up in such a place.

'You, boy. Move your stall back from the gates. You'll block the way for the traders,' an imperious voice snapped at him, breaking into his thoughts.

It was Didric's father, Caspar; a tall, slim man dressed in fine velvet clothing, hand-stitched from purple cloth that had been delicately embroidered with gold. He glared at Fletcher as if his very existence offended him. Didric stood behind him with a grin on his face, his hair plastered with wax into a blond side parting. Fletcher looked at the next stall over, which was considerably closer to the road than his.

'I won't tell you again. Do it now, or I'll call the guards,' Caspar barked. Fletcher looked at Berdon, who shrugged his broad shoulders and gave him a nod. In the grand scheme of things, it would make no difference. If someone needed weapons, they would find them.

Didric winked and made a shooing motion with his hands. Fletcher reddened, but moved to do as Caspar asked. Didric's time would come, but his father was an incredibly powerful man. He was a moneylender and had almost the entire village in his pocket. When a baby needed medicine from the city, Caspar was there. When the hunting season went poorly, Caspar was there. When a fire destroyed a home, Caspar was there. How could a villager who could barely sign his own name on the lengthy contract understand the concept of compound interest, or the complex numbers written above? In the end, they all found the price of their salvation came at a cost higher than they could afford. Fletcher hated that Caspar was revered by many in the village, despite being nothing more than a conman.

As Fletcher struggled to shift the stall backwards, dropping several carefully polished daggers in the dirt, the village bell began to toll. The traders had arrived!

3

It began, as it always did, with the creaking of wheels and the crack of whips. The path up the slope was uneven and steep, yet the traders would push their horses to the limit in the final stretch, eager for the prime locations at the end of the village's main road. Those who were last inevitably ended up by the gate entrance, away from the milling crowds deep inside the village.

Caspar stood at the entrance and waved them through, nodding and smiling to the drivers of the heavy-laden wagons as they rolled through the gates. Fletcher could see the horses had been pushed hard on this journey; their flanks shone with a froth of sweat and their eyes were wild with exhaustion. His face broke into a guilty grin at the state of them, knowing Berdon would be kept busy today. He hoped they had enough horseshoes for all of them.

As the last of the wagons pulled through the gate, two men with heavy blond moustaches and peaked caps trotted into the village. Their horses were not the plough horses that pulled the wagons, but heavy chargers with wide flanks and plate-sized hooves. They tossed their bridles as they moved from the dirt path on to the uneven cobbles. Fletcher heard Berdon curse behind him and grimaced with sympathy.

The men's jet black uniforms with brass buttons identified them as Pinkertons – lawmakers from the city. The muskets they held in their hands left no doubt of their status. Fletcher glanced at the metal-studded truncheons that sat holstered by the panniers in their saddles. They could break an arm or a leg with ease, and they had no qualms about doing so, for the Pinkertons were only answerable to the King. Fletcher had no idea why they were accompanying the convoy, but their presence meant that there would be little need for protection on the route. There would be few sales at his stall that day.

The two men looked so alike they might have been brothers, with curling blond hair and cold grey eyes. They dismounted and the taller of the two strode up to Fletcher, his musket hanging loosely in his hands.

'Boy, take our horses to the village stable and have them fed and watered,' he said with a hard voice. Fletcher gaped at him, taken aback by the directness of the order. The man motioned at the horses as Fletcher paused, unwilling to leave the stall unattended.

'Don't mind him. He's a bit slow in the head,' Caspar's voice cut in. 'We don't have a village stable. My son will see to your horses. Didric, take them to our personal stables and tell the stable boy to take extra care.'

'But, Father, I wanted to—' Didric began, his voice wheedling.

'Now, and be quick about it!' Caspar interrupted. Didric reddened and flashed Fletcher a black look, before taking the

18

bridles of the two horses and leading them down the street.

'So, what brings the Pinkertons to Pelt? We haven't seen any new faces for several weeks, if you are chasing outlaws,' Caspar said, holding his hand out.

The tall Pinkerton shook his hand reluctantly, forced to be civil now that his horse was in Caspar's care. 'Our business is with the military on the elven border. The King has expressed a desire to conscript criminals into the army, in doing so writing off their prison sentences. We are investigating whether the generals would be amenable to that, on his behalf.'

'Fascinating. Of course we knew that the enlistment rates had dropped recently, but this comes as a surprise. What an elegant solution to the problem,' Caspar said with a fixed smile. 'Perhaps we can talk more about it over dinner and some brandy? Between you and me, the local inn is filthy, and we would be happy to provide you with comfortable beds after your long journey.'

'We would be grateful. We have travelled all the way from Corcillum and have not slept in a clean bed for almost a week,' the Pinkerton admitted, doffing his cap.

'Then we must draw you a bath and have a hot breakfast brought to you. My name is Caspar Cavell, I am a village elder of sorts here . . .' Caspar said, leading them down the road.

Fletcher considered the news as their voices faded. Criminals, being pressed into the armed services, was something he had never considered. Rumours had abounded that forced conscription for all young men was right around the corner, something which both worried and excited him. Conscription had been implemented in the Second Orc War, centuries ago. That war had been fought over orc raiding parties that stole livestock and slaughtered the townsfolk in the fledgling Hominum Empire. Hundreds of villages had been wiped out before the orcs were driven back into the jungles.

This time it was Hominum who had started it, by clearing away their forests to fuel the industrial revolution that had just begun. That had been seven years ago, and the war showed no sign of ending any time soon.

'If I could forge those muskets, there would be no need to open the stall at all,' Berdon grumbled from behind him. Fletcher nodded in agreement. Muskets were in high demand on the front line, manufactured by the dwarven artificers that lived in the bowels of Corcillum. The techniques used to create their straight barrels and mechanisms were closely guarded secrets that the dwarves harboured jealously. It was a lucrative business, yet the technology had only been recently implemented in the military. Where before the orcs could endure a hail of arrows, a barrage of musket fire had far more stopping power.

It was then Fletcher noticed a final traveller enter through the gates. He was a grizzled soldier, with grey hair and an unshaven face. He wore a red and white uniform, the cloth tattered and worn, spattered with mud and dust from the journey. Many of the brass buttons from his coat were missing or hanging loose. He was unarmed, unusual for a member of a trading convoy and even more so for a soldier.

He had no horse or wagon, but instead led a mule that was heavily laden with saddlebags. His boots were in a sorry state, the soles worn through and flapping with each staggering step he took. Fletcher watched as he settled in the space opposite him, tying the mule to the corner post of the next stall and glaring at the vendor before he could protest.

He unpacked his saddlebags, spreading out a bundle of cloth and arranging several objects upon it. The soldier was likely on his way to the elven front, culled for being too old to fight as a soldier, yet too incompetent to have been promoted to an officer. As if he could sense his gaze, the old man straightened and grinned at Fletcher's curiosity, showing a mouth full of missing teeth.

Fletcher craned his neck to get a better look at the soldier and his eyes widened as he saw what was for sale. There were huge flint arrowheads the size of a man's hand, the edges pitted to create barbs that would snag in the flesh. Necklaces made from strings of teeth and desiccated ears were untangled and laid out like the finest pendants. A rhino's horn, tipped with an iron point, was arranged at the very front of the collection. The centrepiece was a huge orc skull, twice the size of a man's. It had been polished smooth and bleached by the jungle sun, with a heavy brow-ridge jutting unnaturally over its eyeholes. The orc's lower canines were larger than Fletcher had imagined, extending out into tusks that were around three inches long. These were souvenirs from the front lines, to be sold as curiosities to northern cities, far from where the real war was being fought.

Fletcher turned and looked beseechingly at Berdon, who had also seen what the man had for sale. He shook his head and nodded at the stall. Fletcher sighed and turned his attention back to the arrangement of his own goods. It was going to be a long, fruitless day.

4

A small crowd had gathered around the soldier, children mostly, but also a few guardsmen who had nothing to trade and no coin to spend.

'Come round, all of you! Everything you see here is the genuine article, the real deal. Every item has a blood curdling tale that will make you thank your lucky stars you live in the north,' he yelled with the flourish of a fruit vendor, tossing a spearhead high in the air and deftly catching it between his fingers.

'Perhaps I could interest you in a gremlin's loincloth or an orc nose-ring? You, sir, what do you say?' he said to a young boy with a finger firmly inserted in his nose, who was certainly not qualified to be called 'sir'.

'What's a gremlin?' asked the boy, his eyes widening.

'Gremlins are slaves to the orcs. One might compare them to a squire to one of the knights of old, tending to his every need. Not great fighters; it's in their breeding to be servile. That, and the fact that they barely come up to the height of a man's knee,' he said, demonstrating with his hand.

Fletcher eyed the image with renewed interest. Most people had some idea of what gremlins were, even this far north. They stood on two legs, as the orcs did, but wore nothing but tattered scraps of cloth around their waists. Their large bat-like ears and long crooked noses were distinctive, as were their elongated and nimble fingers, expert at prying snails from their shells and insects from rotten logs. Gremlins had grey skin, just like an orc's, and their eyes were large and bulbous with sizeable pupils.

'Where did you get all this stuff?' asked the boy, kneeling to take a closer look at what was on offer.

'I took it from the dead, my boy. They have no use for it, not where they're going. It's my way of bringing a little taste of the war up here.'

'Are you on your way to the elven front?' asked a guardsman. Fletcher saw it was Jakov, and ducked behind his stall. If Jakov noticed him, he might extract the price of the drink Fletcher had promised. He needed all his money to purchase the jacket.

'I am indeed, but not because I'm a useless bag of bones, no siree. I was the only survivor in my squad. Got caught in a night raid whilst on a scouting mission. We barely had a chance.' His voice had a hint of grief in it, yet Fletcher could not be sure if it was genuine.

'What happened?' Jakov asked, his voice dripping with disbelief as he looked the old man up and down.

'I'd rather not say. It's not a memory I relish,' the soldier murmured, avoiding Jakov's gaze. He lowered his head with apparent sadness. The crowd jeered and began to disperse, taking him for a liar.

'All right, all right!' the soldier yelled, seeing his customers slipping away. This was probably his last stop before reaching the elven front, and he would likely find it difficult to sell his goods to the soldiers there, many of whom would be all too familiar with the goods he had on offer.

'Our orders were to scout out the next forward line,' he began, as the crowd turned back to him. 'The lines were advancing again. You see, the wood behind us had all been cleared, and we needed to move the trenches up.'

He began to speak with more confidence now, and Fletcher could see he was a natural storyteller.

'It was darker than a stack of black cats that night, barely a sliver of a moon to light our way. I can tell you, we made more noise than a rhino charging as we made our way through the thickets. It was a miracle we made it more than ten minutes without being noticed,' he intoned, his eyes seeming to mist over as if he were there again.

'Get on with it!' yelled one of the boys from the back, but his comment was met with glares and shushing as the crowd listened eagerly.

'Our battlemage led the way, his demon had good night vision which helped somewhat; but it was all we could do not to accidentally fire our muskets, let alone keep our footing. A suicide mission if I've ever seen one. A waste of good men, that's for sure,' the soldier continued, twirling the spearhead between his fingertips.

'They sent a summoner with you? Now that is a waste. I thought we had only a few hundred of them?' Jakov asked, his scepticism replaced with fascination.

'The mission was important, even if it was misguided. I didn't know him well, but he was a good enough fellow, although he was definitely not a very powerful summoner. He was fascinated by the orc shamans, always asking the soldiers what they knew about them and their demons. He was constantly scribbling and drawing in his book, investigating the remains of the orc villages we passed over, copying the runes they painted on the walls of their huts.' The soldier must have noticed their faces begin to go blank as he went off topic, so he hurried on.

'In any case, it was not long before we were lost, the few stars we had been using to navigate covered by rain clouds. Our fate was sealed when the drizzle began. Have you ever tried firing a musket with wet gunpowder? It was one disaster after another.' He dropped the spearhead on the cloth and balled his fists together with emotion.

'The chosen weapon of the orc is a javelin. When one hits you, it sends you flying like a cannon ball, pinning you to the ground if it doesn't go clean through and into the man behind. They whistled through the trees and plucked us from the earth like the world had flipped sideways. We didn't even see who was throwing them, but half the men were dead in the first volley, and I didn't want to hang around for the second. The summoner made a break for it, and I followed him. If anyone could make it back in the midst of that god-awful mess, it was him. We ran in a panic, following the chirps of his demon.'

'What kind of demon was it?' asked Jakov, his hands clasped together in rapt attention.

'I never got a good look at it in the dark. It looked like a flying beetle and it was ugly as sin, but I'm thankful to it; without it I would be a dead man. In the end, the summoner stumbled and fell, and I saw a javelin had winged his side. The bugger was bleeding like a stuck pig. There wasn't much I could do for him, but the damned demon wouldn't leave without him, so I picked him up and carried him away. The poor bastard must have died before we reached the trenches, but the demon led me back all the same. The little varmint wouldn't leave his side when I brought the body back. They tried to do me for desertion, but I told them I was carrying the wounded and the rest of the troop got lost behind. They didn't know what to do with me, with my squad dead an' all and my age being what it is, so in the end, they chaffed me. My only consolation was the summoner's pack, full of some of the goodies you see before you. But that wasn't the real gem . . .' He rummaged through the saddlebags by his feet and suddenly Fletcher realised what it had all been leading up to. Perhaps the soldier did this with every crowd, reeling them in with his story, then bringing out the most expensive piece.

Yet what the soldier removed with a flourish was not the shrunken head or preserved demon he had been expecting. It was a book, bound in heavy brown leather, with thick vellum pages. It was the summoner's book!

5

If the soldier had expected to impress his crowd, he was mistaken. Most looked on ambivalently and there were even a few groans. In a small hunting town such as Pelt, learning to read was far down the list of priorities. Many villagers would struggle to get through the first page, let alone the entirety of a thick book. Fletcher, on the other hand, had been put in charge of Berdon's finances, which required him to be both numerate and literate. The many long hours he had spent sweating over his numbers and letters had cost him precious time to play with the other children, but he was proud of his education and was sure he was just as learned as Didric, if not more so.

The soldier smiled as he brandished the book, holding it up in the grey winter light and flicking through the pages, giving Fletcher a tantalising glimpse of scrawled handwriting and intricate sketches.

'What else you got?' asked Jakov, the disappointment clear in his voice.

'Plenty! But they don't get much better than this, if you will allow me to explain. Let me show you, before we move on to the next item,' the soldier implored.

The crowd, though disinterested in the book, was not going to let free entertainment go to waste. There were nods of assent and urging from them, and the soldier broke into a snaggle-toothed grin. He hopped on to an empty crate from the next stall and beckoned the crowd closer, holding the tome above his head where everyone could see.

'This battlemage was the lowest rank a summoner can assume, a second lieutenant to a regiment that hadn't even finished their training. But he volunteered for that fateful mission, and when I looked through his book I understood why. The man was looking for a game changer, a way of summoning something new.' He had their attention now, and he knew it. Fletcher gazed across the street, slack jawed, earning him a warning cough from Berdon. He straightened and busied himself with the stall, though it was already impeccably arranged.

'The orc shamans summon all manner of demons, but they are mostly base, weak creatures, no match to what our own summoners can bring forth. Yet there are only a few species of demon our summoners are able to capture from the other world, with the occasional rare exception. So, although our summoners are more powerful than orc summoners many times over, that leaves us with only a few strings to our bow, so to speak. And what this battlemage was trying to do was to find a way, using orcish techniques, to summon the *really* powerful demons.'

During his night in the barracks on the elven front, Fletcher had overheard reminisced accounts of horrifying demons that slunk in the night, slitting sleeping throats and slipping away.

Beasts that came clawing out of the jungle like wildcats and fought until their bodies were ragged with musket balls. If these were the base and weak creatures that the soldier spoke of, then he would not like to meet the demon of a fully-fledged battlemage.

'So we're to believe that book holds a secret that will change the course of the war? Or contains instructions on how to summon our own demons? Perhaps it is worth its weight in gold,' a familiar voice scoffed, dripping with sarcasm.

It was Didric, back from the stables. He had been standing behind the next stall along, out of Fletcher's view.

'Your words, not mine, my good sir,' the soldier said, tapping his nose with a knowing wink.

'It would be more worthwhile to invest money in the pitiful weapons across the road than in your book!' Didric smirked as Fletcher reddened at the jibe, then Didric strolled around the crate to the front of the crowd, carelessly kicking the rhino horn over as he did so.

'Why would the summoner volunteer for such a mission, if he had already discovered this great secret? And why would you be selling it here, if the book was worth so much? As for it containing summoning instructions, we all know only those of noble blood and a few lucky others are blessed with the ability needed to summon.' He sneered as the soldier gaped in surprise, but then the soldier rallied with surprising alacrity.

'Well now, sire, he probably was eager to see an orc demon up close. I don't know my letters, and so I don't know its worth, and it would be confiscated from me if I tried to sell it to any battlemage, since it was stolen from one of their own.'

He spread his arms, his face a picture of innocence.

'Of course,' he went on, 'I will likely hand it over when I get to the elven front. But if I can make a few shillings on the side, knowing that the book will reach a battlemage eventually regardless, well, who could begrudge me that, after carrying the man halfway across the jungle?' He lowered his head in false modesty, peeking through his greasy locks. The crowd was uneasy, unsure which party to side with. Didric was certainly popular, especially when he was being free with Caspar's money in the tavern. Yet the soldier was exciting, and Fletcher could see the crowd wanted this story to be true, even if they knew in their hearts that it was not.

Even as the crowd jeered and Fletcher began to grin at the bully losing this battle of wits to a common soldier, Didric interjected.

'Wait. Did you not say earlier that you knew the focus of his studies by looking through the book? Surely you would need to read to know about any of this? You are a liar and a fraud, and I have a good mind to send for the Pinkertons. They might even throw a desertion charge at you too.' He laughed as the soldier spluttered.

'You have him dead to rights now,' Jakov said, his hand on the hilt of his sword.

'There are pictures in the book . . .' the soldier stammered, but was immediately shouted down by the crowd, who had begun to mock him. Didric raised his voice and held up a hand for silence.

'I'll tell you what. I like the look of the book. It is curiosity and the need for learning that drives me, not the desire for riches,' he declared nobly, even as the gold trimming on his clothing glinted in the sunlight.

'I will come by later to pick it up. Shall we call it . . . four shillings? I just so happened to sell a pair of fine antlers for the same price last night,' he said, giving Fletcher a gloating look. He did not wait for an answer, but instead strode off in triumph, followed by Jakov and most of the soldier's customers.

The soldier looked after him in fury, but soon dejection took over. He sat down on the crate with an audible sigh, dropping the book on to the ground in defeat. Crestfallen at Didric's victory, Fletcher watched as the wind sent the pages riffling.

He did not know how, but Didric was going to pay that night. One way or another.

6

The day went by excruciatingly slowly. Berdon was having a busy day, but the acrid stench of burning hooves was beginning to become unbearable. Every few minutes a soft pile of horse manure tumbled to the ground behind him, adding to the existing odour. There had only been one sale that day: a small dagger sold to a merchant who had decided to cut his haggling short to get away from the smell, producing a small windfall of twelve silver shillings.

The soldier across the road had not been as vocal as before, but he had still done very well for himself, selling most of the items that had been spread out on the cloth before him. There were only a few trinkets left, as well as the iron-tipped rhino horn and, of course, the book. Fletcher believed most of the soldier's story, yet he suspected that the book did not contain any secrets of value. He did not understand why the man would lie; whatever it contained, the book would provide fascinating insight into the secretive life of the battlemages. That, in itself, was a valuable prize, one that even now Fletcher would be bartering over if he did not so desperately want that leather jacket.

As he stared at the book, the soldier caught his eye and gave him a knowing smile. Seeing there were no likely customers in the vicinity, he sauntered across the road and fingered one of the better swords on Fletcher's stall.

'How much?' he asked, lifting it from its seat and twirling it in a practised manner. It thrummed the air like a swooping dragonfly, the man's dexterity and speed remarkable, given his greying hair and wrinkled face.

'It's thirty shillings, but the scabbard that comes with it is another seven,' Fletcher replied, ignoring the glitter of the spinning blade and eyeing the soldier's other hand. He knew every trick in the book, and the soldier's behaviour reminded him of a classic. Misdirect the eye by making a show of an expensive piece, then slip a smaller item, like a dagger, into a deep pocket while the vendor was distracted. The soldier rapped his knuckles on the table to get Fletcher's attention back to the item at hand.

'I'll take it. It has a nice balance and a good slicing edge. None of this fencing nonsense the officers keep mucking about with. You think stabbing an orc is gonna stop it before it tears your head off? You might as well stab a wolf with a toothpick. I learned quick: you chop at an orc's legs and they'll go down just like any man. Not that I'll need a decent sword for the northern front, but old habits die hard.'

He punctuated his last sentence with a downward stab into the earth, then pulled out his purse and began to count out the money. Fletcher retrieved the scabbard from behind the stall,

33

a simple but sturdy piece made from an oak frame and wrapped in rawhide.

'They don't haggle where you're from?' asked Fletcher, after he'd taken the money.

'Course they do. I just didn't like the way that little bastard was talking about your stall. The enemy of my enemy is my friend, isn't that how the saying goes? I wish the elves thought that way. With them, it's more like the enemy of my enemy is vulnerable, let's stab them in the back whilst they're not looking,' grumbled the soldier. Fletcher remained silent, wary of venturing into politics. There were many who were sympathetic to the elves and a loud discussion on the subject might turn some of the traders away from getting their horses shod.

'I was enjoying your story before he came along. I hope I don't offend in asking, but was any of it true?' Fletcher looked the man in the eye, daring him to lie. The soldier observed him for a moment, then visibly relaxed and smiled.

'I may have . . . embellished a little. I've read the book in parts, but my reading isn't too good so I flipped through it. From what I can tell, he was studying the orcs, trying to learn from them. There's orc symbols all over the place, and mostly half-translated ramblings about their clans and ancestors. There are also sketches of demons, damn fine ones too. He was a good artist, even if he wasn't the greatest summoner.'

The soldier shrugged and took a dagger from the stall, using it to pick at the dirt beneath his nails.

'Shame though. Thought it would be nice to offload it here. I'll have to sell it for cheap on the elven border. There's some who are mad for battlemages in the ranks, but none of them have any coin. Maybe I'll sell it to several of them, page by page.' He seemed to like that idea and nodded to himself, as if his problem was solved.

'What about Didric? His father is a powerful man, and the Pinkertons are staying at his house! If it's your word against Didric's, I'm not sure how the cards would fall,' Fletcher warned him.

'Pah! I've faced far worse than a brat born with a bronze spoon in his mouth. No, those two coppers have seen me try and sell that book before, and they never said a dicky. They like soldiers, do the Pinkertons, think we're cut from the same cloth, even if all they do is beat up dwarves who look at them funny. Put a Pinkerton in front of an orc and they'll do what those horses have been piling on the ground behind you for the past few hours,' he said, wrinkling his nose.

'Well, make sure I'm there when Didric comes back for the book. I'd love to see his face when you tell him he can bugger off.' Fletcher rubbed his hands together with glee.

'Of course.' The soldier winked, then sheathed his sword and strolled back to the other side of the road, whistling a marching tune.

This was going to be good.

7

The sun was beginning to set, and the soldier had become more and more good-humoured as he raked in a small fortune at his makeshift stand. Nothing remained, except for the book left optimistically in the centre of the cloth at his feet. Throughout the day, the soldier had extolled the virtues of Fletcher's goods whenever a customer inspected the stall. Thanks to his cajoling, Fletcher had sold two more daggers and one of their cheaper swords at a good price. The day's sales had not been so bad after all and Fletcher couldn't wait to get his hands on the leather jacket.

'Maybe we can get a drink at the tavern after this and celebrate our good fortune,' the soldier suggested, smiling as he walked across the street again.

'The tavern sounds good, if you'd allow me to make a quick stop first. There is a purchase I have to make,' Fletcher replied with a smile, holding a heavy purse up for the soldier to see and jingling it.

'Is that for the book?' the soldier asked half-jokingly, but with a hint of hope in his voice.

'No, though in all honesty had I the coin to spare I would make you a fair offer for it. There is a jacket I have my heart set on, and I only have just enough. The stall is owned by my . . . master, Berdon, so the money we made today will go to him.'

At the sound of his name, Berdon lifted his head from the hoof grasped between his huge hands and gave the soldier a respectful nod, before returning to his work.

'My name's Fletcher. What's yours?' Fletcher extended his hand.

'My family name is Rotherham, but my friends call me Rotter,' he said, grasping Fletcher's hand with a leathery palm. The grip felt firm and honest to Fletcher. Berdon had always told him that you could tell a lot about a man from his handshake.

'You may go now, Fletcher. You've done well today,' Berdon called. 'I'll put away the stall myself.'

'Are you sure?' asked Fletcher, eager to be away from the horses and hear the soldier's war stories in the warm tavern.

'Be off with you before I change my mind,' Berdon said over the hiss of burning hoof.

The leather stall was not too far away, yet Fletcher's heart fell as he noticed the jacket he wanted was no longer hanging there. He ran ahead of Rotherham down the street, hoping that it had been put away by accident. Janet looked up at him as she counted out the takings for the day; a hefty pile of silver shillings and gold sovereigns that she covered with her arms.

'I know what you're going to ask me, Fletcher, but I'm afraid you're out of luck. I sold it about an hour ago. Don't you worry, though. I know I'm guaranteed a sale so I'll start working on another right away. It will be ready in a few weeks.'

Fletcher balled his fists in frustration but nodded in acceptance. He would have to be patient.

'Come on, boy. I'll buy you a drink. Tomorrow is another day.' Rotherham patted him on the shoulder. Fletcher pushed away his disappointment and forced a smile.

'Hunting season is almost over,' he said, arguing away his dismay. 'Wouldn't get much use out of it this winter anyway, I'll be in the hot forge prepping for my next trip to the elven front. They're in dire need of weapons to fill their quotas.'

'Not that we'll ever use them,' Rotherham laughed.

The tavern was loud and crowded as the locals and traders celebrated the close of business. Despite this, Fletcher and Rotherham jostled their way to the corner with a large flagon each, managing to somehow keep most of the ale inside and off the wooden floors, already sticky with spilled booze. They settled into an alcove with two stools and a rickety table, where it was quieter and they would be able to hear each other speak.

'Do you mind me inquiring about the war, or is it a topic you would rather avoid?' Fletcher asked, remembering the emotion the man had shown when he recounted the night he lost his comrades in the wood.

'Not at all, Fletcher. It's all I've known for the past few decades, I've probably little else to talk about,' Rotherham said, fortifying himself with a deep gulp. The beer ran down his grizzled chin, and he smacked his lips and sighed.

'We hear rumours that the war is not going well for us. That the orcs are growing bolder, more organised. Why is that?' Fletcher kept his voice low. It was seen as unpatriotic to speak pessimistically of the war, perhaps even treasonous. This was one of the many reasons why news from the orcish front travelled so slowly to Pelt.

'I can only answer with more rumour, but likely from better sources than yours.' He leaned in close enough that Fletcher could smell the beer on his breath.

'There is an orc that is uniting the tribes under one banner, leading them as their chieftain. We don't know much about him, other than he was born an albino and is the largest orc ever known. The tribes believe he is some kind of messiah, sent to save them from us, so they follow him without question. There has only been one other like him that we know of, back in the First Orc War two thousand years ago. It is because of this albino that the orc shamans share their knowledge and power so that they can send wave after wave of demons at us, and hurl fireballs into the sky to bombard us in the night.'

Fletcher's eyes widened as Rotherham spoke, his beer already forgotten. Things were even worse than he had thought. No wonder pardons were being exchanged for criminals' enlistment.

'Sometimes they break through the lines and send a raiding party deep into Hominum. Our patrols will get them eventually, but never fast enough. I've seen too many villages burned to the ground, nothing left but charred bone and ash.' Rotherham was in full swing now, spitting as he slurped his beer.

'I'm glad I live so far up north,' Fletcher murmured, trying to shake the images from his mind.

'They get rid of the old veterans like me, put a musket in the hands of a boy, and tell him he's a soldier. You should see what happens when the orcs charge in all their glory. If they're lucky, they fire one volley and then turn and run. It's a goddamned disgrace!' he shouted, slamming his flagon on the table. 'Too many of our boys are dying, and it's all the King's fault. It was Hominum who turned the occasional raid into a full-fledged war. When King Harold was given the throne by his father, he started pushing into the jungles, sending his men to cut down the trees and mine the land.'

Rotherham paused and stared into the bottom of his flagon. He took a deep gulp, then spoke again.

'I'll tell you something. If it wasn't for the summoners, we would be in serious trouble. They're poncey chaps and they think a bit too much of themselves, but we need them more than anything. Their demons keep an eye on the borders and let us know when an attack is coming, and a large demon is the only goddamned thing that can stop a war rhino other than a cannon or about a hundred muskets. When fireballs rain down on us, the battlemages raise a shield over the front lines. It lights up the sky like a dome of shining glass. The shield takes a battering and it cracks something fierce during the night, but the worst we get is a bad night's sleep.' Rotherham took another draught from his flagon, then raised it in a toast. 'God bless those posh buggers.'

He slapped his knee and polished off his tankard of beer. As he stood up to go to the bar and purchase another, a heavy hand pushed him back into his seat. 'Well, well. How very predictable that you two should become friends. They do say that snakes travel in pairs,' said Didric, a sardonic smile on his face.

Jakov removed his hand from Rotherham's shoulder and made a show of wiping it on his trousers, earning a titter from Didric. Both were now wearing their guard uniforms, heavy mail beneath an orange surcoat that matched the glow of the torches in the tavern.

'I believe there was a purchase we previously arranged. Here are the four shillings, as we agreed. More than you deserve, but we must always be charitable to those less fortunate than ourselves. Is that not so, Jakov?' Didric asked, dashing the coins on to the table.

Jakov chuckled and nodded his agreement. Fletcher snorted; Jakov was barely wealthier than Fletcher and was as low born as they came. His face was red from drink, and Fletcher suspected Didric had been plying him with beer all night to turn him to his cause. Not that Jakov had likely needed much persuasion; the man would sell his own mother for a few shillings.

Rotherham made no move to collect the coins, instead staring at Didric until the boy shifted with discomfort.

'Come on now. A deal's a deal. It's not my fault you're a fraud. You're lucky you aren't in chains and on your way to a desertion hearing,' Didric said, as he stepped behind Jakov's bulk. The reality of the situation began to dawn on Fletcher, and he gained new appreciation of Jakov. The guard was a large man, towering over Rotherham by at least a foot and built almost as heavily as Berdon. He had not been hired as a guardsman for his intelligence, that was for sure.

Even Didric was half a head taller than Fletcher, and his flabby body was twice the width of Fletcher's wiry frame.

Rotherham continued to stare, unnerving Fletcher as his steel gaze bore into Didric's pudgy face. The tension in the alcove racked up another couple of notches as Jakov's hand wandered towards his sword hilt.

'Check his satchel. It's probably in there,' Didric ordered, but his voice showed a hint of uncertainty. As Jakov moved for the bag, Rotherham stood abruptly, startling the pair into taking a step back. Fletcher rose with him, his fingers balled into fists. His pulse was racing and he could hear his heart juddering as the adrenaline took hold. He felt a twinge of satisfaction when Didric's eyebrows shot up in alarm as he squared up to him.

'If you're gonna unsheathe that sword, you'd better know how to use it,' Rotherham growled, his own hand resting on the hilt of the sword he had purchased from Fletcher.

Didric's face paled at the sight of it. He had seen that the soldier carried no weapons in the market and had clearly not expected him to be armed now. His eyes darted furtively between Jakov and the old man. In a sword fight, the soldier would have the upper hand.

'No weapons,' he declared, unbuckling his sword and letting it fall to the floor. Jakov's soon followed.

'Aye, no weapons,' Fletcher said, raising his fists. 'I remember how worried you were about getting blood all over your uniform.'

Rotherham grunted in agreement and laid his scabbard on the table.

'It's been a long time since I've been in an old-fashioned tavern brawl,' he declared with relish, grasping Fletcher's tankard and bringing it to his lips.

'Fight dirty, and go for the face. Gentlemen's rules are for gentlemen,' Rotherham muttered out of the side of his mouth, and with that he spun and dashed beer into Jakov's eyes, blinding him. Quick as a flash, he had his knee buried in the brute's groin, and as Jakov doubled over, Rotherham head-butted him with a crack on the bridge of his nose.

Then Fletcher was in the thick of it, swinging at Didric's round face. The target was an easy one and his first blow smashed into Didric's nose, spraying red like an overripe tomato. Fletcher's fist flared with pain, but he ignored it, using the momentum to take his shoulder into Didric's chest and send him to the ground. That was a mistake. As they tussled on the sticky floor, Didric managed to use his weight to his advantage. He wrapped a beefy arm around Fletcher's neck and applied pressure. Fletcher's vision bruised black and consciousness slipped from him. In a last-ditch effort, he sank his teeth into the bare skin of Didric's wrist, so hard that he could feel the bones grinding. A screech of pain resounded in his ear and the arm withdrew. The relief left him dizzy as he gasped like a beached fish. He slammed his elbow into Didric's armoured midriff and then spun into a crouch.

Almost immediately, Didric was on him again, trying to flatten him on to the ground. This time Fletcher was ready, pulling in the same direction as Didric and using the fat boy's momentum to roll on top of him. Then his fingers were around Didric's throat, choking him with all the strength his hands could muster. Didric flapped at his neck, then his hand flew to his side.

'Watch out!' yelled Rotherham, and Fletcher jumped back just in time. A curved dagger sliced across his bright blue tunic and a streak of fire burned across his midriff. Beads of blood sprang up and stained the cloth red, yet Fletcher could feel it was just a scratch. Didric scrambled to his feet and swiped at him again, but Fletcher had backed away.

Then Rotherham was there, his sword held at the base of Didric's Adam's apple.

'What happened to "a deal's a deal"?' Rotherham growled, pressing forward so that Didric had to stumble backwards over Jackov's unconscious body. Fletcher realised that the whole tavern was watching them. The only sound was Didric's shrill gasps as he tried to speak, yet no words left his mouth.

'What do you say, Fletcher? Shall we do to him what he tried to do to you? Your guts would be spilled on the floor right now if I hadn't seen him go for that dagger,' Rotherham proclaimed, so all the crowd could hear. This time, the murmurs were firmly on the soldier's side.

'No. I don't think so, Rotherham. We must always be charitable to those less fortunate than ourselves.' Fletcher's voice dripped with disdain as he pushed Rotherham's sword down. Before the words had even left his mouth, Didric scurried to the door, both Jakov and his sword left forgotten on the floor.

The men in the tavern raised their voices in scorn as the door slammed behind him in his haste to leave. Laughter soon followed and the merrymaking began once again.

'Come on,' Fletcher said to Rotherham, his mind reeling with relief. 'I'll make you a bed in our forge. You won't be safe anywhere else tonight.'

8

Fletcher opened his eyes and immediately regretted it. The light that cut through his open window was glaringly bright. He sat up, shivering, and stumbled to close it, his breath pluming in the chill air. He must have left the window open in his drunken state.

He blinked in the dark room, but could not see the soldier, only the pile of furs he had given him stacked in the corner. With a growing fear, Fletcher pushed his way outside and saw that Rotherham's mule was gone; there was no sign of him anywhere.

'Finally awake, are you?' asked Berdon from behind him, his voice tinged with disapproval. He was standing by the forge with his arms crossed and a bemused look upon his face.

Fletcher nodded, unable to speak as he felt the first wave of nausea hit him. He was never going to drink again.

'The soldier filled me in on last night's events before he left. I can't say I approve of fighting, nor the rather too literal close shave you had. But I'm glad you gave

45

that little upstart a seeing to,' Berdon said with a rueful smile. He tousled Fletcher's hair in rough affection, making his head shake dizzily. Fletcher retched and sprinted outside, before emptying the contents of his stomach on the cobbles.

'Serves you right! Let that be a lesson to you,' Berdon called, chuckling at Fletcher's misfortune. 'Just wait until you try hard liquor. You'll wish you feel the way you do now the morning after that experience.'

Fletcher groaned and tried to cough the bitter taste of acid from the back of his throat, then tottered back into the forge. He gathered up the furs that had constituted Rotherham's makeshift bed and slumped on to the cot in his room.

'I think it's all out now,' he said, wiping his mouth with the back of his hand.

'Aye, you've left a nice meal for the rats outside,' Berdon called from the forge. 'I'll fry you up some pork sausages and collect some ice-cold water from the well.'

Fletcher felt ill at the thought of food, but decided it would do him some good. He rolled over to go back to sleep and lay in the comforting warmth of the fresh furs for a while. The sizzle of frying sausages began and he shifted, trying to get comfortable.

There was something under him, digging into his side. He reached down and pulled it up to where he could see it.

A sack had been left amongst Rotherham's furs, with a piece of parchment affixed to the outside. Fletcher tore it from its purchase and squinted at the near illegible scrawl.

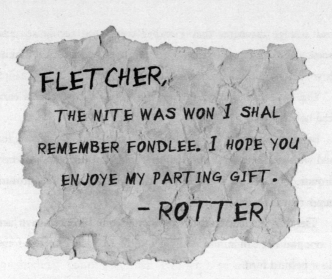

FLETCHER,

THE NITE WAS WON I SHAL
REMEMBER FONDLEE. I HOPE YOU
ENJOYE MY PARTING GIFT.

— ROTTER

The soldier had not been lying when he said he didn't know his letters, but Fletcher understood it well enough. The wily old man had slipped away in the morning, but had left Fletcher a gift in lieu of a farewell. Fletcher didn't mind. He was sure he would see Rotherham soon, although he was not exactly sure what he would do with a gremlin's loincloth, if that was what he had been left with.

He pulled the drawstring of the sack open and his hand felt something hard and oblong. It couldn't be . . . could it? He shook the contents of the sack out and gasped with disbelief, clutching the object with both hands. It was the summoner's book!

He stroked the soft brown leather, tracing his fingers along the pentacle etched on the front. Strange symbols dotted the corners of the star, each one more alien than the last. He flicked through the pages, finding every inch filled with finely scribbled handwriting, broken intermittently with sketches of symbols and strange creatures that Fletcher could not recognise. The book was as thick as an iron ingot and weighed about the same as well. It would take months to go through it all.

The sound of Berdon plating up the food reached his ears, and he rushed to hide the book under the furs.

Berdon brought the sausages in and laid them on the bed with exaggerated care. Fletcher could see they were perfectly browned on all sides and seasoned with rock salt and ground peppercorns.

'Get this down you. You'll feel better soon.' Berdon gave him a sympathetic smile and walked out of the room, closing the door behind him.

Despite the delicious smell that filled the room, Fletcher ignored the food and uncovered the book once again.

A single page slid out from the very back of the volume, the paper made from a strange, leathery fabric, different from the rest. Fletcher opened it at the place where it came from and read the words inscribed in the book there.

It is now a year to this day since Lord Etherington ordered my research to begin; yet I am no closer to discovering a new way into the ether. The pentacles the orc shamans use have different keys from ours, of that I am certain now. Yet they cover their tracks with surprising regularity. I am yet to recreate them with success, but I am sure that should I venture into terrain unmolested by Hominum's touch, clues to what they are may be found. I must therefore make every effort to advance beyond the front lines, where I might see an orc perform a summoning and perhaps catch a glimpse of their pentacle. It is essential we discover which keys they use and in what order.

———

Today my search finally bore fruit, but not the kind I had hoped for. In my digs at the remains of an old orc encampment, I discovered an incantation, etched on a scroll made of human skin. I have found a surprising joy in its translation; the orc language is brutalist in its expression, but there is an untamed beauty to it that I cannot explain.

———

I suspect the scroll imparts a demon to the adept who reads it. In all likelihood this demon will be a low-level imp gifted from an older shaman to his apprentice to start him in the learning of the dark art. This will be a rare opportunity to examine a demon from a different part of the ether. Perhaps through more careful scrutiny, this imp will point me in the right direction. With each failure, my resolve grows, yet I cannot shake the feeling that my mission is perceived by my colleagues as a fool's errand. Though my demon is weak, I will prove to the naysayers that I have just as much right to be an officer as those of noble blood.

———

Now I must away, for my commanding officer has called

me to his tent. Perhaps this will be my first opportunity to cross into enemy territory.

The last few words were an untidy scrawl, as if the writer had been in a hurry. It was clearly a diary of some sort. Fletcher flicked to the front to see if there was a name and indeed there was; inscribed in golden letters were the words *The Journal of James Baker*.

Fletcher recognised the common surname. The man must have been one of the few commoners who had the ability to summon, an occurrence discovered purely by chance when a nosy stable boy had read something he was not supposed to and summoned a demon by accident. With that revelation, most boys and girls of around Fletcher's age from the big cities were now tested for the tiny trace of summoning ability required to control a demon. But Pelt was too small and secluded to warrant a visit from the Inquisition.

He inspected the loose sheet, pulling a face as he realised what the material was made from. Barbaric runes scarred it, with the summoner's neat handwriting below spelling out their pronunciation phonetically.

Fletcher grinned and began to eat his sausages, savouring every slice. It was hard to keep his eyes from straying back to the grisly page. He knew what he was going to be trying his hand at tonight . . .

9

Fletcher was not sure why he had bothered sneaking to the graveyard. It was not like anything was going to happen, after all. For one thing, he knew that most commoners found to be adepts exhibited small signs of special abilities even before they were discovered, like the ability to move small objects or even generate a spark. He was pretty sure that the closest to a special ability he had was a talent for rolling his tongue.

It was exciting nonetheless and perhaps, once he had read the incantation, he would be able to sell it on his next trip to the elven front, with no regrets at not having tried it. He would find Rotherham and split the profits with him, of course. After all, it had been a generous gift and, if anything, it had been Fletcher who was in his debt and not the other way around.

He sat on a broken tombstone and laid the book on an old tree stump a few feet away. He had been of two minds as to whether he should leave the book at home or take it with him. Didric and his goons might have broken in when he was away, or mugged him if they caught him on the way to the graveyard.

In the end he had brought it, if only because he was loathe to let it out of his sight.

The scroll was leathery in his palm, and Fletcher realised with a flash of horror that the symbols must have been carved into the victim's flesh to scar over, before skinning him alive. He shuddered at the gruesome thought and tried to hold it with as few fingers as possible. The surface was surprisingly dry and dusty.

The words on the scroll were nothing more than a list of syllables, more of a musical *do re mi* than any kind of orc language. Then again, he wasn't even sure what language summoning used; perhaps the orcs had translated what he was about to read into their own writings from another language entirely. On top of that, James Baker had written that this demon had already been captured by a shaman and somehow 'gifted'. Who knew what that entailed? Still, he would read the words and then get back to his warm bed, happy in the knowledge that he had tried.

'*Di rah go mai lo fa lo go rah lo . . .*'

He began to speak, feeling slightly ridiculous and glad nobody was watching him, except for, perhaps, the ghosts of people long dead.

The words flowed from his tongue as if he knew them by heart, and he could not stop even if he wanted to, so great was the draw to speak them loud and clear. A heady, drunken feeling suffused his body like a warm cloak, yet instead of the haze that beer brought on, he felt a perfect clarity, like staring into the placid waters of a mountain lake. In Fletcher's mind, the words were more of a mystic equation, each one repeating, in varying cycles, that were almost melodious in their utterance.

'*Fai lo so nei di roh . . .*'

The words droned on and on relentlessly, until at last he came to the endmost line. As the final words were uttered, he felt his mind shift in a way he recognised, that split-second feeling of razor sharpness that he experienced in the moment of his arrow's release, yet twice what he had ever felt then. It was both familiar and alien to experience the world in such a way. Colours became vivid and almost iridescent. The small winter flowers that grew among the graves seemed to glow with ethereal light, so bright were they in his vision.

As his heart thundered in his chest he felt a tugging at his mind, at first tentative, then insistent and so powerful he fell from his perch to his knees.

When he lifted his head he saw the cover of the book glimmer. His eyes widened as the lines of the pentacle glowed, the star within a circle shimmering with purple radiance. Then, as if it had been there all along, a blue orb of light appeared a few inches above it. It was at first the pinprick of a firefly, then the size of a small boulder in the space of a few seconds. It hovered there, so bright that Fletcher averted his eyes, then covered them with his hands as the radiance intensified to a burning ball as bright as the sun. A roaring like the stoked flames of Berdon's forge clamoured in his ears, sending waves of pain into his skull.

After what seemed like hours, it stopped. In the sudden darkness and silence, Fletcher thought he was dead. He kneeled with his forehead in the soft earth, breathing in great sobbing breaths of its grassy scent to convince himself he was still there, though the air was now tinged with a sulphurous odour he did not recognise. It was only the sound of a soft chirp that caused him to lift his head.

A demon crouched on a small hillock in the grass two feet from the book, sitting back on its hind legs. Its tail lashed behind it like that of a feral cat, and its claws gripped the remains of something black and shiny, an insect-like imp of some kind from the other world. It gnawed at it like a squirrel on a nut, crunching into the beetle demon's carapace.

The creature was about the size of a ferret, with a similarly lithe body and limbs long enough that it would be able to lope with the grace of a mountain wolf rather than scuttle like a lizard. Its smooth skin was a deep burgundy, like a fine wine. The eyes were large and round like those of an owl, fiercely intelligent and the colour of raw amber. To Fletcher's surprise, it had no teeth to speak of, but the snout ended sharply, almost like a river turtle's beak. It used it to snap up the last of the beetle, before turning the focus of its gaze on to him.

Fletcher blanched and scrambled backwards, pressing his back into the broken gravestone. In turn, the creature screeched and scampered behind the stump, bounding sinuously as its tail switched back and forth. Fletcher noticed a sharp spike on the end of it, like a slim arrow-head carved from deer bone. The graveyard was silent, not even a breeze breaking the hush that had settled over Fletcher's world like a blanket.

The yellow sphere of its eye peeked suspiciously over the lip of the stump. When their eyes met, he sensed something strange on the edge of his consciousness, a distinct otherness that seemed connected to him somehow. He felt an intense curiosity that was overpowering in its insistence, even as he was suffused with his own desire to flee. He sucked in another deep, sobbing breath and prepared to run.

Suddenly, the demon darted over the stump in a languid leap and on to Fletcher's heaving chest. It peered up at him, cocking its head to one side as if examining his face. He held his breath as it chittered incomprehensibly then patted him with a foreleg.

Fletcher sat there, frozen.

Again the creature trilled at him. Then, to Fletcher's horror, it continued its climb, each claw digging through the fabric of his shirt. It wrapped itself around his neck like a snake, the leathery skin of its belly smooth and warm. The tail whipped past his face, then continued to encircle his nape. Fletcher could feel hot breath by his ear and knew that it would throttle him in that instant, a painful death that Didric had already tried to impart on him. At least they wouldn't have to cart his body very far for burial, he thought morbidly. As the grip began to tighten, Fletcher closed his eyes, praying it would be quick.

10

The minutes ticked by at a snail's pace. The third morning bell must have rung by now and dawn was just a few hours away. Fletcher was beginning to get cold, but resisted his compulsion to shiver for fear of startling the imp. Twin plumes of steam flared to his left with every exhalation from the demon's nostrils. Its chest rose and fell in a continuous rhythm, and he could hear a gentle susurration as its hot breath tickled his ear. It was almost as if . . . the demon was sleeping! How that had happened he did not know, but he was glad he was still breathing.

When he tried to pull it from his neck it growled in its slumber and tightened itself, the claws clamping down near his jugular. He removed his fingers, and it relaxed again, chirring contentedly. It reminded him of one of the village cats that would sneak into his room during a snowstorm, refusing to leave the warmth of his lap and hissing when he tried to get up. The imp was a possessive little thing.

He got up and walked to the book, keeping his neck still, as if he were balancing a jar of water on top of his head. Crouching with difficulty, he picked it up, slid the scroll between its pages, and clutched it to his chest. If he was going to take command of this demon, he would probably need it.

It was then that he heard it: the sound of loud angry voices. He turned and saw a flickering light at the end of the graveyard. How had they found him? Perhaps a local had heard the noise, or seen the light from the orb earlier. This was unlikely: he had chosen the graveyard because it was located on a small outcrop to the north of the main village, accessible only by a treacherous goat path and almost a half-mile from the nearest dwelling.

He looked about in panic, before spotting a crumbling mausoleum in the corner of the graveyard. It was the size of a small cabin, surrounded by ornate columns and embellished with carvings of flowers, though the rain had worn away the detailing long ago. He crept up to it and ducked into the low entrance, sinking into the darkness and hunkering behind the block of stone that covered the crypt at the very end of the chamber. Fletcher knew that an ancient ossuary lay just a few feet below him, the bones of villagers from generations ago stacked like so many pieces of kindling.

He was not a moment too soon, for the glow from the burning torch tinged the ground outside his hiding place a few seconds later.

'I am beginning to think you have led us on a fool's errand, wandering around this graveyard,' came Didric's voice, thick with frustration.

'I'm telling you, I saw him walking up through the back

gates of the village.' Fletcher recognised the voice as that of Calista, a newer guard and one of Didric's drinking companions. She was a hard-faced girl with a sadistic streak almost as bad as Didric's.

'Surely you understand how absurd this is,' Didric scoffed. 'That he would be wandering around the graveyard, of all places, in the dead of night. He's got no family to speak of, who would he be visiting?'

'He's got to be here. We've checked the orchards and the storehouses, and he's not in any of them. This is the only other place north of the village,' Calista insisted.

'Well, search the place. Maybe he's creeping about behind some tombstones. Come on, you too, Jakov. I'm not paying you to just stand there,' Didric commanded.

Jakov grunted, and Fletcher ducked down as he saw the man lumber past the mausoleum, Didric's torch casting a long shadow ahead of him.

This was bad. Didric and Calista he might have been able to fight off, but with Jakov . . . his only option was to make a break for it. Even then, Calista had been hired as a guard for her athletic build, and Fletcher was not sure if he could outrun her, especially with an unpredictable demon wrapped around his neck. The good thing was that Didric seemed to be the only one with a torch. Fletcher might be able to lose them in the dark.

He sunk down to the cold marble floor and waited, hoping they would leave before checking the mausoleum. It seemed such an obvious place to look, but then it probably appeared empty at first glance, with him hiding behind the stone cover.

The torch light from outside dimmed as Didric wandered down the rows of graves and a heavy drizzle of rain began to patter on the roof. Fletcher allowed himself to relax; they wouldn't search for long in this downpour.

The cracked ceiling began to leak, and a thin trickle of water splattered beside him. He edged away from the growing puddle and tried to stay calm, though it was not easy knowing who was searching for him outside. He hoped this was not how the animals he hunted felt when he tracked them through the forest.

Just when he thought he had escaped them, he noticed the dark around him retreat as the light from the torch drew closer. Didric was returning! Fletcher heard swearing as the boy ducked into the mausoleum and held his breath as Didric wrung out his cloak. The torch spluttered from the rain, then finally died and cast the room in darkness. Didric swore viciously. A few moments later Jakov and Calista followed, both of them just as foul mouthed and wet.

'Did I say you could stop searching yet?' Didric growled in the darkness, but he sounded resigned.

'He's not here. He must have doubled back when I went to get you.' Calista's voice was tinged with misery.

'Don't think you're going to be paid for this,' Didric spat. 'No Fletcher, no money.'

'But we're soaked!' Jakov whined, his teeth chattering.

'Oh grow up. We're all wet. That little sneak may have given us the slip, but all that means is it will be worse for him when we do catch up with him. Come on, let's get out of here.'

Fletcher breathed a silent sigh of relief as their departing footsteps echoed through the chamber. Then, just when Fletcher thought the ordeal was over, the demon stirred. It yawned with a loud mewl and unravelled itself from his neck. With an affectionate lick of Fletcher's face, it tumbled into his lap and stretched languorously.

'What was that?' Didric hissed.

Damn.

11

Fletcher stood up and squared his shoulders, tipping the imp on to the floor. It yelped in protest and darted into the back corner of the mausoleum.

'Is that you, Fletcher?' asked Didric, squinting into the darkness. The entrance was the only part of the chamber that was visible in the dim moonlight, so Fletcher was likely just a dark shape in the shadows. Didric began to walk towards him.

'What do you want, Didric? Isn't it past your bedtime?' Fletcher asked, his voice filled with confidence he did not feel. It was better he announce himself now than allow Didric to come closer to investigate. He wanted to keep the tombstone in between them.

'The little sneak is in here!' Didric called out, but there was no need; Jakov and Calista were already standing behind him. Their black silhouettes were stark against the moonlit graveyard, giving Fletcher the small advantage of knowing where they stood. But the fact that they were barring the way out definitely did not help his chances.

'Caught like a rat in a trap,' Didric said with sadistic relish. 'Not so clever now, are you, Fletchy?'

'I see you've brought your two nannies with you,' Fletcher said, wracking his brains to think of some way out of there. 'Three against one is it? Why don't you fight me like a man? Oh wait . . . we've already tried that.'

'Shut up!' Didric snapped. 'You sucker punched me. If it had been a fair fight, I would have beaten you into a pulp.' His voice was taut with hurt pride and anger. Fletcher knew his only way out of this was to take Didric on, one on one.

'So fight me now. Let Jakov and Calista see what would have happened if I hadn't,' Fletcher said with as much conviction as he could muster. He clenched his fists, and took a step forward. There was silence for a moment, then a chuckle.

'Oh no, Fletcher. I know what you're trying to do,' Didric laughed. 'I won't be fighting you today.' His cackling echoed in the chamber, sending a shiver up Fletcher's spine.

'Fine, don't fight me. Let's hurry up and get this beating over with. I have things to do,' Fletcher challenged over Didric's laughter. He ran his hand along the lip of the stone covering the crypt entrance, frantically calculating. He knew that there was another entrance to the catacombs below, in an abandoned chapel just outside the graveyard. If he could somehow get this entrance open, he might be able to get out through there. He felt the telltale crack underneath that told him that a heavy tablet sealed the entrance. It was a long shot, but he would need to lever the lid off in slow stages so the others didn't notice. It was a good thing Didric loved the sound of his own voice.

As Jakov and Calista joined in the laughter, Fletcher eased

the tablet a fraction away from him, flinching as he heard the scrape of stone against stone. This was going to take longer than he thought.

'You idiot, we aren't here to beat you up either,' Didric said with glee, barely containing his mirth. 'No, we're here to kill you, Fletcher. How perfect that you chose a graveyard to come to tonight. Hiding your body will be easy.'

Fletcher's blood froze as he heard the rasp of swords being drawn from their scabbards. He gritted his teeth and heaved, succeeding in pushing the tablet back another inch, but it wasn't enough. He needed more time.

'Kill me? With Pinkertons in town? You're more of a fool than I thought. Berdon knows where I am, he will go straight to them if I'm not home soon,' he bluffed. But Didric ignored him and took a half-step forward.

Fletcher tried again. 'Half the village saw our fight last night. You're going to spend the rest of your lives in prison over a disagreement that only started two days ago?'

He spoke loudly, trying to cover the grating sound as he managed another few inches. Didric paused and laughed.

'Oh, Fletcher. My dear father has the Pinkertons wrapped around his little finger,' Didric said, unconcerned. 'They'd sooner arrest each other than the son of their new business partner.' Fletcher paused and tried to think. Business partner? What was Didric talking about?

'In fact, perhaps I will tell you what transpired over dinner a few hours ago, just so you know what is going to happen to your precious village after you're six feet under,' Didric continued, blocking Jakov and Calista with his arms as they began to stride past him. 'You two are going to learn why sticking with me is a good career move.'

'Go on then. Enlighten me, why don't you?' Fletcher said, pushing the stone tablet far enough so that there was a crack of empty space below it. He caught a waft of trapped air from the crypt below, stale as old parchment.

'As I'm sure that fraud soldier has told you, convicted criminals are going to be press-ganged into the army. A pessimal idea in my opinion, but where others see stupidity, my father sees opportunity,' Didric boasted, leaning on his sword. 'The prisoners will be transported by day, bedding down in each city's prison at night, where they are safe and secure. Yet when they reach the northern-most city of Boreas, it is another two days to the elven front lines. That means they will have to overnight in the forest, not ideal at all. Why, any band of marauders could attack the convoy in the dead of night, and there would be no jail cells to keep the prisoners from escaping. But do you know what stands right between Boreas and the frontier? Our fair village of Pelt, of course.'

Fletcher was getting sick of Didric's pretentious tone, but he knew that his life depended on the boy's bragging.

'So what? They can't stay here. It's too small. What are you going to do, hire out some of the spare rooms in your house?' Fletcher said. He managed to slide his hands into the crack and grip the bottom of the stone lid, getting more leverage. He might be able to throw off the lid in one motion and dive in, but he would rather wait until Didric was in full flow and get a silent head start. He was probably going to need it, as the tablet covering the other entrance would need removing too.

'You miss the point, as I knew you would,' Didric said with exaggerated exasperation. 'We're going to call in our debts, Fletcher. Seize everyone's houses and turn this whole village into a prison. Imagine charging the same price as a luxurious inn, whilst serving gruel and bedding made of straw. Full bookings every night, all payments guaranteed from the King's treasury. Think of the profits! Our redundant guards will become the warders, the palisades will keep people in, not out! And if a prisoner escapes, the wolves will take them, if they don't get lost in the forest. The Pinkertons have already signed the agreement. Even if the law doesn't go ahead, our prison will be the most remote and secure ever made, away from the good people of the city.'

It took a few seconds for the words to sink in. Their beautiful home, hundreds of generations old, made into a prison. Most of the townsfolk would have their properties seized, unable to pay the debts that were ten times more than they had borrowed. It was too horrific to even contemplate, yet he clung on to one hope, a glaring problem that Caspar must have overlooked.

'It will never work, Didric. The elven front doesn't need conscripts. They send the dregs up to wait there until retirement. And even the chaffed don't visit Pelt, travelling through the night or making camp in the woods to save paying for an inn,' Fletcher pointed out, pushing the tablet far enough that he could now climb through the gap. But he waited – he needed to know more. The villagers had to be warned.

'Not so stupid after all, Fletchy. But you're wrong. Dead wrong.' Didric chuckled at his little joke and gave his sword a threatening swing. 'You see, the elven front is the perfect place for a training ground. Get them prepared for war in a relatively safe place with experienced warriors to teach them, then ship them down to the south when they're ready. No, Fletchy, this plan is going to be perfect. But there's one thing I haven't told you. I think you'll like this.' Didric paused, waiting for Fletcher to ask him what it was.

Fletcher's heart sank. Of course, if the prisoners went directly to the orc front, it would be chaos. The King's army couldn't fight a war and try to contain thousands of freshly released criminals at the same time. If there was a riot, the soldiers would end up fighting on two fronts. Better to teach the new recruits discipline and indoctrinate them up here, before sending them to reinforce Hominum's beleaguered army in the south.

'What is it, Didric?' Fletcher snarled. He could feel anger bubbling, caustic and hot in his chest. Didric's family were like ticks, sucking the life from Pelt. Now they were infecting it too.

'Just before the deal was done, I remembered you, Fletchy. You and that great oaf, Berdon. I reminded my father that the new recruits were going to need to be equipped, then suggested a rather elegant solution. So the Pinkertons made an addendum to the agreement – giving *us* exclusive selling rights to the new conscripts on the elven front. Only weapons and armour sold by our family can be purchased by their quartermasters. We begin shipping from Boreas within the week, and trust me when I say that, in the quantities we will be buying, our prices will be half what Berdon is charging. So, you see, as that redheaded fool mourns your death, he will become penniless. Who knows, maybe we will let him work as a stable boy. That's all he's good for, after all.'

Even in the darkness, Fletcher could see the satisfied grin on Didric's face. The rage inside him burned like Berdon's furnace, quickening his heart until he could almost hear the blood rushing in his ears. Hatred throbbed in his body with each heartbeat, pulsing at his temples. He had never wanted to kill someone before, but now he understood the compulsion. Didric needed to die.

With that thought, he felt the link between him and the imp, as if it were a house spider hanging from a thread of gossamer. His anger flowed through it with a potent ferocity, and he felt the demon's consciousness fill with the same intent as his own. Didric was an enemy, a threat.

'Nothing to say? That wasn't as satisfying as I thought it would be.' Didric sighed to the others, lifted his sword and stepped forward. 'Right . . . let's kill him.'

12

Even as the words left Didric's mouth, the imp came flying out of the shadows. It squealed as it dug its claws into his face, scrabbling and scratching. Didric gave a shriek and dropped the sword with a clatter, spinning around the room like a man possessed.

'Get it off, get it off!' he howled, blood streaming down his face. Jakov and Calista batted at the imp with their fists, wary of hurting Didric. With each punch, Fletcher felt a flare of dull pain on the edge of his consciousness, but the demon clung on doggedly, emitting barks of rage. Fletcher's anger continued to radiate from him like roaring fire, filling him with righteous fury. As it reached its zenith, he felt that moment of clarity once again; Didric's dark blood turning ruby red in his vision.

The imp silenced, then opened its mouth as wide as a snake's. Liquid fire burst from the creature's maw, flowing over the side of Didric's face and setting his hair alight. An unearthly, orange glow flared in the cavern as Didric collapsed, his choked scream cut short when his head cracked on to the marble floor. Jakov and Calista fell to their knees and beat at the flickering flames, yelling Didric's name. As the imp scampered into Fletcher's arms, he vaulted into the crypt and made for the exit, his heart fluttering beneath his ribs like a caged bird.

It was black as a sinner's soul down there, the air stale and ice cold. He ran on and on, stumbling deep into the bowels of the earth. Clutching the book under his arm, Fletcher's hand brushed along stacks of bones as he felt his way through the darkness, held together by rusting wire and centuries of dust. He knocked a skull from its alcove, his finger catching in its empty eye socket. It bounced down the corridor, then shattered into grisly fragments. They crunched underfoot as he lurched onwards, desperate to get out of there. The air was stifling, and Fletcher felt he was suffocating with each dust-laden breath. The demon was not helping matters, digging its claws into the fabric of his shirt and hissing in displeasure.

After what felt like an eternity, his shin cracked painfully into a stone ledge. He groped forwards and found another. Relief flooded through him as he realised he had found what must be the stairs to the chapel. He reached above and felt the flat surface of another stone tablet. With a colossal effort, he heaved it upwards and sideways, sending it to the floor with a crash.

The dim glow of the moon was glorious as it shone through the chapel's broken windows, bathing Fletcher in silver. He gulped down lungfuls of fresh air, grateful to be out of that deathtrap. Yet even as he began to relax, he remembered what had just happened. He needed to get back to Berdon as soon as possible. He would know what to do.

Fletcher ran through the dark, using the moonlight to guide

him down the goat path. He was sure that the others would not be far behind, probably carrying Didric with them. He would have ten minutes at most before the word got out. If the guards heard that one of their own had been attacked, whatever the circumstances, it was unlikely Fletcher would live long enough to stand trial. Even if he did, with Caspar's connections he wouldn't get a fair hearing, and the only two witnesses would have no problem lying.

The village was silent as a shadow; everyone was asleep in their beds. As he jogged up to the main gates, he was overjoyed to see the gatehouse above lay empty. One of his attackers must have skipped their shift to hunt him down.

The forge was lit by the soft glow of coals, smoking gently as they burned themselves out. Berdon was asleep in the wicker chair, in the exact same position he had been in when Fletcher sneaked out.

There was no time to waste; he needed to escape. The thought of leaving Pelt cut him to the core, his heart clenching at the notion. For a moment he could see the life of a vagrant ahead of him, wandering from town to town, begging for scraps. He shook the thoughts from his head. One thing at a time.

With a heavy heart, Fletcher shook Berdon awake.

'What is it?' he slurred, slapping at Fletcher's hands. 'I'm sleeping. Wake me in the morning.' Fletcher shook him again, harder this time.

'Wake up! I need your help. There isn't much time,' Fletcher said. 'Come on!'

Berdon gazed up, then started as the curious imp dropped from Fletcher's shoulder on to his chest.

'What the hell is that?' he yelled, leaning as far away from it as possible. The demon squawked at the noise and gave a half-hearted swipe at Berdon's beard.

'It's a long story, but I'll have to make it quick. You should know I'm going to have to skip town for a while,' Fletcher began, picking up the imp and laying it on his shoulder. It curled around his neck and emitted a soft purr.

He spoke as quickly as possible, skipping the details but making sure Berdon understood all the facts.

In the retelling, Fletcher realised what an idiot he had been to walk through the centre of the village, where anyone could have seen him. When he had finished, he stood there woodenly, hanging his head in shame as Berdon rushed around, lighting a torch and then packing things into a leather satchel. Berdon only had one question.

'Is he dead?' he asked, looking Fletcher in the eye.

'I . . . don't know. He hit his head pretty hard. Whatever happens, his face will be badly burned. They'll say I attacked him with a torch; lured him to the graveyard, then tried to kill him. I've let you down, Berdon. I've been a fool,' Fletcher cried. Tears welled in his eyes as Berdon handed him the deep satchel, the same one he had used to transport the swords to the elven front. He threw the book into the bottom with a sob, wishing it had never come into his possession. Despair seemed to be crushing his heart like a vice. The big man put his hands on Fletcher's shoulders and gripped them, sending the demon skittering to the floor.

'Fletcher, I know I've never told you this, but you are neither my apprentice nor a burden. You are my son, even if we do not share the same blood. I am proud of you; prouder than ever tonight. You stood up for yourself and you have nothing to be ashamed of.' He gripped Fletcher in a bear hug, and Fletcher buried his face in his shoulder, sobbing.

'I have some gifts for you,' Berdon said, brushing tears from his cheeks. He disappeared into his room and came back holding two large parcels. He shoved them down into Fletcher's satchel and gave him a forced smile.

'I was going to give these to you on your sixteenth birthday, but it's best I give them to you now. Open them when you're far away from here. Oh, and you're going to need protection. Take this.'

A rack of weapons lay against the far wall. Berdon selected a curved sword from the back, where the rarer items were kept. He held it up to the light.

It was a strange piece, one that Fletcher had never seen before. The first third of the blade was the same as any sword, a leather hilt followed by four inches of sharp steel. But next part of the sword curved in a crescent, like a sickle. At the end of the curve the sword continued on with a sharp point once again.

'You've no formal training, so if you end up in trouble . . . well . . . let's not think about that. This sickle sword is a wild card. They won't know how to parry it. You can trap their blade in the curve of the sickle, then move in past their guard and hit them with the back edge of it. The point is long enough for stabbing, so don't be afraid to use it in that way too.' Berdon demonstrated, swiping the sickle down and to the side, then bringing the back edge up at head height and stabbing violently.

'The outer edge of the sickle is curved like a good axe head.

72

You can use it to split a shield or even chop down a tree if you need to, far better than any sword could. You can take a man's head from his shoulders with a good backswing.' He handed the blade to Fletcher, who strapped it to the back of his satchel with a leather belt.

'Keep it oiled and away from the damp. Because of its shape it won't fit in a conventional scabbard. You'll have to get one made when you get a chance. Tell the blacksmith it's a standard sized khopesh. They will know how to make one if they know their trade,' Berdon said.

'Thank you. I'll do that,' Fletcher said gratefully, stroking the leather pommel.

'As for that demon, keep it hidden,' Berdon instructed, peering into the imp's amber eyes. 'You'll never pass for a noble, nor should you try to. Even if someone hasn't heard about Didric, it's best to avoid attention.'

Fletcher gathered the demon into his arms and examined it, wondering how exactly he would keep the unruly creature out of sight.

Suddenly, the bells began to toll, their brassy knells reverberating in the streets outside. Even with the bells clamouring, Fletcher heard distant shouts down the road.

'Go! But not to the elven front, that's where they will expect you to run. Head south, to Corcillum. I'll bar the forge's door, make them think you're still in here. I will hold them off as long as I can,' Berdon said, shoving him out of the forge and into the cold night air.

'Goodbye, son.'

Fletcher caught one last glimpse of his friend, mentor and

father, silhouetted in the doorway. Then the door slammed shut and he was alone in the world, but for the sleeping creature around his neck. A fugitive.

13

It had been two days. Two days on the run, cutting back and forth to leave false trails. No food, no sleep, only drinking when he waded down the mountain streams, trying to kill his scent and leave no footprints. Whenever he stopped to rest, he could hear the bark of the hunting dogs in the distance.

At night he would climb to the top of a tall tree to check his direction by the constellations in the sky. When he did, he saw the flicker of campfires in the valleys above him. The whole town guard and probably most of the hunters were chasing him. Didric's father, Caspar, must have put a huge bounty on his head.

Now, on the third night, he could only see tiny pinpricks of light halfway up the mountain. They had turned back, the trail gone cold. He breathed a sigh of relief and began the long climb down, careful not to lose his footing. Any injury, even a sprained ankle, could mean death now.

He did not let himself become too complacent. Lord Faversham, a powerful noble, owned most of the land around the base of Beartooth. He was notorious for sending patrols of his men through the forest to catch poachers. Fletcher would have trouble explaining to them why he was travelling alone, so far away from the safe mountain paths.

The demon hissed with displeasure at being disturbed when he dropped to the ground. It had stayed in its customary position around his neck since he left the village. Fletcher was glad that it had. He had been cold and wet through for far too long, but the furnace in the demon's belly kept his neck and shoulders warm at least.

Fletcher looked around, then decided that the base of the oak tree was as good a place as any to camp. The ground was flat and covered in springy moss. The tree's canopy would keep off the worst of any rain and, although it was too late to build a shelter, there were plenty of dead branches lying around for a small fire.

He stacked a pile of kindling together, then used a flint and the steel of his blade to spark at the tinder.

'You couldn't spare us some of that fire now, could you?' Fletcher asked the demon, as the damp leaves he was using spluttered against the sparks. The demon unravelled at the sound of his voice, slinking down his arm to the ground. It yawned and looked at him with curiosity, cocking its head to the side like a confused puppy.

'Come on. There's got to be a way we can communicate,' Fletcher said, curling his fingers under the demon's chin and scratching it. The demon chirped and rubbed his hand with the side of its head. With each rub, Fletcher could feel a hint of a deep satisfaction on the edge of his consciousness, like an itch being scratched.

'Fire!' Fletcher announced, pointing at the woodpile. The demon yapped and whirled in a circle.

'Shhh,' Fletcher hushed, a flash of fear running through him. The lower mountains were notorious for wolves. He had already heard their howls in the distance. They had been lucky so far to avoid them.

The demon silenced and cowered, crawling between his legs. Had it understood? Fletcher sat cross-legged in the damp, wincing as the back of his trousers became wet. He closed his eyes and wracked his brains, trying to remember if Rotherham had mentioned anything in his stories about how summoners controlled their demons.

As he did so, he sensed the consciousness of the demon, just as confused, scared and alone as himself. He sent it a wave of comfort and felt the demon stiffen, then relax, the fear and loneliness replaced by simple tiredness and hunger. Then it clicked. That was how: it didn't understand his words, it sensed his emotions!

He sent the demon a feeling of coldness, but the demon simply shrilled in discomfort and wrapped itself around his leg. Given how warm its body felt, Fletcher suspected it was not very familiar with any temperature other than one of warmth. Perhaps . . . an image? He pictured fire, bringing back memories of the hot furnace in Berdon's forge.

The demon chirruped and blinked its round, amber eyes at him. Perhaps fire reminded the little creature of home. Fletcher rubbed his numbed hands together in frustration; this was going to be harder than he'd thought. He slumped and pulled his threadbare jacket closer around his shoulders.

'If I had managed to buy that jacket at the market, we wouldn't even need a fire,' Fletcher grumbled. He stared at the woodpile, willing it to burst into flame. Without warning, a gout of fire shot from between his legs, flaring the dank wood into a cracking blaze.

'You clever little thing!' Fletcher whooped, gathering the imp up in his arms and hugging it close to his chest. Already he could feel the warmth seeping back into his frozen limbs. He smiled as the mellow glow brought back fond memories of Berdon's forge.

'That reminds me,' Fletcher said, dropping the demon into his lap and rummaging through the satchel. With the constant pursuit, he had almost forgotten the gifts Berdon had given him. He took the larger of the packages out and tore into it, his hands still clumsy from the cold.

It was a bow, lacquered with clear varnish and strung with a fine braid of conditioned rawhide. The wood was intricately carved, the two ends curving in and then outwards at the ends, for extra power when bent back. The wood was yew, an expensive timber that Berdon must have purchased from a trader the year before; it did not grow on the mountains. He had treated and dyed it so that the usually pale bow had become grey, preventing it from catching the eye when the hunter crouched in the shadows. It was a beautiful and valuable weapon, the kind a master huntsman would pay through the nose to own. Fletcher smiled and looked up at the top of Beartooth, giving silent thanks to Berdon. It must have taken him months to make, working on it in secret when Fletcher was out hunting. There was even a slim quiver of fine, goose feather arrows. He might be able to catch a mountain hare in the morning.

With that thought, Fletcher's stomach rumbled. He put aside the second gift and delved into the bottom of his rucksack, taking out a weighty packet wrapped in brown paper. He opened this one with more care and smiled as he saw the jerky from the elk that Didric tried to blackmail from him. He put a few strips on the fire to heat up, then passed another to the demon.

It gave it a wary sniff, then jerked its head forward and snapped at it, lifting its head upwards and gulping it down whole like a hawk.

'Almost took my fingers off there,' Fletcher observed as the smell of cooking venison wafted under his nose.

He reached into the bag again to see what other food was in there. He felt something that jingled and pulled out a heavy purse.

'Oh, Berdon, you didn't,' Fletcher murmured in wonder.

But he had. From what Fletcher could see, it was over a thousand shillings, almost a year's wage for Berdon. Even knowing that his business would soon be under threat, the man had given Fletcher a good chunk of his savings. Fletcher almost wished he could go back and return it, then remembered the three hundred shillings he had saved up for the jacket, still sitting in his room. Hopefully Berdon would find it, and the rest of Fletcher's old possessions would likely fetch some money as well.

'What else have you given me . . . ' Fletcher whispered. He picked up the second gift and shook it, feeling something soft and light. There was a note pinned to it, which Fletcher tore off and read by the flickering firelight.

FLETCHER,

WE HAVE ALWAYS KNOWN THAT THE DAY WE CALL YOUR BIRTHDAY IS LIKELY NOT THE DAY YOU WERE BORN. YET TO ME, IT WILL ALWAYS BE THE MOST IMPORTANT DAY OF MY LIFE. IT IS THE DAY I BECAME A FATHER, AND YOU BECAME MY SON. TONIGHT WE SHALL GO FOR A DRINK TOGETHER AND DISCUSS THE FUTURE OF THE BUSINESS. I AM GOING TO MAKE YOU A FULL PARTNER. HEAVEN KNOWS YOU DESERVE IT. THIS GIFT IS JUST A SMALL TOKEN OF MY APPRECIATION FOR EVERYTHING YOU HAVE DONE FOR ME OVER THE YEARS. I AM SO PROUD OF YOU.

HAPPY BIRTHDAY, SON,

BERDON

Tears dripped on to the letter as Fletcher folded it, his heart full of longing for home. He opened the gift and sobbed as he saw the jacket he had wanted, burying his hands in the soft inner lining.

'You were a better father to me than my true father could ever have been,' Fletcher whispered, looking up at the mountains. Somehow, the words he had left unsaid over the years were what he regretted the most.

The demon began to mewl at Fletcher's misery, licking his fingers in sympathy. Fletcher patted its head and shuffled closer to the fire, allowing himself a few minutes of sadness.

Then he wiped tears from his eyes, put on the jacket and pulled the hood over his head. His heart filled with resolve. He was going to make a new life, one that Berdon would be proud of. He was going to make it to Corcillum.

14

The tavern reeked of unwashed men and stale beer, but then Fletcher supposed he didn't smell too rosy himself. Two weeks of travelling in a wagon full of sheep did that to a body. The only fresh air he had managed the entire time was when he went out to buy cheap bread and thick slices of salted pork from the locals. He had been lucky; the cart driver had asked no questions, only charging five shillings and asking that Fletcher muck out the dung from the back every time they stopped.

Now he sat in the corner of one of Corcillum's cheap taverns, relishing the taste of warm lamb and potato broth. He had barely seen any of the city yet, instead entering the first tavern he could find. Tonight he would pay for a room and have a hot bath brought up; exploring could wait until tomorrow. He felt like the stink of sheep had become permanently ingrained in his skin. Even the imp was reluctant to venture out from its customary place within the confines of his hood. In the end he had to bribe it with the last of his salt pork, feeding it until it fell asleep.

Still, the little creature had made the long, dark journey bearable, curling up in his lap to sleep in the cold of night. Fletcher could share in its feelings of warmth and contentment, even while he shivered in the soiled straw of the cart.

'One shilling,' said a woman's voice from above him. A waitress held out a grimy hand, pointing at his food with the other. Fletcher dug into his bag and pulled out the heavy purse, then dropped a shilling into her waiting fingers.

'No tip? With all that silver?' she screeched, then strode off, drawing looks from other patrons in the tavern. Three hard-looking men paid particular attention. Their clothes were dirty, and their hair hung in greasy locks around their heads. Fletcher grimaced and stowed his purse.

They had never needed pennies up in the mountains. Everything was priced in shillings; pennies complicated things. It was one hundred copper pence to a silver shilling and five shillings to a gold sovereign in the big cities of Hominum, but Fletcher's purse contained only silver. He would ask for change when he paid for his room, so that this didn't happen again. It was frustrating to make such an obvious mistake, but he couldn't exactly tip her with the same cost as his meal now, could he?

Another man seated behind the three vagrants was still staring at Fletcher. He was handsome but fearsome looking, his chiselled face marred by a scar that extended from the centre of his right eyebrow down to the corner of his mouth, leaving a blind, milky eye in its wake. He had a pencil-thin moustache and curling black hair that was tied in a knot at the nape of his neck. The uniform he wore marked him as an officer of some kind; a long blue coat bordered with red lapels and gold buttons. Fletcher could see a black tricorn hat laid on the bar in front of him.

Fletcher sunk into the shadows and pulled his hood further over his head. The demon shifted and grumbled in his ear, unhappy at being kept in the dark for so long. The hood did a good job of hiding it, especially when he raised the collar of his shirt, but the way the officer stared at him was disconcerting.

He gulped down the last of his broth and stuffed the bread that came with it into his pocket to give to his demon later. Perhaps another tavern would be a better place to stay, away from everyone who had seen the weight of his purse.

He ducked into the cobbled street and hurried away, looking over his shoulder. Nobody seemed to be following him. After a few more paces, he turned his jog into a stroll, but kept in mind the need to find another inn. It would be dusk soon and he didn't like the idea of sleeping in a doorway that night.

Already he was marvelling at the tall buildings, some over four storeys high. Almost every one had a shop on the ground floor, selling a multitude of goods that had Fletcher itching to get his purse out once more.

There were red-faced butchers with strings of sausages decorating their store, bloodied to the elbows as they portioned heavy haunches of meat. A carpenter put the finishing touches to a chair leg with magnificent carvings, like a tree entwined with ivy. The alluring scent of cologne wafted from a perfumery, the glass shelves on display filled with delicate, coloured bottles.

He stumbled to the side as a horse-drawn carriage pulled up, exited by a pair of girls, their hair ringleted in pretty curls and their lips painted like red rose petals. They were gone into the perfumery with a swish of their petticoats, leaving Fletcher open mouthed. He grinned and shook his head.

'Not for the likes of you, Fletcher,' he murmured, continuing on his way.

His eye was caught by the shine of metal. A weapon store bristled with pikes, swords and axes, but that was not what drew him. It was the firearms, gleaming in velvet-lined cases on a stall in front of the shop. The stocks were carved and dyed red, with each of the barrels engraved with stampeding horses.

'How much?' he asked the vendor, his eyes fixed on a gorgeous pair of duelling pistols.

'Too much for you, laddie; these weapons are for officers. Beautiful, aren't they, though?' said a deep voice above him.

He looked up and blinked in surprise. It was a dwarf, of that Fletcher was certain. He stood on a long bench so that his head was level with Fletcher's, but without it he would have only reached Fletcher's midriff.

'Of course, I should have known. I've never seen finer. Did you make them?' Fletcher asked, trying not to stare. Dwarves were not common outside of Corcillum, and Fletcher had never seen one.

'No, I'm just a vendor. Still doing my apprenticeship. Perhaps someday, though,' the dwarf said.

Fletcher wondered at how the dwarf could still be an apprentice. He looked much older than him, with his heavy beard and whiskers. His beard reminded Fletcher of Berdon's in colour, but the bristles were much thicker and longer, plaited and braided with beads throughout. The dwarf's tresses were just as long, hanging halfway down his back in a ponytail kept by a leather thong.

'Are your masters looking for any new apprentices? I have plenty of experience in the forge, and I could use the work,' Fletcher said, his voice hopeful. After all, what else was he going to do to find money in this expensive city? The dwarf looked at Fletcher as if he were stupid, then his face softened.

'You're not from around here, are you?' the dwarf asked with a sad smile. Fletcher shook his head.

'We won't hire any men, not while we don't have the same rights and not while we still hold the secrets to gun making. It's nothing against you personally. You seem like a nice enough fellow,' the dwarf sympathised. 'You'd best go to one of Corcillum's human blacksmiths, though there are only a few. They do well enough; plenty of soldiers refuse to buy from the dwarves. But I hear they aren't hiring these days; too many applicants.'

Fletcher's heart dropped. Blacksmithing was the only profession he knew, and he was too old now to become an apprentice in another trade. There were no forests near the city to hunt in either, unless the jungles over the southern frontier counted.

'What rights are you denied?' he asked, suppressing his disappointment. 'I know the King granted you the right to join the military last year.'

'Oh, there's plenty. The law dictating the number of children we can have each year is the most galling. We can only have as many children as the number of dwarves who died the previous year. Given that we can live almost twice as long as

86

you humans, that's just a handful. As for the right to join the military, aye, that's a step in the right direction. The King is a good sort, but he knows his people don't trust us, especially the army, thanks to the dwarven uprisings eighty-odd years ago. The thinking goes, once we've proven our loyalty by shedding blood beside his soldiers, well, then the King will revisit giving us equal citizenship. But until that time, this is how it has to be.' The dwarf's voice was tinged with a hint of anger, and he turned away as if overcome with emotion, rummaging in a box behind him.

Fletcher remembered the scorn from the other villagers in Pelt when it was announced that dwarves would be fighting in the Hominum army. Jakov had been joking that they could barely brush his balls if they walked between his legs. The stout dwarf's arms were thicker than most men's thighs, and his barrel-like chest reflected his deep booming voice. If Jakov took this dwarf on, Fletcher knew who he'd put his money on. The dwarves would make formidable allies indeed.

'Do you know anywhere cheap and safe to stay around here?' Fletcher asked, trying to change the subject.

The dwarf turned back and handed him something, closing Fletcher's hand over it before anyone saw.

'There's a place not far from here. It's a dwarf-friendly tavern, called the Anvil. Maybe somebody can find work for you there. Say Athol sent you. Take the third right down the street, you can't miss it.'

The dwarf gave him an encouraging smile and turned to another customer, leaving Fletcher holding a square of paper with an anvil printed on the centre. Fletcher smiled and headed in the direction the dwarf had pointed, then remembered he had forgotten to thank him.

As he turned, he locked eyes with the scruffy men from the tavern, their faces lighting up in recognition. They careened towards him and Fletcher began to run. People stared as he jostled through the street, earning himself a clip round the ear as he brushed past a well-dressed man accompanying a young lady.

Just as he was about to reach the turning for the tavern, the street was blocked ahead by two carriages, the horses wheeling and neighing as their drivers yelled at each other. Cursing his luck, Fletcher was forced to turn down a side street. He sprinted into it, glad to at least be away from the thronging crowds. The street was empty, the shops on either side already closed for the night. Then he stopped short, his heart hammering in his chest. It was a dead end.

15

Fletcher used the time he had before the thieves arrived to coax the demon on to his shoulder. It dug its claws into the leather of his jacket, sensing his agitation.

'Be ready, little fellow; I think this is going to get messy,' Fletcher murmured, nocking an arrow to his bow and kneeling for better aim. The men rounded the corner and stopped, staring at him.

'Back off or I'll put this through your eye. I've no qualms about putting down a cutpurse,' Fletcher shouted, squinting down the arrow at the largest of them. The man smiled, showing a mouth full of yellowed teeth.

'Aye, I've no doubt. But you see, we're not so much cutpurses as cutthroats, if ye catch my meaning.' The man sneered and held up a curved blade. 'All we wants is yer purse and we'll be on our way, no harm done.'

He took a few steps forward, putting himself within ten feet of Fletcher. The demon hissed and huffed twin plumes of flame from its nostrils that flared just a few inches from the man's face, sending him stumbling back into the others.

'I'm not messing around here. Leave now or you'll regret it!' Fletcher shouted again, though his voice trembled. He glanced at the silent houses around him. Why hadn't anyone heard? Someone needed to call the Pinkertons. How wretched it would be to have made it this far, then to die in a dank alleyway on his very first night.

'Ah, a summoner. You're one of them adepts from Vocans Academy, aren't ye? Little past yer bedtime now, isn't it?' the man said, brushing himself off.

'Leave!' Fletcher said, realising the demon could probably only breathe fire a certain distance. He didn't want to test that tonight.

'Well now, ye've shown me yours. Let me show ye mine,' the man said, then whipped out a pistol and pointed it at Fletcher's chest. Fletcher almost loosed the arrow then and there, but the muzzle jerked as the man walked forward once again.

'Now which one do ye think will hit faster, the gun or that there bow?' the man asked with easy confidence. Fletcher eyed the pistol. It was an ugly thing, the metal rusted and the barrel cracked and worn.

'It doesn't look too accurate,' Fletcher said, backing away.

'Aye, yer right there. But say it missed, and you put that arrow through my eye? My two friends here will come at you sharp like, and slit you from ear to ear. We could both die here, or ye could make it easy and give us what we want. There's nowt spellcraft or a demon can do against a bullet, summoner,' the man said, his voice steady and confident. Something told Fletcher the thief had played this game before.

'I'll take my chances,' Fletcher said, loosing his arrow. The pistol belched smoke with a clap and Fletcher heard the crack of an impact near his chest. Light flared across his vision, yet he could feel no pain – perhaps that would come later. The demon's squeals rung in his ears as he crumpled to the ground, smiling grimly as he saw the thief fall with an arrow in his skull. The two men behind stood frozen; they had not been expecting Fletcher to go through with it.

'Wrong, actually,' came a well-spoken voice from the shadows at the end of the street. 'There's plenty spellcraft can do. Like throwing up a shield, for example.'

The scarred officer Fletcher had seen in the tavern emerged, striding in between the two men left standing. A growl came from the gloom behind him, so loud that Fletcher could almost hear it, rumbling in his chest.

'I would run if I was you,' advised the officer. Without a second look, the men turned tail and sprinted around the corner. From what Fletcher could hear, they did not make it very far. A loud snarl echoed from out of sight, followed by screams that swiftly descended into a horrid gurgling sound.

Fletcher covered his face with his hands and took deep, sobbing breaths. That had been a close call.

'Here,' said the officer, holding out his hand. 'You're not injured. My shield saw to that.'

Fletcher took it and was pulled to his feet. He patted his chest, finding no damage. Instead, a glowing crack seemed to hang in the air in front of him, like broken ice on an opaque lake. It was embedded in a large, translucent oval, floating in front of him, which was barely discernible to the naked eye. Even as he reached out to touch it, the shield faded into nothingness. He noticed the bullet had fallen to the ground, its round shape flattened by the impact.

'Follow me,' said the officer, striding off without looking at him. Fletcher paused for a moment, then shrugged. The man had saved his life; he wasn't going to question his intentions.

The imp clambered up Fletcher's back and slid into his hood as he followed, exhausted by the excitement of the encounter. He was glad, for the officer had been staring intensely at the demon.

'Sacharissa!' the officer yelled. A shadow detached from the gloom and nuzzled the officer's hand. The officer tutted in disgust as the creature's muzzle bloodied his fingers, then pulled out a handkerchief from his pocket and wiped them fastidiously. Fletcher darted a glance at the demon and caught sight of a dog-like creature with four eyes – a normal set, with a smaller set about an inch behind. However, the paws were more like a feline's than a dog's, with claws over an inch long and caked with blood. Its fur was black as a starless night, with a thick mane that ran along the ridge of its spine down to a bushy tail that put Fletcher in mind of a fox's. It was as large as a small horse, its back coming up to Fletcher's chest. He had imagined other demons to be the same size as his own, yet this one was large enough to be ridden. The enormous creature's flanks rippled with muscle as it prowled beside them, making Fletcher almost sympathetic to the men who had died at its hands.

He and the officer walked on in silence. Fletcher considered the tall man. He was hard-faced, yet handsome, perhaps in his thirties. The battlescar that adorned his face filled Fletcher with imagined scenes of battles being fought, arrows whipping overhead.

The streets were already beginning to empty, and though the creature attracted a few furtive looks, they were soon alone as they turned off the main road and down an empty street.

'What kind of demon is that?' Fletcher asked, if only to break the silence.

'A Canid. If you'd paid attention in your classes you would know that. It's probably the first demon they introduced you to, God knows it's the most common. So . . . you're a truant *and* a dunce! I would expell you on the spot if we didn't need every adept we can get, no matter how sorry an excuse they are for a summoner.'

'I'm not from the school. I only arrived in the city this morning!' Fletcher said indignantly. The officer stopped dead in his tracks and turned to face him. The man's unblinking milky eye stared at him for a moment, before he spoke.

'Our Inquisitors said that all the commoners who tested positive as adepts arrived at the school last week. If you're not one of them, who are you? A noble? And who gave you that demon?'

'Nobody gave me the demon. I summoned it myself,' Fletcher replied, confused.

'Ah, you're a liar,' the officer said as if he had finally understood, then continued walking.

'I'm not!' Fletcher growled, grabbing the man by his coat-tails.

In an instant the officer had him up against the wall, holding him by the scruff of his neck. Fletcher's imp hissed, but a warning growl from Sacharissa silenced it.

'Don't ever presume to touch me again, you little prig. I've just saved your life, then you decide to tell me a preposterous lie. Everybody knows that summoners must be given a demon by someone else before they can capture their own. Why, next you'll claim you walked into the ether yourself and plucked a demon out like a pea from a pod. Now tell me, which summoner gave you the demon?'

Fletcher kicked at the air, choking as his windpipe was crushed. A name floated, unbidden, to his mind.

'James Baker,' he gasped, patting at the officer's hands. He let Fletcher down and smoothed some imaginary wrinkles on his jacket.

'I'm sorry, I let my anger get the better of me,' he apologised, his face filled with regret as he saw the welts his fingers had left on Fletcher's neck. 'The war takes a toll on the mind. Let me make it up to you. I'll book you a room at my inn and I'll send you up to Vocans Academy on one of the supply wagons tomorrow. My name is Arcturus. And yours?' He held out his hand.

Fletcher took the hand and shook it, the violence instantly forgiven at the mention of the academy. Its reputation was legendary; the training ground of battlemages since Hominum was first founded. What took place there was a closely guarded secret, even to the soldiers that fought alongside them. Arcturus's invitation was far beyond anything Fletcher had dreamed possible for him and his demon.

'Fletcher. No harm done; I'd have far worse than a bruised neck if it wasn't for you. The way in which I received my demon is rather a complex one, which is why I was confused by your question. I'll explain it all to you tonight if you'll let me,' Fletcher replied, wincing as he rubbed his throat.

'Yes, you can tell me over dinner and a drink. My treat, of course. If I remember correctly, James Baker was not a very powerful summoner, so capturing a rare Salamander demon like yours would certainly have been beyond his means – though I suspect he would have kept it for himself if he'd managed to get hold of one,' Arcturus mused, continuing down the street.

'Is that what it is?' Fletcher asked, looking at his demon. He grinned as Arcturus turned into an expensive looking inn, smelling the telltale scent of cooking from inside. Tonight he would stuff himself with food and soak away his troubles in a hot bath. Then, tomorrow, it was on to Vocans Academy!

16

Fletcher did not learn much more from Arcturus that night. The man was as good as his word, buying Fletcher a steak and kidney pie and listening to his story – leaving out Didric's part, of course. No sooner had Fletcher finished speaking than Arcturus excused himself and disappeared to his chambers. Fletcher didn't mind; he bathed in a steaming hot bath with a full belly and slept between silk sheets. Even the imp had feasted on a fresh, minced steak, devouring it in seconds before nosing his bowl for more. If Arcturus could afford such finery, surely the life of a summoner could not be all bad.

In the morning he was woken by an impatient man, who claimed that he had been instructed to take Fletcher to the academy. When Fletcher emerged into the street, the man bade him hurry up and sit beside him in the front of the wagon, or he would be late for his morning delivery of fruit and vegetables.

The journey took over two hours but the driver evaded Fletcher's attempts at small talk, his face pinched with worry at the traffic on the road. Instead, Fletcher passed the time by allowing the imp to ride proudly on his shoulder, grinning at the curious glances from people as they trotted by. After Arcturus had allowed Sacharissa out in the open so brazenly, Fletcher did not see why he couldn't do the same.

He tried to picture Vocans, but he knew so little about it that his mind ranged from imagining a sumptuous palace to a comfortless training ground for fresh recruits. Either way, his excitement mounted with every turn of the cart's wheels.

Finally, they arrived at the frontier with the southern jungle, the boom of cannon echoing in the distance. Whereas before the dirt road they were travelling on was surrounded by green fields, this land was thick with weeds and pitted with heavy gouges in the earth, evidence of the war that had since passed this land by.

'There's the castle,' the driver said, breaking his silence. He pointed at the murky shadow of what looked like a mountain ahead of them, obscured by a thick fog that hung in the air. The wagon had joined a queue of others, though these were delivering heavy barrels of gunpowder and crates full of lead shot.

'Is that where the King lives?' Fletcher asked.

'No, boy. That's Vocans Academy. The King lives with his father in a fancy palace in the centre of Corcillum,' the driver replied, giving him a curious look. But Fletcher wasn't listening. Instead he gazed open mouthed, as the fog was dissipated by a heavy gust of wind.

The castle was as large as one of Beartooth's peaks. The main building itself was a giant cube, made up of blocks of marbled granite, with terraces and balconies layered into the sides, like decorations on a wedding cake. There were four round turrets on each corner, each one with a flat, crenulated top, stretching hundreds of feet into the sky above the main structure. A deep moat of black, murky water surrounded the castle, twenty feet wide with a steep bank on each side. The drawbridge was down, but all the wagons passed it by, moving towards the cannon fire that still boomed in the distance.

As they moved closer to the academy, Fletcher could see that the walls were thickly latticed with creeping ivy and tinged with lichen and moss; it must have been built centuries ago. The boards of the drawbridge emitted a dangerous creak as the driver clucked his skittish horses over the top of it, but they made it to the other side in one piece.

The courtyard was shadowed by the four walls around it, with only a small square of sky illuminating it, from several storeys up. It was dominated by a semicircle of steps that led up to a heavy set of wooden double doors; the entrance to the castle.

As soon as the horses' hooves clopped on the cobbles, a fat man in an apron, with a puffy, red face, emerged from the shadows. He was flanked by two nervous looking kitchen boys who sprang to work unloading the wagon.

'Late, as usual. I shall have a word with the quartermaster about getting a new supplier if this happens again. We've only half an hour to prepare and serve breakfast now,' the fat man said, plucking at his apron strings with his pudgy fingers.

'It's not my fault, Mr Mayweather, sir. An officer forced me to bring this noviciate up, which took me half an hour out of my way. Here, boy, tell him,' the driver spluttered, prodding Fletcher in the small of his back. Fletcher nodded dumbly, the reality of where he was beginning to hit home.

'All right then. We'll let this one slide, but you're on my list,' Mayweather said with an appraising glance at Fletcher and an even longer look at his demon. Fletcher dismounted as the last of the fruit and vegetables were removed from the back of the wagon and stood, unsure of what he was supposed to do. The driver left without a second glance, eager to be away and on to his next pick up.

'Do you know where you're going, lad?' Mayweather asked gruffly, but not unkindly. 'You're not a noble-born, that's obvious. The commoners have already been here a week and I know all the second years by now. You must be new. Did you turn down the offer to come here, then change your mind?'

'Arcturus sent me . . .' Fletcher said, unsure how to answer.

'Ahh, I see. You must be a special case then. We've already got two more of those upstairs,' Mayweather said, his voice low and mysterious. 'Though they're a little stranger than you, I'll grant you.

'We don't get many noviciates brought in personally by a battlemage,' he continued, stepping closer to peer at Fletcher's imp. 'It's usually the Inquisitors who find the gifted and bring them in. Battlemages rarely enlist any adepts themselves, because it means they have to give away one of their demons to them. They need every demon they can get their hands on at the front lines. Seems strange for Arcturus to give you a rare demon like this one, though. I've never seen the like!'

'Is there someone I need to present myself to?' Fletcher asked, eager to get away before Mayweather pried further. The more people who knew how Fletcher had become a summoner, the more likely that his whereabouts would get back to Pelt.

'You're lucky. The first day starts tomorrow, so you haven't missed much,' Mayweather said. 'The noble-born candidates will arrive tonight; they tend to spend the week before in Corcillum, it's more comfortable for them there. As for the teachers, they'll be arriving from the front lines tomorrow morning, so you're best off speaking to the Provost. He's the only battlemage that doesn't spend half the year on the front lines. Go straight ahead through the front doors and one of the supporting staff will let you know where to find him. Now if you'll forgive me, I have breakfast to prepare.' Mayweather spun on his heel and waddled away.

Despite the demon nestled around his throat, Fletcher did not feel like he belonged here. The ancient stone spoke of opulence and history. It was not for the likes of him.

Fletcher mounted the wide stairs and pushed through the double doors. Best to find the Provost before breakfast was served; then he could introduce himself to the other students over the morning meal. He was not going to be a loner again.

He stepped into a huge atrium with twin spiral staircases to his left and right, stopping on each floor. Fletcher counted five levels in total, each one bordered by a metal railing. The ceiling was supported by heavy oak beams; massive struts that held the stone above in place. A dome of glass in the ceiling allowed a pillar of light into the centre of the hall, supplemented by crackling torches set in the walls. At the very end of the hallway was another set of wooden doors, but it was the archway above them that drew Fletcher's eye. The stone was carved with hundreds of demons, each one more breathtaking than the last. The attention to detail was extraordinary, and the eyes of each demon were made up of coloured jewels that sparkled in the light.

It was a huge space, almost wasteful in its design. The marble floors were being polished by a young servant, who gave Fletcher a weary look as he walked his dirty boots over the wet surface.

'Could you point me in the direction of the Provost?' Fletcher requested, trying not to look behind him at the footprints he had left.

'You'll get lost if I don't show you,' the servant said with a sigh. 'Come on. I've got a lot of work to do before the nobles arrive, so don't dawdle.'

'Thank you. My name is Fletcher. And yours?' Fletcher asked, holding out his hand. The servant stared at him with surprise, then shook it with a happy smile.

'I can honestly say I've never been asked that by a student,' the servant said. 'Jeffrey is the name, thank you for asking. If you're quick I'll show you up to your quarters afterwards, and sort out any laundry for you that you might need doing. Begging your pardon, but from the smell of your garments it seems you need it.' Fletcher reddened but thanked him all the same. Although he had washed himself the night before, he had forgotten that his clothes still smelled like sheep.

Jeffrey led him up to the first floor on the east side and down a corridor opposite the stairway. The walls were lined with suits of armour and racks of pikes and swords, left over from the last war. Every few steps they would walk past a painting depicting an ancient battle, which Fletcher would have to tear his eyes away from as Jeffrey pulled him onwards.

They passed by a set of large glass cabinets, stacked with jars of pale green liquid. Each one contained a small demon, suspended eternally within.

Finally, Jeffrey slowed down. The servant pointed to a huge mace hung up on the wall. It was studded with sharp stones, each the size and shape of an arrowhead.

'That's the war club that belonged to the orc chieftain of the Amanye tribe, taken as a trophy in the Battle of Watford Bridge. It was actually the Provost who struck him down,' Jeffrey said with pride. 'A great man, our Provost. Strict as a judge, though. You be careful of him; look him in the eye and don't backchat. He hates both the spineless and the insolent in equal measures.'

With those words Jeffrey stopped at a heavy wooden door and banged on it with his fist.

'Come in!' shouted a booming voice from inside.

17

The room was stiflingly hot compared to the chilled corridors. A blaze crackled in the corner of the dim room, spitting sparks that were sucked up into the flue of the chimney.

'Shut the damned door! It's bloody freezing out there,' the voice boomed again. Fletcher jumped to obey as he noticed a figure sitting behind a large wooden desk in the centre of the room.

'Let's be having you, step lively now. And remove that hood from your face. Don't you know it's rude to cover your head indoors?'

Fletcher hurried into the room and pulled his hood down, revealing the demon that had taken refuge there soon after Fletcher had set foot in Vocans.

The figure harrumphed and then struck a match, lighting a lamp on the corner of his desk. The glow revealed a walrus of a man with a white handlebar moustache and thick mutton-chop sideburns that dominated his features.

'I say, that's a rare demon you've got there! I've only seen one of those, and that wasn't on our side, either.' The man snatched some glasses from the desk and peered at the imp. It shied away at his gaze, causing the old man to chuckle.

'They're fragile little things, but powerful. Who gave it to you? I'm supposed to be informed whenever someone manages to summon a demon outside of the usual species,' the Provost boomed.

'Arcturus sent me,' Fletcher said, hoping that answer would be enough.

'Impress him, did you? We haven't had a novice brought in by a battlemage for quite some time; two years now, I think. You're lucky, you know. Most of the commoners are given weaker demons to start off with. Mites, usually. They're easier to capture and, when we need a new one, a battlemage is chosen at random to provide it. Doesn't put them in a generous mood, unfortunately. Not the best system, but it's the only one we've got. In any case, I shall be having words with Arcturus about it.'

Fletcher nodded dumbly, earning himself a stern glare.

'There's no nodding here. You say "Yes, Provost Scipio, sir"!' the man barked.

'Yes, Provost Scipio, sir,' Fletcher parroted, standing up straight.

'Good. Now, what do you want?' Scipio asked, leaning back in his chair.

'I want to join up, sir; learn to become a battlemage,' Fletcher replied.

'Well, you're here, aren't you? Be off with you. Registration is tomorrow, you can make it all official then,' Scipio said, waving him away. Fletcher left, dumbfounded. He was careful to close the door behind him this time. It had all been so easy.

Somehow, everything was falling into place.

Jeffrey was waiting for him, an anxious look on his face.

'Everything OK?' he asked, leading Fletcher back to the stairs.

'More than OK. He's allowed me to join up,' Fletcher said with a grin.

'Not surprising. We need every summoner we can find, that's why we started making all the changes. Girls, commoners, there's even . . . well . . . you'll see for yourself. It's not my place to say,' Jeffrey muttered. Fletcher decided not to pry, instead being careful not to lose his footing on the dark stairwell.

'There aren't many fires or torches here,' Fletcher observed as they trudged up the steep stairs.

'No, the budget is strained as it is. When the nobles arrive we will warm the place up. Everything has to be just so for them, or they complain to their parents. Half of them are spoiled little popinjays, but don't get me wrong, some are nice enough fellows,' Jeffrey panted, pausing when they reached the fifth and final floor. Fletcher noticed Jeffrey was even skinnier than he was himself, with dark brown hair that contrasted starkly with a pallid complexion that was almost verging on the sickly.

'Are you all right? You don't look so well,' Fletcher asked him. The boy coughed and then took a deep, rattling breath.

'I have terrible asthma, it's why they won't let me join up. But I want to do right by my country, so I serve here instead. I'll be all right, just give me a second,' Jeffrey said, wheezing.

Fletcher felt a growing respect for Jeffrey. He had never felt particularly patriotic, with Pelt being so far removed from any major cities, but he admired it in others.

'I didn't see Scipio's demon. What kind does he have?' Fletcher asked, making conversation as Jeffrey began to breathe more easily.

'He doesn't. He used to have a Felid, but it died before he retired. They say it broke his heart when he lost it. Now he just teaches and manages Vocans,' Jeffrey said.

Fletcher wondered what a Felid might be. Some sort of cat, perhaps?

They walked on past dimly lit corridors to the very corner of the castle, where another staircase spiralled upwards. Jeffrey eyed it with apprehension.

'Don't worry, I can manage from here. Just tell me where I need to go,' Fletcher volunteered.

'Thank God. You can't miss it; the commoners' quarters are at the very top of the southeast tower. I'll send someone up for your laundry later; for now, there's a spare uniform in every bedroom upstairs, try a couple on and see which of them fits. You don't want to be known as the smelly one on your first day,' Jeffrey said, already hurrying away.

Fletcher resisted the temptation to shout the question that had come unbidden to his mind. *Why did the commoners have separate quarters?* He shrugged it away and began his long journey up the stairs, knowing from what he had seen outside that it was quite a way.

At intervals off the staircase there were wide, round chambers, each one filled with old desks, chairs and benches, amongst other bric-a-brac. The wind whistled through the arrow slits in the walls, chilling Fletcher to the bone and causing him to put his hood up once again. He hoped it would be warmer upstairs.

As he rounded what felt like the thousandth step, he heard a boy's voice above him.

'Hang on, that's one of the servants. I think they're going to call us for breakfast!' The boy's voice reminded him of Pelt, the accent common, and hinting at a rural upbringing.

'I'm starving! I hope they don't make us sit in silence like last time,' a girl's voice followed.

'Nah, it's only because crusty old Scipio was there that they wanted us quiet, but he complained about the cold so much I doubt he'll break his fast in the canteen again,' the boy replied.

Fletcher rounded the corner into a large room and almost ran straight into a boy with bright blond hair and the ruddy complexion of a northerner.

'Whoops, sorry, mate. Guess I spoke too soon. Here, let me help with your bags,' the boy said, pulling at Fletcher's satchel. Fletcher unstrapped it and let him carry it to a long table that sat in the middle of the room.

'Rory Cooper, at your service,' the boy said, shaking Fletcher's hand. 'Welcome to our humble abode.'

It was a round chamber, with a high ceiling and two large doors on either side of the back wall. Paintings of battlemages and their demons lined the walls, the faces stern and disapproving. Fletcher grimaced as a draught from the arrow slits blew across the room.

A fetching looking girl with bright green eyes smiled at him through a mass of freckles and wild ginger hair. A blue, beetle-like demon flickered its wings on the table in front of her. Another of them, with an iridescent green carapace, hovered beside Rory's head, filling the room with a soft hum.

The demons were larger than any insect Fletcher had ever seen, so large that they would barely fit on a hand. They sported fierce-looking pincers, with an armoured shell that shone like burnished metal. Fletcher's demon stirred under his hood at their presence, but was not interested enough to come out of hiding.

'My name's Genevieve Leatherby. What's your name?' the girl enquired, flashing him a welcoming smile.

'Fletcher. It's nice to meet you. Is it just the two of you? I thought there would be more of us . . . commoners,' Fletcher said, hesitating at the term.

'There's some more of us downstairs, waiting in the breakfast hall, and the second years eat later than we do, so they are still sleeping. We decided to wait till the servants come and announce it, as the time they serve breakfast hasn't been very consistent so far,' Genevieve said wistfully. 'I thought there would be more students too, when I got here. But there's only five of us first years, including you. I guess I shouldn't be surprised, the lack of summoners is the main reason they let women join the army all those years ago—'

Rory interjected. 'There's seven if you count the other two. We heard them last night but they haven't come out of their rooms yet. Don't know what a laugh they're missing,' he said with a wide grin. 'They'll come round. Everyone loves me eventually.'

'Come off it. You're an annoying little prig if ever I've seen one,' Genevieve teased, pushing him playfully. Rory gave Fletcher a cheeky wink and pointed at the furthest door.

'Why don't you introduce yourself? Maybe see if they can join us for breakfast.'

18

Fletcher pushed the door open to find a short corridor with a row of doors on either side. The door slammed shut behind him as a draught came gusting in from a loophole at the very end of the passageway. He frowned at the sight of it; it was going to be a long, cold winter if this kept up.

He heard movement from the nearest room and knocked, hoping he was not waking them. The door opened at his touch; perhaps the wind had blown it ajar.

'Hello?' he asked, pushing it open.

Suddenly he was on his back, slavering teeth snapping at him as a heavy weight held him down. He managed to grip the creature by its throat, but it took all his strength to keep the fangs from closing on his neck. As saliva dripped on to his face, Fletcher's imp clawed across the monster's muzzle with a screech, but all that did was cause the creature to yawp in pain with each gnash of its teeth.

'Down, Sariel! He has learned his lesson,' came a lilting voice from above. Immediately the creature stopped its attack and sat back on Fletcher's chest. Still helpless, Fletcher gazed up at it, seeing a Canid almost as large as Sacharissa; the size of a small pony. Yet where Sacharissa had wiry, black fur, this demon's hair was as blond and curling as a Corcillum lady's ringlets. Its snout was longer and more refined, with a wet black nose that sniffed at him.

'Get it off me!' Fletcher managed to gasp through gritted teeth. It felt like a tree had fallen on him and was crushing his chest.

The creature stepped off and sat panting behind the door, its four malevolent eyes still fixed on Fletcher's face.

'I shall be writing to the clan chieftains about this! Put with the commoners in a room smaller and less comfortable than a jail cell, which of course is broken into by a young ruffian on the first morning. I had thought when they gave me Sariel that they were taking our peace talks seriously. Now I know I was mistaken,' the voice railed, full of bitterness and anger.

Fletcher sat up and looked at the speaker, dazed as the blood rushed back to his head. His eyes widened as he saw long diamond shaped ears that cut through silvery hair. A delicate face looked at him through large eyes that were the colour of a clear blue sky. They were filled with distrust and almost looked on the verge of tears. Fletcher was talking to a pale elfish girl, dressed in a lacy nightgown.

He averted his eyes and turned away, speaking up in his defence. 'Steady on. I was only trying to say hello. I didn't mean to frighten you.'

'*Frighten* me? I'm not frightened; I'm angry! Didn't anyone tell you that these are the girls' quarters? You're not allowed in

110

here!' the elf screeched like a banshee, and slammed the door in Fletcher's face. He cursed at his stupidity.

'You moron,' he muttered to himself.

'That didn't sound like it went very well,' Rory said from behind him, a sympathetic look on his face as he poked his head through the common-room door. Fletcher felt a fool.

'Why didn't you tell me these were the girls' quarters?' Fletcher snapped, his face reddening as he stormed back into the main chamber.

'I didn't know, honest! I guess it makes sense though, now that I think about it, with Genevieve in this bit and there being a spare room next door . . .' Rory trailed behind him.

'It's fine. Just make sure you smarten up before teaching starts, or you'll embarrass us in front of the nobles,' Fletcher said, then regretted it. Rory's cheerful expression faded, and Fletcher took a deep breath.

'I'm sorry. You're not to blame. It's not every day you get a Canid trying to tear your throat out.' He forced a smile and patted Rory on the back. 'You were saying something about a spare room?'

'Sure! Since you're the last here, all the best rooms have gone. I had a look when I moved in; it's not great.'

They walked into an almost identical corridor, except for an extra door that had been built at the very end. It looked like an afterthought, more a glorified broom cupboard than anything else.

But the inside was more spacious than Fletcher had hoped for, with a comfortable-looking bed, a large wardrobe and a small writing desk. He grimaced at the open loophole in the wall; he was going to have to stuff it later. There was a uniform folded up on the end of the bed; a navy coloured double-breasted jacket with matching trousers. Fletcher shook it out and groaned. It was threadbare and torn, the brass buttons hanging so loosely that one dangled an inch beneath where it was supposed to be.

'Don't worry. I'll take a look at it for you after breakfast. My mother was a seamstress,' Genevieve said from the doorway.

'Thanks,' Fletcher said, though he wasn't sure how salvageable it was.

'So what was she like?' Genevieve asked, her eyes flashing with curiosity. 'Is she a southerner like me?'

'She's . . . I'm not sure exactly,' Fletcher said, avoiding the question. Now that he had ruined the girl's morning, he didn't want to start gossiping about her as well. Best to let her present herself to the others in her own way. His mind was still reeling from the presence of an elf at the academy. Weren't they the enemy?

His thoughts were interrupted by the emergence of the imp, who tumbled from his hood to inspect their new abode. The little demon brushed the uniform on to the floor with a flick of its tail, then hummed with content as it rolled on to its back and scratched itself against the rough fabric of the bed covers. Rory's eyes widened at the sight and Fletcher smiled to himself.

'What's a Canid?' Rory pondered aloud as they walked back into the main chamber. They were soon followed by the imp, who clambered on to Fletcher's shoulder and surveyed their surroundings with a protective glare.

'You'll find out soon enough. They aren't easy to describe. If your Mites are beetle-demons then I would say a Canid is a dog-demon, if that makes sense,' Fletcher replied proudly, glad to finally know more about summoning than someone else.

'Our demons are called Mites?' Genevieve asked, holding out a palm and letting her blue beetle settle on her hand.

'I'm not sure; I heard the Provost use the word,' Fletcher replied, sitting down at the table.

'Oh well, I just call mine Malachi. Like malachite. You know, because of his colouring,' Rory said, letting the green beetle scuttle up his arm.

'Mine is called Azura,' Genevieve declared, holding the demon to one of the torchlights so that Fletcher could see the cerulean blue of the creature's carapace. Fletcher paused, feeling awkward as they looked at him expectantly.

'What's yours called?' Rory prompted, as if Fletcher was slow.

'I . . . I haven't really had a chance to name him yet,' Fletcher muttered with embarrassment. 'I know he is a Salamander demon, though. Maybe you can help me think up a name over breakfast.'

'Of course! He's got a lovely colour to him; I'm sure we can think of something,' Rory exclaimed.

'Could we stay away from colours?' Fletcher said, hoping to come up with something more original. 'He's a fire demon. Maybe we can use that.'

As Rory began to answer, a stern-looking matron walked into the room with a heavy basket of sheets and linens.

'Be off with you! I need to clean. You can wait downstairs with the others instead of getting into mischief up here,' she scolded, shooing them down the stairs.

'Shouldn't we tell the other two?' Genevieve looked back up

as they tramped down the winding staircase.

'No,' Fletcher blurted, hoping to avoid the elf for at least another few minutes. 'The matron will let them know when she gets to their rooms.'

They shrugged and led him the long way down the corridor, making suggestions for names. Fletcher's imp went back to sleep with a yawn, oblivious to the debate. Fletcher was starting to wonder whether he was allowing the demon to be lazy, as he watched Malachi and Azura zipping around their owners' heads.

They eventually reached the ground floor and Fletcher was led through the atrium, mouthing an apology at Jeffrey, who was still polishing the floor they were treading on. The boy rolled his eyes with a sad smile and went back to his work.

They walked through the set of large double doors opposite the main entrance across the atrium. This room's ceiling was substantially lower, yet it was still a huge space that echoed with their footsteps. Large, unlit chandeliers hung at intervals above three rows of long stone tables and benches. The centre of the room was dominated by a statue of a bearded man dressed in elaborate armour, carved with startling attention to detail.

Fletcher was surprised to find only two boys sitting there, spooning porridge into their mouths with gusto. One had black hair and olive skin; he must have been from a village on the border of the Akhad Desert in eastern Hominum. He was handsome, with a chiselled jaw and lively eyes that were hooded with long lashes.

The other boy was chubby, with closely cropped brown hair and a hearty red face. Both waved at him as a servant handed him a tray of porridge, jam and warm bread. When he sat they immediately introduced themselves; the fatter boy was called Atlas and the other Seraph.

'Is it just you two? Where are the second years?' Fletcher asked, confused.

'We eat before they do, thank heavens!' Atlas mumbled, abandoning his spoon to slurp the porridge up from the edge of the bowl.

'They need their extra sleep, what with the stress of their more . . . practical lessons,' Seraph explained, looking at Atlas with a bemused expression. 'They even have field trips to the frontier once a week. I can't wait to be in their shoes.'

'Wait until you've been there,' Genevieve muttered, a hint of sadness in her voice, Fletcher noticed. He knew enough about the front lines to sense that she might have lost someone close to her. Perhaps she was an orphan, like him.

'Where are your demons?' Fletcher changed the subject. 'Have you got Mites like the others?' He was desperate to see more demons.

'No, none yet,' Atlas said with a hint of jealousy. 'We're still waiting. They said the teachers would be giving us ours tomorrow. They only had two demons on the day we all arrived.'

'It was the smart move,' Seraph said, half to himself. 'They asked me if I wanted to take one of the Mites or wait. I did my homework, asked some of the servants. Mites are the weakest. It's better to wait for the chance of a bigger prize.'

Fletcher was intrigued by the mention of better demons. He tried to remember what he had glimpsed in the paintings and carvings around the castle. If only Jeffrey hadn't been in such a hurry. Still, there would be plenty of time for that later.

'I wouldn't have it any other way,' Rory replied, defensive. 'I wouldn't trade Malachi for anything.'

Seraph held his hands up in surrender. 'I meant no offence. I am sure I will feel the same way about my demon when I eventually receive it, Mite or no Mite.'

Rory grunted and went back to his meal.

'What other kinds of demons do you know of? I've only heard of four,' Fletcher asked Seraph, who seemed to know the most in the group. But before the handsome boy could answer there was a gasp from Atlas. The fat cadet was staring at the door. Fletcher turned and saw what had caused it. A dwarf had entered the room . . . and he had a demon with him.

19

The dwarf looked very much like Athol had, with a dark red beard and a powerful, stocky body. He glared at them from beneath his bushy eyebrows and then took a tray from a nervous servant's hands. He sat away from the group on another table, turning his back on them. Though Fletcher was sure that the dwarf was the source of everyone else's fascination, he was more interested in the demon that had trailed in behind him.

At three feet high, the creature was shaped much like a young child, were it not for its squat profile and hefty arms and legs. Yet what was most fascinating was its colouring. The creature looked as if it was made from misshapen rock, the effect made more striking by a dusting of moss and lichen that grew on its surface. Its hands were like mittens, with a thick opposable thumb that could be used for grasping. With every movement it made, Fletcher could hear the dull rasp of stone against stone.

As the commoners gawked at it, the demon turned around and looked back through a pair of small black eyes that were set deep in its head.

'A Golem! Those are difficult to capture. The servants said they grow over time, so you have to catch them young,' Seraph whispered. 'I hope I get gifted one of them.'

'Not likely,' Atlas said. 'They must have given it to him as a favour to the Dwarven Council, a show of good faith as dwarves are incorporated into the army. I didn't realise they had been accepted into all branches of the military. God knows what they would ride if any join the cavalry; their little legs would barely be able to grip a horse's sides!'

Atlas laughed at the thought. Fletcher ignored him, looking at the dwarf sitting hunched and alone. He stood up.

'What are you doing?' Rory hissed, snatching at Fletcher's sleeve.

'I'm going to introduce myself,' Fletcher said.

'Did you see the look he gave us? I think he wants to be left alone,' Genevieve stammered.

Fletcher pulled out of Rory's grasp, ignoring them. He had recognised the look of resentment on the dwarf's face when he walked in. He himself had worn it many times before, back when he had been ostracised by the other village children in Pelt.

As he approached the bench the Golem rumbled threateningly, its craggy face opening to reveal a toothless mouth. The dwarf turned at the noise, a look of apprehension on his face.

'I'm Fletcher.' He held out his hand for the dwarf to shake.

'Othello. What do you want?' the dwarf replied, ignoring it.

'Nice to meet you. Why don't you sit with us? There's plenty of room,' Fletcher asked. The dwarf looked at the others, who were staring at them from the other table, their faces full of apprehension.

'I'm fine here. Thank you for making the effort, but I know I'm not welcome,' the sullen dwarf muttered, turning back to his meal. Fletcher decided to make one last attempt.

'Of course you are! You're going to be fighting the orcs just like the rest of us.'

'You don't understand. I'm nothing more than a symbolic gesture. Hominum's generals don't mean to let us join the military for real. They sent most of our recruits to the elven front to rot with the chaffed. The King meant well by forcing them to let us join, but the generals are still the ones who decide what to do with us. How can we change their minds when they won't let us fight?' Othello murmured, so only Fletcher could hear.

'Vocans has girls, commoners too. In fact, everyone you see here is a commoner. The nobles are arriving tomorrow,' Fletcher replied, his heart going out to the unhappy dwarf. He paused for a moment, then leaned closer to the dwarf and whispered.

'They need adepts, no matter where they come from. There's even an elf! I don't think the battlemage division is very picky, as long as you can fight.'

The dwarf smiled at him sadly, then took Fletcher's hand and shook it.

'I know about the elf. We had an . . . interesting conversation when we were waiting to be gifted our demons. Anyway, I hope you're right. I'm sorry for my rudeness earlier; I must sound very jaded,' Othello said, picking up his tray.

'Not to worry. I met another dwarf yesterday and he felt much the same as you did. He gave me something,' Fletcher said, pulling the card he had been given from his pocket.

'Put that away!' Othello hissed under his breath as soon

119

as he saw it. Fletcher stuffed it back in his trousers. What was the big deal?

They sat down at the table with the others, their conversation suddenly muffled by the dwarf's presence. Fletcher introduced them all.

'Good morning,' Othello said awkwardly, nodding to everyone. They all nodded back in silence. After a few beats Rory piped up. It seemed to Fletcher that he hated awkward silences.

'I'll tell you what, I wish I could grow a moustache like that. Did you always have one?' Rory said, stroking his own bare face.

'If you're asking if I was born with it, no,' Othello said, cracking a wry smile. 'It's our belief that cutting our hair is a sin to the Creator. We are made just as he wished us to be. If he gave us hair, then we must keep it.'

'Why don't you let your nails grow too then? Sounds like madness to me,' Atlas said bluntly, pointing at Othello's stubby but neatly trimmed fingers.

'Atlas!' Genevieve scolded.

'That's OK, it's a fair question. We consider the white part of the nail dead and therefore no longer part of us. Of course it is considered more of a tradition than a religious belief these days: many dwarves trim their beards and hair; some of the younger dwarves even dye it. This is quite common knowledge in Corcillum. Where do you hail from?' Othello asked in a measured voice.

'I'm from a village to the west, close by the Vesanian Sea,' Atlas retorted. 'Are you from Corcillum originally?'

Othello paused, looking bemused. Seraph answered for him.

'The dwarves were here before the first man even set foot in this land. They cleared the forests, flattened the earth, diverted the rivers, even put up the great marker stones that map out Hominum's territory.'

Othello smiled, as if impressed by the young commoner's knowledge of his people.

'Mankind moved here two thousand years ago, when they made the long journey across the Akhad Desert.' Seraph continued, encouraged by the rapt attention of the others. 'Corcillum was the dwarf capital, so we moved in with them, working and trading. But then a great sickness swept through the city, hitting the dwarves particularly hard. Soon after, our first King took power, with help from what now are the noble families. They were a small group of summoners who controlled powerful demons, far stronger than the demons our modern day summoners control. That is why every royal and noble-born is able to summon; they inherited their ancestors' abilities.'

'It is also why we rebelled so often,' Othello said in a hushed tone. 'Foolish though it was, with our population so low and no summoners in our ranks. We never recovered our numbers after the sickness, thanks to a law forced on us by your King's forefathers. We must live in the ghetto and may only have a certain number of children each year. We cannot even own our own land. The royals said we have brought it on ourselves after so many rebellions.'

A sombre mood settled over the others, but Fletcher felt angry, the same anger he had felt at Didric's injustice. This was . . . inhumane! The hypocrisy of the situation sickened him. So this was what Athol had been talking about. Atlas opened his mouth to speak again, a look of disagreement on his face.

'So, Seraph, you said you have done your research. Tell us a bit about what we should be expecting over the next few months,' Fletcher interjected, before Atlas could start an argument.

Seraph leaned forward and beckoned everyone closer, smiling at the opportunity to show off what he had learned.

'They are very fair here. Commissions are given based on merit, so the better you perform in the exams and challenges, the higher the officer's rank you are given when you graduate. The problem is that it is weighted against us commoners. The demons we get given are not particularly strong, whilst the demons the nobles receive are from their parents, who take more care to capture powerful ones for their children. Some are even fortunate enough to be given one of their parent's main demons, but that is rare. Fletcher's demon I'm not so sure about – I've never seen one of those before. But, Othello, your demon will be very powerful when it is full grown, from what I have heard of Golems.'

'So . . . we're always going to only have our Mites?' Genevieve asked, confused.

'Not necessarily,' Seraph answered. 'It's possible to capture another, more powerful demon in the ether, and add it to your roster. I don't know much about how to do that, and apparently it is harder and riskier to do it with a weak demon. I'm hoping for something other than a Mite. They make great scouts and their pincers pack a nasty punch, but their mana levels are quite low and physically they would be no match for even a juvenile Canid.'

'I see,' Genevieve said, looking slightly less proudly at Azura as she took off and buzzed around the room. They all watched as she settled on the huge statue in the centre of the hall, crawling on to the stone man's eye.

'Who is that anyway?' Fletcher asked the table.

'I know,' Othello said, pointing at the plaque beneath the statue. 'It is Ignatius, King Corwin's right-hand man and the founder of Vocans Academy, back when it was nothing more than a tent in a field. He died in the First Orc War a couple of thousand years ago, but he is credited with leading the charge that broke the orc ranks and ultimately led to their defeat.'

'That's it,' Fletcher said under his breath, looking at his imp. It had crawled down his arm and was licking at the remains of the porridge in his bowl with relish.

'What's it?' Rory asked.

'Ignatius. That's what I will call my demon.'

20

With breakfast over, the others decided to go back to their rooms for more sleep, but Fletcher was loath to sit in the cold. The conversation over breakfast made him realise how little he knew about Vocans. He was going to find Jeffrey. If Seraph knew so much about Vocans from the servants, he was going to tap that source of information for all it was worth. He was in luck; Jeffrey was still polishing the atrium floor.

'Care to show me around? There's not much point in cleaning that floor now, it's just going to get dirty when the second years come down for breakfast,' Fletcher said to the tired looking servant.

'I'm only polishing it so that Mr Mayweather doesn't yell at me. If I can say I was showing a noviciate round then I'm off the hook! Let's just take it easy on the stairs this time,' Jeffrey said, grinning. 'What would you like to see?'

'Everything!' Fletcher said. 'I've got all day.'

'Then so have I.' Jeffrey beamed. 'Let's go to the summoning room first.'

The room was on the same floor within the east wing. The large steel doors were difficult to open, the screech of rusted hinges echoing around the atrium. Jeffrey took a torch from a sconce outside and led him in, lighting their way with the flickering orange flame. The floor was sticky underfoot, which upon closer examination turned out to be made of heavy strips of leather. There was a large pentacle painted in the middle of the room, the epicentre of a spiral of gradually smaller stars. Each was surrounded by the same strange symbols that Fletcher had seen on the summoner's book. Perhaps these were the keys that James Baker had written about?

'Why leather?' Fletcher asked.

'The pentacles and symbols need to be drawn on or with something organic, otherwise they don't work. We used to have wood but it kept burning and needed to be replaced. The Provost decided that leathers were a better idea. It's worked so far; they smoke and smoulder a bit and it smells something awful, but it's better than risking a fire every time someone's demon enters the ether.'

'I had no idea!' Fletcher said, examining a row of leather aprons that hung on hooks beside the door.

'I don't know much else about this room. You're better off asking a second year, but I wouldn't bother. The competition for ranks is fierce, and they don't like to help first years in case you steal what would have been their promotion. I hate that way of thinking, but the Provost says that it's brutally competitive on the front lines, so why shouldn't novices get a taste of that here?'

Jeffrey lingered by the door, refusing to venture any deeper into the room.

'Let's go. This place gives me the creeps,' he muttered.

He led Fletcher out and they trudged up to the second floor of the east wing.

'This is the library.' Jeffrey pushed open the first door. 'Forgive me if I don't go in. The dust; it's terrible for my asthma.'

The room seemed as deep and long as the atrium was tall. Row upon row of bookshelves ranged along the walls, full of tomes even thicker than the book that lay at the bottom of Fletcher's satchel upstairs. Long tables sat between each bookshelf, with unlit candles spaced at intervals along them.

'There are thousands of essays and theories written here by the summoners of old. Diaries mostly, dating back over the last thousand years or so. This place doesn't get used much, there is so much work to do already, without the extra reading. But some do come here for tips and tricks, usually the commoners who don't have the coin to spend in Corcillum on the weekends,' Jeffrey said leaning against the doorway. 'They need to catch up anyway; the nobles always know more than they do, growing up with it and all.'

'Fascinating,' Fletcher said, eyeing the piles of books. 'I'm surprised that this room is used so rarely. There must be a treasure trove of knowledge here.'

Jeffrey shrugged and closed the door.

'I wouldn't know, but I think the teaching in the school has become far more practical, out of necessity. There is just no time for research and experimentation any more; all they care about is getting you to the front lines as quickly as possible.'

As they walked out, Fletcher saw a string of boys and girls walking through the hall.

'Those are the second years,' Jeffrey said, nodding at them. 'They've had a hell of a time this year, the competition for ranks is fiercer than ever. Now that convicts are likely to be drafted into the army, dwarves too, they're going to need officers. And if the second years don't perform well, that is who they will be leading into battle . . . or rotting away with on the elven front.' Fletcher wasn't sure what would be so bad about leading dwarves into battle, but he wasn't going to get into a debate with Jeffrey, not when he still had so much to learn.

He stared at the second years as they descended the dark stairs, without their demons. Tiny spheres of light floated around their heads like fireflies, emitting an ethereal blue glow.

'What are those lights? And where are their demons?' Fletcher exclaimed, as he and Jeffrey followed them down the steps. The second years ignored him, rubbing their eyes and murmuring amongst themselves.

'Demons aren't allowed out other than in your quarters or during lessons, you'll be told about that once you first years have settled in. Although where the demons go when they aren't with their summoners I haven't a clue. As for the lights, they're called wyrdlights. It's one of the first skills noviciates learn, I think. In a few days you guys will be zipping those things all over the place.'

'I can't wait,' Fletcher said, eyeing the little blue lights as they floated aimlessly around the atrium. 'No wonder there's only one candle in our rooms.'

Jeffrey dragged him away from the atrium and down some stairs beside the entrance to the summoning room.

'The castle is huge, but the rooms are mostly used as

accommodation for the nobles, teachers and servants. The rest are either empty or used as storage, except for a few lecture halls,' Jeffrey said as their footsteps echoed down the dark steps.

When they reached the bottom of the stairs, the first thing Fletcher noticed was a chain of manacles that were embedded in the wall of a long, dank corridor that stretched into the darkness. As they walked down it, Fletcher could see dozens of cramped, windowless prison cells, barely a few feet wide.

'What is this place?' Fletcher asked, horrified. The conditions for people kept imprisoned there would have been appalling.

'This part of the castle was built in the first year of the war eight years ago, for deserters. We didn't know what to expect, so whenever troops were sent to the front lines, we made sure they would bed down here for the night beforehand. That way, they would know what awaited them if they ran away in cowardice. We only ever had a few dozen prisoners in the first two years, or so I'm told. Nowadays, deserters are just flogged when they are caught and then sent back to the front lines.' Jeffrey ran his hand along the bars as he spoke. Fletcher shuddered and followed him down the long corridor.

He was surprised when the claustrophobic tunnel opened out into an enormous room. It was shaped like the inside of a coliseum, with concentric rings of stairs that also served as seats, encircling a sand-covered enclosure. Fletcher estimated it could easily fit an audience of five hundred.

'What the hell is this doing here?' Fletcher asked. Surely there could be no explanation for a gladiatorial arena such as this in the basement of the academy.

'What do you think, boy?' came a rasping voice from behind

him. 'Executions, that's what it was for. To give the soldiers and novices heart whenever we captured an orc, so they could see that they die just like any other creature.'

Fletcher and Jeffrey spun to see a near toothless man with greying hair, leaning on a staff. He was missing his right foot and hand, which had been replaced by a thick peg and wickedly sharp hook. Stranger still, he wore the chain mail armour of the unmodernised army, resplendent in dark green and silver from one of the old noble houses.

'Of course it was never used. Who ever heard of an orc being captured alive!' He cackled to himself and held out his left hand, which Fletcher shook.

'We captured a few gremlins, but watching them cower and piss their loincloths wasn't very gratifying. They probably have more of a quarrel with the orcs than we do, what with them being enslaved and all,' the man said, limping down to the arena with a lopsided gait.

'Well come on, let's see what you can do with that khopesh. Long time since I've seen one of them.' The man brandished his staff and pointed it at Fletcher's sword. 'I may have lost my good hand in the war, but I can still teach you a thing or two with my left. Hell, I must be able to; that's my job, isn't it!'

'Who the hell is that?' Fletcher whispered, wondering what kind of madman would choose to spend his free time down in the dungeons. Jeffrey leaned in and whispered back.

'That's Sir Caulder. He's the weapons master!'

Sir Caulder scraped a line in the sand with his staff and beckoned Fletcher closer.

'Come on. I may be a cripple, but I've got things to do.'

129

Fletcher jumped into the arena and advanced towards him, cautioning Ignatius to stay beside Jeffrey with a thought. Sir Caulder winked at him and raised his hook in mock salute. 'I know officer material when I see it, but can you fight like one?'

'I don't want to hurt you, sir. This sword is sharp,' Fletcher warned him, unbuckling it and holding it out for him to see. It was the first time he had really held his weapon in his hand. The sword was far heavier than he had expected.

'Aye, I may be old, but with age comes experience. This staff here is twice as dangerous a weapon in my one hand than that khopesh is in both of yours.'

Fletcher doubted it. The man was as skinny as a rake and about as tall too. He gave a half-hearted swipe at him, aiming so that he wouldn't hit anything. The man made no move to defend himself, allowing the sword to graze harmlessly in front of his chest.

'All right, boy, enough playing,' Sir Caulder snapped.

The staff came thrumming through the air at Fletcher's head and dealt him a stinging blow. Fletcher cried out and slapped his hand over his ear, feeling the blood as it ran in a hot trickle down his neck.

'Come on, that sword wouldn't even pierce this chain mail,' the old man said with glee, prancing in front of Fletcher like a billy goat.

'I wasn't ready for that,' Fletcher snarled, then stabbed at Sir Caulder's stomach, two-handed. The staff came down like a hammer, knocking his sword so hard that it stabbed into the sand. Fletcher was rewarded with another swat to his cheek, leaving a wide welt.

'That's not going to look pretty in the morning,' Sir Caulder cackled, jabbing at Fletcher's stomach and causing him to stumble back.

'You see, Jeffrey, they carry around their swords as if they're just for show. Let me tell you, when an orc charges at you from the bushes, don't think a musket ball is going to stop it. It'll be using your rib as a toothpick before it even realises it's been shot,' Sir Caulder ranted, punctuating each word with a prod of his staff.

Fletcher's patience had run out. He swung his khopesh in a wide arc, catching the staff in the curve and pushing it to the side. Then he charged in under Sir Caulder's guard, shoulder barging the man to the ground, landing on top of him.

Before a shout of triumph could leave his lips, Sir Caulder's knees scissored around his neck, choking off the words. His peg leg knocked against the back of Fletcher's head. Fletcher dropped his sword and tried to pry open Sir Caulder's thighs, but they were like twin bars of steel. The man tightened his hold, until Fletcher's vision bruised. Then the world faded to black.

21

When consciousness returned, Fletcher could hear the sound of Ignatius hissing. He opened his eyes to find Jeffrey and Sir Caulder watching him from across the arena. Sir Caulder was swearing foully and there was the stench of burning in the air.

'Goddamned demons, they should all be shot. It's good, solid fighting that will kill orcs, not these abominations,' he grumbled, fingering a blackened patch of cloth in the breast of his surcoat. Ignatius must have flamed at him when Fletcher fainted.

Fletcher rubbed his bruised throat ruefully and sat up. What was it with people trying to strangle him? Even Ignatius liked to wrap himself around his neck.

'There's something you're forgetting,' Fletcher croaked. 'The orc shamans have twice the number of these abominations, as you call them. Do you think good solid fighting will beat them too? Why do you even teach here if you hate them so much?'

Sir Caulder and Jeffrey crossed the arena towards him, pausing every few steps in case Ignatius attacked again. Fletcher calmed

Ignatius with soothing thoughts and then picked up the khopesh, buckling it back on to his belt.

'I'm sorry, laddie. I was just blowing steam. The surcoat was my old uniform. It's all I have left of the old days,' Sir Caulder said, kicking at the sand with his stump.

'Well, it is my fault too. I should have told Ignatius that this was a play fight, though I think we stretched the definition of the word *play* this time round. I'm sorry about your uniform. Can I replace it?' Fletcher asked.

'No. I fought under the Raleighs,' Sir Caulder said, as if that explained everything.

'The Raleighs?' Fletcher asked. 'Are they a noble family?'

'Aye, that they were. Not any more though,' Sir Caulder muttered. Fletcher could see pain in the man's eyes, but his curiosity got the better of him.

'Why? Did they fall out of favour with the King?' Fletcher had never heard of that happening before, though Pelt was so far removed from the machinations of Hominum's upper class it could be a regular occurrence for all he knew.

'No, nothing like that, you idiot! I served under Lord Edmund Raleigh, a long time before the war. He was one of the nobles who owned estates on the southern frontier, so our lands were being constantly raided by orc marauders. In those days the military was too focussed on keeping the dwarves in check to send us any help, so as part of Raleigh's bodyguard we had to deal with it on our own. Lord Raleigh was a good man and a close friend to the King, so don't you go thinking he wasn't!' Sir Caulder ranted.

'I meant no disrespect,' Fletcher said, trying to be polite, 'but I don't understand how the Raleighs fell out of power.'

'The orcs, boy. That's who are to blame. They came in the dead of night, sneaking by all the livestock and the grain and everything else that my lads were protecting. We thought that was what they wanted, so why protect anything else?' he said bitterly, clenching his fists at the memory.

'They slaughtered everyone in the Raleigh family home; the women, the young children. When we got word of it, they were gone, taking the dead with them as trophies and tying them to the trees on the borders of their territory. Lord Raleigh put up a terrible fight. His Canid took three of the orcs out before they slit its belly open and left it to bleed to death. I put it out of its misery myself, poor thing. So don't be thinking I have something against summoners either!'

Sir Caulder shuddered at the memory, then walked up the arena steps to an open door in the wall.

'You're not a bad fighter, but you're going to need to learn how to fight against an orc. That shoulder barge wouldn't have any effect and you'll be fighting against heavy clubs and axes, not precision weapons. Come see me again and I'll show you how,' he said from the doorway, then disappeared inside with a satisfied grunt.

Jeffrey walked him to the entrance and lifted the torch to Fletcher's face so he could see better in the dim light. Ignatius crawled on to Fletcher's shoulder and purred at the sight of the flame.

'He really did a number on you. That's swelling up something fierce,' Jeffrey said.

'It doesn't hurt that much.' Fletcher touched the welt on his face and winced.

They returned in silence to the atrium, pondering Sir Caulder's story as they made their way back up the tall staircase.

'Tour's over,' Jeffrey groaned as they emerged into the atrium. 'I need to get back to work now.'

'Did you know about Sir Caulder and the Raleighs?' Fletcher asked Jeffrey as the servant began to clean the floors again.

'I knew about the Raleighs, but I had no idea Sir Caulder served under them. I do know the Raleigh incident was what set the war in motion. The King and his nobles began to expand Hominum's borders in retaliation; cutting down their trees and razing their villages year after year. It was only when the albino orc began uniting the tribes that it became a proper war though,' Jeffrey replied, scrubbing at the floor.

'I can't believe I hadn't heard of it before.' Fletcher scratched his head. It seemed that living so far north of Corcillum had limited his education on the politics of the wider world.

'You wouldn't. It was kept very hush-hush. The King doesn't like the commoners to know that a noble line can be snuffed out, just like that. It's only because noble offspring go here that I know about it; Sir Caulder never mentioned anything like that before,' Jeffrey replied.

'He must have cared about that uniform very much,' Fletcher said, stroking Ignatius's head.

'Speaking of which, I can't believe you haven't had your clothes cleaned yet! It was a little nauseating in the confines of the corridor downstairs, Fletcher. Go back to your quarters and I'll send someone to collect your clothes and take you to the baths. Seriously.'

22

The moon was full and bright in the cloudless sky. Fletcher shivered and pulled at his uniform's collar; it was the only clothing that hadn't been taken away for cleaning. Still, he had to wear something; it was freezing in the room and the tattered blanket on his bed did little to keep him warm. He leaned out of the glassless window and into the cold night air, thinking on the day.

The elf had remained in her room, which had suited Fletcher just fine. The rest of the group had been cheerful during lunch and dinner, eager for tomorrow and what wonders it would bring. Fletcher found that he enjoyed the company of the others, although the tension between Atlas and Othello left a strained undertone to the otherwise cheerful evening. He was particularly drawn to Seraph, whose clear charisma and knack for storytelling had everyone hanging on to his every word. Rory's happy-go-lucky attitude had also endeared him to Fletcher, and although her efforts at salvaging his uniform had been in vain, he had found Genevieve to be a kind person with a dry sense of humour.

It was strange to know that they would all be risking their lives in the hot jungles of the south in just a few years. Although Fletcher tried to avoid thinking about it, the others were eager for battle. Genevieve was the only one who did not openly flaunt her wish to fight, although she spoke of the orcs with a dark fury that belied tragic experience.

Fletcher knew he should go to sleep, yet he felt too exhilarated to do so. Even the usually lazy Ignatius had caught his mood, playfully chasing his tail in the darkness of the room.

Fletcher held out his candle for Ignatius to light, then went out into the common room. As he entered, he saw a fading light in the stairwell, with the sound of hasty footsteps echoing from below.

'Come on, Ignatius, looks like we aren't the only ones who can't sleep,' Fletcher said. If it was going to be a restless night, he might as well have company.

The corridors were eerie at night, the chill draughts of air whistling through the arrow slits that peppered the outside of the castle. Fletcher's candle flame flickered with each gust, until he had to cup it with one hand to keep it from going out.

'I could do with one of those flying lights right now, don't you think, Ignatius?' he whispered.

The shadows shifted unnaturally as he moved down the corridor, the dark slits of every suit of armour staring at him as he walked past.

It seemed strange that whoever was ahead was moving so quickly, their pace closer to a jog than a midnight stroll. Fletcher hurried to keep up, his curiosity getting the better of him. Even when he reached the atrium, all he saw was the dim light and a swish of cloth as a figure darted out through the main entrance.

The courtyard was silent as a grave and twice as eerie when Fletcher set foot outside, but there was no sign of the mysterious person. He walked to the drawbridge and peered out at the road, looking for the candlelight. As he stared into the wavering gloom, he began to hear the steady clop of hoofbeats on the ground, coming towards the castle.

Fletcher darted into a small room built into the drawbridge's gatehouse, blowing out the candle and pressing himself against the cold stone wall. Whoever it was, Fletcher didn't want their first impression of him to be that of someone who liked to sneak around in the dead of night.

He quelled Ignatius's excitement, impressing on him the need for silence with a stern thought. He remembered what happened the last time he had been in a cold stone room, hiding in the dark. At that memory, the imp responded with agreement and even a hint of what felt like regret. Fletcher smiled and scratched Ignatius's chin. The imp understood more than he thought!

The chirr of spinning wheels and the crack of whips announced the arrival of carriages, rumbling as they crossed the old drawbridge. Fletcher peered through a chink in the stone of the room, hugging his arms to his chest for warmth. Was it the nobles? Perhaps one of the teachers was arriving early?

There were two carriages, both ornately decorated with golden trimming and lit by crackling torches. Two men rode on top of each, wearing dark, brass-buttoned suits and peaked caps that put Fletcher in mind of the Pinkertons' uniforms. All of them carried heavy blunderbusses in their hands, ready to blast buckshot into anyone who ambushed their convoy. Precious cargo indeed.

The doors opened and several figures got out, wearing perfectly tailored versions of the Vocans uniform. In the dim glow of the torches it was hard to see their faces, but the one closest stepped in clear view.

'Oh, dear,' he said to the others in a posh, drawling voice. 'I knew this place had gone to the dogs, but I didn't think it was going to be this bad.'

'Did you see the state of it, Tarquin?' said a girl from the shadows. 'It's a wonder we made it over the drawbridge.'

Tarquin was a handsome boy with chiselled cheekbones and angelic blond hair that fell in curls down to the nape of his neck. Yet his blue-grey eyes seemed to Fletcher as hard and cruel as any he had seen before.

'This is what happens when you let the riffraff in,' Tarquin stated with a contemptuous sneer. 'Standards are slipping. I'm sure when Father was here this place was twice what it is now.'

'Still, at least the commoners can be given the commissions we don't want,' the girl said, out of Fletcher's sight.

'Yes, well, that is the silver lining,' Tarquin said in a bored sounding voice. 'The commoners can have the criminals and, if, heaven forbid, they allow dwarves to serve as officers, then they can command the half-men too. Keep everyone in their rightful place, that's the way to do it.'

A girl stepped out from the gloom and stood beside him, squinting at the tall castle in front of them. She could have been Tarquin's twin, with razor sharp cheekbones and cherubic hair curled in delicate blonde ringlets.

'This is a disgrace. How can every noble child in Hominum be forced to live here for two years?' she asked out loud, tucking an errant strand behind her ear.

'Dear sister, this is why we are here. The Forsyths have not set foot in Vocans since father graduated. We are going to show this place how real nobles are meant to be treated,' Tarquin replied. 'Speaking of which, where are the servants? Be a dear and fetch them for us, would you, Isadora?' he joked, pushing his sister towards the entrance.

'Ugh! I'd rather have my head shaved than spend one second in the servants' quarters,' she spat.

With those words the side door opened and Mayweather, Jeffrey and several other servants stumbled out, many still rubbing sleep from their eyes.

'My apologies for our lateness, my lord,' Mayweather said in a humble voice. 'We had thought you would be arriving in the morning when you did not arrive before the eleventh bell.'

'Yes, well, we decided that Corcillum's drinking houses were a far more enticing place to be tonight than this . . . establishment,' Tarquin said icily, then pointed at Jeffrey. 'You, boy, take my bags up to my quarters and be careful with them. The contents are worth more than you'll make in your lifetime.'

Jeffrey hastened to obey, giving the golden-haired nobles an awkward bow as he passed them.

'Let me show you to your quarters, my lord. Follow me, both of you,' Mayweather said, waddling up the steps as the servants unloaded the carriages. Fletcher caught a glimpse of the two nobles following Mayweather, then his view was obscured as the carriages wheeled around and thundered out of the courtyard.

Soon Fletcher was alone again, filled with disgust at what he had just witnessed. He had always pictured nobles as generous and fair, leading their own men to fight in the war and giving up their adolescent children to serve as battlemages. He knew that many of the nobility of fighting age risked their lives every day on the front lines, leaving their families at home. But he had found these spoiled brats to be the complete opposite of what he had expected. He hoped that not all the noble-born novices would be like the two specimens he had just encountered.

Fletcher waited a few minutes, then snuck out of the gatehouse, making his way back to the main entrance in the shadows of the courtyard walls. Just before he stepped into the moonlight, he heard a creak from the drawbridge behind him.

He spun round to see a figure just before it vanished out of sight, running down the road. A figure with long red hair.

23

The nobles arrived late for breakfast, sitting on the other side of the room and completely ignoring the group of commoners. Tarquin and Isadora led the way, clearly having established themselves as the ringleaders, although the casual backslapping and guffawing made Fletcher think that most of the nobles already knew one another.

'Why are they ignoring us?' Atlas asked, looking over his shoulder as the nobles began to make loud comments about the poor quality of the food.

'This is normal,' Seraph said matter of factly. 'The nobles always stay separate from the commoners. I snuck past one of their rooms the other day. They're the size of our entire quarters and then some!'

'I don't think it should be this way,' Rory said. 'Are we not going to be living together for the next two years? There are only five of them. Surely they will get bored of each other's company?'

'I doubt it,' Fletcher ventured. 'One of the servants told me that the nobles often spend their free time in Corcillum. It is us who will be stuck in this castle with little to do. Our best bet will be to befriend some of the older commoners.'

Even as he spoke, a dozen second years began to stream into the hall, talking loudly. They split into two groups and sat on separate tables, but unlike the first years, the two cliques seemed to be talking to each other with no clear animosity. Yet judging by the quality of their uniforms, Fletcher suspected the table divide was between nobles and commoners once again.

'They're down for breakfast early,' Seraph commented as both tables of second years looked them up and down, with special attention placed on Othello. One of them nudged another and pointed at Ignatius and the Golem, who Othello had named Solomon. The dwarf shifted and lowered his head over his meal, uncomfortable under their gaze.

'I wish we could have breakfast at the same time as they do every day. There's enough room for hundreds of us to eat in here.' Genevieve yawned, resting her head in her hands. Fletcher eyed her red hair with suspicion. Was she the figure he had seen leaving Vocans last night?

As the servants finished laying out breakfast for the new arrivals, the room suddenly hushed. Looking up from his meal, Fletcher saw the Provost stride into the room, followed by two men and a woman who were dressed in officers' uniforms. With a start, he recognised one of them to be Arcturus, his milky eye staring resolutely ahead. The man showed no sign of recognition. The elf girl strode in behind them, causing a stir. She walked with her head high to a seat further down from the commoners' table. Her Canid curled beneath her, its bushy tail stiffening as it glared around the room protectively.

The four officers stood with their arms crossed and stared at the room until absolute silence had fallen.

'Welcome to Vocans! I trust you have all settled in,' Provost Scipio announced gruffly through his bristling moustache. 'You are privileged to be the latest generation of students to grace the hallowed halls of Vocans Academy.' Fletcher looked around, counting the other novices. The second years numbered twelve students, the same as them.

'Our traditions date back to the first King of Hominum, over two thousand years ago,' Scipio continued. 'And though we are few in number, the battlemages that graduate from this institution go on to serve as the finest officers in the military, whether it be at the King's pleasure or under the banner of one of our great noble houses.'

Fletcher saw Tarquin lean in and whisper to Isadora, whose tinkling laugh rang out across the room. He was not the only one to notice. Scipio's face reddened with anger, and he pointed at the young noble.

'You, stand up! I will not abide rudeness, not from anyone, noble or otherwise! Stand up, I say, and give account of yourself.'

Tarquin stood up, yet he seemed unshaken by the Provost's anger. He dug his thumbs into the pockets of his trousers and spoke in a clear voice.

'My name is Tarquin, the first in line for the Dukedom of Pollentia. My father, Duke Zacharias Forsyth, is the general of the Forsyth Furies.' He grinned as the second years began to murmur when they recognised his family name. Clearly his father was one of the oldest and most powerful nobles in Hominum. Fletcher recognised the name Pollentia, a large, fertile tract of land that ran from the Vesanian Sea to the centre of Hominum.

Scipio remained silent, looking at Tarquin expectantly under two bushy white eyebrows. Tarquin waited for a few moments until the silence weighed heavily on the room. Finally, he spoke.

'I apologise for my rudeness. I was only saying to my sister that I am . . . proud to be part of this fine institution.'

'It is only out of respect for your father that I don't send you up to your room like a child,' Scipio harrumphed. 'Sit back down and keep your mouth shut until I have finished speaking.'

Tarquin inclined his head with a smile and sat down, unfazed by the exchange. Fletcher was not sure whether it was confidence or arrogance that gave the boy his dauntless attitude, but he suspected the latter. Scipio stared at Tarquin for a while longer, then turned to the three officers behind him.

'These are your three teachers; Major Goodwin and Captains Arcturus and Lovett. You will treat them with the respect they deserve and remember that whilst they are here educating you, good soldiers on the front lines suffer without their leadership or protection.'

Fletcher examined the two teachers he did not recognise. Captain Lovett was a raven-haired woman with cold eyes and a strict appearance, yet when she smiled at the noviciates as her name was announced, her face lost all of its harshness. Major Goodwin looked almost as old as Scipio, with a large, portly figure and a thick white goatee. He sported a pair of gold-rimmed spectacles that rested on a red nose that hinted at a penchant for hard liquor.

'Now, you second years must be wondering why you have

been called down early,' Scipio announced, causing the bored-looking second years to sit up in their seats. 'I have an announcement that concerns you all. It may not be a particularly popular decision that we have made, but it is one made out of necessity. In the final exams and tournaments this year, both first years and second years will take part. Should any first year acquit themselves to a high standard, then they too shall be offered a commission and sent to the front lines a year early, where they are sorely needed.'

Immediate uproar ensued, but it was quelled with a bellow from Scipio. He held up a hand as the muttering continued.

'I understand that this increases the competition for the few high-level commissions on offer for you second years. I remind you that you have had a year's head start. Should one of the first years beat you, you don't deserve the commission at all.'

Fletcher frowned at the announcement. So much for befriending the older commoners.

'As for the first years, you may be worrying that you will be given poor commissions this year, when you might have been given better if you'd stayed on next year. To counteract this, you will only be given good commissions of a First Lieutenancy or higher, with the optional choice of a less prestigious Second Lieutenancy should you decide to take it. The winner of the tournament shall be given a Captaincy, the highest an untested battlemage can achieve.'

This received more muttering from the second years. Fletcher suspected that they would have been happy for the first years to take part if they would be filling all the second lieutenancies, the lowest and most common of ranks.

'The King has offered an added incentive to this year's tournament. The winner will also receive a place on the King's council and be given the right to vote on matters of state. He wishes to have a representative that comes from the next generation of battlemages. If a commission as a high-ranking officer doesn't motivate you, I know this will,' Scipio announced, giving the room a solemn look.

Fletcher saw Othello clench his fists as Scipio spoke, though whether it was the council seat, the commission or both that had affected him, Fletcher couldn't tell. Tarquin and Isadora were especially incensed by Scipio's revelation, whispering excitedly despite a warning glare from Arcturus.

'Which divisions will the commissions be in? Will the first years be at equal risk of being put in the dwarven and criminal battalions?' asked a tall, second-year commoner, standing up from his table.

Othello bristled at the implication, but Scipio beat him to the punch.

'You'll go in whatever division you're damned well put in! And don't speak out of turn!' the Provost roared. The boy sat down hurriedly, despite dissatisfied murmurs at the answer. Scipio seemed to relent at the grim faces that stared at him from around the room.

'They'll have just as much chance as you do. That's all I will say on the matter,' he said.

A dainty hand was thrust into the air and the fingers fluttered for attention. Scipio rolled his eyes and gave an irritated nod. Isadora stood and curtsied prettily.

'Excuse me for interrupting, Provost Scipio sir, but what is *she* doing here?' she said, pointing an accusatory finger at the elf.

'That was the next announcement I was going to make,' Scipio said, walking over to the silver haired girl. 'The peace talks between Hominum's envoys and the elves' various clan chieftains have been a long struggle, but recently we have had a breakthrough. Instead of paying the tax, the elves plan to join the fight themselves, sending their own warriors to be trained as soldiers, just as the dwarves have done.'

As he mentioned the dwarves, Scipio gave a respectful nod to Othello, who gave him a level nod back.

'But there is still a lot of distrust, as is to be expected,' Scipio continued, walking back to the entrance to stand by the other teachers. 'So, in an act of good faith, a chieftain's daughter has been sent to train as a battlemage, the first of many elves that we hope will be incorporated into our military over the next few years.'

He gave the elf a forced smile.

'Her name is Sylva Arkenia, and you should all make her feel as welcome as possible. We were never really enemies with the elves, though it may have felt that way. Let us hope this is the first step in a long and fruitful alliance.'

Sylva's face remained expressionless, but Fletcher noticed Sariel's tail wagging under the table. He wondered at the courage of this young girl, to leave her country and home to fight in a war that was not her own, amongst people who distrusted her ilk. As he planned his apology to her, Scipio's voice cut in once again.

'Now, be off with you. Lessons start in a few minutes. Oh, and Fletcher,' Scipio said, turning his eyes towards him. 'Come and see me in my office. Immediately.'

24

Scipio's office was as hot as it had been the last time, but today the shutters on the window had been opened, leaving a bright beam of light that cut between Fletcher and the Provost's desk. He had been staring at Fletcher through steepled fingers for the past minute, and Fletcher was beginning to feel uncomfortable.

'Why did you lie to me, boy?' Scipio asked, his eyes flicking between Ignatius and Fletcher's face.

'I did not mean to,' Fletcher said, then, after a moment, adding, 'Provost Scipio, sir.'

'I asked you where you got that demon, and you replied that Arcturus had sent you. Do you think that answered my question? Do you think that the answer you gave did not have certain implications? Didn't you think that after I spoke to Arcturus I would know the truth?' Scipio's voice was calm and composed, a deep contrast to the bellowing man he had seen in the canteen just a few minutes before. Fletcher wasn't sure which he preferred.

'I . . . don't know why I said it. It was true that Arcturus had sent me, but I knew what you meant. It was wrong of me to lie to you. I just wanted to be allowed to study here so badly. I am sorry, sir.'

Fletcher hung his head, feeling foolish. If he had simply told the truth, perhaps he would be in a lesson with Arcturus right now, learning how to produce a wyrdlight. Instead, he was now at risk of being expelled from Vocans on the very first day, for lying to a superior officer. Scipio harrumphed in what Fletcher hoped was approval and then beckoned him over to his desk.

'I am at fault as well. I should have pried a bit closer. After all, researching how to capture new species of demons is something that every battlemage has been tasked with. I assumed that you would not know the magnitude of the implications that your Salamander signified . . . I have been doing far too much assuming of late,' he said with a sigh. 'Arcturus has explained how you came by your demon . . . an orc shaman's summoning scroll, of all things. I suspect my frustration has stemmed from my disappointment that we have not made some great breakthrough, only got lucky. However, I must ask that you leave the book Arcturus told me about with the librarian, in case she can glean some knowledge from it. James Baker was obviously a secretive man.'

Fletcher stood in hopeful silence as the old warrior considered him. Eventually, Scipio pulled out a sheet of paper and laid it on the desk in front of him.

'This is the pledge that all officer cadets must sign before they join Hominum's military. Once you have signed, you will officially be a student soldier at this academy and working at His Majesty's pleasure. Your annual income will be that of one thousand shillings, minus room, board and tuition. It's all there in writing. Make your mark and be off with you.' He held a large quill out to Fletcher, who scrawled his name on the dotted line at the bottom, his heart filled with joy.

'No surname?' Scipio asked, peering at the writing.

'I was never given one,' Fletcher muttered with some embarrassment.

'Well, put something. Officers are usually known by their surname, not their first,' Scipio said, tapping at the empty space beside Fletcher's name. Berdon's surname had been Wulf, so he scribbled that down.

'Get to the atrium, Cadet Wulf. Your sponsor is teaching your first lesson, and you are five minutes late,' Scipio said, giving him a rare smile.

When Fletcher got to the atrium the room was already dotted with the wandering wyrdlights, blue orbs that drifted around the room like fireflies. In the bright teal light, he saw the nobles laughing and floating one after the other from their fingers, competing to see who could create the largest. Othello, Genevieve and Rory were the only commoners there, but they stood away from the nobles in miserable silence.

'That was quick. Is it as easy as all that?' Fletcher asked, watching as Tarquin released a ball of light the size of a fist, much to the amazement of the other nobles.

'No, we haven't even been shown yet. Having summoners as parents has taught the nobles a thing or two,' Rory whispered, his face a picture of disappointment and jealousy.

Arcturus was standing in the middle of the room, watching

the nobles with impassive eyes. He clicked his fingers and the balls were snuffed out, sending the room into pitch-blackness. The atrium slowly glowed again as a small wyrdlight appeared at the end of Arcturus's finger. Thin strands of blue blossomed from his fingertips and pulsed into the light, expanding it to a sphere the size of a man's head. He released it above him, where it floated, motionless, as if suspended from the ceiling. The room was immediately filled with a warm blue light.

'I did not ask you to demonstrate; I asked if any of you were versed in the technique already. Clearly your noble parents have already taught you this. As such, you may leave if you wish. Your timetables will have been left on your beds. I suggest you memorise them. Tardiness is unacceptable.' Arcturus gave Fletcher a telling look at those last words.

'I knew this lesson would be a joke. Come on, Penelope, let the amateurs play catch up,' Isadora snickered. There was another noble girl, a brunette with large hazel eyes who nodded after a moment of hesitation. Isadora flounced off, followed by the girl, who cast an apologetic look over her shoulder at Arcturus.

Tarquin sauntered behind with the two other nobles, a large sable-haired boy with skin as dark as Seraph's and another, slighter boy with mousy brown hair and a cherubic face. As Tarquin passed by, he looked at Fletcher's ragged, ill-fitting uniform and the bruises on his face. He wrinkled his nose in disgust and walked on. Fletcher was in too good a mood to let himself care at that moment.

'Let them leave,' Arcturus said once the nobles were out of earshot. 'They have not learned to control the movement of their wyrdlights. Next lesson, it is they who will be playing catch up. The principles of wyrdlights follow the same principles as all spell casting.'

He turned to the commoners and gave them an appraising look.

'The first lesson is very important; you will find that you all have different capacities for spellcraft. Your demons are the source of all your mana, and the species, experience and age of your demon will determine how much they have and how quickly it recharges.'

Mana. That was the word that Seraph had used yesterday. Fletcher guessed that it meant some kind of energy, used to power spells. Now Arcturus was walking towards them, the wyrdlight above him moving in unison. Under the ethereal glow, his scar looked grislier than ever.

'Excuse me, where are Seraph and Atlas?' Fletcher asked, pushing his way in front of Rory and Genevieve so that Arcturus would finally notice him.

'Sir,' Arcturus prompted.

'Sir,' Fletcher parroted with exasperation.

'I suspect they have gone to collect their demons. Since I chose to sponsor you but did not give you one of my demons, as is usually our way, the Provost decided it would be only fair if I provide an imp for one of the other commoners. I captured it yesterday, at great risk to Sacharissa. I hope you are worth it,' he said with a hint of regret in his voice, much to Fletcher's discouragement.

'Does that mean it was a powerful demon, sir?' Rory asked.

'Not necessarily. It will be in time, but it was too rare for me to pass up. One of your friends is very lucky to have received it.

I had never come across one before. Now, enough questions. Sit down on the floor and close your eyes.'

They did so, and Arcturus's steps echoed as he walked behind them. 'Let your mind go blank. Listen only to the sound of my voice.'

Fletcher tried to still the excited beating of his heart, listening to Arcturus's words. The captain's voice was mellifluous, washing over him like a warm breeze.

'Reach out to your demon, feel the connection between you. Be gentle. This will likely be the first time you have touched it. Don't worry if you struggle to find it at first, the more you practise the easier it will be.'

Fletcher did as he asked, searching for the other consciousness that seemed to float on the edge of his mind. He felt the demon's psyche and, as he touched it, Ignatius twitched in discomfort from around his neck. This was not the pulse of emotion that Fletcher had sent him before, but something else entirely.

'As you grasp it, you will feel the demon's mana flow through you. You must take it and focus it all through the index finger of your dominant hand. For now, that is all you must do.'

Fletcher felt that feeling of clarity suffuse his body once again, even stronger than when he had summoned the demon in the graveyard. It raged through him like a hurricane, and he could feel his body shaking.

'Through your finger, Fletcher! You are taking too much! Control yourself!' Arcturus shouted. His voice sounded a long way away.

Fletcher took a deep breath and exhaled through his nose, raising his finger and channelling the current to it. As he did so, his finger tingled and felt both burning hot and freezing cold, all at once. The black behind his eyelids turned to a dim blue.

'Open your eyes, Fletcher,' Arcturus said, putting a steadying hand on Fletcher's shoulder. He realised he was breathing heavily and calmed himself, then opened his eyes with trepidation.

The tip of his finger was a blue that shone so bright, it verged on white. As he moved his finger, it left a trace of light in the air, like the afterimage of a burning cinder being waved in the dark.

'I said *through* your finger, Fletcher, not to it,' Arcturus said, but there was a hint of pride in his voice.

'Will I be OK?' Fletcher asked, horrified as he traced a figure eight in the air. The others had by now opened their eyes, obviously having taken far longer than Fletcher to harness their demon's mana. Before he became big headed, Fletcher reminded himself that he had been with his demon for over a week longer than they had.

'You have managed something that we are several lessons away from; the art of etching. Watch closely.'

Arcturus lifted his own finger and the tip glowed blue. He drew a strange triangular symbol, made up of jagged lines. He moved his finger around in front of them and the symbol followed it, as if it were attached by an invisible frame. Just as it began to fade, he fired threads of wyrdlight through the gap between his finger and the symbol. Yet when it passed through, a stream of ghostly, opaque tendrils emerged, forming a circular shield in front of him that Fletcher recognised as the very same that had saved his life just two days ago on the streets of Corcillum.

'When we use our mana without a symbol, it becomes nothing but wyrdlight, otherwise known as raw mana. But when you etch a symbol and channel your mana through it, the more useful aspects of a battlemage's tool chest become available. It is not easy; it takes time and practice to create a shield like mine, rather than a misshapen mass. Even forming a ball of wyrdlight will take a while for you to master.'

Fletcher's finger faded back to pink and he hugged it to his chest. Ignatius purred and leaped to the ground. The demon licked at Fletcher's finger with a triangular tongue that was surprisingly soft, soothing the strange tingling he still felt on his fingertip.

'So what did we miss?' Seraph's joyful voice rang out from behind them.

Fletcher turned to see Seraph, Atlas and Captain Lovett walking out of the summoning room. They had their demons with them.

Seraph was grinning like a madman, his happiness complete. His demon crawled along the ground beside him, its lumbering gait and stature putting Fletcher in mind of an overgrown badger. Yet that was where the similarity ended. The creature was covered in rough skin that appeared like bark, with a layer of mildew dusted over the top. A thick ridge of spines ran along its backbone, each one an inch long and as sharp as a surgeon's knife. They reminded Fletcher of the thorns from a gorse bush, vicious green blades that easily punched through the skin.

'What is it?' Rory breathed in wonder as it ran ahead of them and sniffed at Arcturus's boots in recognition. Its short pug snout opened to reveal a strange, ridge-filled mouth. Fletcher could see the pulped remains of leaves within, which were subsequently swallowed with the help of a leathery brown tongue.

'It's a Barkling,' Arcturus replied. 'They are masters of camouflage, hence why it is so rare to come across one. You will have trouble feeding it; they need to get through at least a pound of leaves a day. I'm sure Major Goodwin will teach you all of this in your demonology lessons.'

Arcturus looked at the demon with mixed emotions, then rubbed its head with some reluctance. Seraph caught up and gave Arcturus a grateful smile.

'I would have dearly loved to keep this for myself and capture another demon for you, Seraph, but the wily creature shot Sacharissa full of splinters from its back when she got close to it. She was too injured to make a second trip into the ether. Poor girl almost couldn't hold it down once she'd dragged it through the portal. I had barely enough time to perform the harnessing. It is too late to capture another now. I wish you well of it.'

'Thank you so much, sir!' Seraph exclaimed, scooping the demon up into his arms and wincing at the weight. 'You have no idea how much this means to me. I will name him Sliver.'

Atlas had been lingering behind, a smile plastered across his face. His demon was the size of a large dog, with thick, bristling fur and two sharp incisors that jutted from the front of its mouth. It looked like an enormous, bucktoothed otter, but for a ratlike tail with a spiked ball on the end, in the shape of a morningstar. It was incredibly agile, almost flowing along the ground as it circled Atlas's feet.

'Mine is a Lutra. I called him Barb, after his tail!'

'Barb,' Arcturus remarked. 'You might want to think a while on that. It is not a . . . traditional demon name. Why not

157

Barbarous? I know of at least one other demon that goes by that name.'

'Perfect!' Atlas replied, sweeping the demon into his arms.

Captain Lovett had disappeared back inside the summoning room, but not before Fletcher glimpsed a flash of brown feathers as the door was closed shut. He wondered what it could be. It appeared that there were more species of demons available to Hominum's summoners than he had thought.

As Arcturus took a breath to continue the lesson, Fletcher held up his hand. There was one thing he had to know.

'Where is Sacharissa now, sir? And where are the nobles' demons? Are they sitting in their rooms, waiting for them?' he asked, his curiosity finally reaching a boiling point.

'Do you know what infusion is?' Arcturus asked, giving him a level look. Fletcher shook his head.

'Infusion is when a summoner absorbs a demon into themselves, allowing them to heal and rest. The summoner can still communicate with their demon and even use mana, but it remains within them, out of way. When orc javelins are raining down around you, infusion is the best defence for your demon. You will learn how to do it in your summoning lesson with Captain Lovett tomorrow. I specialise in spellcraft, so it is not my place to teach you infusion. Is that answer enough?'

'Yes, sir. Thank you.'

As Arcturus turned away and began etching another symbol in the air, Fletcher reached for his shoulder, stroking Ignatius. He could feel the flesh and bone beneath his fingertips. Infusion. He would believe that when he saw it.

25

The group was boisterous when they left their lesson, laughing and smiling as they made their way up the stairs. Fletcher, Othello and Seraph were the only ones who had been able to create wyrdlights; small but serviceable ones, that floated by their shoulders. The others had managed to project a thread of blue light, but were unable to find the focus to form the ball. In spite of this, their first taste of spellcraft had been exhilarating, and Rory and Genevieve were not the sort to be jealous of their friends. Even Atlas was rubbing Barbarous's head with a happy smile plastered across his face.

'I'm going to practise wyrdlight control in my room,' Seraph announced as they reached their chambers. 'I could push it about, but I'll never keep it as still as Arcturus did!'

He disappeared into the boys' chambers, Sliver following in his wake. There was no sign of Sylva, once again having disappeared. Fletcher was not sure why she had been allowed to skip the first lesson, but he was eager to make amends.

'I wonder if we should have waited,' Rory said in a morose

159

voice, looking at Malachi in a different light.

'I love Azura to bits, but I can't help thinking that we are going to struggle now. If Arcturus finds it difficult to capture a new demon, what hope do we have?' Genevieve mumbled in agreement. Fletcher could think of little to lighten their spirits, yet it was the usually taciturn Othello who spoke next.

'You might not be able to capture a demon as powerful as a Barkling yet, but maybe you could capture another Mite. Living so close to the front lines, one hears things about the different kinds of battlemage. Some have one powerful demon that is difficult to control, whilst others have many smaller imps, as the orc shamans do. Would you not prefer to send a swarm of Mites at your enemies? You might even be able to send several Mites into the ether and use their combined strength to bring a more powerful demon back,' Othello said, scratching his chin.

'Hey, you're right,' Rory said, an enormous grin on his face. 'Imagine a thousand little Malachis. That would be something to see!'

Seraph walked back into the room, brandishing a sheet of paper in one hand and a small cloth bag in the other.

'Look at these!' He displayed what turned out to be a timetable in front of them. 'Just three all-day lessons a week after breakfast, with optional arms training in the basement on the fourth day. The rest is free study! We can do whatever we want for the rest of the time.'

Rory laughed and slapped the table, sending Malachi flying away with a reproachful buzz.

'Whoops!' Rory said, holding out his palm for the aggrieved insect to land on. He gave him a light kiss on its green carapace.

'That's not all! They paid us what's left of our first month's wages. Who needs university when you can join the military and get paid to study?' Seraph said, jingling the bag. 'There's sixty shillings in here.'

'I think a trip to Corcillum is in order!' Genevieve exclaimed, her face lighting up with a bright smile. 'That's more than my mother earned in a month and she worked all day long. Let's go after lunch.'

'I could definitely do with visiting a tailor,' Fletcher agreed, fingering the ragged hem of his shirt collar.

'My family will be worried about me. I would welcome the chance to let them know I have . . . some friends here.' Othello tugged at his beard shyly.

'It's agreed then. Who said that we wouldn't have the coin to go to Corcillum? It will probably cost us an arm and a leg to get there, but it will be worth it,' Seraph said, rushing back to his room.

Footsteps echoed on the stairs behind them, followed by the sound of voices.

'Who could that be?' Fletcher wondered out loud.

'So you see . . . they've stuck me in with the commoners when my blood is as pure as yours. It's an absolute disgrace! I'm sure if you talk to the Provost on my behalf I can move in next to you.' It was Sylva, followed by Isadora and the other noble girl.

'Ugh, this place is smaller than my bathroom,' Isadora sniffed, wrinkling her perfect nose as if she could smell something foul in the room.

'I know! You should see my bedroom. Let me show you,'

Sylva said, trying to drag Isadora towards the girls' quarters. Isadora stopped and looked at the group, narrowing her eyes when they settled on Othello.

'Hang on,' she said, stamping a delicate foot. 'It's time I told these commoners how things are going to go down this year.'

Isadora stalked around them like a mountain lion on the hunt. She exuded an easy confidence that put Fletcher on edge.

'Here's what's going to happen. You commoners are going to keep your heads down and not give the nobles any trouble. When it comes to the tournament this year, you will all bow out in the first round and let your betters take their rightful places. After all, it is our taxes that fund the King's army and then we pay for our own noble battalions. It's only fair that we lead the soldiers that our families pay for. You have no right and no chance of becoming a senior officer. You just don't have the breeding. So stay out of our way and we might just let one of you serve as our lieutenant. Sound good?' She smiled sweetly when she had finished speaking, as if she had just paid them a compliment. Fletcher was the first to speak.

'Sounds like you're scared of a little competition,' he said, stretching with exaggerated nonchalance. The others remained silent, wondering what the girl would do next. Isadora pouted like a spoiled child, a strange contrast to the self-assured she-devil of just moments ago.

'Rare does not equal powerful. Remember that, Fletcher,' she hissed in his ear.

As she straightened, Seraph came back into the room and smiled at the sight of the girls.

'Lovely, nobody told me we had guests. Welcome to our

humble abode! We haven't been introduced. I'm Seraph Pasha.'

Isadora gave him a look of pure disgust, and then strode off down the stairs, ignoring Sylva, who was halfway to her room. The elf glared at Fletcher as if he were at fault, then rushed after her. The brunette stood indecisively in the stairwell, biting her lip at Seraph, whose face was a picture of incredulity.

'I'm sorry about that,' she said in an almost imperceptible voice.

'Come on, Penelope!' Isadora's voice shouted from below. The girl turned and left, the back of her neck flushed red.

'Nice to meet you,' Rory called, as she disappeared from sight.

'What the hell was all that about?' Seraph asked, slumping into a chair.

'She was feeling us out, wanted to see if we were pushovers. Guess she was wrong,' Othello said, his fists clenched with anger.

'What is Sylva doing cosying up to the nobles?' Genevieve asked, equally distressed.

'I guess as a chieftain's daughter she considers herself a noble too,' Fletcher said, the half-formed apology now gone from his thoughts. Although Isadora and Tarquin seemed to be the source of all the noble superiority so far as he could see, the fact that Sylva had jumped on that bandwagon did not place her in his good graces.

'Come on, get your stuff together – let's skip lunch and go to Corcillum now,' Fletcher said.

'Good thinking. I've lost my appetite,' Othello replied, shaking his head with disappointment.

26

A carriage to Corcillum would have cost an extortionate six shillings per person, but Othello knew of a town a bit further down the main road that might be cheaper. Half an hour's walk and another ten minutes of negotiation later and the group had found transport on the back of a horse-drawn cart for one shilling each. They purchased a basket of apples for another shilling and munched into them, enjoying the sweet tartness. Even the shower that beat down on them could not dampen their spirits as they laughed and tried to catch the raindrops in their mouths. Atlas's Lutra enjoyed the rain the most, yapping and rolling on the wet boards of the cart.

They were dropped on the main road, which was thronging with vendors and customers despite the downpour. As they huddled in a street corner, people stared at their demons and uniforms, some smiling and waving, others hurrying past with fear in their eyes.

'I want to go to the perfumery,' Genevieve said, as two girls walked by under pink parasols. They wafted an exotic fragrance that reminded Fletcher of the mountains. His stomach twisted as he realised how little he had thought of Berdon over the past few days. He needed to get in contact to let him know everything was OK.

'I need to run some errands, send some messages, that sort of thing. Othello, do you know someone who might be able to make a scabbard for my sword?' Fletcher asked.

'Sure . . . as long as you don't mind stopping by my family home on the way,' the dwarf replied, tugging on his beard in excitement.

'Why not? I haven't been to the Dwarven Quarter yet. Are there tailors there too?' Fletcher asked.

'The best in Hominum,' Othello said firmly.

'Well, someone has to come with me to the perfumery. I can't go alone,' Genevieve wheedled as more young ladies walked past. Seraph's eyes lit up at the sight of them, and he volunteered without hesitation.

'I'll go. Perhaps there is some cologne that will help me melt Isadora's cold heart,' he said with a wink.

'Rory? Are you with us or them?' Fletcher asked.

'I think I'll go with Genevieve. It would be interesting to see what they do with all the flowers. My mother collects mountain flowers and sells them to perfume merchants,' Rory said, with a sidelong look at the pretty girls walking by. Fletcher was sure Rory's motive was based on more than the art of scent making, but he didn't blame him. It was only two days ago that he had been awestruck by the beauty of Corcillum's girls and their painted faces. Atlas had already begun to wander down the street, but Fletcher assumed he would not want to come with them to the Dwarven Quarter, given his animosity towards Othello.

'Meet back here in about two hours. There's plenty of carts on their way to the front lines along that road, so just leave if the other group is late,' Othello called.

They parted ways and increased their pace as the downpour intensified, ducking under the awnings in front of shops and keeping close to the walls. Ignatius purred in the dry warmth beneath Fletcher's hood while Solomon followed several feet behind, struggling to keep up on his stumpy legs. The dwarf had the foresight to bring a hooded jacket of his own, but poor Solomon looked miserable in the wet.

'So what do you need other than a tailor and the blacksmith? Did I hear you need to send a letter?' Othello asked, looking over his shoulder to make sure Solomon was still in sight. As Othello threaded his way through the narrow alleyways, Fletcher realised that the dwarf would be the perfect guide to help him make the best of their trip to Corcillum.

'Yes, I need to send a letter to the elven front,' Fletcher said. It would be best not to send anything directly to Berdon in case Caspar or Didric intercepted it. Maybe if he sent it to Rotherham, then the soldier could pass on the message in secret.

'Well, if that's the case you'd be best sending it from Vocans. The military couriers stop by there all the time. As for the blacksmith, trust me when I say he is the best. He designed this for me.'

Othello paused and opened the leather pouch he carried on his shoulder and pulled a hatchet from inside. The handle was made of black, fire-hardened wood and painstakingly carved to conform to the shape of Othello's hand. The axe head was thin but devastatingly sharp, with a keen blade coming from the back that made for a lethal backswing.

'This is a dwarven tomahawk. Every dwarf is given one on their fifteenth birthday, to protect them in their adulthood. It was decreed by the first of our holy elders that all adult male dwarves must carry one at all times, ever since our persecution began two thousand years ago. Even our female dwarves own a torq, a spiked bangle that is carried at all times on the wrist. It is considered part of our tradition, heritage and religion. Now you know the high esteem I hold for the blacksmith's skill.'

Fletcher's eyes widened as he saw the beautiful weapon.

'Can I hold it?' Fletcher asked, eager to try the axe for himself. Perhaps he would have the same carved handle added to his khopesh.

There was a high pitched whistle and the sound of running feet. Two Pinkertons were sprinting towards them, studded truncheons drawn and pistols levelled at Othello's face.

'Drop it! Now!'

The first Pinkerton took Othello by the throat, lifted him off his feet and pushed him up against a brick wall. He was a huge brute of a man, with a bristling black beard that covered an ugly, pockmarked face. Othello's tomahawk clattered to the ground as he struggled to breathe against the sausage-like fingers constricting his windpipe.

'What have we told you dwarves about carrying weapons in public? Why can't you get it through your thick, dwarven skulls? Only humans have that privilege!' the second Pinkerton said in a reedy voice. He was a tall, skinny man with a pencil moustache and greasy blond hair.

'Let him go!' Fletcher shouted, finding his voice. He stepped forward as Ignatius dropped to the ground, hissing viciously. The demon blew a warning plume of flame into the air.

'Release him, Turner,' the thin Pinkerton said, registering the danger and rapping his truncheon against the wall.

'All right, Sergeant Murphy, we'll have more fun with him in the cells anyway,' the large man grunted, releasing Othello to leave him wheezing on the street cobbles. He gave the dwarf a sharp kick in the side, making Othello cry out in pain. As he did so, an unearthly roar blasted from behind Fletcher.

'No!' Othello gasped, holding his hand up as Solomon pelted round the corner, stopping the Golem just a few feet short of Turner. 'No, Solomon, it's OK!'

The dwarf stood with difficulty, leaning against the wall.

'Are you all right?' Fletcher asked as the Golem rushed to his master, rumbling with worry.

'I'm fine. They've done worse before,' the dwarf croaked, patting the Golem on the head.

Fletcher spun and scowled at the Pinkertons, his hand straying towards his khopesh.

Murphy stepped in and prodded him in the chest.

'As for you, you can wipe that look from your face,' Sergeant Murphy growled, lifting Fletcher's chin with his truncheon. 'Why are you defending a dwarf anyway? You want to be more careful who you make friends with.'

'I think you should be more worried about trying to arrest an officer of the King's army for carrying a weapon! Or did you expect him to fight the orcs with his bare hands?' Fletcher said with confidence he did not feel. Turner was swinging his truncheon back and forth.

'Who are you to tell me what I can and can't do?' Murphy, pointed his pistol at Fletcher's face. There was nothing that Ignatius was going to be able to do against a bullet. Fletcher weighed the odds of being able to perform a shield spell on his first try, but decided against it. Better to take a beating than risk death. He cursed under his breath; this was the second time he had found himself cornered in the streets of Corcillum with a pistol in his face.

'What did you just say? I think he just swore at you, Sergeant Murphy,' Turner growled, raising his own pistol.

'Nothing! I was just cursing my luck,' Fletcher stammered. The two barrels were like a pair of snakes' eyes, ready to strike.

'You have no idea who you're messing with,' Othello growled, straightening with a wince. 'You'd better put those pistols down and get the hell out of here.'

'Enough, Othello!' Fletcher hissed. The dwarf must have gone mad! It was easy for him to be cocky, he wasn't the one staring down two gun barrels!

'Just wait till we tell his father about you. Lord Forsyth will be very displeased to find out that some low-level Pinkertons held his son Tarquin at gunpoint,' Othello continued, unbuttoning his jacket to show the uniform underneath. Fletcher tried not to look too surprised, but inside he was horrified at the gamble the dwarf was taking. Even so, it was too late now. Then Fletcher detected a hint of hesitation in Murphy's face.

'Of course, you are aware of the dwarven battalions forming on the elven front. If the Forsyths have to incorporate one of them into our forces, we will want the best dwarf officers available,' Fletcher said in a confident voice, pushing Turner's pistol away from his face. 'Now I find you assaulting our newest officer in the street, for carrying a weapon that Zacharias Forsyth himself gave him? What are your names? Murphy? Turner?'

Murphy's pistol wavered, then lowered to the ground.

'You don't speak like a noble,' Murphy challenged, his eyes focussing on the ragged hem of Fletcher's uniform trousers. 'Nor do you dress like one.'

'Your uniform would look like this too if you were fighting on the front lines. As for my voice, if you grew up amongst the common soldiers, your language would be as coarse as mine. We can't all be fancy boys like you.' Fletcher was getting in the swing of it now, but Othello prodded him in the small of his back. He reined it in, worried he had gone too far.

'Now, if you will excuse me, I will be on my way. Ignatius, come!' Fletcher said, scooping Ignatius into his arms and striding off down the street. He didn't look back, but heard the click of a pistol's flint being pulled.

'Keep walking,' Othello whispered from behind him. 'They're testing us.'

Fletcher continued onwards, every second imagining a bullet was going to come bursting through his chest. The moment they rounded the corner they ran down the street, Solomon just managing to keep up with his stubby legs.

'You're a genius,' Fletcher gasped, when they were a safe distance away.

'Don't thank me just yet. Next time they see you, they will

probably beat you to a pulp. They won't be able to tell who I am, all dwarves look the same to them. I've been arrested twice before by that pair and they didn't even recognise me,' Othello wheezed, clutching his injured side. 'I think they might have cracked a rib though.'

'The sadistic brutes! We need to get you to a doctor. Don't worry about me. My hood was up, and it was dark. As long as they don't see Ignatius and Solomon next time our paths cross, we should be OK. We'll need to learn how to infuse our demons straight away. Shield spells too, for that matter,' Fletcher said.

'Too right. Come on, let's go. The Dwarven Quarter is not far from here. My mother should be able to bind my chest.' Solomon gave a throaty groan as they set off once again. Clearly, he was not used to this much exercise.

'I'm going to need to get you into shape,' Othello chided, pausing to rub the Golem's craggy head.

They walked on, the streets getting narrower and filthier. Clearly the cleaners no longer bothered to come this way, not with the Dwarven Quarter so close. The dwarves must have been allocated the worst part of the city to live in.

'Why were you arrested before?' Fletcher asked, stepping over a tramp who was sleeping in the middle of the street.

'My father refused to pay the protection money the Pinkertons asked of him. Every dwarf business gets turned over by their officers, but those two are the worst. They threw me in the cells both times, until my father paid up.'

'That's insane! How can they get away with that?' Fletcher asked. Othello walked on in silence and Fletcher kicked himself.

What a stupid question.

'What does your father do? Is he a blacksmith? My father was a blacksmith,' Fletcher said, trying to fill the awkward silence he had created.

'My father is one of the artificers who developed the musket,' Othello said with pride. 'Now that we hold the secret to their creation, the Pinkertons tend to not bother the dwarven blacksmiths. I can't say that for all dwarf businesses though. The creation of the musket was the first step in the long journey to equality. Our joining the army is the second. I will finish what my father started.'

'You must be the first dwarf officer in Hominum, even if you are just a cadet at the moment. That is something to be proud of,' Fletcher said.

He meant every word; the more he found out about the dwarves, the more he respected them. He endeavoured to emulate their resolve to better their situation.

Othello stopped and pointed ahead of him.

'Welcome to the Dwarven Quarter.'

27

The tall buildings fell away to reveal row upon row of huge white tents, exquisitely embroidered with kaleidoscopic shapes of red and blue. Springy green grass replaced the cobblestones, and each pavilion was surrounded by lovingly tended gardens. The vividly coloured flowers wafted sweet scents in the air, reminding Fletcher of his youthful summers in the mountains. Unencumbered by the dingy buildings, the winter sun cast a pale but warm light across Fletcher's face.

'It's beautiful,' Fletcher said, amazed by the sudden transformation. He had expected the Dwarven Quarter to be a squalid and miserable place, given the standard of the buildings that surrounded it. Othello smiled at his words and limped on, waving at nearby dwarves as they sat talking in the gardens.

'This is mine.' Othello pointed to a nearby tent. 'My whole family lives in here.'

'How many are there of you?' Fletcher asked, trying not to mind the stares he was receiving from the other dwarves as they passed by.

'Oh, there are probably around thirty of us in each tent, but ours contains my father's workshop, so there are only twenty of us in this one. He needs his space.'

Fletcher tried to wrap his head around how a pavilion tent could house twenty people and a workshop. Each one was about the size of a large barn but, unless they slept in bunk beds, there was no way that could be true.

'Take down your hood and remove your shoes before you go in. In our culture that is polite,' Othello said. Fletcher helped him take off his boots; the poor dwarf had begun to turn pale from the pain of his injury and bending over was difficult for him. As he kneeled and struggled with Othello's thick-knotted bootlaces, a short figure in flowing robes ran up the path towards them, crying out in shock. Her face was obscured by a pink veil, held in place by a delicate silver chain.

'Othello, what happened?' the figure wailed in a high-pitched voice.

'I'm OK, Thaissa. We just need to get me inside. It's best not to let the others see me injured. They will think I am being mistreated at Vocans, which is not the case.'

Thaissa parted the tent flap and ushered them in. Strangely, it was not the tightly packed room that Fletcher had expected. Instead, the floors were lined with ornate floor mats and cushions. In the centre, there was a thick metal pipe that extended to the top of the tent like a chimney. Understanding dawned on Fletcher when he saw the spiral staircase that wound around the pipe, going deep into the earth. They lived underground!

Thaissa, who could only be Othello's sister, continued to fuss around him, piling cushions on the ground for him to lean against.

'You have a lovely home,' Fletcher commented as another figure came up the stairs. He caught a flash of a rosy-cheeked face with bright green eyes before the female dwarf uttered a shriek and pulled a veil over her face.

'Othello!' she cried out. 'How can you bring guests here without letting us know? He has seen my face!'

'It's OK, Mother, I don't think a human counts. He is my friend and I ask that you treat him as such.' Othello slumped to the ground and clutched at his side.

'You're hurt!' she gasped and ran to him.

'Please, get the bandages. Constable Turner and Sergeant Murphy attacked me again. This time I think they may have broken a rib. I will need you to bind my chest.'

He spoke in short bursts of breath, as if it hurt to breathe, as he removed his jacket and the top half of his uniform. His broad chest and shoulders were covered with a thick pelt of curly red hair, which also extended halfway down his back. The skin of his shoulders was latticed with scars; evidence of more brutality from the Pinkertons. Fletcher shuddered at the sight.

Othello's mother ran downstairs as Thaissa dabbed at his forehead with her sleeve. She returned soon after with a roll of linen and began to wrap it tight around his chest. Othello winced with each swathe, but bore it stoically. Fletcher could already see a black bruise blossoming on the dwarf's chest.

'Othello, what are you doing back so early? Someone told me they had seen you in town,' came a voice from behind them.

'I'm just getting patched up, Atilla,' Othello said. 'The

Pinkertons had another go at me. Lucky I had Fletcher here to help me out.'

Another dwarf stood in the doorway. He looked the spitting image of Othello, almost identical in fact. The dwarf gave Fletcher a look of pure hatred and helped Othello to his feet.

'The humans will never accept us. We should move out of this goddamned city and create our own settlements, away from here. Look where fraternising with this human has got you,' Atilla ranted. 'Get out of here, human, before I do the same to you.'

As if Ignatius could understand the words, he leaped on to the floor and hissed, allowing a thin stream of smoke to waft from his nostrils.

'Enough! I have had it with your antihuman rhetoric!' Othello shouted. 'I will not have you insult my friend in my own home. It is you who needs to leave!' He coughed with pain at the outburst and leaned on Fletcher. Atilla gave Fletcher another glare and then swept out of the tent, muttering under his breath.

'You will have to forgive my twin brother. He too passed the testing, but his hate for your people means he will never fight for Hominum, not even as a battlemage. We both desire freedom for the dwarves, but that is where our agreement ends,' Othello said miserably. 'I worry about him, what he might do. I can barely remember the number of times I turned myself in when they put out a warrant for his arrest, enduring his punishments. If they tried to arrest him, he might have fought back. Then they would have killed him. What else could I do but go in his stead?'

'It's OK. How can I blame him for feeling that way after what

I saw today? I hope that I'll get a chance to change his mind some day. We aren't all bad.'

'Aye, you're all right,' Othello said with a grin. 'We've been keeping Atilla out of trouble, working with Dad in the workshop. I might as well take you there now. My father will take a look at that sword for you. He's the best blacksmith in all of Hominum.'

'The inventor of muskets and pistols? I don't doubt it,' Fletcher said, then remembered his manners. 'I would be honoured if you would allow me to visit your home,' he said to the two female dwarves, inclining his head.

Othello's mother's veil hid her expression, but she nodded after a few moments.

'I trust my boy's judgement, and I am glad he has found a friend at the academy. We had feared that he would be unhappy there. My name is Briss. It is a pleasure to meet you.'

'He has many friends. I am just one of them,' Fletcher said, patting Othello on the back. 'I am honoured to meet you, Briss, and you too, Thaissa.'

'We must seem very strange to you with our veils,' Thaissa's voice was shy and hesitant. 'It is not often that dwarven women meet humans. Why, many still think that dwarf women grow beards and cannot be told apart from the men!'

She giggled and even Briss let out a light, tinkling laugh.

'I must admit, I was wondering why you wear them. Would it be rude of me to ask?' Fletcher enquired.

'Not at all. We wear them so that dwarves marry for love and not out of lust,' Briss said. 'Our spouses cannot see us until our wedding night, and so they must love us for our personalities

177

and not our looks. It is also a mark of modesty and privacy, so that we do not flaunt our beauty for everyone to see. That is a privilege reserved for our husbands—'

'Speaking of husbands, I must take Fletcher to see Father right away,' Othello interrupted, flustered by his mother's forthrightness. 'Come on, Fletcher. He's downstairs.'

28

The steps opened up into a chamber, as wide and as tall as the tent above. The pipe in the centre contained a crackling fire resting over a grate, the gush of hot air and smoke from below sending sparks rushing upwards. The walls were made of bare earth, propped up by strong oak beams that held the room in place. Small chandeliers with wax candles hung from the ceiling, giving the room a warm orange glow. Seven doors were built into the walls of the round room, each one made of solid steel.

They continued down into a near-identical chamber, this one containing a stone dining table. Instead of a fireplace, the pipe was connected to what looked like a large oven and kiln. Vases and pots of all sizes were stacked against the walls. Each one was painted with an intricate floral pattern.

'This is where my mother spends most of her time. She likes baking, both food and porcelain. A man comes to buy her goods in bulk every week so he can sell them in his shop. The housewives of Hominum turn their noses up at dwarf-made pottery, so he pretends he makes them himself. We make a tidy profit,' Othello boasted. Fletcher was astonished at how quickly the dwarf was recovering. They were a hearty people, of that he was certain.

They continued deeper and deeper into the earth, as the stairwell became more narrow and constricted. Fletcher was glad that Solomon had decided to rest with Thaissa and Briss; his stumpy legs would never have managed the steep steps.

They passed two more chambers on their way down, each one smaller than the last. The first was layered in stone and full of residual steam, with copper tubing that twisted around the central pipe column; baths of some sort.

The next room was too dark to see much, but Fletcher could just make out the outline of pikes and swords. He guessed it was a storage room, full of Othello's father's weapons. The stairs became so steep that Fletcher almost had to clamber down, fumbling in the dim light.

'Sorry about the stairs. They were designed for defence, you know. The stairs go down clockwise so any men fighting their way down would have to fight with their left hand and would only be able to come one at a time. One dwarf could hold this stairway against a thousand foes, if he was warrior enough,' Othello said, knocking the pillar in the centre that prevented a right-handed fighter from manoeuvring his sword. It rang hollow beneath Othello's knuckles, and Fletcher reckoned he could hear the sound of hot air rushing within.

'Have your homes always been this way?' Fletcher asked, starting to feel claustrophobic as the low ceiling scraped against his head. For someone used to open skies on top of a mountain, this was not a comfortable experience.

'Yes, as far back as we can remember. We think it was at first to defend against the wild animals and orcs, but in time we preferred to sleep below the earth. It's so quiet and peaceful down here. I must confess, I have been having trouble sleeping in the top of that tower, with the wind blowing into my room.'

'Yes . . . me too,' Fletcher said, thinking back on the figure from the drawbridge last night.

'Here it is,' Othello said as they reached the bottom of the stairs. There was a large steel door surrounded by stone, as if it had been embedded into a natural sheet of bedrock underground.

'Even if they dug around this, they would have to chip their way through the stone to get in. My father takes his privacy very seriously. There are many others just like this, to house the factories that produce the muskets. But this one is special. It is where the first musket was ever created.'

He knocked his fist against the door with a rhythmic booming pattern, a secret code of some sort. A few seconds later, there were a series of bangs as locks were removed. Then a familiar face opened the door.

'Athol!' Fletcher exclaimed, smiling at the familiar face. 'Othello's father is your boss? I should have guessed, what with those beautiful guns.'

'What are you doing here?' Athol's face filled with surprise and confusion. 'And with Othello of all people?'

'He's my friend from Vocans,' Othello said, pushing his way into the room. 'I want to introduce him to my father.'

'Uhtred is busy now, Othello. You'd best be coming back another time,' Athol warned. 'Wait out here, Fletcher. I don't think he would want you in the workshop.'

The dwarves disappeared inside, leaving Fletcher to peer in. The room was filled with tools and piles of metal ingots. In contrast to Berdon's forge, everything was organised to an almost obsessive degree. The inside of the room radiated heat, as if Fletcher had his face a few inches away from a bonfire. Just out of sight, a murmured conversation went on, but Fletcher could not make out what they were saying over the muffled roar of the forge's flames. Then rumbling like the bellows of the forge itself, a voice rang out.

'WHAT?' the voice thundered. 'HERE?'

Footsteps thudded through the chamber and Othello's father stood in front of him. The dwarf's naked chest was enormously broad, with brawny arms spanning the doorway as he blocked the view into the room. The red beard that hung from his chin was split into a fork that hung in two braids down to his waist, and his long, droopy moustache hung almost to his stomach. His thick pelt of chest hair glistened with sweat in the orange glow of the forge's fire.

'Athol tells me you asked to work as my apprentice just a couple of days ago.' Uhtred's deep booming voice echoed in the tight confines of the stairwell. 'Now I find you're chumming up to my boy, wheedling your way into our forge. I don't trust you, not even as far as I could throw you, and I warrant I could chuck you a good long distance.'

Ignatius stirred from beneath Fletcher's hood, sensing the threat. Fletcher took a few steps back. He was horrified by the implication. Yet he understood how suspicious the situation appeared.

'I swear, I had no agenda in coming here. I worked in the north as an apprentice blacksmith. I had just arrived in Corcillum and was seeking employment! Othello and I only met when I enlisted at Vocans. I need a scabbard for my sword, and your son offered to take me to a trustworthy blacksmith. I did not even know he came from a smithing family until just a few minutes ago, nor that Athol worked here until just now. I will go upstairs. My deepest apologies for disturbing you.'

Fletcher bowed and turned to leave, but had only made it to the first step when Uhtred cleared his throat.

'I may have . . . been hasty. My son is a good judge of character, as is Athol. But I must test your story first and see if you were really an apprentice. Athol, hide the musket-making tools and fetch one of the smaller hammers for Fletcher. If he is a spy, best to find out now so we can take the proper precautions. In the meantime, show me this sword. I have not seen a khopesh of quality for a while.'

Fletcher removed his sword and handed it to Uhtred. It looked tiny in the dwarf's meaty hands, more like a sickle for pruning flowers than a deadly weapon. He was almost five feet tall, practically a giant for a dwarf.

'You need to look after this better. When was the last time you oiled it, or sharpened it?' Uhtred asked, turning the blade this way and that in the dim light. 'A sword is a tool, just like any other. I will leave you an oilcloth to wrap it in whilst the scabbard is prepared, should your story check out. Look after your weapons, boy! Would you let your demon starve?'

'I guess I have been lax of late,' Fletcher said with embarrassment. He had barely given the khopesh a second thought since he had received it, other than during his fight with Sir Caulder. Another twinge of guilt ran through him as he thought of how much time and effort Berdon must have put in to make it.

'All right. Athol should be done by now,' Uhtred said, stepping out of the way. 'Let's see what you've got.'

29

Fletcher grimaced as the red hot metal on the anvil slowly turned grey once again. Every time he removed the bar of steel from the roaring fire of the forge, it returned to a cool state after just a few hits with his hammer. He had shaped it into a rough sliver of metal, but it looked nothing like the dagger he wanted to create.

'That's dwarven steel for you,' Othello said with a hint of pity. 'It's harder and sharper than any metal known to man, but it cools fast. You need to have a dwarf's strength to make an impact on it before it hardens again.'

'It was an unfair trick to play on you, Fletcher,' Uhtred said, not unkindly. 'I knew you wouldn't be able to do it. Athol, fetch some of the pig iron from the back.'

'At least he didn't know what dwarf steel looked like, I could tell from the look of surprise on his face,' Athol replied. 'A spy from the Hominum military would know that. Now we will find out if he really was an apprentice.'

'Wait,' Fletcher said, an idea forming in his mind. 'I can make this work.'

He pulled Ignatius from around his neck and prodded him awake. The imp yawned and scratched at his cheek with his back leg like a dog. Fletcher smiled and waited until Ignatius's consciousness went from fuzzy to clear as he roused from his slumber.

'Time to give you a work-out, you idle thing,' Fletcher teased. Then he concentrated on the steel, willing it to become red hot once again. Ignatius chirred with excitement. He took a deep breath and blew a blue-tinged fan of flame on to the metal.

Slowly but surely, the metal turned red, then pink.

'Wow . . . I could do with one of those,' Uhtred breathed in wonder as the demon gulped in another breath, then intensified the flame. It turned the metal almost white and filled the room with an acrid, sulphuric scent.

Fletcher hammered away, the dagger taking shape with each swing. After what felt like an age, he calmed Ignatius with a thought. Exhausted, the demon crawled back up under his hood, its energy spent. Fletcher also felt drained, his arm aching from the rain of blows he had pounded on to the blade.

Uhtred took some tongs and held the weapon up to the light. The handle was a plain metal pommel with a round end, ready to be wrapped in leather for a firmer grip. The blade itself was a simple stiletto, the long, thin blade preferred by assassins.

'Where did you learn to make one of these?' Othello asked, prodding the tip with his thumb. 'It's not exactly standard issue.'

'We sold to traders mostly. They liked an easily concealable weapon, so they could take highwaymen by surprise,' Fletcher said, admiring his handiwork. It was one of his better pieces.

'All right, lad, you're free to go. It's not like you've discovered much anyway. To make amends for my bad manners, we will make you a scabbard free of charge. You will need to leave your blade with us, but it should be back with you in a few days. My wife will organise a new uniform for you too. It won't be tailored but it's better than that moth-eaten thing you're wearing now. We won't have anyone saying our son's companions are vagrants. No offence,' Uhtred asserted with a smile.

'How much do I owe you?' Fletcher asked, digging out his purse.

'Just this dagger and your promise to look out for my boy. You seem like a rare sort, Fletcher. It is people like you that give me hope for reconciliation between dwarves and men,' Uhtred said.

Rain had begun to pour when they reached the meeting place, but there was no sign of the others. Othello kicked the wall as they shivered in a narrow doorway, planning their next move. There were no carts in sight, and the streets were nearly deserted.

'Damn this rain,' Othello grumbled. He was in a foul mood and the rain and lack of transport were not the only causes. In their rush to leave the Pinkertons, Othello's tomahawk had been left on the ground. It had not been there when they returned the same way.

'Damn the Pinkertons too. My side is as stiff as a ramrod and I've lost one of my father's finest pieces,' Othello continued, squinting through the deluge.

'I'm sorry, Othello. I'm sure your father will make another one for you,' Fletcher said, grimacing with sympathy.

'How would you feel if you lost your khopesh?' Othello sounded bitter, striding out into the street.

Fletcher didn't know how to answer, so he kept his mouth shut. He followed the dejected dwarf through the rain. They were now chilled to the bone despite their jackets, and Fletcher knew that the journey home was going to be a cold and miserable affair.

'I think our best bet is Valentius Square,' Othello shouted as thunder began to rumble in the air. 'That's where most of the stables are.'

'All right, let's go! I just want to get a move on.' Fletcher yelled back, eyeing the tumultuous sky.

They ran down the empty streets, splashing in the puddles that gathered on the road. Every few seconds the street would freeze with a flash of lightning, followed by a loud crash of thunder.

'The lightning is close, Othello! There must be a rèal storm brewing,' Fletcher cried, his voice almost snatched away by the wind.

'Nearly there!' Othello yelled back.

Finally they turned into a small square with an enormous awning, which kept the worst of the rain at bay. It was filled with a crowd of people, taking shelter from the storm and listening to a man on a raised platform. He was shouting, but Fletcher was too tired to listen.

'They auction the horses off from that stage, if you ever feel the need to buy me one,' Othello joked, wringing out his beard.

'Hah, maybe a potbellied pony, that's all you could manage,' Fletcher joked back, glad that the dwarf had perked up again.

As they looked around for a cart, Fletcher caught the last words of the irate man's speech.

'. . . yet the elves drag the war on, costing both nations many times over what the tax would have been! But instead of taking the war to them, our King talks of peace, never realising the elves' true intentions! They want us to lose the war, don't you see? When Hominum falls, they will be free to take our lands from us! The orcs don't want it, they just want us dead. When blood runs in the streets of Corcillum, the elves will rejoice in our deaths!'

The crowd roared back in approval, waving their fists in the air. Fletcher looked on, distracted from the task at hand. He had never seen a man talk so openly against the King, nor with such hatred for the elves. Not even Rotherham had been as vehement.

'So what do we do about this? How do we force the King's hand? I'll tell you! We march on their embassy and kill every one of those pointy-eared bastards!' the man howled, his passion so fervent that it verged on a scream.

This time the audience was less incensed. This suggestion was so audacious that a shocked hush fell on the crowd, accompanied by perturbed muttering. The man raised his hand as if he needed silence.

'Oh, I know, the first step is always the hardest. But let us take it together. Let us seize this moment!' he roared, accompanied by a smattering of cheers from the crowd, warming to his rhetoric. 'But first, let me show you how it is done. Grindle, bring out the prisoner!'

A fat, baldheaded man with arms as big as Uhtred's emerged from a door behind the stage and dragged a screaming elf on to the front of the platform. Even from his position, all the way at the back, Fletcher recognised the struggling figure.

'Sylva!' he cried.

30

The crowd pulsed with excitement, both outraged and thrilled at the same time. The fat man on stage flourished a club in the air, drawing fresh cries from the mob. Fletcher began to shove his way to the front, but was held back by Othello.

'Let go!' Fletcher shouted at him, struggling in the iron grip of the dwarf.

'We don't have any weapons, Fletcher. We need to go and get help!' Othello yelled back as the mob around them heaved.

'Who are we going to call, the Pinkertons? If we don't do something right now, Sylva is going to die,' Fletcher retorted, wrenching his arm away and barging forward.

He pushed and elbowed, but the crowd began to thicken as he got closer to the stage. Soon he was crushed in the mass of surging bodies, barely able to see above the heads of those in front of him.

'The elves are so bold that they walk our streets, like the war means nothing to them!' the man on stage shouted. 'Grindle, bring her here so we can show everyone what we do with elves who don't know their proper place.'

The crowd roared, some in favour, others in disagreement. The mood was as electric as the lightning that lit up the awning above them, freezing their screaming faces in place with every flash. The sun was almost set, with the sky the dark blue of winter dusk.

'What's going on?' Othello shouted from behind him, jumping up and down to try and see what was happening. Solomon was crouched between his legs, growling at the feet that stamped in the wet mud around him.

'I don't know. We need to find a way of getting through this crowd!' Fletcher yelled. The air was filled with the sound of thunder, angry shouts and rain drumming on the stretched cloth above. Sylva's scream cut through it all, a long screech of mindless fear that cut straight through Fletcher's core.

He gritted his teeth with frustration and tried to push forward once again, but all he managed was a few inches.

'Othello, get Solomon to make some noise! If we can't get past, we'll have to disperse them,' Fletcher hollered over his shoulder.

A bellow blasted from behind him, a deep bass roar that reminded Fletcher of a mountain bear. The people around them turned and scrambled away, leaving a few feet of empty space.

'Ignatius!' Fletcher shouted, sending the demon on to his shoulder with a thought. The imp discharged a heavy plume of flame into the air, scaring the rest of the crowd into giving them a wider berth. As a path opened, they hurled themselves up the stairs and on to the stage.

Fletcher took in the scene at a glance. Sylva's head was being held on a block by the angry speechmaker, who was kneeling beside her prone figure. Grindle had his club raised, about to smash her head to pieces. The poor girl was blindfolded – she wouldn't even see it coming.

Ignatius reacted instinctively, spitting a ball of fire that took the fat man high in the shoulder and blasted him off his feet. As the heavy body collapsed to the ground, Othello sprinted in and kicked the speechmaker in the side of the head with a sharp crack, knocking him out cold.

Three more men charged at the dwarf, armed with cudgels not unlike those the Pinkertons carried. Othello took a blow to the face and went down like a puppet with its strings cut. Before the man could swing again, Solomon punched the man in the leg, bending it sideways with a sickening crunch. The Golem clambered on to his chest and stamped down. The pop of snapping ribs made Fletcher's stomach churn.

The other two began to advance, swinging their cudgels with practised ease. Fletcher blanched and danced backwards to buy himself more time, wishing he had not left his bow in his room. This was going to be tricky.

'All right, Ignatius. Sic 'em,' Fletcher said. Ignatius leaped from his shoulder, a whirlwind of claws and flame. He landed on the closest man's face and hissed, his thin tail-spike stabbing back and forth like a scorpion's sting.

Before the other man could interfere, Fletcher ran in. As the cudgel swung at him, he blasted a flash of wyrdlight from his hand, blinding the man with a beam of blue light. He kicked him in the fork of his legs, then kneed him in the nose as he doubled over. Rotherham had been right; gentlemen's fighting was for gentlemen. Ignatius had torn the other man's face apart; he was rolling on the floor moaning whilst Ignatius lapped at his bloody snout with relish. Gone was the demon's puppy-like innocence.

Sylva was trussed up like a turkey, but she struggled wildly on the floor. Solomon was wailing, burying his stony face in Othello's beard.

Fletcher tugged off Sylva's blindfold, then plucked at the knots with fingers made clumsy by the cold. The ropes were swollen from the wet, but they loosened as he tugged at them. All the time the crowd watched on, as if he were an actor on a stage and they the theatregoers.

'Get them off, get them off!' Sylva screamed. Her eyes were rolled back in her head. How on earth had she got herself into this situation? The last time he saw her she was with Isadora, back at Vocans.

Then the side of Fletcher's head erupted in pain and he was on his back, the white of the canvas above filling his vision. Grindle's gross bald head swam into focus, his club raised once more. It was an ugly, misshapen thing, all knotted and pitted like a roughly-hewn tree branch.

'Race traitor,' Grindle hissed. His shoulder was a mess of blackened cloth and burned flesh.

He clutched Ignatius by the neck as if he were holding a chicken, the demon's tailspike stuck in his flabby arm. Fletcher's heart filled with hope as Ignatius's chest expanded, but nothing left the demon's nostrils but a thin trickle of smoke. The fat man laid his foot across Fletcher's neck to hold him still, then centred the club at his head. Fletcher closed his eyes and prayed it would be a quick death.

He heard a scream and then a thud. A weight fell across him, crushing his chest and knocking the wind out of him. He opened his eyes to see Sylva, holding a bloody cudgel in her hands. The fat man gurgled in Fletcher's ear.

He struggled to lift the body, but it felt like he was trying to shift a tree.

'I can't breathe,' Fletcher gasped with the last of the air in his lungs. Sylva crouched and pushed with all her might, but the body barely budged. Fletcher's heartbeat pounded in his eardrums, the pulse erratic and frantic. The edges of his vision began to darken as he wheezed, snatching tiny mouthfuls of air.

Then Othello was there, staggering on to the scene with blood running down the side of his face. The elf and the dwarf heaved at the body until Fletcher could breathe once again, deep sobbing gasps that tasted sweeter than honey.

'You monsters!' Sylva cried, spitting at the silent onlookers.

'Let's get the hell out of here,' Othello said, looking at the crowd in disgust.

They lifted Fletcher to his feet then staggered down the steps like three drunks, almost unable to stand. This time, the rabble parted to give them a wide berth.

They lurched down the deserted streets, rain beating down on them in waves as the wind blew and ebbed. Othello seemed to know the way, leading them down tight alleyways and backstreets until they arrived at the main road that had brought them into Corcillum. They had no idea if they were being followed. Sundown would arrive at any minute, yet with Sylva in tow there was no way they could stay overnight in a tavern.

The trio walked for two hours without seeing a single cart or wagon. Sylva was dressed in nothing more than a silken gown, and she had somehow lost her shoes in her capture. She was shivering so violently that she could barely get her arms through Fletcher's jacket when he offered it to her.

'We need to stop and rest!' Fletcher shouted over the roar of the wind and rain. Othello nodded, too tired to even look up from the road. His face was ashen white, and red-tinged rivulets of water trickled down the side of his face. The head wound was too wet to close up of its own accord.

There were green cornfields on either side of them, but Fletcher could see a wooden roof peeking out over the top, a few hundred yards to their right.

'This way!' he yelled, pulling them off the road. They brushed through the heavy stalks, snapping their brittle stems underfoot. Solomon led the way, desperate to get his master to safety.

It was nothing more than a glorified shed, long since abandoned. Fletcher's heart dropped for a moment when he saw the outside had been locked up with a rusted chain, but Solomon snapped it with a blow from his stone fist.

The inside was damp and musty, filled with old barrels of flour that had succumbed to rot. Yet to be out of the torrent that pelted down on them was bliss.

Sylva and Othello collapsed to the floor, huddling together to keep warm. Fletcher slammed the door behind him and slumped down to the ground too. This was not how he had imagined his trip to Corcillum would go.

'Don't worry, guys, I'm going to warm you up. Ignatius, come down.' The imp scampered down his arm and looked at him miserably. The little creature's neck was bruised a dark red from Grindle's grip. He took a deep breath and let out a thin plume of flame, but in the damp air it did nothing but illuminate their near pitch-black surroundings. The only light came from cracks in the walls, which also let in chilling draughts of wind. There had to be another way. If Fletcher didn't do something, they would likely catch their death.

Solomon growled, then began to tear apart some of the barrels. The Golem's hands were like stone mittens, but the opposable thumb gave him enough dexterity to crack the rotten timbers and throw them into the centre of the room.

'Stop, Solomon, save your energy,' Othello muttered. The demon paused, then gave Othello an apologetic rumble. He growled and motioned at the barrels, pointing with his stubby hands.

'Oh, all right,' Othello said, waving his hand in defeat. Solomon continued his work, but more methodically this time. What on earth was he doing?

'He's building a fire! Come on, before Sylva goes into shock,' Fletcher said. The elf was still shuddering, hugging her knees to her chest. He couldn't imagine the day she'd had. The escape had left the tips of her ears wind-bitten and red with cold.

Soon the wood was stacked high, but Fletcher put most of it aside for later. Solomon pummelled some planks into splinters to work as tinder, then Ignatius blew repeated bursts of flame until the fire flickered into life. Soon a warm light filled the shed, the smoke wafting up and out of the cracks in the corners of the roof. The wood was punky and slow burning, as rotten timber so often is. Though it added to the musty smell in the air, the chill slowly left their bones and their wet clothes began to dry on their bodies. Even so, it was going to be a long night.

196

31

Fletcher started, then looked around the room. Othello was moodily poking the flames with a stick. He was topless, his shirt and jacket left to dry out beside the fire.

'I must have drifted off. How long was I out?' Fletcher asked, sitting up. His clothes were still damp, but he decided to leave them on. He supposed that Sylva would not be pleased with such a lapse in decorum. Yet, to his surprise, she was sitting on the other side of the fire, ripping the bottom of her dress off in a long strip. Ignatius was curled up beside her, his back warmed by the flames.

'Only a few minutes, Fletcher,' she said, handing the strip to Othello. 'Here, use it to wrap your head. It will help it heal.'

'Thanks,' Othello said, with a look of happy astonishment on his face. 'I appreciate it. I'm sorry you had to ruin your dress.'

'That's the least of my worries. How stupid of me, to think I could walk the streets of Corcillum in the middle of a war and not suffer the consequences.'

'Why did you?' Fletcher asked, furrowing his brow.

'I thought I would be safe with the Forsyths. They walked with their demons in plain sight and we were given a wide berth. In hindsight, I am not surprised.' She wrung her hands in frustration. 'I am sure if a man was to saunter into elven territory, he would suffer a similar fate. There are race haters on both sides of the frontier.'

'I'm glad you feel that way. I wouldn't blame you for thinking the worst of us and convincing your father to end all chances of an alliance between our peoples,' Fletcher said, shuffling over to the fire and warming his numbed hands.

'No, it has only strengthened my resolve,' Sylva replied, gazing into the flames. Gone was the haughty girl who had looked down her nose at them. This person was someone entirely more righteous.

'How so?' asked Fletcher.

'If even the false war we pretend to fight has created so much hate between our peoples, what would a real one do?' she explained, pushing more wood into the fire.

'What is the feeling amongst the elves?' Othello asked, removing his boots and letting his socks dry by the crackling fire. Solomon dutifully picked them up and held them close to the flames.

'Some understand it, saying that joining with humans to fight in the south is worth it if it keeps the orcs from our doorsteps. Others claim that the orcs would never raid so far north, even if the Hominum Empire fell,' Sylva answered, wrinkling her nose at the cheesy smell of the dwarf's feet. 'But my father is an old chieftain. He remembers the stories his father told to him, of the days the orcs laid waste to our villages, slaughtering us for sport and gathering our warriors' heads as trophies. The younger elves are barely aware that it was the orc marauders that made us make our homes in the great oaks of the north in the first place, thousands of years ago. Even when we did, that only slowed the orcs down. It was the first humans who allied with us, driving them back to their jungles and patrolling the borders. Our alliance existed since the first men crossed the Akhad Desert, yet over time and countless generations it fell into non-existence.'

'We were allied with the elves?' Fletcher asked, wide-eyed with incredulity.

'I studied the history of our two peoples before coming here on my diplomatic mission. We elves can live for two hundred years, so our historians' memories are longer than yours. King Corwin, the first King of Hominum, led a war against the orcs on our behalf. It was the elves who taught him and his ilk how to summon in exchange for his protection, creating the first noble houses of Hominum.'

'Wow. I had no idea you had a hand in creating our empire,' Fletcher marvelled. 'Nor that elves were the first summoners.'

'Not so,' Sylva murmured. 'The orcs were summoning long before we were. But theirs was a rough, nascent art, small imps and nothing more. Would that it were so today—'

'I have a question,' Othello interrupted. 'Why didn't you bring your own demon? Surely you must have your own demons over there, if you taught men how to summon in the first place?'

'That is a difficult question to answer. We had a long period of peace after the Hominum Empire was founded. Whilst the dwarves were rebelling and the orcs were raiding the kingdom of man, the elves remained in relative safety. So, our need for using demons to defend ourselves passed. Of course there were other factors. For example, the summoning of demons was banned for a brief period four centuries ago, when duelling came into fashion amongst our clan chieftains' heirs. Eventually there were no more demons to gift as they were either killed in these duels or released back into the ether.'

Othello's stomach rumbled and Sylva laughed; the sombre tone of the room rushed away.

'I've got an idea,' Fletcher said, standing. After a moment's hesitation he jumped outside. Thirty seconds later he rushed back into the shed, soaked to the skin once again but holding an armful of corn.

As he settled back down Fletcher noticed something he hadn't before. Othello's back was tattooed in black, depicting a hammer crossed with a battle-axe. The level of detail was extraordinary.

'That's a beautiful tattoo, Othello. What does it mean?' Fletcher enquired.

'Oh, that. It's a dwarven sigil. They are the two tools that dwarves use. It represents the axe for our prowess in battle and the hammer for our skill as craftsmen. I never liked the idea of tattoos though. I don't need marks on my skin to tell the world that I am a true dwarf,' Othello grumbled.

'Why did you get it then?' Sylva asked, spitting a few ears of corn on a rusted pitchfork and holding it over the flames.

'My brother had it tattooed on him, so I had to do the same. Sometimes I need to take the rap for him. It makes more sense that we look identical. The Pinkertons take off your shirt when they . . . punish you.'

Sylva continued to look at him with a mix of bafflement and

horror, then her eyes widened as they settled on Othello's scars.

'We're twins, not that the Pinkertons could tell the difference usually anyway; one dwarf is the same as another to them,' Othello explained.

'So . . . you're like Isadora and Tarquin then,' she ventured. 'I've always wondered what it would be like to be a twin.'

'I thought they were twins, but I wasn't sure,' Fletcher said, trying to picture the two nobles.

'Of course they are,' Othello said. 'It's always the first-born who inherits the ability to summon, twins included. The other children have a much smaller chance, although it happens sometimes. Nobody is quite sure why, but it has certainly helped consolidate power in the noble houses. Firstborn sons and daughters inherit the entire estate, so the lands are not portioned out to multiple children in the majority of cases. The Forsyths have enough land for two though, that's for sure.'

The dwarf pulled an ear of corn from the pitchfork and bit into it greedily, blowing on his fingers.

'So tell me, Sylva, what were you doing in Corcillum? Did you see Genevieve and the others in the perfumery?' Fletcher asked, trying to put aside the fact that she had almost got them killed.

'The nobles took me in a carriage to the town square. Then Isadora and Tarquin brought me to the flower district, as they wanted fresh roses for their rooms. I was wearing a headscarf to cover my ears and hair, so I did not think there would be a problem. But my eyes, they must have given me away. That fat man, Grindle, he tore my shawl from my head and dragged me down an alleyway with his friends. Isadora and Tarquin ran at the first sign of trouble. They did not even look back. I didn't have a summoning leather with me, so Sariel remained infused within me. I'll never make that mistake again.'

'Summoning leather?' Othello questioned, finishing off the last of his cob and reaching for another. Sylva slapped his hand away playfully.

'Greedy! Fletcher, have some. I noticed none of you came down for lunch at the canteen earlier, you should eat something.'

'Thanks. All I had for lunch was an apple,' Fletcher said, grabbing an ear for himself. He bit into the soft kernels, each one bursting with cloying sweetness in his mouth.

'A summoning leather,' Sylva turned back to Othello, 'is just a pentacle printed on a square cut of leather, which would allow me to summon Sariel when she has been infused within me. I'm not sure if your summoners call it that today. The documents I found on summoning practices were pretty ancient.'

'I can't believe that Tarquin and Isadora ran away!' Fletcher exclaimed through a mouthful of corn.

'That's not the worst part. They both had their demons out when I was captured. I suspect it was the sight of them that attracted so much attention in the first place.'

'Those cowards,' Othello growled.

'And their full-fledged demons are inherited from their mother and father,' Sylva continued. 'They could have taken several times the number of men that attacked me. If I had been standing closer to them, the men would have never attacked, but I was getting sick of their narcissistic chatter so I walked away for a moment.' Sylva paused, delicately biting into her own cob.

'Why did you try and befriend them if you didn't like them?' Fletcher asked.

'I am here as a diplomat. Who would you think it best to befriend if I am to broker an alliance between our two peoples? I know now of course that the best way is to become an officer as soon as possible and make a name for myself in battle, not suck up to spoiled children with no real power. That will get the word out, if it is known that the elves have some fight in them.'

'Ah,' said Fletcher. It made sense, yet the way she had treated him before still hurt. Then again, if he were alone in his enemy's land with such a huge burden of responsibility, being considerate might be the last thing on his mind, too.

'Right, we should bed down for the night. We're probably going to get in trouble for staying out all night, but there's no way we can walk back in this weather,' Fletcher said, stretching out by the fire.

'Oh, I don't know about that,' Othello said, rolling his jacket into a makeshift pillow and lying back on it. 'There are no guards or anything at the academy entrance. If we get there before the deliveries, we should be able to sneak in without a soul seeing us.'

As Sylva curled up beside the fire and pulled up the jacket's hood, a thought crossed Fletcher's mind. How did Othello know that?

32

'Where the hell have you been?' Seraph hissed. Fletcher, Othello and Sylva had just stumbled into the summoning room, attaching themselves to the others as quietly as possible when the students made their way in from the atrium. The trio looked a mess but there was nothing they could have done. They had arrived whilst the deliveries were being made, so they were only able to sneak in after breakfast, just as lessons were about to begin.

'It's a long story. We'll tell you later,' Fletcher whispered. Isadora turned at the commotion, her eyes widening when she saw Sylva. She prodded Tarquin, who looked around and jerked in shock. Sylva stared blankly at them and then turned to face Captain Lovett, who was waiting for everyone to settle down. The tall woman was wearing a leather apron over her officer's uniform, as well as heavy leather gloves.

'Let's get some light in here,' Lovett said, releasing several balls of blue wyrdlight into the air. Unlike Arcturus, she allowed them to float around the room aimlessly, casting the room in a bright but eerily shifting light.

'So, as I understand it, Arcturus allowed those of you who were already practised in wyrdlights to leave early yesterday. This will not happen in my classes. My motto is practice makes perfect, and considering your short tenure here, you should be making use of every second under our tutelage.' She paced back and forth in front of them, her hard eyes ranging across each of their faces. This was not someone Fletcher wanted to cross.

'The first order of business will be to teach you the art of infusion. I see that some of you do not have your demons with you, so I assume you have already been taught this. However, the speed at which you can release your demon from within can be the difference between life and death. Trust me, I know. Those of you who have been trained by your parents are to practise on the summoning circles on the other side of the room. I will come and check on you later.'

The nobles peeled off with smug expressions, talking and laughing amongst themselves. Lovett had split the room into two with a large curtain, so they were obscured from view once they ducked through the central parting. After a few moments, Fletcher saw bright lights flashing underneath. What manner of demons did the nobles possess?

Sylva raised her hand and stepped forward.

'I was self-taught. Would it be possible to stay with the others and learn the proper technique?' the elf asked.

Lovett eyed her torn dress and dishevelled hair and arched an eyebrow. After a long, hard look, she relented.

'All right. But please note that in future, I expect you in uniform,' she said, before turning to the rest of the commoners.

'Go and get yourselves a summoning leather each, as well as a leather apron. There should be gloves and goggles in the compartment below too.' She motioned at the back of the room and one of the wyrdlights shot over and hung above a row of cupboards built into the wall.

'What happened to you?' Genevieve muttered out of the corner of her mouth as they walked over. 'We waited for as long as we could, but we had to go before the last carriage left.'

'We missed the last carriage and had to walk home this morning,' Fletcher murmured back, rummaging through several rolls of leather until he found one with a pentacle that was not too faded. He didn't know if Sylva wanted her assault to become common knowledge.

'Did you get mugged on the way or something?' Genevieve asked, unconvinced.

'What makes you say that?' Fletcher retorted, shrugging a leather apron over his head.

'Well, leaving aside Othello's bandaged head, you have a goose egg-sized lump on the side of yours too,' Genevieve pointed out as they walked back. Fletcher reached up to his temple and winced as he realised she was right. Fortunately, they had arrived back in front of Lovett again, who silenced them with a look.

'I hear some of you have had your demons for at least seven days. They should be quite tired now, so it would be best to infuse them straight away so that they can rest. Raise your hands those of you who received your demon last week,' Lovett announced. Genevieve and Rory raised their hands. After a few moments Fletcher raised his too.

'What's the hesitation? Fletcher, is it?' Lovett asked, beckoning Fletcher to step forward.

'I have had my demon for two and a half weeks,' Fletcher answered. 'Is that normal?'

'No; it must be very tired indeed! Let's have a look at it,' she chided. Fletcher woke Ignatius with a mental prod. The imp mewled in annoyance and leaped on to the ground from Fletcher's hood. He looked around with curiosity and then licked his chops. The demon must be quite hungry, having turned his nose up at the roasted corn the night before.

'He's been a bit sleepy, but he usually is anyway,' Fletcher explained, feeling a pang of guilt as the little demon yawned.

'A Salamander,' Lovett breathed. 'Rare indeed! Major Goodwin will be very interested in this. It is not often that he gets to examine a new species of demon.'

'Is Ignatius going to be OK?' Fletcher asked, still worried about the supposed exhaustion.

'It would appear so,' Lovett replied. 'The more powerful a demon is, the longer it can survive without rest in our world, although it will be several months before their tiredness becomes life threatening. I had thought, as a commoner, your demon would be one of the weaker species. Although by all accounts it seems you have been a lucky bunch. Last year most of the commoners were given Mites, but you have a Lutra, a Barkling, a Salamander and a Golem.'

'A Canid too!' Sylva exclaimed, unrolling her mat on the floor. Fletcher smiled, glad she had put herself in with the commoners.

Rory shuffled his feet and clenched his fists.

'I'm sick of being told how unlucky I am to have Malachi,' he whispered with obvious frustration.

'Why don't you begin, Sylva?' Lovett suggested. 'It is a relatively simple act, once you know what to do.' Lovett suggested.

Sylva kneeled on the floor without hesitation and laid her gloved hands on the leather mat. The goggles sat awkwardly over her long ears, but she didn't seem to mind. Fletcher was sure she couldn't wait to be under Sariel's protection once again after last night's debacle. Taking a deep, steadying breath, Sylva stared at the pentacle until it flickered with soft, violet light.

'Watch how she pushes the mana through her hands, into the leather and through to the pentacle. She will know when it is time to push the demon through once the pentacle is glowing steadily.'

The pentacle gleamed with blue light, yet nothing happened for almost half a minute. The only sound was Sylva's laboured breathing as she glared at the shining star. Then, without warning, a Canid's form grew into the space out of nothingness, expanding from a pinprick of light to a large glowing shape in half a second. The figure shone white, then the colour faded and Sariel stood above the pentacle.

Her four eyes focussed on Sylva, and then the Canid leaped on to her master, sending them both tumbling to the ground. The demon licked her face and howled. Fletcher wondered whether Sariel was aware of what Sylva had gone through yesterday. Maybe she had just missed her owner.

'Obviously your demon needs some discipline and training, but good work none-the-less! I shall summon my demon,

Lysander, so that I can demonstrate how to infuse. Stand back please!' Lovett announced. Sylva and Sariel moved aside, and the rest of the group took several steps backwards.

'The larger your demon is, the more difficult the summoning. Of course, in the field, you won't be able to wear protective clothing, but it is best to take precautions when we can, especially with untrained noviciates such as yourselves,' Lovett said, kneeling on the corner of the summoning leather. 'The main reason for all the protection is for using keyed pentacles, but we won't get on to that until later.'

She fished a pair of black-lensed goggles and a leather cap from a pouch in her apron, then put them on firmly.

The pentacle glowed again, white sparks spitting and sizzling on the leather around it. A white orb appeared above it and, to Fletcher's astonishment, a demon formed in just a few seconds. The creature had the body, tail and back legs of a lion, but the head, wings and front talons of an eagle. It was the size of a large horse, with tawny brown feathers that blended into the golden fur halfway down the creature's back.

'I too was blessed with a rare demon, a Griffin. But he was not given to me. I started with a Mite, just as some of you have. Do not be disheartened by your modest beginnings. Mites are fiercely loyal creatures, and you can control many of them at once. Lysander requires all my concentration just to keep him under control. Major Goodwin will teach you more on demon control in your demonology classes.'

Genevieve smiled and lifted Azura to her lips, kissing the beetle's cobalt carapace.

'Does that mean you were a commoner too?' Rory asked,

barely able to tear his eyes away from the majestic creature.

'No . . . although I was present when the first commoners arrived at Vocans. I am the third daughter of the Lovetts of Calgary, a small fiefdom in northern Hominum. By strange coincidence, my father was blessed with several adept children. I was the youngest, so I was given the weakest demon by my father. I'm glad he did though. If he had not, I would never have specialised in demonic capture. You can all own a powerful demon such as this, as long as you work hard.' She wrapped her arm around Lysander, who nuzzled his beak against her chest fondly. The Griffin's eyes were deep amber, as large and intelligent as an owl's. They flicked from student to student with curiosity, at last resting with special attention on Ignatius.

'Now, I shall demonstrate how to infuse. It is almost a reverse of the procedure. The pentacle must be pointed directly at the demon and it cannot be too far away. This is why we have them stand on the summoning leathers. However, if Lysander were to hover several metres above the pentacle, I would be able to manage it.'

She kneeled and laid her hands on the leather once more, sputtering the pentacle into life.

'You must first push mana into the pentacle. Soon you will feel an obstacle between your demon's consciousness and your own. Once you feel that, pull the demon through it . . .' She heaved with effort, and Lysander glowed, then dissipated into strands of white light that flowed into her hands.

'That's all there is to it,' Lovett announced, her forehead beading with sweat. They applauded her skill, but Fletcher was filled with apprehension when she turned her steely eyes on to him.

'Fletcher, you shall try first, as your demon needs to rest the most. Arcturus tells me you are unusually gifted at spellcraft. Let us see if the same holds true for infusion.' Lovett pointed at the floor in front of him.

Fletcher slowly unrolled his summoning mat and sent Ignatius on to it. The demon sat there, uttering a nervous chirr as he felt Fletcher's anxiety. Fletcher did as he had been instructed, channelling the mana into the leather mat. It glowed a fierce violet, steady and unwavering.

'Do you feel it, Fletcher?' Lovett asked, placing a steadying hand on Fletcher's shoulder.

'I feel it,' Fletcher grunted back through gritted teeth. In his mana-charged state, the light was almost blinding, filling his vision with the glowing star.

'Pull him through. You may struggle initially, but that is normal for the first infusion.' Lovett's voice sounded as if it were coming from a great distance. The mana pulsed through his veins with each beat of his heart, thundering in his ears. His link with Ignatius was blocked. He grasped at the demon's mind, then, with a colossal effort, drew him in. For a moment, he strained, hissing between gritted teeth. It felt as if Ignatius was caught in an elastic web. After what seemed like an age there was a gentle snap, and the demon's consciousness merged with his own. It was like sinking into a warm bath.

'Well done, Fletcher! You can rest now,' Lovett whispered in his ear.

Fletcher pressed his head into the soft leather, breathing in

211

deep lungfuls of air. He could hear the others clapping and yelling incoherently. His mind was filled with extraordinary happiness and clarity, as if he were drugged to the gills.

'What Fletcher will be feeling now is the temporary exhilaration of merging consciousnesses with another being. His demon is within him, yet he will be barely aware of it in a few minutes. Ignatius will see everything that Fletcher is seeing, though he will understand very little of it. This can be extremely useful should you need to summon in the midst of battle, as demons are prepared for the situation as soon as they reappear,' Lovett lectured, pacing back and forth behind him.

'Some summoners experience flashes of demonic memory in the months after they first infuse their demons. This too shall pass, but is an important part of how we learn about the ether. If this happens to you, make sure to take note of every detail and tell myself and Major Goodwin all of it. We need every bit of information about the life of demons we can get,' she continued.

Fletcher stood with difficulty and walked back to the others, his head still spinning. Seraph patted him on the back with a jealous grin on his face.

'Well done. I guess you're the one to beat,' he whispered.

'Not likely. I think that almost killed me,' Fletcher replied, feeling the warm glow of Ignatius within him. It was strange, he could barely distinguish between Ignatius's consciousness and his own. The thread no longer connected them; they flowed into each other like the meeting of two rivers.

Othello gave him an encouraging smile and even Sylva touched him lightly on the arm before turning her attention back to Sariel. The elf buried her face and hands in her demon's golden fur, clinging on to the Canid as if her life depended on it. Fletcher suspected it would be a long while before she would want to infuse Sariel again.

'Now. Othello and Fletcher, let's have a look at those heads of yours,' Lovett said, beckoning them forward. Once they were in front of her, she whispered under her breath, 'Is there anything you boys need to tell me? You and Sylva look like you've been in the wars, and I should know.'

'It's nothing we couldn't handle,' Fletcher assured her, looking to Othello for support.

'We dealt with it,' the dwarf agreed.

Lovett eyed them for a moment, before inclining her head in acceptance.

'Well, if you ever change your minds, you can talk to me,' she murmured, looking them in the eyes. 'You don't have to fight your battles alone.'

Then she stepped back and raised her voice.

'Gather round, everyone. I'm going to use the healing spell; you might as well watch.'

The rest of the commoners approached them, chattering with excitement at the opportunity to see another spell. Othello removed his bandage, revealing a jagged cut across his temple.

Fletcher winced at the sight of it. He hadn't realised how bad the wound was.

'Watch closely now,' Lovett announced. She etched a heart-shaped symbol in the air with wyrdlight, then pointed it at Othello's gash.

'The healing spell is perfect for cuts, bruises and even internal

213

injuries, although it won't do anything against poisons and diseases,' Lovett declared, knitting her brows together in concentration. 'It requires a lot of mana and takes a while to perform, especially for deeper injuries.'

She exhaled and golden light flowed from the symbol to Othello's head. Nothing happened for almost thirty seconds. Then, to Fletcher's astonishment, the wound began to stitch together, sealing itself until the skin was completely healed, leaving nothing but a crust of dried blood.

The group clapped, cheering at the feat. Lovett turned her eyes to Fletcher's forehead, but shook her head.

'You'll have to let that heal on its own, Fletcher,' she explained, pointing at the swelling. 'You may have a fracture. The healing spell can cause broken bones to fuse incorrectly, leaving you permanently disfigured. Best not to risk it.'

Fletcher nodded in agreement, fingering the lump on his head with a wince.

'Right, let's get the rest of you trained up. Once you've mastered infusion we can move on to the fun stuff,' Lovett exclaimed, clapping her hands.

'What happens then?' Rory asked as he unravelled his summoning leather on to the floor.

Lovett removed her goggles and smiled at them mysteriously.

'We're going to enter the ether.'

33

Their next lesson was with Major Goodwin, a blustering but strict old man with a red nose and bristling, white goatee. He strode energetically around the lecture hall, belying his portly frame.

'Demonology is key in supporting your spellcraft and etherwork. It concerns the identification, understanding, and upbringing of all demons, as well as the study of the geography and diversity of the ether. This includes demonic impact upon the summoner's mana levels and their fulfilment.' He spoke in short bursts that left the front row of nobles flecked with spit. Fletcher was glad to see that Tarquin was directly in the firing line, and judging by the disgusted look on his face, he did not enjoy being bathed in saliva.

Unfortunately, Fletcher's smile drew Goodwin's attention.

'You boy, what is a summoner's fulfilment?' he asked, pointing at Fletcher.

'Ummm . . . his happiness?' Fletcher suggested. Wasn't it obvious?

'A laughable answer. A summoner's fulfilment relates to how many demons they are able to harness. I had hoped that someone fortunate enough to be gifted with a rare demon would take time to research this before their first lesson. Obviously I was mistaken. A shame,' Goodwin said, shaking his head. Fletcher felt his face burn as he reddened with embarrassment. Isadora turned and smirked at him from the row below.

'Could someone who came prepared explain? How about you, Malik?' Goodwin questioned.

'Sir, every summoner is born with varying capacities to absorb demonic energy,' a tall, dark-skinned noble said. 'For example, Captain Lovett only has the capacity to harness and control one Griffin and one Mite. Another summoner might be able to harness and control two Griffins, because they have a higher fulfilment level than she does.'

'Correct. The old King Alfric has a fulfilment level of one hundred, the highest ever recorded since we began classifying demons. Using the example of Captain Lovett again, we know that she has a fulfilment level of eleven, given that her Griffin is a class ten demon and her Mite is a class one demon. What else?'

'Fulfilment levels can improve,' Malik said after a pause.

'How?'

'I don't know, sir.'

Goodwin took a long angry sniff through his nose.

'Not good enough. The answer is that fulfilment levels grow naturally at varying rates for each summoner as time goes by. This process can be sped up by the hard work of the summoner in question. Captain Lovett was not born with the fulfilment level required to harness and control a Griffin. She had to work up to it by the constant use of spellcraft, entering the ether and regularly battling and harnessing other demons. Some summoners spend their entire lives with a fulfilment level of no higher than five, whilst others start at five and work their way up to twenty or so. Well, why aren't you writing this down?' Goodwin shouted, sending a fresh spray of spit into the crowd.

The others pulled parchment from their satchels and began to scribble. Fletcher stared at his hands miserably, realising he had none. Everyone else had known they were coming to Vocans weeks ago and had brought the correct materials, but Fletcher had forgotten to buy some in the few days he had been there. Goodwin bristled as he saw Fletcher's inactivity.

'Fletcher, is it?' he growled.

'Yes, sir,' Fletcher replied, ducking his head in embarrassment.

'Whilst the others are busy learning, perhaps you can tell me what happens to a demon once his summoner is killed?'

Fletcher contemplated the question, eager to redeem himself, even if by guesswork. He knew that dead demons were often preserved in jars and sold as curiosities. But surely something must happen when the summoner died and left the demon unharnessed . . . unless it was a trick question? Fletcher remembered Rotherham's story about Baker and the demon that would not leave his side, even in death. Perhaps it was a trick!

'Nothing, sir,' Fletcher replied confidently. But his heart sank as he saw Tarquin smirk. He knew he was wrong before Goodwin had even opened his mouth.

'Preposterous. Do you know anything about demons at all? When a summoner dies, his demon will remain in our world for just a few hours, before it is reabsorbed back into the ether.

To remain in our world alive, a demon must be harnessed. It is that bond that keeps them here. Otherwise, they will simply fade away. Or did you think there were wild demons running about out there?' Goodwin spoke loudly for the benefit of the others, and in response, the scratch of their quills increased in intensity. Goodwin turned away from him in disgust and stalked to the wall behind him. There were several long scrolls stacked against it, one of which he picked up, unrolled and pinned to the wall. On the front of it was a detailed diagram of a Mite in black and white, with various statistics and numbers below it.

'Today we are going to learn about Mites, the very lowest level of demon, other than their various cousins at the bottom of the food chain, which are not worth capturing. I know we have two Mites here today, specifically Scarabs, the most powerful of the Mite family. Low in mana, size and strength, but useful as scouts. Very good at distracting the enemy during a fight, especially if they go for the eyes. Genevieve and Rory own juvenile Scarabs, but in a few months they will develop stingers, which can cause low-level paralysis and not an insignificant amount of pain. A swarm of ten stings can take down a bull orc, so do not underestimate the power of their poison.'

'Terrific!' Rory said aloud, then covered his mouth with his hands. The others laughed, except for Goodwin, who sniffed irritably.

The lesson continued in this vein for another hour, noting down various statistics and discussing the feeding and breeding habits of the Scarab. Fletcher watched despondently as page after page of notes piled up on the others' desks, until Othello nudged

218

him with his foot and whispered, 'Don't worry, you can copy mine later.'

During lunch, Fletcher managed to borrow a spare quill from Rory and a swathe of parchment from Genevieve, so he was better prepared for the second half of the lesson. But when they returned, Fletcher was surprised to find Scipio waiting in the room for them, with an impatient look on his face.

'Fletcher, you are to report to the library. You are yet to hand in James Baker's book, despite being told to bring it to the librarian several days ago,' he said irritably. 'Major Goodwin, do you mind at all?'

'Not with this cadet,' Goodwin harrumphed. 'He has been a disappointment.'

Scipio raised his eyebrows at Fletcher but said nothing. Fletcher gathered up his things, feeling himself flush with humiliation. Had he really made such a bad impression?

'Bloody hell, they take late books very seriously at the library here, huh?' Rory muttered in his ear.

'I will meet you there. Be sure to bring the book,' Scipio said to Fletcher, then strode from the room without a backwards glance.

Fletcher hurried up the stairs, cursing his forgetfulness. He had forgotten to write to Berdon, forgotten to hand the book in and, more importantly, he had forgotten to examine the book itself.

He reminded himself that the sheep wagon had been too dark to read in, a fact that had annoyed him greatly. It had been a torrid and fetid journey with nothing to distract himself with, other than his own thoughts. Even so, Fletcher had definitely had time to read it last night.

By the time he had rushed to the top of the tower, collected his book and made his way back to the library, Fletcher was panting. He steadied himself against the wall and tried to compose himself. He didn't want to lower Scipio's opinion of him any more than he already had by walking in all hot and flustered.

'What are you waiting for, Fletcher, in with you!' Scipio barked from behind him, making him jump. The Provost laid his hand on Fletcher's shoulder and propelled him forward.

They walked into the library together, the musty smell of old books bringing memories of Pelt's crypt back to Fletcher's mind. Had all that only happened a few weeks ago?

'Ah, here you are. I must say I have been looking forward to this. Thank you for bringing him, Provost Scipio,' came a voice from behind the shelves. A middle-aged woman with curly blonde hair and gold-rimmed spectacles emerged. She had a matronly appearance and an open, honest face.

'This is Dame Rose Fairhaven, the librarian and nurse at Vocans. She has been with us a long time,' Scipio murmured.

'Come now, Provost, you make me sound like an old lady. It hasn't been that long! Well, bring it over here. Let's have a look.'

She beckoned them both over to a low table illuminated by a plethora of bright candles.

'Set it down here where we can all see. Arcturus has explained the book's origin to me. I remember James Baker. Quiet boy, always drawing. He had the heart of an artist, not a warrior. He was never cut out to be a soldier. I'm sorry to hear what happened to him.' She sighed and sat down beside the table.

Fletcher set the book down and they joined her, leaning over as she flipped through the book with a practised air.

'This is incredible,' she breathed. The pages were filled with intricate sketches of demons and spidery handwriting underneath. The level of detail was extraordinary, with statistics and measurements much like the large Mite scroll that Major Goodwin had been teaching from.

'He'd been studying demons from the orc's part of the ether, their physiology, their characteristics. He must have been dissecting any preserved orc demons he could find! This is exactly what we need for our archives. Most battlemages seem to have forgotten one of the most important of a soldier's sayings – *know thy enemy*. Perhaps now that it is all on paper they will actually take that to heart.'

Fletcher grinned, glad that he had finally been able to contribute, even indirectly.

'That is excellent news, Dame Fairhaven, although I had hoped he would have given us more information on how he found the summoning scroll for Fletcher's Salamander,' Scipio said, with a hint of disappointment in his voice.

'Actually Dame Fairhaven, if you turn to the back, there should be something about it there. I think Baker began a diary towards the end,' Fletcher suggested.

She flipped through the book until the very last few pages, where the diagrams ended and the pages were filled with lines of text.

'Wait, what's this?' Dame Fairhaven said, pulling out the leathery summoning scroll and turning it over in the light.

'I . . . wouldn't touch that if I were you,' Fletcher stuttered.

'I know what this is, Fletcher,' Dame Fairhaven said, stroking the material. 'I have seen one before, many years ago. Inscribing a scroll through scarification of an enemy's skin was the usual way the old orc shamans used to gift demons to their apprentices. It's not so common these days though. Let's see what Baker had to say on the matter.'

Her eyes scanned the pages as Fletcher and Scipio waited patiently. She seemed to be reading at a terrific pace, but then she was a librarian after all. It wasn't long before she shut the book and laid it aside.

'Poor James,' she said, shaking her head. 'He became very depressed by the end – nobody would take his research seriously. The other battlemages didn't respect him because he was such a weak summoner. He was cursed with a fulfilment level of three, poor fellow. I suspect his ill-fated mission into the forest was a desperate attempt to encounter an orc shaman and somehow discover the keys that they use.'

'Foolish of him,' Scipio scoffed, throwing his hands in the air. 'The orc shamans know we want to find out what keys they use, so they never enter the ether anywhere near the front lines. Now tell me about this scroll. It's what all the fuss is about after all.'

'It says here he found the scroll buried underground in an old orc encampment. Earlier in the diary, it says that he had found a lot of bones at the same site, both orc and human. My suspicion is that the orcs' encampment was attacked in the middle of the demon-gifting ceremony and the scroll was buried underground in a mass grave. The men who filled the grave probably did not know its significance,' Dame Fairhaven said, peering at the scroll with morbid fascination.

'Useless!' Scipio grumbled, his voice full of disappointment. 'A fluke event. I doubt we will find any other scrolls by digging up old bones. Make a copy of the book without the diary and send it out to the battlemages.'

'Yes sir, I will start it tonight. Although I will need to hire a few scribes to get these drawings right,' Dame Fairhaven replied, flicking through the book absentmindedly.

'Do it. At least some good has come of all this,' Scipio said as he walked from the room. 'As well as having you of course, Fletcher,' he added from the corridor outside.

Fletcher eyed the book greedily. He couldn't believe he had waited so long to read it, long though it was. Dame Fairhaven continued to finger the pages, then as Fletcher shifted on his feet she looked up at him, as if she had forgotten he was there.

'Sorry, Fletcher, I am just so taken with this book. Thank you so much for bringing it to me. I'm afraid I will have to keep it until enough copies have been made, which should take a few months. You can have it back after that.'

34

Fletcher had hoped to see what demons the nobles possessed when Lovett finally decided that all the commoners had mastered infusion. Sadly, she always ordered them to infuse their demons before parting the curtain.

He had been surprised to find that Rory and Genevieve were adept at infusion, whilst Seraph, Othello and Atlas had taken several tries to manage it. It made a lot of sense, as the more powerful the demon, the more difficult it was to infuse them.

As the lessons progressed, Fletcher had begun to size up his fellow students. The nobles were proficient yet lazy, content with their current level of expertise and complacent in their learning.

In contrast, the commoners were learning at a furious pace, absorbing every bit of information that they could. Unfortunately, practice was the greatest teacher in both spellcraft and infusion, so progress was slow.

Still, there were several frontrunners amongst Fletcher's friends. Sylva and Othello were naturals, earning approving remarks from the teachers in almost every lesson. The same was true for the more cerebral demonology classes. The pair practically lived in the library, hunting through old tomes for hidden knowledge. Fletcher learned as much from them as he did from Major Goodwin.

As for the human commoners, Fletcher and Seraph led the pack, though it was through the dint of hard work rather than natural talent. The others had taken to whiling away their weekends in Corcillum, buying gifts and necessities and sending them back to their family. Seraph's family appeared to be wealthy already and he had visited Corcillum in the past, so he preferred to spend time studying with Fletcher.

He was a good-natured lad with a shameless sense of humour, earning many a disapproving stare from Sylva and Othello as they read in the dusty silence of the library.

'Gather round, everyone,' Lovett shouted, tearing Fletcher away from his musings.

Four servants had brought a round stone table to the centre of the room. It was covered in a white sheet, but Fletcher could see a large convex bump in the centre of it. Everyone found a place along the edge, although it was tight. Isadora made a face as a sweaty Atlas squeezed in beside her, then pointedly held a lacy handkerchief to her nose.

'Sorry,' Atlas muttered with embarrassment.

Lovett left her place at the table and kneeled beside the largest pentacle in the very centre of the room. Unlike the summoning leathers that they had been using, this pentacle was surrounded by the strange keys that had been etched into the front of James Baker's book.

'You are never to use a keyed pentacle without a teacher present, is that understood?' she growled, pointing at the star in front of her. 'Breaking this rule is grounds for immediate expulsion. You have been warned!'

The students nodded dumbly as she powered up the pentacle, the lines crackling with energy and spitting sparks in all directions. This time Lovett stayed with her head bowed for several minutes, her face contorted with concentration. The pentacle was pulsing with a volatile buzz, wavering like the incessant humming of a madman.

'Wow, if it takes Lovett this long, I don't think I could use a keyed pentacle even if I wanted to,' Seraph whispered next to him. 'I can barely infuse Sliver without almost passing out.'

'Don't worry. I'm sure with practice we will manage it,' Fletcher murmured back.

Finally, a sphere expanded in the centre of the star and hung in the air like a dim blue sun. Lovett panted and then shuffled over to the next pentacle on her knees. With a soft touch, she released a demon into existence above it.

'A Mite!' Genevieve whispered to Rory. Lovett heard and turned around with a tired smile.

'That's right. They make the best scouts, always needed when hunting in the ether. Valens is the first demon I ever owned. Without him, I would never have managed to capture Lysander, or any of the demons I had before him for that matter.' She strode back to the table and placed one hand on the white sheet that covered it. In the other hand, she held a long strip of leather that connected to the base of the keyed pentacle. Fletcher suspected it was so she could keep the mana flowing to it.

'What I am about to show you is the most expensive equipment in the entire academy. Do not touch it. Don't even breathe on it. Just watch,' Lovett hissed, looking them each in the eye until they were all nodding. With that last warning, she whipped off the cloth and revealed what was underneath.

An enormous gemstone was set in a white marble counter. The crystal was as clear as a mountain stream and its colouring was the deep purple of wild heather.

'The gemstone is a very rare type of crystal called Corundum,' Lovett said. 'It forms in almost every colour, but large, transparent pieces such as this are incredibly hard to find. We call them scrying stones, although this particular gem is known as the Oculus. We will provide you with one if you cannot afford to buy one for yourself, although you may find the quality and size of the academy's pieces quite . . . lacking.'

Lovett beckoned Valens over, and the little creature flew over their heads, settling on the gem. Unlike Malachi and Azura, the Mite's shell was a boring dark brown. As if she could read Fletcher's mind, Lovett smiled at him knowingly and stroked the beetle demon's carapace.

'Valens is well suited to his job. He won't look pretty on my shoulder, but he will be harder to spot if a hungry demon comes by in the ether.'

Fletcher had a brief recollection of Ignatius eating a brown beetle when he had first summoned him, but that thing had been much smaller than any of the Mites he had seen. It was probably a different species.

'Right, let's get this show on the road. You must push the

mana through the demon and into the stone like this,' she said, laying her free hand over Valens.

The gemstone turned black. As she removed her hand the colour changed again. At first, Fletcher thought the gemstone had become a mirror, finding himself staring at an image of his own face. But soon the image flicked to Seraph's.

'You are now looking through Valens's eyes. It is a technique that we call scrying, very useful for scouting and controlling your demons from afar. We can already sense the demon's thoughts. Now we can also see and hear what they can in the crystal. It is essential to check what is on the other side of the portal with your least important demon before entering the ether. Should there be something dangerous on the other side when he comes through, it will be Valens at risk rather than Lysander. Because a Mite is smaller and more agile, he is less likely to be noticed and can escape more easily.'

The image shook as Valens buzzed into the air and hovered just in front of the spinning blue orb. Lovett clicked her tongue, and with that, the demon whipped into the orb like a gunshot.

The first thing Fletcher saw in the stone was the red-tinged ground. Fine grains of rusty sand swirled above it, churned into dust devils by a seething wind. The sky was the orange of sunrise, yet it held no warmth, nor was there a source of light in the sky. Stunted trees dotted the landscape, their sparse branches contorted in rigor mortis. There was no life here, just a dry husk of a land long dead.

'Perfect,' Lovett said. 'We have emerged in the deadlands.'

'Deadlands?' Rory asked in an awestruck voice.

'Entering the ether is not an exact science. There is a large margin of error in where we might come out. The deadlands come with positives and negatives, depending on your purpose. There will be nothing to surprise you here, but if you are trying to capture a demon, you will have to drag it quite a distance to get back to the portal. If I was hunting, I would close this portal and open a new one, but for the purposes of this exercise it is ideal. The deadlands are between the void and the outer circle of the inhabited ether.' Lovett's voice was strained. Fletcher could see a vein pulsing in her forehead. Entering the ether must take a lot of power and concentration.

Valens turned and flew away from the portal, his altitude rising steadily. It was silent in the room, the only sound Lovett's heavy breathing, as the minutes ticked by. The landscape seemed to get even more desolate, with fewer and fewer trees until all they could see was flat, raw earth.

'How do you know where to go?' Tarquin asked. 'It all looks the same to me.'

Fletcher realised that was a good question. The young noble was a lot of things, but he was not stupid.

'The portal always faces the centre of the ether when your demon comes out, so you are orientated as soon as you enter. Additionally, all demons are drawn to the centre instinctually and they have an internal compass that tells them where it is. I can guide myself using this, but it takes practice and is not very accurate. That is why it is always risky entering the ether. I can only hold the portal open for so long and if I close it before Valens gets through, our bond will be broken, and I will lose him,' Lovett lectured back. Tarquin opened his mouth to ask another question but Fletcher got there first.

'What do you mean by the centre? Does that mean the ether has a shape?' he asked, trying to understand.

'As far as we know, the ether is disk shaped. The weaker demons tend to stay in the outer rings, with more powerful demons gravitating to the centre. There seems to be a rudimentary food chain, with low-level Mites on the very bottom, closest to the deadlands.'

Tarquin began to speak again but Lovett held up a hand to silence him.

'Save your questions for later. It is hard enough holding the portal open and guiding Valens without thinking of answers for you.' Even as she spoke, the pentacle flickered. She grunted and it glowed a steady violet once again.

Despite the intensity of the lesson, Fletcher felt himself relax, perhaps for the very first time. Everyone was learning something here, even Tarquin. It all made so much sense to Fletcher, as if he were remembering something long forgotten. He was meant for this.

The horizon began to fall away, darkening dramatically. The glow of the sky faded into a pure, starless black, yet the little Mite flew higher and higher. Finally he stopped and turned his view downwards once again.

'Look closely. You will see them,' Lovett said, her voice taught with exertion.

The land cut off in a neat line, creating the perfect precipice of a cliff that fell away into murky darkness below. Fletcher could see that the cliff line stretched on far into the distance, almost imperceptibly curving as they faded out of sight. He realised that the disk must be enormous, larger than a thousand Hominums. This would not be a good place to get lost, he thought grimly.

His line of thought was broken as he saw something stir in the abyss. As the beetle demon's eyes adjusted to the dark, a seething mass came into view. It twisted and writhed tortuously, a tangled chaos of tentacles, eyes and jagged teeth.

'Ceteans,' Sylva breathed in quiet horror.

'Aye, Ceteans. You've done your homework, Sylva,' Lovett uttered darkly, wiping sweat from her brow. 'Some call them the Old Ones. They starve down there, cannibalising each other as they wait. The Ceteans will snatch any demon that wanders this far, usually the sick or the injured trying to find somewhere to recover. That is why we must fly so high. This is the one and only time I will risk coming near them, so learn this lesson well. Stay away from here.'

Valens turned and flew back the way they had come. This time there were no questions as the group mulled over the nightmarish creatures they had just seen. The giant monsters were grotesque and tortured beings, of that Fletcher was certain. Though he could not hear anything, he could imagine their tormented screams in his head.

The blue orb that was the portal hovered beneath them, but Valens flew over it. With his current height, they made good time, the land rushing underneath like fallen leaves in a river. Fletcher wondered what it was like for Lovett, riding on a Griffin over the battlefield, then felt a pang of jealousy when he realised he would never be able to ride Ignatius.

'I will quickly show you where the hunting grounds

begin, then I must get back,' Lovett spat through gritted teeth. 'Normally I can go for much longer, but I am not yet recovered from the capture of Atlas's Lutra a few days ago. I was lucky that Provost Scipio was there to harness it.'

'Harness?' Rory asked. Lovett ignored him, instead pointing at the gemstone.

The world had turned green. Valens was looking over a forest, though the vegetation was not one Fletcher recognised. Above it, he saw flocks of flying demons in the distance, swooping and turning like starlings. A swarm of tiny Mites flew low above the trees, before scattering as a large Mite not unlike Valens snatched one of them from the air. Far in the distance, ash clouds stained the sky. Below them, lava-tipped volcanoes spewed pillars of smoke, hanging in the air like columns supporting the heavens.

Something hit Valens with brutal force, knocking him out of the sky. Lovett cried out in pain as the image spun like a kaleidoscope, trees rushing up to meet them.

The stone turned black as ink.

35

The group stared at the black stone in horror, holding their breaths. Lovett was clutching her tether with a white knuckled grip as the pentacle spat violet sparks, sizzling and smoking on the leather around them with the stench of burning hair.

The Oculus flickered into life. The image was fuzzy and unfocussed, but it panned slowly as Valens looked at the iridescent treetops above. The little demon was alive!

'I was afraid of this,' Lovett muttered. 'This is the time of year that the Shrikes migrate across our hunting grounds. In previous years I would wait until next month to begin with your lesson in the ether, but with you first years taking part in the tournament I had to move it up. Damn Scipio and his rush to get you on the battlefield! In his day, there were five years of study before graduation. He should know better!'

She cursed long and hard, her tirade blacker than a Vesanian sailor's. Fletcher's ears reddened at her colourful language, but he smiled to himself. Lovett could swear with the best of them!

He tried to picture a Shrike from his studies, but could only remember that it was a dangerous, birdlike creature that visited Hominum's hunting grounds in the ether seasonally.

'The Shrike will be coming back, but I can feel Valens has hurt one of his wings. He's going to have to race to the portal. There's no way he can fight a Shrike; it is three classes above him. Maybe five if it's the matriarch in their flock.'

The last sentence meant little to Fletcher, but he wondered what class ranking Ignatius would fall under. As the Mite buzzed into life and jerked into the air, his thoughts turned back to the task at hand.

The poor demon flew slowly, hampered by his injured wing. He skimmed over the barren desert, buffeted by the low winds that spun the dust across his vision. As the minutes ticked by excruciatingly slowly, Fletcher noticed something ahead of them. It was a shadow, though of what he was not certain.

'There's something above us,' he said, pointing at the black shape on the stone.

'I know. It has been with us since the forest. Shrikes like to injure their prey with a surprise attack, then follow the victim from above until it collapses from its wounds. It is an effective technique, but it will work to our advantage today. Wild demons have an almost instinctual fear of portals, so it is rare for one to come through unless we drag it in. If we can get Valens to return through the portal, the Shrike will leave him alone. Then I can infuse him, and he will heal just fine. I just hope he can make it,' Lovett replied, pushing a sweaty strand of hair from out of her eyes.

Finally, the portal appeared on the horizon. It was not a moment too soon, for Valens's flight was becoming jerky and the Oculus's image was dimming with worrying frequency.

'Just a little further,' Lovett hissed, her brow furrowed in concentration.

But the Mite had gone as far as he could go. Valens tumbled to the ground a few feet from the portal, landing in a puff of dust. He lay motionless, the only sign he was still alive was the glow of the stone, still showing the plumes of dust as they twisted in the wind's eddies.

'Quick, get me the ether gear, now! It's in the last cupboard on the far wall. I don't know how long we have left!'

Seraph was the first to react, sprinting to the back of the room and heaving out a bulky package.

'I need help, it's heavy!' he shouted. Othello hastened to his assistance and together they hauled it to Lovett. Fletcher continued to stare into the stone. The shadow had swooped by again.

'Can't I send Ignatius in to get him?' Fletcher asked.

'No, our manas would merge if your demon entered through my portal. Mixing manas is difficult to master. If you fail on the first attempt, the portal will close, and we will lose Valens for good.'

Lovett was struggling to get into what looked like a bulky one-piece suit. It was made of heavy leather with steel-capped boots at the bottom and a metal ring around the neck at the top. Once her feet were in, Lovett attached the long leather tether that powered the pentacle to another that extended from the back of her suit, several metres in length. There was a long, empty hose connected to a helmet on the floor, coiled in several loops.

'Stretch my air pipe out, Seraph. I need a clear airway,' Lovett demanded, lifting the helmet. As Seraph unravelled the hose, she clicked it into place above her neck.

'It needs to be airtight!' she shouted in a muffled voice. 'The ether's air is poisonous to us. If I get a hole in my suit, pull me out immediately using the tether, whether I have collected Valens or not!'

'It's just a Mite. Why risk your life for something you could capture another of tomorrow?' Tarquin asked, his voice filled with scepticism.

Lovett turned towards him, her face barely visible. The helmet was made of copper, with a round pane of thick glass on the front. There was a cage built over the small window to keep it from shattering.

'A demon is not an item to be tossed aside like an old shirt,' she snapped. 'When you have battled side by side with yours, maybe you'll understand.'

With those parting words, she stepped into the portal.

They saw Lovett step out on the gemstone, a hazy brown figure swimming into Valens's view. It was so strange, to see her move from the blue-tinged gloom of the summoning room to the scorching sky of the ether in just a few seconds. Yet there she was, stomping through the dust towards the Mite with slow, measured strides.

Soon her gloved hand scooped up Valens and brought the demon to the front of her helmet. They could see her grey eyes flashing through the glass with equal amounts of fear and concern, before she turned and trudged back to the portal.

'Why is she moving so slowly?' Genevieve whispered.

'She's wearing a heavy suit in a scorching desert whilst maintaining a portal to another world and controlling a dying demon simultaneously. It's a miracle she is still standing at all,' Tarquin said in a lofty tone. 'If that portal closes she will be trapped there for as long as it takes for the poison to kill her after her air pipe gets snipped in two. Foolish woman.'

'She's going to make it,' Fletcher murmured, willing her onwards as she took step after staggering step.

It was Othello who saw it first, a small black spot in the sky, growing larger by the second. He pointed at it with curiosity then wide-eyed horror as a feathered demon expanded into view. Lovett had seemingly noticed too, for her pace quickened and the pentacle crackled dangerously as her concentration slipped.

The Shrike was a giant bird with long black feathers. The wingspan was as wide as Fletcher was tall, the endmost feathers tipped with bleached white. Its lethal beak was hooked cruelly, with a bright red wattle underneath its neck and a red ridge along the top of its head like that of a rooster. It reminded Fletcher of an enormous, ugly vulture.

The bird demon dived towards Lovett, its bright orange talons outstretched. She ducked down, but it was too late; the talons scored along her helmet with brutal accuracy. They caught in the helmet's cage, dragging her over on to her back. The hooked beak stabbed down again and again, yet all it did was dent the copper helmet.

'Pull her in!' Fletcher yelled. 'She has Valens in her hand!'

He grabbed the tether and heaved, stretching the thick leather until it creaked under the strain. The others soon followed suit, even Isadora daintily clutched the lead and pulled with the others. They made fast progress, extracting several feet of it through the crackling portal. Fletcher glanced back at the scrying stone, but could only see flashes of feathers against the bronze sky as the demon continued to peck violently.

The strain on the leather lifted as Lovett managed to stumble to her feet, then she fell through the portal in a tangle of limbs. Even as the group began to cheer, their voices caught in their throats as realisation dawned. She was not alone.

The Shrike emitted a harsh *caw*, then spread its wings wide and stepped on to the ground, standing almost as tall as a man. It squinted its fierce yellow eyes in the dim light then advanced in a strange, hopping motion, like it was playing a macabre game of hopscotch. Lovett lay motionless on the ground – something was terribly wrong.

'Stand back!' Tarquin yelled, putting himself squarely in the Shrike's way. Fletcher may have disliked the boy, but he was impressed. Tarquin had some courage.

The young noble kneeled quickly and put his hands on the ground, powering up the nearest pentacle. In moments a demon formed above it, then charged at the Shrike without hesitation.

Tarquin's demon was a Hydra, with three reptilian heads on long, powerful necks, like a trio of snakes attached to the body of a monitor lizard. They weaved and snapped at the Shrike, darting this way and that as the bird demon was driven back towards the portal. They were well matched, since Tarquin's demon was large enough to ride, though much of its height comprised of neck. The Hydra's legs were short, but each foot was equipped with thick black claws that tore into the leather with every step.

'Nothing can stand against Trebius!' Tarquin yelled as the Shrike squawked with confusion at the three pronged attack.

Fletcher ignored the fight and circled around to Lovett. She must have been conscious, as the portal was still open, but her body was as still as a corpse. Valens was twitching in her open hand, buzzing as the Shrike battled Tarquin's demon. The little Mite wanted to help, but did not have the strength.

'I'll get a teacher!' Genevieve yelled, then ran out of the door.

Fletcher kneeled beside Lovett and dragged her out of harm's way, then removed her helmet with care. His eyes widened at what he saw beneath. Her mouth was foaming with froth and both eyes were rolled so far back that all he could see was white. The poor woman's head bounced punishingly on the leather as her body was wracked with convulsions. Fletcher had no idea how she was still holding the portal open.

'The poison!' Fletcher gasped with horror, trying to cushion the back of her skull with his hands. His eyes fell on the helmet and he saw a deep crack in the glass on the front. The Shrike's claws must have damaged it in the first attack.

He turned to the bird demon in anger, watching as it stopped just a few feet from the portal. In such close proximity, the fear of the portal seemingly outweighed its fear of Trebius. The Shrike took a hesitant step forward and stabbed its beak at the nearest Hydra head, drawing blood and a cry of dismay from Tarquin. But the noble did not need to fight alone.

'Ignatius!' Fletcher yelled, powering up the pentacle nearest to him and summoning his demon with an angry blast of mana.

The Salamander formed in but a moment, then leaped into the fray with a screech.

Despite the fact that the Shrike was many times his size, Ignatius bit into the bird demon's leg, stabbing it repeatedly with his tail spike. The Shrike squawked with pain and alarm, losing its footing and falling back towards the pentacle. The Hydra took the opportunity without hesitation, lumbering forward and sinking all three sets of fangs into the Shrike's neck. The momentum took the demons, in a tangle of writhing claws and teeth, to the very edge of the portal, screeching and howling like banshees.

'Now, Ignatius!' Fletcher yelled, wary of the demons falling through the unstable portal and losing them all for good. The imp rolled away from the melee and blasted a plume of flame, scorching the air above Trebius and the Shrike. That was the last straw. The bird demon took one last swipe at the Hydra with its talons, then leaped back into the portal with a disappointed squawk, leaving Trebius snapping at thin air. Moments later the portal closed up, shrinking into nothingness. The wyrdlights soon followed suit, dissipating in threads of blue light, until the room was pitch black. Lovett gave a deep sigh, then her body relaxed. Fletcher was relieved to feel her chest continue to raggedly rise and fall.

The noviciates roared in triumph, but their happiness was short-lived as they heard Lovett's choked breathing in the darkness. As Fletcher sat her up and rubbed her back, Tarquin's voice echoed beside him.

'You idiot, Fletcher! The Shrike was going to be my next demon!'

240

A wyrdlight flickered the room into light from Tarquin's hand, then the boy pointed an angry finger at him.

'You're so worried about our stupid teacher. Don't worry, I'll teach you a lesson you won't soon forget!'

36

The Hydra advanced on Fletcher, hissing from its forked tongues. The heads waved hypnotically, swaying back and forth like cobras about to strike.

'Solomon!' Othello shouted, materialising the Golem into existence. The stone demon stomped in front of Trebius and squared up against it. Ignatius soon followed, snarling furiously. Together the two stood, daring the Hydra to try and pass.

'So the dwarf decides to put his cards on the table. I'm not surprised. The weak often stick together,' Tarquin drawled.

'I'll show you how weak I am. Come try me,' Othello growled. He circled around to stand beside Fletcher.

'There is no time for this! Can't you see Captain Lovett is dying?' Fletcher yelled, furious at both of them. The teacher's breathing was becoming more and more difficult, her prone figure taking choking gulps of air as if every second was a struggle.

'Let the half-man fight if he wants,' Tarquin said, drawing a gasp from the others at his racial slur. Even Fletcher knew that the word 'half-man' was a hugely offensive term for dwarves.

Othello's hands balled into fists but he did not rise to the bait.

'Shut your mouth! You don't talk to him that way!' Fletcher roared, rage flooding his veins like liquid fire.

'The dwarf thinks that because one of his betters was forced to give him a demon of value, he is now their equal,' Tarquin continued, unfazed. 'I am going to show him he is wrong. Then I'll kill your ridiculous little imp, Fletcher. Its fire tricks don't scare Trebius.' At the sound of its name the Hydra hissed and pawed at the ground.

'Brother dearest, don't hog all the fun. I want to duel too!' Isadora stepped into the light. She curtsied, scraping the edge of the nearest pentacle as she did so. Thin strands of white light flew from the leather to form a shape, twisting and curling until her demon stood in the centre of the pentacle.

It appeared to be much like a large feline, yet it seemed to be almost bipedal, walking in a hunched crouch, like a jungle chimpanzee. Its thick fur was striped orange and black like a tiger, with powerful muscles that rippled underneath. A sabre-tooth's enormous canines extended on either side of its mouth, both over four inches long and ending in needle points. Just like a Canid, this demon had an extra set of eyes behind the first.

'Never seen a Felid before?' Isadora said, catching Fletcher's expression of wonder. 'My Tamil is quite the specimen. You won't see another like him in your lifetime. Mother dearest was kind enough to bequeath him to me. It was the least she could do after Tarquin was given Father's pride and joy.'

Tamil yowled in excitement, his tail switching back and forth. He turned his blazing eyes on Ignatius, unsheathing a set of deadly claws with practised ease.

Fletcher gulped as the two demons advanced, his anger ebbing as reality sunk home. Both had likely been their parents' primary demons, meaning they were extremely powerful. Even with Solomon supporting him, Fletcher was sure that Ignatius was outclassed. He willed Ignatius into firing a burst of orange flame in the air, but the noble demons barely flinched as the fire flared above them.

'Now, Trebius!' Tarquin shouted, sending the Hydra charging towards them with a hiss, followed by a bounding Tamil. Solomon spread his legs and unleashed a guttural roar, raising his stone fists. Ignatius reared back on his hind legs and took a deep breath, ready to let forth a gout of flame.

Suddenly, a flash of golden fur raced between the four demons; Sariel had arrived on the scene. Her aureate mane was standing on end, all four eyes blazing with anger. The Canid's usually elegant snout was wrinkled in a fearsome snarl that was all teeth and dripping saliva. She pawed the ground with her front claw, leaving four grooves in the leather. This time, the Hydra paused.

'Stop this!' Sylva cried out. 'Have you forgotten who the enemy is? We are all on the same side!'

'Not officially; or have the elves surrendered already?' Tarquin spat maliciously. 'You are a glorified hostage, nothing more.'

Sylva bristled at his words and Sariel barked, feeling her anger.

'Come now, Tarquin, let us not forget ourselves,' Isadora said, laying a calming hand on Tarquin's shoulder. 'The elves may very well soon be our allies. The Forsyths and the elven clan chieftains could greatly benefit each other . . . remember?'

Fletcher saw her squeeze Tarquin's arm, digging her nails into his flesh. Tarquin paused and then bowed his head, beckoning Trebius to take a few steps back.

'I apologise, I was caught up in the moment. Battle fever, you understand,' Tarquin muttered, but his face was still flushed with anger. He gave Fletcher a menacing look.

'So, Sylva, what is it to be? The dwarf and the pleb . . . or us?' Isadora asked. But she would never hear the elf's answer.

The door slammed open and Arcturus stormed in, followed by Genevieve and two servants bearing a stretcher.

'What is going on here?' he roared. Sacharissa loped in and stopped beside Sariel, standing a full head taller than her. With a snap of her jaws she sent the other Canid back to Sylva.

'Take her up to the infirmary now,' Arcturus murmured, picking up Lovett and laying her gently on the stretcher. He brushed a curl of hair from her forehead and closed her eyelids, for they stared unseeing at the ceiling. The servants hurried her away, stumbling in their haste.

'Now . . . someone is going to tell me what is happening here,' he uttered, with barely restrained anger.

'We were scaring off a Shrike that had come through the portal,' Tarquin lied smoothly. 'It's gone now.'

Arcturus's eyes turned to Fletcher, but Fletcher was loath to get the others in trouble. He kept his mouth shut, but he shifted guiltily. Arcturus narrowed his eyes and strode forward, throwing blue wyrdlights around the room. As the noviciates squinted in the electric glow, he spoke in a loud voice.

'I hope you haven't been thinking about duelling. The elves liked to duel. They lost demon after demon, until they didn't have any left. Do you know what happens when there are no demons left? There's no mana to open a portal. No way of replenishing numbers. That's it, the ether is lost forever. You, Sylva, of all people, would be a complete fool if you were to duel here. The concessions your people had to give to get you here alone . . . you are to be the founder of a new generation of elven adepts, to whom you will be tasked with gifting their first demons. You are the first elven summoner in a thousand years. Do not take that lightly. If you lose your Canid, we will not gift you another.'

Sylva hung her head in shame, and Sariel whined, her tail between her legs. Fletcher was grateful that Sylva would take such a risk on his behalf and silently thanked her from across the room. They could have been in the middle of a duel and subsequently expelled if it had not been for her.

'Any instance of duelling will be rewarded with instant expulsion. Commoners will have to join the rank and file with no further training. Maybe, if you are lucky, you will become a sergeant. As for the nobles, you will have the right to purchase a commission as an officer, shaming your noble house into bribing your way into the military. Even then, you will have to be privately tutored.'

Tarquin scoffed at Arcturus's words and whispered something to his sister.

'Is that what you want, Tarquin? The great Zacharias Forsyth, forced to buy his son's way into an officership?' Arcturus's scathing voice was layered with sarcasm. Tarquin blanched at the thought, then rallied as he felt everyone's eyes on him.

'Pocket change.' He shrugged, then his voice took a more

sinister tone. 'And half-nobles? What happens to them? I mean, you are the man to ask about that . . . or am I mistaken, Arcturus?'

Tarquin smiled as if he had won the exchange and Arcturus paused with shock. Then his face turned scarlet with rage and Sacharissa growled with deep menace, so loudly that the sound reverberated in Fletcher's chest. Tarquin took a step back, realising that he had gone too far. Fortunately for him, Scipio ran into the room, his walrus face red from exertion.

'I came as soon as I heard,' he wheezed, panting for breath. 'Is she all right?'

Arcturus took a deep, calming breath and turned to him.

'No, sir, she is not. It's ethershock, that much is certain. We will have to wait for her to come out of it, but there is no telling when she will be back on her feet. I will take over her lessons in the meantime.'

Scipio closed his eyes and sighed with frustration. Then he turned to the noviciates and spoke.

'Take heed, cadets. Now you understand the dangers of the ether, the risks your parents and donors took to give you your demon. Be thankful and work hard to make their gifts worthwhile.' With those words, he took a few steps towards the door, then paused and spoke again.

'Tarquin Forsyth, you are to come with me. Do not think you got away with speaking so disrespectfully to a superior officer. There will be consequences for your insolence.'

Tarquin's face fell and he stared at the ground, but Scipio's tapping foot sent him walking to the door. Fletcher could not help but smile. Serve the spoiled little upstart right.

His happiness was short-lived, however.

'Wipe that smile from your face, Fletcher.' Arcturus's voice cut into his thoughts. 'As your sponsor, your behaviour reflects upon me. Go directly to my office and wait for me there. We are going to have words.'

37

Arcturus's office was as cold as Scipio's had been hot, with no fireplace and a glassless arrow slit in the wall. It was surprisingly bare, but then both he and Fletcher had only arrived a few weeks ago, hard though it was to believe. Fletcher felt like he had been at Vocans for years.

The minutes ticked by, and soon he got bored. Ignatius was sleeping on his neck, having exhausted himself in all the excitement earlier. Listening out for approaching footsteps, Fletcher walked around the large oak desk that seemed to be the only piece of furniture in the room, other than two chairs and a large cushion for Sacharissa in the corner. Papers were scattered haphazardly on the desk, yet one caught Fletcher's eye.

It was a list of names, all beginning with Fletcher. He looked below it in confusion and, to his horror, found another list, this time all ending with the name Wulf. This was not good news. If Arcturus were to dig deeper, he might find out about Fletcher's crime. Worse still, he might leave a trail that Caspar could follow to track Fletcher down. He wracked his brains, trying to remember if he had mentioned Pelt by name.

Footsteps rang in the corridor, sending Fletcher scurrying back in front of the desk. Moments later, Arcturus strode in, followed by a bounding Sacharissa. Fletcher could tell from his movements that Arcturus was agitated, though his face revealed nothing. He sat down at his desk and shuffled his papers, giving no sign that they had anything to do with Fletcher. Then he looked up and steepled his fingers.

'Do you know why I sponsored you, Fletcher?' he asked, looking Fletcher in the eye.

'Is it because I already had a demon so you wouldn't need to capture one for me?' Fletcher suggested.

'No, I do not mind doing that. Sacharissa is adept at hunting in the ether, though the Barkling did prove a tricky customer, didn't it, Sacha?' Arcturus said, ruffling the Canid's head.

'Guess again,' he ordered, leaning back in his chair.

'Ummm . . . my rare Salamander?' Fletcher hesitated.

'That was an added bonus, but it's not why,' he said, eyes twinkling with mild amusement.

'My bravery in the face of certain death?' Fletcher joked, catching Arcturus's expression and hoping to lighten the mood.

'No, not that!' Arcturus replied with a chuckle. 'Some might say that you made the wrong decision there. An officer must learn to sacrifice good men so that the rest of his command can survive. So too could you have given up your money in exchange for your life. But I must say I was impressed. You were cool under pressure and you took a calculated risk. Good officers are pragmatic and calm under fire. But the men and women who rise to greatness are the risk takers, the gamblers. Those who take all or nothing. Perhaps you too will rise to their station if you play your cards right.' Fletcher grinned at Arcturus's words, but then they took a more sombre turn.

'Today you played your cards wrong, Fletcher. Very wrong. Duelling Tarquin could have resulted in instant expulsion.'

'I'm sorry, sir. I was only defending myself. If I knew how to shield myself I would have used that instead,' Fletcher muttered, hanging his head.

'A shield would not be much use against a demon, but that is neither here nor there. You need to understand that the nobles will do anything they can to get rid of you. Better to take a beating than rise to their bait. Trust me, I know.' Arcturus sounded bitter. He looked as if he was going to continue, but then thought better of it and shook his head. He stood suddenly and beckoned Fletcher closer to the desk.

'We need summoners, Fletcher, but they do not need to be battlemage officers. A summoner in the rank and file is just as good as one in the officer's mess, in the grand scheme of things. Commoners being trained alongside nobles is not a popular practice. Many believe that you should have a separate academy. Do not give Scipio a reason to demote you.'

Fletcher nodded grimly. He couldn't help but glance at the papers on the desk. Arcturus made no move to hide them.

'The reason I sponsored you, Fletcher, was because you remind me of myself. More importantly, it is because I know who you are. Or *what* you are, at least.'

He swung the papers round for Fletcher to see and ran a finger along them.

'There are few Fletchers of your age listed in Hominum, and

none of them have the surname Wulf. You are not on any official census that I can find. Am I right in saying that you are an unregistered orphan?'

Fletcher nodded his head, not understanding.

Arcturus sat back down, nodding to himself as if Fletcher had confirmed his suspicions. He pointed at the chair opposite him. Fletcher sat and watched as Arcturus stared at him through hooded eyes.

'Do you remember Tarquin suggesting that I am a half-noble?' Arcturus asked, smoothing his hair back and readjusting the bow that held it in place at the back of his neck. Fletcher assented and, after a long pause, Arcturus continued.

'Many years ago, a young noble was on his way to Vocans, coming from his home in the northern territories that border the elven lands. He was spending his first night in Boreas which, as you know, is not too far from your Beartooth Mountains.' Fletcher was not sure if he should be glad or upset that Arcturus had mentioned Beartooth instead of Pelt. There were hundreds of villages there, but word travelled fast. Arcturus would put two and two together if he found out a young fugitive had escaped from there.

'This noble boy had been gifted a Canid by his father, Lord Faversham,' Arcturus continued. 'But he did not want to read his summoning scroll until he arrived at the school, where the teachers could supervise the transfer. He therefore left his summoning scroll in his saddle bags and bedded down for the night.'

Arcturus stopped for a moment, rubbing Sacharissa's ears. The demon rumbled with pleasure and nuzzled his hands.

'That night, a stable boy decided to rob the noble for all he was worth. He had nothing to his name. He was an orphan who had been raised in a workhouse, then sold to the stable master for twenty shillings. He didn't even own the clothes on his back. The theft was a last, desperate bid to get enough money together to escape and make a new life for himself. But fate had a different plan for him.'

Fletcher furrowed his brow. This story sounded familiar, but he could not place where he had heard it before.

'The boy could read somewhat. He had taught himself so that he could learn about the world, devouring every book left abandoned by passing travellers in the tavern that owned the stables. So when he found the scroll and summoning leather that came with it, he laid them out and read them, more out of curiosity than anything else. Fortunately for the boy, he still struggled with his reading, so he said each word under his breath as he read them. Nobody was more surprised than him when he summoned a Canid pup, with black fur and shining eyes. She was the most beautiful thing he had ever seen.'

Fletcher looked from Sacharissa to Arcturus, then realisation dawned on him.

'You were the first commoner to own a demon since . . . well, since forever!' Fletcher gasped. 'If it wasn't for you, none of us would be here! Your discovery tripled the number of battlemages!'

Arcturus nodded gravely.

'But hang on,' Fletcher said with confusion. 'What does this have to do with me? Or you being a half-noble?'

'That is the story you already know, with a little more detail. But there is a second half to it, one that is only known by the nobility and a few select others. You see, some years after I was discovered, there was a great meeting between the noble houses, the generals of Hominum and King Harold. The war was going poorly in its first year, the orc shamans were uniting under the albino orc's banner and they outnumbered our own battlemages many times over. The nobles were loathe to put their firstborn sons and daughters in harm's way, for with each heir's death their bloodlines would come under threat. They were being forced to have several children, so that if the firstborn died, there might be a sibling with the ability to summon. After the firstborn, there is only a one in three chance of a noble child being an adept. Many noble houses will have three or four children in case of a death, so that the next adept can become the heir. On top of this, many young nobles are forced to marry and have children as soon as they graduate from the Vocans, so that if they die fighting they leave an heir to take their place.'

Fletcher had never given much thought to the idea of succession and noble bloodlines. He could imagine the noble families, desperately aware that with a single death, their entire house could disappear in one generation. For a moment he pitied Tarquin and Isadora, with all the pressures that their noble blood brought with it. But only for a moment.

'Believe it or not, it was Obediah Forsyth – Tarquin's grandfather – who was the noble who led the charge on introducing commoners into the ranks of battlemages, using his own money to fund the great Inquisition, bringing children in from across the land and looking for hints of mana in them. He was the most powerful and wealthiest noble at the time, and still is today. His son, Zacharias, married another firstborn from another great house, Josephine Queensouth, uniting their neighbouring lands under the Forsyth banner. This effectively dissolved the Queensouth house. Usually heirs will marry a second- or third-born from another noble house so as to keep their legacy, but the Queensouths were near bankruptcy and were close to selling off their land. It was the only solution for them at the time. I explain this to you, Fletcher, because nobility, marriage and succession are key to understanding who you are.'

Fletcher nodded sagely, trying to keep track of it all. The political machinations of the nobility were interesting, but he still did not understand what it had to do with him, or Arcturus for that matter.

'In any case, Obediah's search bore fruit and commoners were introduced to Vocans, myself included. The old King's Inquisitors took over the search, but they noticed a curious trend, one that Obediah had missed. There were strange clusters of adepts, most noticeably in the orphanages in the northern cities. Now why do you think that is, Fletcher?' Arcturus asked him, the milky orb of his eye staring unseeingly through Fletcher's head.

But Fletcher's mind was blank. What was so special about orphans?

'What differentiates the orphans from everyone else?' Arcturus asked, parroting Fletcher's thoughts.

'Nobody wants them?' Fletcher suggested.

'That's right, Fletcher. Now who usually don't want their children?' Arcturus murmured, talking him through it.

'People who can't afford to keep them.' Fletcher's memory flitted to the long, lonely nights where he had wondered about that very thing.

'True, Fletcher, there are some who abandon their children for that reason. There are also orphans whose parents have died. But there is another group who abandon their children regularly. The Inquisition found this was the one commonality between almost all the orphaned adepts.'

Arcturus took a deep breath. 'Almost all of their mothers were courtesans. Including mine.'

Sacharissa whined, and Arcturus hushed her gently. Fletcher could see that he was touching upon something that caused him great pain.

'You see, Lord Faversham was . . . shall we say . . . an insatiable man. His wife could not bear him children for a long time. Lady Faversham eventually grew cold and distant, turning him away from her bed. So he sought the beds of those who would not.'

Fletcher sunk into his chair, finally understanding.

'So the firstborn children of the courtesans he slept with became adepts? Is that how it works?' Fletcher asked, trying not to think about what it might mean about his own heritage.

'Yes, although he had mistresses as well. A man can have adept children with several different women, as long as it is the woman's first child too. So too can a woman have several adept children with different fathers, if the men are yet to father a child. It was pure coincidence that a small number of commoners were also being born with the gift. I set the search in motion, but I was not born with the gift independently, like

256

other commoners are. I was an adept because I was one of Lord Faversham's firstborn sons.'

Fletcher's mind raced, thinking of the circumstances of his abandonment. Not even a blanket to protect him from the cold. It seemed a fitting explanation. Arcturus interrupted his moody thoughts.

'Of course the discovery caused a scandal. Proof of infidelity cast shame over various noble houses, especially the Favershams. Noblewomen went on strike and refused to go to war unless a law was passed that orphans could not be tested by the Inquisition. They could not bear the shame, to see their husbands' other children fighting alongside them and their true-born sons and daughters.' He whispered now, his voice layered with complicated emotion.

'I hear Lady Faversham was aggrieved when she learned that the demon meant for her son was actually passed on to me. Her hatred for me is even greater than that of the other noblewomen. She has only given birth to one child, meaning that should her son die, I will be next in line as Lord Faversham by Hominum law. She was forced to request special permission from the old King to take her son from the front lines, in case I should try to murder him and take his place as the next heir. You won't be surprised to hear that she was the one who organised the strike.'

Fletcher was shocked by the cool way Arcturus spoke about the suspicion he was under. He wondered whether Arcturus would be capable of such a crime. Lord Faversham owned most of the lands around Beartooth and was a rich and powerful man.

'Of course, most orphans had been identified and trained up by the time they found out about all this, so as a compromise

257

those that had already been discovered were allowed to stay,' Arcturus continued. 'The only condition was that we would not be referred to by our noble surname, hence why I am known as Captain Arcturus, my first name. I have three half-brothers of about my age, also fighting in the army. There are probably more out there, completely unaware of who they are. I am not allowed to test children in the orphanages, much as I would wish to. Yet somehow, fate has brought you to me.'

Fletcher barely comprehended these last words. He was too deep in thought. Could his father be Lord Faversham? Did that mean his mother had been alive in Boreas his whole life?

'Fletcher, I may be wrong,' Arcturus's voice floated by. 'You may be just another orphan, you are many years younger than me after all. I don't even know if Faversham continued his infidelity after he had his first child with Lady Faversham. But what are the chances of an adept orphan that was abandoned near Boreas being one of the few not descended from the nobility?'

'So you are saying I am the bastard love-child of Lord Faversham, and my mother is either a mistress at best or a courtesan at worst?' Fletcher said bitterly, coming out of his reverie.

'And my half-brother . . .' Arcturus Faversham said.

38

Fletcher had stormed out of Arcturus's office. He was full of anger; but who with, he did not know. Ignatius spent much of the night hissing, small rings of smoke puffing from his nostrils as the others laughed and joked at dinner.

'I may not be sure who I'm angry at but you definitely haven't a clue, have you?' Fletcher murmured under his breath, scratching Ignatius's chin. It was quite funny to see the little demon's confused agitation, which cheered Fletcher up somewhat.

Fletcher had managed to laugh off his meeting with Arcturus to the others, claiming that he had just been scolded like a naughty schoolboy. Of all his new friends, only Othello noticed his despondency, knocking on his door after they had all gone to bed. Fletcher decided to tell him everything – after all, he needed to return the level of trust Othello and his family had placed in him. But Othello was unimpressed with Arcturus's story.

'It sounds like Arcturus is reading too much into it if you want my opinion,' Othello said, scratching at his beard. 'He must be desperate to find more of his family and is ignoring several things to make your story fit with his own. I have heard of Lady Faversham, for entirely different reasons. She is the old King's cousin and was famous for her great beauty, back in the day. I sincerely doubt that after Lord Faversham's behaviour came to light that old King Alfric would have allowed the lord to continue shaming his royal cousin in this manner. Nor would his son, King Harold.'

'But what if he did? What if he had a moment of weakness, years after it all came out?' Fletcher asked.

'Even assuming that he would be so foolish, why were you abandoned just outside of Pelt? Surely the desperate woman in question would leave you in an orphanage or doorstep in Boreas, not somewhere as obscure and far from the city as Pelt. I mean, it's almost on the elven border!' Othello exclaimed.

'Maybe she didn't want me to end up in a workhouse like Arcturus did,' Fletcher replied, equally as stubborn, although he was not quite sure why he was supporting Arcturus's side of the argument.

'If she cared enough to do that, then why did she leave you to freeze in the snow, with not a stitch of clothing or a blanket? No, Fletcher, there is more to it than that. Don't be disheartened by Arcturus's theory. Just be glad you have him on your side and that you had the good fortune to run into him in Corcillum.'

With those words, Othello went to bed and left Fletcher feeling considerably better but a lot more confused.

'Who the hell am I?' Fletcher whispered in the darkness. Ignatius mewled in sympathy and burrowed his head into Fletcher's chest.

Despite the events of the day, Fletcher's sleep that night was the undisturbed and dreamless sleep of the exhausted.

The noviciates waited in the summoning room for their next lesson in etherwork. Fletcher was hoping to see Lovett, but knew that it was far more likely that Arcturus would be taking the lesson. His attempts to visit the infirmary had been in vain – Dame Fairhaven had seen to that. She informed Fletcher that she was sure Captain Lovett would not like to be pestered by her students whilst in her paralysed state, and that her reading to Lovett was enough to keep the captain entertained. The discovery that Lovett was completely paralysed but conscious of her surroundings only increased Fletcher's desire to see her, but the door was closed firmly in his face.

'Nice togs,' Genevieve said, giving him a thumbs-up. Fletcher smiled and fingered the collar of his new jacket.

Uhtred had been as good as his word, sending Fletcher a beautiful dark blue uniform as well as his sword with the morning deliveries. The gold buttons on his jacket and pants had even been embossed with the curling silhouette of a Salamander, much to Fletcher's delight. The scabbard was of the finest quality, made from firm black leather and burnished steel. Fletcher saw that the sword had also been whetted and was accompanied by an oiled cloth and a reminder for Fletcher to look after his weapon, as it was a tool of the finest workmanship.

He was glad to have it, as he had been forced to use a wooden stick whilst Sir Caulder took him and the other commoners through the basics of swordplay. The noble children had all been tutored from an early age and had not accompanied them, though Malik and Penelope had briefly watched from the sidelines before becoming bored and leaving. When Fletcher asked why they were being taught to battle each other after what Sir Caulder had told him about fighting orcs, Sir Caulder had snapped, 'The tournament, boy. They'll be having you fencing and God knows what else. No use having all you commoners lose in the first round because you've only been taught how to fight a seven-foot savage instead of a noble with a rapier.'

The reminder of the tournament had filled Fletcher with dread and sent him running to the library, where he had buried himself in books. He had not been alone – most of the other commoners accompanied him. Growing up with fully-qualified battlemages for parents had put the noble noviciates far ahead of their common counterparts, breezing through most of the teachers' questions with little difficulty.

There were thousands of demons to learn the names, measurements, strengths and weaknesses of, even if most of them could not be found in the part of the ether that Hominum's summoners had access to. The eighteen Canid breeds alone had taken Fletcher most of the weekend.

The sound of the door slamming behind him broke into his thoughts. A tall, slender man had entered the summoning room. At first Fletcher thought that it was Arcturus, but when the man stepped into the wyrdlight, he saw that his uniform was different, cut from black cloth with silver trimming. His face was sallow and bearded, with small black eyes that glittered as they surveyed the students.

'My full title is Inquisitor Damian Rook, but you may call me sir. I will be instructing you in the art of etherwork until

Captain Lovett has recovered from her . . . accident. Fortunately for you, Scipio has decided to hire a more competent teacher this time around.'

His words earned a smirk from Tarquin and a discreet titter from Isadora, much to Fletcher's disgust. Rook ignored this and turned to the commoners, studying them through hooded eyes.

'My my, it feels as if it was only yesterday that I tested you,' Rook said, in a low voice that commanded absolute obedience. 'Genevieve, Rory, Seraph, Atlas, as well as the dwarf and the elf, will stand in a line over there.'

Fletcher's friends moved with alacrity, lining up against the far wall. Rook ignored them and instead scrutinised Fletcher and the nobles, walking around them as if they were horses on sale.

'A good turnout this year. Tarquin, Isadora, it is good to see you here. I hope your father is well?' he inquired.

'Aye, sir, though it has been several months since last I saw him,' Tarquin replied, with unusual politeness. Fletcher wondered what kind of man would command the respect of a noble like Tarquin. How did they know each other?

'You are clearly a Saladin, if I am not mistaken,' Rook continued, stopping in front of the olive-skinned boy.

'I am Malik Saladin, son of Baybars Saladin, hailing from the lands of Antioch,' Malik replied, jutting his chin out proudly.

'Of course. Your father's Anubid fought right alongside my Minotaur at Watford Bridge. Were you fortunate enough to be gifted it?'

'No, sir, Father has more use for it than I. But I have been given a juvenile Anubid, that was captured before I came here.'

263

'Good. You will have need of it soon.' Rook turned to the next noble, Penelope.

'And you are?'

'Penelope Colt . . . from Coltshire.' She curtsied nervously. This earned her a noncommittal grunt from Rook, who moved on to the last noble, the small, mousy haired boy who Fletcher had seen following Tarquin around like a lapdog.

'I'm . . . My name is Rufus Cavendish, from the Cavendish Downs,' the boy stuttered.

'Cavendish Downs. I have not heard of it. Who are your parents?' Rook asked, his black eyes boring into Rufus's face like a hawk's.

'My mother died when I was young. She was Captain Cavendish. My father is not of noble blood.'

'I see,' Rook said disinterestedly, then turned away. Clearly the Cavendishes were not a noble family of significant standing or importance.

He turned his baleful gaze upon Fletcher, his small eyes flicking from his sword to the golden buttons of his uniform.

'And you? Where are you from?'

Fletcher hesitated, then ventured. 'I am from the north, sir, near Boreas. My name is Fletcher.'

'A Faversham, then? I did not know that they had a child who was of age. How have you escaped my notice?'

Tarquin's voice cut in before Fletcher could respond.

'He's not a noble, sir. He's just a pleb.'

'Preposterous. I am an Inquisitor, I know the name of every common adept. Who are you, boy?'

'I . . . was sponsored, sir. I read a summoning scroll that

264

I . . . found . . . and summoned a demon. Arcturus discovered me and brought me here.'

'Did your parents not think to send you to the Inquisitors as soon as they discovered you were an adept? And Arcturus found you? He is not allowed north of Corcillum, how did he come by you?'

'I'm an orphan, si—'

'An ORPHAN!' Rook hissed, interrupting him.

'Yes, but it's not what you think!' Fletcher cried, realising what Rook must be imagining.

'He's broken the rules! The arrogant bastard thinks he can cheat the agreement he made with the old King, sending summoning scrolls to Boreas's orphans in secret! Oh, I've got him now!' Rook spat with glee.

'He didn't!' Fletcher shouted.

'Quiet! We thought we had seen the last of your ilk long ago. Lady Faversham shall hear of this,' he hissed, prodding Fletcher hard in the chest.

'You're wrong! Ask the Provost!' Fletcher yelled.

'Oh, I will, don't you worry. But it can wait. We have to measure everyone's fulfilment levels first. Follow me, all of you!'

They trooped behind Rook as he led them out of the summoning room and up the stairs of the west wing, all the way to the top and then down the corridor to the southwestern tower. Only Othello understood what had just transpired, laying a comforting hand on Fletcher's shoulder.

'Don't worry, it will all get straightened out,' he whispered in Fletcher's ear.

The others eyed him with a mix of suspicion and confusion,

but the silence that hung in the corridors prevented them from asking him any questions. Tarquin and Isadora were positively skipping, though whether it was because of Fletcher's public humiliation or the coming lesson, he was not sure.

This tower contained no spiral staircase. Instead, it was a huge tube of empty space, with the floors knocked through on every level. An enormous pillar stood in the centre of the room, made up of many segments that were embedded with multicoloured Corundum crystals. It stretched all the way to the top of the tower, glittering as beams of light cut across it from arrow slits in the old tower walls.

'This is a fulfilmeter, the largest of its kind. Each segment represents one fulfilment level. By touching the base, a summoner or demon can discover what level they are. Now, who shall go first?' he mused, looking only at the nobles. 'Malik, if you are anything like your father, you will impress. Lay your hand on the base stone. Let us see what calibre of summoners we have here today.'

Malik strode forward without hesitation, kneeling at the first segment and pressing his hand into the base of it. For a moment nothing happened, then suddenly the crystals on the first segment glowed with fierce intensity, lighting the room with kaleidoscopic beams of light. A dull pulse of sound echoed in the room, followed by another as the next segment flared into light. More followed, until fourteen segments had been lit. Malik held his hand there for a further minute before Rook pulled him to his feet, flickering out the lights as the hand was removed.

'Well done, boy. The average for a noble-born is eight

266

when they first start, so you are above the curve. Soon you will be a level twenty like your father. Next!'

Isadora flicked her mane of ringlets and stepped forward, pressing her hand to the fulfilmeter. Again the dull sound echoed, followed by the scattered lights. Twelve this time.

'The Forsyth blood is strong. Zacharias will be proud,' Rook said, helping Isadora to her feet.

Tarquin followed suit, lighting up twelve again.

'Twins usually have the same fulfilment level, but it is worth checking,' Rook muttered, half to himself, as he shook Tarquin's hand. Fletcher's heart felt like a stone in his chest as Tarquin pushed past him roughly to stand at the back. They were all so powerful – Lovett was only level eleven!

Penelope was a level seven, but she seemed happy, smiling and nodding as she stood up. Rufus was a level nine, a result that earned him a backslap from Tarquin and a grunt of approval from Rook.

'Now for the commoners. You first, dwarf. A level eight, at least, from what I hear, given that you were able to summon a Golem. The average for commoners is five of course, but then you are a special case.'

'Why do commoners have lower fulfilment levels, sir?' Rory asked, shuffling his feet.

'I say bad breeding,' Rook sneered. 'But the official answer is that nobles grow up amongst demons and are gifted their own well in advance of arriving at the academy, allowing them to increase their fulfilment level over the years by practising basic spellcraft and infusion. You will be starting with the level you were born with, since you have had no time to build yours.

That is another reason why commoners usually start with Scarab Mites. No use capturing a demon you might not even be capable of controlling – not that you deserve anything better. It seems as if some of you have been particularly lucky this year.'

Othello had pressed his hand to the fulfilmeter by then, interrupting Rory's response as it began to glow again. The segments lit up one by one, vibrating the room with ten dull throbs.

'Ten! It looks as if dwarves may have a knack for summoning! I shall let the King know at once. Very interesting indeed . . .' Rook said, motioning for Sylva to take Othello's place. Fletcher caught Othello's worried expression. Why tell the King? Would Othello's result mean the dwarves were better allies than the King had thought . . . or an even greater threat?

'Elves usually start at seven, or at least they used to. Go ahead anyway. You've had your Canid for a few months now.' Sylva was indeed seven, though the eighth segment flickered for a brief second.

'Good, you're close to moving up a level. Work hard and you will be able to capture a Mite in addition to your Canid.'

Genevieve was exactly five. Seraph surprised everyone with a seven and Atlas managed a four, much to his chagrin.

'I hope you're better off than me,' Atlas groaned as an ashen-faced Rory hurried past.

This time the fulfilmeter stuttered, then two segments glowed into life. After a full thirty seconds, a third segment flickered on. Rook grabbed his arm and began to pull him away.

'No!' Rory yelled. 'Give me a little more time, there's more!'

'There's no more, boy. That's all the demonic energy you

can absorb. You are a level-three summoner. Be happy it's not less.' He wrenched Rory up and pushed him back into the crowd of commoners.

'Now for the bastard. Let's see what we have here,' Rook said, pushing Fletcher to his knees.

Fletcher closed his eyes and pressed his hand on to the fulfilmeter. The gems were cool against his palm, like polished ice. He felt the draw of mana as it was sucked away, pulsing through his veins and out through his fingers. Then something else was pushed back into him. It was not mana, for it was like fire that boiled his blood and tingled his skin.

He didn't want to look up, but the dull vibration let him know exactly how many segments were lighting up. Five so far. Then six. On the seventh he felt the flow ebb, but still it pushed into him. Eight . . . the gush slowed to a treacle. Finally, just as he thought there was nothing left, a ninth buzz echoed through the room. Relief flooded through him, but he felt pity for Rory at the same time. James Baker had been a level-three summoner.

'Well, well, colour me surprised. Who would have thought it? No matter. Fletcher will be here as long as it takes for me to discover evidence that Arcturus sent him a summoning scroll. Bastard children have not been allowed to attend Vocans since old King Alfric decreed it, on the bequest of Lady Faversham. Nor are any of the old bastards allowed to search new bastards out. That includes Arcturus.' Rook's words drew a gasp from the commoners. Arcturus's secret was out.

'No doubt you will have a new teacher soon, once I have got rid of him,' Rook said with a grin.

'For the last time, he did not send me a summoning scroll. If you must know, it was an orc shaman's scroll that I was given by a passing tradesman,' Fletcher said through gritted teeth.

Rook stared at him for a moment, then unclipped a leather cylinder from his belt. He removed a brown roll from inside and unravelled it on the stone floor. It was a summoning leather.

'Show me,' he said, pointing at it.

Ignatius materialised as soon as Fletcher released him, as if he was eager to come out. He snapped at Rook's hand, causing the man to jerk back with a scowl.

'Well . . . isn't this a turn up,' Rook murmured, rubbing his chin broodily with long, spindly fingers. 'All right, let's find out what fulfilment level it is. Major Goodwin will want to know. We have never tested a Salamander before.'

Fletcher gathered up Ignatius in his arms and touched the demon's tail to the fulfilmeter. It hummed into life. The first four segments lit up in quick succession. But then, to Fletcher's shock, the fifth segment flickered almost hesitantly. Tarquin burst out laughing.

'Hah! Salamanders are barely level five. And you thought you could take on a level-eight Hydra and a level-seven Felid with only a Golem to help you! That's a two-level difference, you foolish pleb bastard.'

'I thought you said our demons were out in order to scare the Shrike away,' Fletcher replied, fighting to keep his rage in check. Nobody, not even Didric, had ever spoken to him in that manner. 'Would you like to change your story?'

Tarquin spluttered, but was interrupted by Rook.

'Silence! We will return to the summoning room immediately! The lesson is not over yet.'

The journey back to the summoning room was even more tense than the last. Othello was lost in deep thought, whilst Rory's face was the picture of abject misery as he trudged at the back of the group. Genevieve tried her best to console him, but he stared ahead blankly, as if he could not hear what she said. Gone was the boisterous boy with his playful banter.

When they arrived, Rook had already instructed some servants to carry in a heavy column, which they struggled to lift upright. It was similar to the fulfilmeter, only instead of several gemstones, each segment was made up of a single red gem the size of a man's fist. Rook tapped it nonchalantly, lighting one of the stones with each touch of his finger.

'Your teacher preferred to do things the old way, powering the portal herself. But I consider the risks of entering the ether differently. This is a charging stone. One can fill it with mana, to use at a later date. It is one of the tools we use for powering the great shields over the front lines, charging it in the day so that we do not need to power them all night. But we will be using it for a different purpose. Together we shall keep it on a constant full charge and attach it to the portals we use when entering the ether. That way, if someone's concentration slips, their portal will not close prematurely. We can't afford to lose a Hydra now can we? They no longer exist in our part of the ether.'

Tarquin smirked and nudged Isadora. Seraph raised his hand.

'Why are they extinct in this part of the ether? Surely we haven't captured them all?'

Rook sighed dramatically and then nodded his head, as if he had decided to humour a stupid question.

'See these keys on the edge of the pentacles? Those are

coordinates, rough ones to the same piece of land in the ether. Every summoner for the past two thousand years has hunted the same land, capturing multitudes of demons. Of course, during that time we went to war with the orcs, not to mention the dwarven rebellions after that. Many of our demons died in battle, and we needed more to replace them. Soon the wild demons learned to stay away from our part of the ether, or maybe we wiped out all the rarer ones. Whatever happened, only a few species remain. Every now and again, a rare demon, such as a Griffin, will wander into the land. Usually it will be a demon that has been injured or is sick. Other times demons migrate over our tract of land, like the Shrikes.'

'So that's why we need the orc keys,' Genevieve sighed, as realisation dawned on her.

'We don't need the orc keys!' Rook snapped. 'The common, weak demons are for commoners. Nobles inherit the older and rarer demons from their parents. It keeps everyone in their natural place. The orcs send nothing but low-level demons at us anyway, which just goes to show that their coordinates are no better than ours. It is a waste of time and resources trying to find out what their keys are.'

Genevieve bit her lip and stepped back, cowed by his sharp tongue. Fletcher did not understand why Rook was so against finding the keys. Surely it could benefit Hominum? But all the man seemed to care about was the petty imbalance of power and rank between common adepts and nobles.

'Now, the charging stone will only have enough power to work with five students a week. So, until the tournament is over, the nobles shall be the only ones allowed to enter the ether. After

272

that we shall see about allowing you commoners to use it.'

As Rory let out a sob of despair and the others began to cry out in protest, Fletcher could only think one thing.

I wish Captain Lovett were here.

39

Fletcher hissed in frustration as the symbol he had etched flickered in the air, then died.

'Again, Fletcher. Concentrate!' Arcturus barked. 'Remember the steps!'

Fletcher lifted his glowing finger and drew the shield spell glyph again. It hung in the air in front of his hand as he fed it a slow stream of mana.

'Good. Now fix it!' Arcturus growled.

Fletcher focussed on the symbol, holding his finger in its exact centre. He held it there until the symbol's light pulsed briefly and Fletcher felt it lock into place. He moved his hand and watched the symbol follow his finger, as if held in front of it by an invisible frame. Sweat trickled down his back like a creeping insect, but Fletcher ignored it. It was taking everything he had to hold his concentration.

'Push the mana through, steady now! You need to feed the glyph at the same time.'

This was the hardest part. Fletcher felt as if his mind would split in two as he tried to juggle a simultaneous flow of mana both to and through the glyph.

It wavered once again, but Fletcher gritted his teeth and forced a thin stream of opaque substance through it and out of the other side.

'Yes! You've done it. Now, while we are ahead, try shaping it,' Arcturus urged.

There was not much shield energy to work with, but Fletcher didn't want to risk pushing more through, in case he destabilised the connection. Just as he had done with the wyrdlight in his first lesson, he rolled it into a ball.

'Well done! But this isn't wyrdlight. For shields, you need to stretch them out. Go on, you might not get another chance to try this lesson.'

But Fletcher could not hold the glyph steady any longer. It flared briefly, then dissolved into nothingness. Moments later, the shield ball did the same.

'All right. We will try again next lesson. Take a break, Fletcher,' Arcturus murmured, his voice laced with disappointment.

Fletcher clenched his hands into fists, furious with himself. All around the atrium, the other students were having much greater success. The nobles were the best, of course, practising by varying the thickness and shape of their shields, having already been versed in spellcraft at home. Malik was particularly gifted, producing a curved shield so thick that it was hard to see through it.

Most of his friends were already able to create a shield with every attempt, except for Rory and Atlas, who managed on every other try. Fletcher, on the other hand, had only succeeded once in the past three hours.

He settled on a bench on the far side of the atrium and watched despondently. Ever since Rook's lesson all those weeks ago, things had been going steadily downhill.

First there had been the scrying stones. Rook had gone down the line of commoners, allowing them to pick stones from a box of spares. Fletcher had been purposely left for last, leaving him with only a purple fragment the size and shape of a silver shilling. To see anything at all, he had to hold it up to his eye and peer through it like a peeping tom at a keyhole. On top of this, the commoners were forced to practise scrying in the summoning room while the nobles sent their demons to explore the safer parts of the ether.

Of course, there had been the next lesson with Arcturus. The captain had not been angry with Fletcher, but he had given Fletcher much to worry about.

'I've never liked Inquisitors, and Rook is the worst of them. There were three institutions set up by old King Alfric: the Inquisition, the Pinkertons and the Magistrate Judges, all of them rotten to the core. King Harold inherited them when his father abdicated the throne, but rumour has it that he does not like the way they do things. If Rook tries to stir up trouble, King Harold won't take notice. I'm more worried about old Alfric getting involved, but he rarely leaves the palace, so hopefully he won't get to hear anything. Don't worry, Fletcher. You haven't done anything wrong. I just hope that Rook doesn't send Inquisitors to your old home and start tearing the place apart.'

Those words had haunted Fletcher for several weeks and had changed his mind about sending Berdon any letters, in case they were traced back to him, or vice versa. If Rook found out about his crime . . . he didn't want to think about what might happen.

Of course that hadn't been the only thing that had dampened Fletcher's spirits. Goodwin had loaded them down with work, demanding endless essays on demonology and giving them scathing criticism if they ever got even the slightest thing wrong.

The silver lining was that Fletcher had earned Goodwin's grudging praise in their second demonology lesson; his study of Canid breeds and their cousins had paid off. He had correctly identified and waxed eloquently about both Penelope and Malik's demons. Penelope's was a Vulpid, a three-tailed fox demon that was a little smaller than a common Canid but far more agile. Its snout was elegant and pointed, with a soft red coat that shone like burnished copper.

Malik's Anubid was one of the rarest cousins to the Canid, a demon that crouched on two legs, much like a Felid, with the head of a jackal and a smooth pelt of black hair. It was a close relative to Major Goodwin's chosen demon, the Lycan, a similar creature with thick, grey fur and the head of a wolf. The Anubid was a popular demon amongst the battlemages that originated from the Akhad Desert, although the species had now been hunted to near extinction in Hominum's part of the ether.

Rufus's demon was another Lutra, much to Atlas's disappointment. Unusually, Rufus's demon had been gifted to him in the same way that the commoners had been, through the forced donation of a summoning scroll. This was because his mother had died when he was a child and his father was not a summoner.

The only thing Fletcher felt he had any natural ability in was swordsmanship. Sir Caulder had invited him for extra lessons, learning techniques specific to the khopesh. His main sticking point was controlling his aggression. According to Sir Caulder, patience was one of a swordsman's most important virtues.

'All right, everyone, gather here please!' Arcturus yelled, snapping Fletcher from his reverie.

The group gathered around him, their faces glowing with the exhilaration of finally learning one of the most practical lessons of spellcraft. The past few weeks had been more wyrdlight practice, channelling their mana and controlling its movement, size, shape and brightness. Arcturus's reasoning had been that mastering the techniques learned with wyrdlights put them in good stead for when they eventually etched glyphs.

'Now, many of you have been struggling with every attempt to produce a spell. More have struggled to do so in a timely fashion. Let me make myself clear. Both speed and reliability are essential for success as a battlemage,' Arcturus said in a grave voice, looking them each in the eye. 'Now, who can tell me which four spells are the staple of a battlemage?'

Penelope raised her hand. 'The shield spell, the fire spell and the lightning spell.'

'Very good, but that is only three. Who can tell me the fourth?'

'Telekinesis?' Seraph suggested.

'That's right, the ability to move objects. Watch closely.' Arcturus grinned.

He raised his hand and etched a spiral in the air, as if he were stirring a cup of coffee. Suddenly he whipped his hand out and the hat he was wearing flicked up to the rafters, then floated down slowly to land on his head again. Fletcher could see a disturbance in the air below it, like a heatwave on a sunny day.

'The art of moving objects is tricky, for, unlike the shield spell, fire spell or lightning spell, the telekinesis spell is nearly invisible to the naked eye. It's much harder to lasso something and then manipulate it when you can't see the rope you are using, so to speak. Most battlemages will simply blast it out; sending their opponent flying, but using a lot of mana.'

Arcturus, looking slightly guilty, eyed a pile of scrolls that Penelope had brought with her. They were full of other symbols that Arcturus had instructed them to learn.

'Of course there are hundreds of other spells. The healing spell for example, difficult but useful. It's slow acting, so not much use in the heat of battle.' Arcturus etched the heart symbol in the air to demonstrate. 'There will be some symbols that you will need next year, but won't be able to perform now, like the barrier spell. You'll see that one in action during the tournament. In any case, stick with the four staples, and you won't go far wrong in the challenge. You will need the others in the written exams, so you must learn them all! Class dismissed!'

With those words, Arcturus turned on his heel and strode towards the door. The others began to chatter happily, but Fletcher did not feel like socialising. Instead, he chased after Arcturus and tugged on his sleeve.

'Sir, do you mind if I ask, is Captain Lovett OK?'

Arcturus turned and looked Fletcher in the eye, his brow furrowed with worry.

'She's in ethershock. She might never recover, or she may recover tomorrow. I try and read to her as often as I can,'

Arcturus said, tapping a book he held under his arm. 'Fortunately for the captain, one of her demons, Valens, was not infused when the accident happened. She might be able to see through his eyes using her mind. Only extremely skilled summoners have managed to learn that ability, but Lovett is one of most skilled I have ever had the honour of knowing. If anyone can do it, she can.'

He gave Fletcher an encouraging squeeze on the shoulder and forced a smile. 'Now get some rest, you've worked hard today.'

Fletcher nodded and wandered away, trudging up the stairs of the west wing. He was eager for the solitude of his room and the company of Ignatius, who was only allowed to be summoned during the occasional lesson.

With Captain Lovett unconscious he felt more alone than ever. Although his friends were supportive and good company, they all had their own problems to deal with. Even Arcturus had been withdrawn lately, although whether it was because of Rook's presence, disappointment in Fletcher or Lovett's condition, was yet to be seen. Lovett had been fair and fearless, completely ambivalent to the differences in race and class of her students. Fletcher knew that he could have confided in her if he ever had any problems. Now . . . it was as if she were gone.

His mind dulled by exhaustion, Fletcher turned on to the wrong floor, where the nobles had private rooms. As he groaned and turned back to the stairs, something caught his eye. It was a tapestry, depicting armoured figures in the midst of battle. He walked over to it and admired the intricate stitching that had brought it to life.

The orcs were charging across a bridge, riding their war

rhinos full tilt at a small group of men armed with pikes. At the very front of them stood a dominating figure, his arm outstretched with the spiral symbol etched in front of him. Beside him, a leonine Felid bared its fangs and seemed to roar at the oncoming horde.

Fletcher leaned forward and read the plaque below it. *The Hero of Watford Bridge.*

'Incredible. Scipio blasted aside an orc rhino charge,' Fletcher murmured.

Suddenly, he heard the sound of footsteps. Realising he was on a noble floor, Fletcher darted into a doorway and hid in the shadows. He did not want to have another encounter with Tarquin; not in the mood he was in.

'. . . Did you see that buffoon's face when his spell failed? I could have wept with laughter. The bastard thought he was so special. Now look at him,' Tarquin drawled. The resultant titter revealed that he was with Isadora.

'You are funny, Tarquin darling.' Isadora giggled. 'But we have not had time to talk today, not with those useless lessons. Tell me, what did Father's letter say?'

'You know he cannot tell us much, not in something as incriminating as a letter. But I could read between the lines. It is happening tonight. By tomorrow morning we will be the largest weapons manufacturer in Hominum. Then all we need to do is get rid of Seraph's father and take over the Pasha munitions business. After that we will have the whole damned pie!'

'Good. Our inheritance will be secure once again. But did he tell . . .' Isadora's voice faded as they entered one of the rooms and the door shut behind them. Fletcher realised he was holding his breath and let it out in a deep sigh. Whatever he had heard tonight, it was not good news at all.

Fletcher was about to move out of his hiding place when he heard more footsteps. The steps came gradually closer until they stopped just outside the room Tarquin and Isadora had entered, then there was a deep breath.

'Come on, Sylva. You can do this,' Sylva's lilting voice said.

Fletcher gaped in surprise. Why was Sylva going to see the Forsyths at such a late hour?

'Do what?' Fletcher said, stepping out of the shadows.

Sylva gasped and clapped her hands to her mouth.

'Fletcher! What are you doing here?'

'Do what?' Fletcher repeated, furrowing his brow.

'I'm here to . . . make peace with the Forsyths,' she muttered, avoiding Fletcher's eyes.

'Why? What on earth could have possessed you to do that? They abandoned you when you needed them most!' Fletcher exclaimed.

'I have forgotten why I am here, Fletcher. I am an elf, the first summoner of my kind in hundreds of years. Not only that, but I am an ambassador. You and Othello have been good to me, and I bear you no ill will. But I cannot alienate the nobility, not with the relations between our countries at stake. Zacharias Forsyth is one of King Harold's closest and oldest advisors and it is the King who will broker an alliance between our nations. Being friends with Zacharias's children will sway him to our cause.' Sylva spoke firmly, as if she had rehearsed the speech before.

'But, Sylva, they don't even like you. They only want your friendship for their own ends!' Fletcher insisted.

282

'As I do theirs. I'm sorry, Fletcher, but I have made up my mind. This doesn't change anything between us, but it is how things must be,' she stated.

'Oh yes it does! You think I'll trust you when you're friends with those two vipers?' Fletcher blurted, pushing past her.

'Fletcher, please!' Sylva begged him.

But it was too late. Fletcher stormed away, his misery replaced with fury that boiled inside him.

Damn the elf and her politics. Damn the nobles too! Everything was falling apart; his friendships, his studies. He couldn't even contact Berdon with Rook looking over his shoulder.

At the top of the stairs Rory, Seraph and Genevieve were chatting, elated by their success. Fletcher sunk into a chair behind them, hoping they would not notice him. He was in no mood to talk.

'I think that maybe my fulfilment level is increasing!' Rory said, full of joy. 'I was doing pretty well! Maybe Malachi is going up in levels too!'

'I don't think you understand how fulfilment levels work, Rory,' Seraph said mildly. 'Your ability to perform the spell has nothing to do with your level. Fulfilment just impacts how much demonic energy you can absorb. Malachi will never go up in level. He will always be level one. Every demon remains at the same level for the rest of their lives. Even if your demon becomes stronger or bigger, that will never change.'

'Oh . . .' Rory muttered. 'But why was Tarquin yelling at Fletcher about how Ignatius was a lower level than Trebius, if it doesn't have anything to do with their power?'

'Because it's usually a rough guide. A level-seven demon is probably going to be stronger than a level six, just as a rule of thumb. It's not a hard and fast rule. For example, a Felid will beat a Canid in a fight nine times out of ten, even though they are both level seven. Or look at Othello's Golem. When it is full grown, it will be many times more powerful than a Canid, even though it is a level eight and a Canid is level seven.'

'Right . . . never mind then.' Rory's face was glum once again.

'Don't worry, I'm sure *you* will go up in level,' Seraph said, noticing Rory's change in mood. 'Major Goodwin told me it is very rare for a summoner to remain at the same level their entire lives. It is only the ones who never capture other demons or who are very unlucky in their natural fulfilment growth who stay that way.'

'How am I supposed to capture other demons if Rook won't let us go hunting?' Rory howled, jumping to his feet.

'Rory, wait. It's just one year!' Genevieve tried to reason, but Rory ignored her and left for his room in a huff. She gave Seraph an exasperated look and then followed Rory into the boys' quarters.

Seraph bit his lip and sighed. 'I've put my foot in it again. I was just trying to temper his expectations, nothing more,' he muttered.

The room was silent then, as Seraph scribbled notes for their next demonology essay. Eventually, Seraph grew tired and snuffed out his wyrdlight, casting the room in shadow. He stood and began to walk to his room.

'Wait,' Fletcher said, holding up his hand. 'I need to ask you something.'

'Sure, what's up?' Seraph asked with a yawn.

'What does your father do? I ask because I overheard Tarquin mentioning something . . . It was about taking your father down and it has something to do with his business.'

Seraph froze. Fletcher could see some kind of internal struggle, then Seraph relaxed and sat down in the chair next to him.

'I guess if I know your secrets it is only right I tell you mine. Just promise me you will not breathe a word of this to anyone.'

Fletcher nodded in assent and Seraph continued.

'I was born and raised in Antioch, the same city where Malik and his family, the Saladins, are from. Malik's family do not own great tracts of forest and farmland like the other nobles, but rather they hold many businesses and properties in Antioch. This is because the city is surrounded by desert, where nothing grows and there is little water.'

'So the Saladins are involved?' Fletcher asked.

'Not quite. My father took a risk. He bought up huge parts of the desert. It was cheap land, but virtually useless. I remember my parents arguing all night long when he spent all of our savings on it. Then one day, a dwarf came to visit us. He told us that the dwarves do not have the right to own land outside of what they were allocated in Corcillum, but he and his people needed it. The nobles would not do business with the dwarves, but perhaps we would.'

'I knew the dwarves had something to do with it!' Fletcher exclaimed, then realised how loud he was being and put a finger to his lips. For a moment he thought he heard a noise from the boy's quarters. When they were confident no one was there, Seraph spoke again.

'It turned out the dwarves needed metals and sulphur, in large quantities. They had surveyed our land and found deposits underneath the sand, deep underground. Without their expertise, we wouldn't be able to extract it, but without our land, neither would they. So we struck a deal . . . they would help us set up the mines and lend us the money we needed to hire men and the equipment. In exchange, we would partner with the dwarves exclusively, not selling to anyone else. They process the materials and then we split the profits fairly.'

'But why sulphur?' Fletcher asked. Everything was starting to make sense.

'It is used in the production of gunpowder. The best part is, only the Akhad Desert seems to have any significant quantities of it and we own all the land that is near enough to civilisation for mining to be viable. Every lead bullet fired and every barrel of gunpowder used is produced in a Pasha mine or factory.'

'So why do the Forsyths care about any of this?' Fletcher asked.

'Don't you know anything? Their biggest business is arms production. They are the chief supplier of swords, armour, helmets, even the uniforms. When the dwarves developed muskets . . . their business began to shrink. Dwarven weaponry is slowly becoming more popular, and when they're fighting with muskets, soldiers don't need to wear armour any more, as they can do battle from a distance. I don't think the Forsyths know how to take us down just yet, but I wouldn't be surprised if they are planning it.'

'They mentioned something about an important event happening tonight, but they spoke about dealing with your father afterwards,' Fletcher warned, trying to remember

Tarquin's exact words.

'It's too late to do anything about it, but my father is well protected. I wouldn't worry too much. I was hoping Tarquin and Isadora wouldn't know who I was, but I think I might have some idea of how they found out.' Seraph smiled as he spoke, as if he had been waiting for an excuse to tell his secret.

'First we lost a noble family called the Raleighs, then the Queensouths and the Forsyths united into one house. King Harold had suddenly lost two of his oldest noble families. He wanted to create new noble houses, taking the few second and third-born nobles who had also been born adepts and giving them their own titles. But the nobles hated this idea, since they usually married them to firstborns of other noble houses. So the King looked elsewhere. My father has a good relationship with the dwarves, owns plenty of land and is now almost as wealthy as a noble himself. But that is not enough. To become a noble, you must be an adept. Then one day the Inquisitors came by, to test me . . .'

'. . . And they discovered you were an adept,' Fletcher said, realisation dawning on him. 'You can start a new line of nobility, since your firstborn children will be adepts too.'

'Exactly. He will make the announcement publicly next year, but the nobles have already been told. I don't think I am very popular with the twins right now, or even Malik for that matter.'

Fletcher sat in silence, trying to process everything he had just been told.

'Goodnight, Fletcher,' Seraph said, padding out of the room. 'Remember . . . it's our little secret.'

40

The war drums beat with a mad fervour, throbbing the night air with pulsing intensity. Row upon row of orcs clapped and stamped to the rhythm, punctuating the end of each cycle with a guttural ululation.

The Salamander curled around an orc shaman's neck, watching the proceedings below. The raised platform they stood upon was the epicentre around which all the orcs were gathered, lit by roaring bonfires on each corner. Gremlin slaves scampered back and forth, dragging wood from the surrounding jungle to keep the fires stoked high.

Suddenly, the drumbeat stopped. The imp started at the abrupt silence and yawned noisily. The orc shaman hushed him and slipped a morsel of flesh into his mouth, stroking the Salamander's head with affection.

A groan cut through the silence behind them. An elf was lashed to a crosspiece, his hands and feet cruelly bound to the wood. His face was swollen and covered in crusted blood, but his worst injury was a large square of raw flesh on his back, where a piece of skin had been removed. Behind him, another orc was scraping the skin with a serrated rock, removing any residual traces of fat, flesh and sinew.

The elf croaked desperately, but his throat was too parched to form words with any meaning. The orc shaman lashed out with a foot, kicking the elf in the stomach. He choked and hung against his restraints, gasping like a fish out of water.

A whispering began from the mass of orcs below. The crowds parted, revealing a procession entering the encampment. There were ten orcs; large, muscular specimens whose grey skin was painted with red and yellow ochres. Their weaponry was primitive yet fearsome; heavy war clubs that were studded with jagged rocks.

Yet they were not alone. Another orc walked behind the others, dwarfing them in size. His skin was a pale white and his eyes glowed red in the firelight. He walked with easy confidence, accepting the awed looks from the surrounding orcs as his due.

As the group approached the platform, the elf began to cry out, struggling against his bindings. This time, the orc shaman made no move to silence him. Instead, he kneeled, bowing his head deeply as the albino orc climbed the platform, leaving his bodyguard below.

The albino orc lifted the shaman to his feet and embraced him. As he did so, the crowd roared in approval, stamping their feet until the platform shook. Even through all the noise, the elf's desperate cries could be heard as he pulled at the leather straps that held him in place.

The cheers died out as the albino orc walked over to the captive elf. He lifted the prisoner's face and peered into it, grasping the head as easily as if it were a grapefruit. Then he released it with a disinterested grunt.

The elf was silent now, as if resigned to his fate. The crowd watched with baited breath as the white orc was handed the piece of skin, now stretched out on a palette of wood. As he lifted it to the light, a pentacle could be seen tattooed on to the white orc's hand, the black ink contrasting starkly with his pale skin. His fingers were tattooed as well, the tip of each fingerpad embossed with a different symbol.

The imp was lowered to the ground by his master, who stepped away and bowed low once again. The albino orc extended his hand, pointing his tattooed palm up at the sky. Then, with a deep and booming voice, the orc began to read from the skin.

'*Di rah go mai lo fa lo go rah lo . . .*'

The pentacle on the orc's palm began to glow a searing bright violet. Threads of white light materialised, a twisting umbilical cord between the shaman and the Salamander. The invisible bond that held the two together unravelled, then snapped with an audible crack.

'*Fai lo so nei di roh . . .*'

But those were the last words the white orc spoke.

An elven arrow whistled through the air and speared his throat, spurting hot blood across the platform. More arrows thudded into the ranks; long, heavy shafts that were fletched with swan feathers. The orc shaman roared, but without his demon he was powerless. Instead, he rushed to the side of the fallen albino orc, trying to stem the blood that gushed from his neck.

Another hail of arrows fell, sending the orcs into disarray, milling about aimlessly as they brandished war clubs and bundles of javelins. Then, with a brassy knell, trumpets sounded from the forest and a great crowd came charging from the trees, screaming their battle cries. But these were not elves that came stampeding out of the darkness . . . they were men.

Men wearing heavy plate armour, armed with broadswords and shields, fearlessly plunging into the heart of the camp. They gave no quarter, hacking and stabbing at the orcs in a whirlwind of steel. The encampment was transformed into a charnel house, the ground thickly coated with entrails, bodies and blood. Behind them, hail upon hail of arrows flew overhead, peppering the orcs with deadly accuracy.

The orcs were no cowards. They waded into their assailants, crushing helmets and breastplates with blows from their clubs as if they were made of tinfoil. It was a desperate, vicious melee. There was no skill or tactics here – death was decided by luck, strength and numbers.

Orcs roared their defiance as the men's blades rose and fell. Each flailing smash from their clubs sent men flying, shattering their bones to leave them crippled where they fell. The orcs fought on through the storm of arrows, snapping the shafts from their bodies and hurling them defiantly into the faces of the enemy.

The abino orc's bodyguard carved a wide path of destruction, sending scores of opponents to their deaths. Their strength was unmatched as they ducked and weaved in the firelight, using their studded warclubs to lethal effect. They rallied other orcs behind them, bellowing orders as they took the fight to the enemy. Somehow, the orcs were now winning.

But then something stirred in the jungle, a dark mass that had been waiting just out of sight. What at first had appeared to be tree branches became antlers, tossing and jostling as they charged into the clearing. It was the elves, sitting astride giant elks, full-chested beasts with strong legs and sharpened antlers. They wore no armour, but wielded the bows that had blackened the sky with arrows not so long ago. The foremost elf held a great pennant that streamed behind them, made from green cloth with gold stitching. The broken arrow it depicted rippled as the elks stampeded over the shattered bodies on the ground.

They hit the orcs like a battering ram, the antlers impaling the front ranks and hurling them overhead. Arrows whistled into skulls and eye sockets as the elves fired nimbly from the backs of their steeds. The men cheered and followed behind, stabbing the fallen orcs who had been trampled under the charge.

The tide had begun to turn again, but it was far from over. The orcs surrounded the platform, a last knot of resistance that would not surrender. They hurled their javelins into the foray, great shafts of wood with sharpened ends that cut down elk and elf alike.

The men put up their shields, one row kneeling and the other standing to provide an interlocking wall that was two rows high. The elves sent their elk back into the trees and fired their arrows from behind the wall, arcing them over the top to fall on their enemy with practised ease. It was a deadly war of attrition as the missiles on both sides took their toll. But there could only be one outcome.

It took dozens of arrows to take down each orc, but die they did. They fell, one by one, twitching and bleeding in the dirt. At last, the albino orc's bodyguard made a final, desperate bid, charging at the enemy. They barely managed ten steps.

On the platform, the orc shaman pawed at his lost Salamander, desperate for the mana that might give him a chance to live. Realising it was useless, he drew a knife and crawled towards their captive elf, perhaps hoping to gain a hostage.

As he lifted the knife to the elf's throat, the bows were raised once again. The arrows whistled for the last time.

Fletcher woke with a start, his body soaked with cold sweat.

'What the hell was that?'

41

What Fletcher had just seen . . . it wasn't a dream, of that he was certain. He had smelled the blood, heard the screams. The images were Ignatius's memories, one of the infusion flashbacks that Lovett had warned him about.

'I'm kind of jealous,' Fletcher murmured to Ignatius. 'I had almost forgotten you once belonged to an orc.'

The little demon gave a soft growl and burrowed deeper into the blankets. It was freezing in the room – Fletcher had yet to find anything adequate to stuff into the arrow slit in his wall.

With a flash of revulsion, Fletcher realised that the summoning scroll he had left with Dame Fairhaven had been made from the elf in the memory. Somehow, seeing the actual victim made the relic twice as disturbing.

He contemplated the scene he had just witnessed. What had elves been doing in orc territory? Was the albino orc he had seen the same one that led the tribes now? It couldn't be. James Baker had written that the scroll was buried amongst bones from long ago. The battle must have happened hundreds of years in the past, perhaps in the Second Orc War; there had been no muskets then after all. But that did not explain what the elves were doing there, nor the albino orc.

'You're probably hundreds of years older than me, that's all I know,' Fletcher murmured, warming his hands on Ignatius's belly.

He lay back down on the bed, but sleep would not come to him. He kept turning over the facts in his mind, again and again. Were there any clues? There had been no demons present other than Ignatius . . . did that mean anything? Surely an army of men would have had battlemages, especially for a battle as crucial as that one.

Then it hit him. The banner that the elves had used: the broken arrow! Surely that would reveal which clan the elves had belonged to. Sylva would know who they were; she knew more about the history of their peoples than anyone.

Fletcher's heart fell as he remembered their argument. Perhaps he had been too hard on her. It was easy to forget the position she was in and the responsibilities she had to her people. Hell, if her friendship meant an end to the war on the elven front, what did it matter if she was being friendly to the Forsyths? At the very least, it would throw a spanner in Didric's works. There would be no need to send all the prisoners north for training if the elven front didn't exist any more.

He rolled from his bed and got dressed. Wrapping the still-sleeping Ignatius around his neck like a scarf, Fletcher padded quietly to the girls' quarters.

'This time, I'm definitely going to knock,' Fletcher murmured to himself, not wanting another encounter with Sariel.

Sylva answered the door immediately. Her room was almost identical to Fletcher's, though twice as large and furnished with an additional chest at the foot of her bed. Sariel was curled up on a sheepskin rug in the centre of the room, watching Fletcher warily. Sylva matched her demon's expression and Fletcher noticed she was still dressed in her uniform. She must have only just got back from her meeting with the Forsyths. He swallowed his annoyance at that realisation and spoke to her levelly.

'Can I come in?'

'Of course. But if you're here to change my mind you might as well go back to bed. Tarquin and Isadora were willing to put aside our differences, and I hope you are willing to do the same with me!'

'I'm not here about that,' Fletcher said, ignoring his desire to contradict her. 'I had a flashback, like Lovett warned us about. I need to ask you about when the elves and humans last fought together.'

Sylva listened in rapt attention as Fletcher told her about his dream. He tried to recount it in as much detail as possible, hoping that he might remember some other clue.

'Fletcher . . . are you sure you weren't dreaming?' Sylva asked when he finished. 'It's only . . . what you told me is impossible.'

'Why is that?' Fletcher asked. 'I'm telling you, it was all real!'

'If what you say is true . . . Ignatius is more than two thousand years old!' Sylva breathed. She rushed over to the trunk at the end of her bed and rummaged through it.

'I know it's here somewhere,' she muttered, piling dusty books next to her on the stone floor.

'Here!' she announced, heaving a heavy tome on to the bed.

Fletcher sat next to her and she flicked through it, before settling on an illustrated page in the middle. The scene it depicted made him feel dizzy: elves riding elks, charging into a horde of orcs. The broken arrow pennant streamed behind them. Men on foot assaulted from the other side, wearing the exact same armour as in Fletcher's vision. Even the albino orc's bodyguard was featured, the red and yellow war paint unmistakeable.

'Do you remember what I told you that night in the cornfields? About how the elves taught the first King of Hominum how to summon in exchange for an alliance against the orcs? This was the final battle they fought, the Battle of Corcillum, so called because of its proximity to the dwarven city. Your demon's namesake, Ignatius, would have led the charge in that battle. Apparently it didn't happen too far from here, but the site of the battle has been lost in time. The fact that you got to see it . . . it's incredible!' She stroked the page, tracing the outline of an elk's antlers.

'But I don't understand. Why was there an albino orc . . . and why was Ignatius the only demon there?'

'Only the elven clan chiefs were summoners, and the whole reason they made their deal with your first King was so they didn't have to risk themselves in battle. The elves weren't supposed to do any fighting after the agreement, but the Battle of Corcillum was fought because a clan chief's son was kidnapped, so the elves sent their own soldiers in to help. They hadn't taught King Corwin the art of summoning yet either, as the conditions of the agreement clearly stated that the orcs had to be utterly defeated first. As for the albino orc, I have no idea. All I know is that after the Battle of Corcillum, the orcs fell back to the jungles.

It was the decisive victory that heralded an age of peace, lasting until the Second Orc War, three hundred years ago.'

Fletcher was glad he had come to Sylva. She seemed to have learned everything about human and elf relations in her preparation for coming to Vocans.

'I think we need to go to the library and research if there have ever been any reports of another albino orc,' Fletcher said. 'It seems as if after the last one was killed, the orcs fell into disarray. Maybe the white orcs aren't just their leaders; there could be something more to it!' Fletcher said.

'You're right. Ignatius was about to be gifted to him and it seemed to be an important ceremony. We need to research what we can about the orcs and their past leaders, maybe we can turn something up.' Sylva stood and strode to the door.

'Where are you going?' Fletcher asked as Sariel bounded after her, nearly knocking him to the ground.

'To the library, of course. I said, as soon as possible!'

Fletcher had no choice but to follow her.

It was dank and cold in Vocans at night, but their wyrdlights lit the way well enough. The use of spells no longer gave Fletcher the joy it had before, for he was still dwelling on his performance in Arcturus's lessons.

He tried to stay positive and concentrate on the task at hand. At least he had the chance to redeem himself by providing useful information about the orcs.

If only they had access to the summoner's book. Fletcher would have loved to be able to read more about the site where Ignatius's scroll had been found.

As they descended the spiral staircase, Fletcher saw the glow of another wyrdlight behind them.

'Hide! It might be Rook!' he hissed.

They snuffed out their own lights and ducked into one of the upper corridors. Holding their breaths, they pressed themselves into a doorway. Sariel whined at the sudden darkness but was silenced with a tap on the muzzle from Sylva.

Hasty footsteps soon followed, accompanied by heavy breathing. Whoever it was, they were in a hurry. After what seemed an age, the steps faded, and they were shrouded in darkness once again.

'Come on, let's go,' Fletcher muttered when he was sure they were out of earshot.

'Who would be wandering the corridors at this time?' Sylva asked.

'I think I have some idea,' Fletcher said, leading the way down the stairs again, careful not to trip in the dark.

'What do you mean?' Sylva asked.

'The first night I was here, I saw someone leaving our common room and eventually the castle. It looked like they were in a hurry and didn't want to be seen,' Fletcher replied, turning into the corridor that lead to the library.

'That's so suspicious, Fletcher. Why haven't you told anyone?' Sylva asked, disapproval clear in her voice.

'Because I didn't think anything of it. It could have just been someone going for some fresh air. That's why *I* was out that night. Now it's happened again though . . . maybe I should have said something.'

Fletcher pushed at the door to the library. It shook on its hinges, but remained firmly closed.

'Well, it looks like we've just wasted a trip downstairs. Dame Fairhaven must have locked it when the last student left for bed . . . which we should do too,' he said, kicking the door in frustration. 'The library can wait until after Rook's lesson.'

'I'm not going to bed! There's somebody sneaking about the school at night. I'm going to find out who it is. If I can bring a traitor to justice, everyone will know that the elves are trustworthy.'

With that, she strode back down the corridor and bounded down the spiral staircase.

'Sylva, it's not safe for you out there! Those men who attacked you in Corcillum could be watching the castle!'

But it was too late. Sylva was gone.

Fletcher cursed as he tripped in the darkness.

'Sylva!' he hissed, trying to be loud and quiet at the same time. He had been following her trail for the past hour, though the thin sliver of moon in the night sky gave him barely enough light to see her trail. There was a flattened patch of grass here, a broken twig there. At one point he thought he had lost her, but the ground had been softened by a recent rain, allowing him to feel the soft indent of footprints that slowly filled with water. If he had not been a practised hunter, he would have lost her.

He could have kicked himself for not following her immediately after she had left. Instead, he had chosen to run back upstairs and get his khopesh, in case they ran into any trouble. Who would have thought she would move so fast?

Now he had reached the edge of a small forest, tall trees

growing in some craggy hills half a mile from Vocans.

'Sylva, I'm going to kill you!'

'Not likely,' whispered a voice from behind him.

Fletcher felt cold steel press into his back and froze.

'I'm perfectly aware of the dangers I face because of what I am. But I refuse to live in fear, or change my behaviour to accommodate my enemies.'

Sylva stepped in front of him and flashed a long stiletto blade, not dissimilar to the one he had made in Uhtred's forge.

'I came prepared, of course,' she said, smiling. 'But Sariel is worth a bodyguard of ten men and two trackers to boot.'

As Fletcher's pride stung from being caught unawares, Sariel wandered into view from behind a crop of rocks ahead, snuffling at the ground.

'Sylva, let's go back. This is none of our business! It could be Genevieve visiting her family, we know she lives near here,' Fletcher reasoned, eager to get back to Vocans. It was freezing out there, even with his jacket on.

'Not when we are so close,' Sylva replied stubbornly. 'They're just ahead of us; come on!'

She jogged away before Fletcher could stop her. Groaning with exasperation, he followed.

The wyrdlight came into view almost immediately. It floated above a small rocky cliff, which Sylva crawled up before poking her head out to see. Her eyes widened and she motioned for Fletcher to join her.

He looked apprehensively at the muddy ground. What could Sylva possibly be seeing below that had got her in such a state? Curiosity got the better of him and he lay flat in the dirt, before sliding himself up the incline to lie beside Sylva. The front of his uniform and jacket were soon soaked with cold mud, but it was nothing compared to the cold that trickled down his spine when he saw what was below.

Othello and Solomon stood in front of a cave. There were two mounted dwarves guarding it, sitting astride boars, the chosen steeds of the dwarven people. The boars had coarse, rust-coloured fur, with heavy tusks that jutted dangerously from their snouts. They were nothing like the wild pigs that Fletcher had hunted in Pelt; these were muscled chargers, with red, baleful eyes that seemed full of rage and malice.

The dwarves themselves were armoured, with horned helms on their heads and two-handed battle-axes clenched in their fists. A bandolier of hurlbat throwing-axes hung from their saddles, deadly projectiles with an additional blade in the top of the axe and a sharpened handle.

And then they heard a clear, booming voice announce, 'Othello Thorsager, reporting for the war council. They are expecting me.'

42

The mounted dwarves followed Othello into the cave, the clomp of the boars' hooves echoing beneath them until the sound faded underground.

'They must have been waiting for him. Still think it's none of our business?' Sylva whispered.

'Well, it isn't. This war council could be about anything. They have just joined the military after all.' Fletcher's voice was low and sullen. He was disappointed in Othello. The dwarf knew all of his secrets, down to the last detail. How could his best friend keep this from him?

'The dwarves could be plotting a rebellion,' Sylva argued back. 'Think about it. Old King Alfric created the harshest laws against the dwarves there have ever been, even if his son Harold has started to repeal them. They have revolted against Hominum for less in the past, not to mention the fact that they now have a monopoly on musket production.'

'I can't believe that. Othello is so set on peace between our races; he would never jeopardise that!' Fletcher hissed, furious at the suggestion.

'Are you willing to risk a civil war on that?' Sylva asked. Fletcher paused, then thumped his fist into the wet earth.

'Fine. But there's no way we can follow him. He's under armed guard. Warning the Pinkertons isn't a good idea, they would burst in and start the civil war tonight,' Fletcher pondered, exploring the options. 'What would you suggest?'

'We're summoners, Fletcher. Let's send Ignatius in to sneak past the guards and scry what's happening. You'll have to tell me what they are saying. I won't be able to hear it.'

'Why not send Sariel?' Fletcher argued.

'Because Sariel will barely fit in that cave, let alone be able to get by the guards. Besides, we need someone to protect us out here.' Sylva sounded exasperated.

'You're doing this so you can find out if there is a plot and use that information to curry favour with the King,' Fletcher accused.

'It's not the only reason, Fletcher. If a civil war were to break out in the middle of our current war against the orcs . . . who knows how the cards would fall then. You and I both know that we need to see what's happening at that war council. Now stop wasting time, and use my scrying stone on Ignatius. If we used your tiny one we would barely be able to see a thing.'

Sylva removed a shard of crystal from the pocket of her uniform. It was oval shaped and at least four times larger than the coin-sized scrying stone that Fletcher had been given.

'Hurry, we've probably already missed the start of their meeting,' she urged.

Fletcher tapped the scrying stone against Ignatius's head, waking the little imp from slumber.

'Come on, buddy. Time to put all that practice to use. At least some good will come of Rook not allowing us to do anything but scry.'

Ignatius yawned in complaint but immediately woke up when he sensed Fletcher's mood. The demon leaped from his shoulder and ran to the edge of the cliff. Digging his claws into the earth, Ignatius crawled vertically down the lip of the cave mouth. Then, as if it was the easiest thing in the world, he scampered upside down along the roof of the cave and ventured deep into the earth.

'Wow. I didn't know Ignatius could do that,' Sylva whispered, flipping the scrying stone in Fletcher's hands so that the inverted image made more sense.

'Me neither. Ignatius still manages to surprise me,' Fletcher replied, his chest swelling with pride.

Controlling Ignatius was easy. Their mental connection had been honed by the many hours of practice in Rook's lessons and it required barely a thought to adjust the roving demon's path this way and that. The cave was dark, but Ignatius's night vision was far better than a human's. It was possible to make out the long, winding passage easily enough.

In just a few minutes, the tunnel widened and the flickering glow of torches could be seen ahead. Fletcher urged Ignatius to slow down, for he could hear the click of the demon's claws through their connection. It would be best not to give the guards a reason to look up.

The two mounted dwarves who escorted Othello were waiting

by the torches with over two dozen others. They stood in a row, watching the tunnel ahead like hawks. Fortunately for Ignatius, their torchlight did not extend as far as the cavern's ceiling. He crawled on in the gloom, unnoticed by the vigilant guards.

The tunnel's roof became higher and higher. Now Ignatius was almost eighty feet above the floor. One misstep and he could fall to his death, but the demon clambered onwards, making his way through the stalactites that hung from the ceiling like icicles. Finally, the tunnel opened up into a dome-shaped cavern, lit by hundreds of torches.

The cave was the central nexus of a network of similar tunnels, like the hub and spokes of a wheel. The glimmer of torchlight at the end of each entrance indicated that they too were guarded by mounted dwarves.

'Whatever this meeting is about, they aren't leaving anything to chance, are they?' Sylva whispered.

Fletcher hushed her, for Ignatius had looked below him. Dozens of dwarves were gathered there, seated on benches made of roughly hewn stone. In the middle, there was a raised stone platform, upon which a dwarf stood. Fletcher could barely make out his booming voice.

'We need to get closer. I can't hear what he's saying,' Fletcher murmured, directing Ignatius to look around the cavern. The walls were illuminated by the torches flickering light, there was no way the demon could climb down them without being seen.

'Get him to climb down that,' Sylva suggested, pointing at a large stalactite that extended a third of the way to the base of the cavern.

Fletcher ordered Ignatius down the pointed stone, urging him to be careful. Then he closed his eyes and began to whisper the words he heard.

'. . . I say again to you, the time is ripe for rebellion! We have not been in a better position for two thousand years. Hominum's army is caught between two wars, the elves to the north and the orcs to the south. They cannot fight a third. From a tactical point of view, we are well placed to storm the palace and hold the King and his father hostage.'

The speaker was a large, heavyset dwarf with a commanding presence. He stared down his nose at the seated dwarves, then descended the platform steps. Another dwarf waited below, this one older, with grey streaks in his beard. He shook the younger dwarf's hand and then took his place on the rostrum.

'Thank you, Ulfr, for those rousing words. You speak the truth, but there is more to it than that. As you all know, we dwarves are the only manufacturers of firearms. At this moment, nine out of every ten men in Hominum's army are only trained in the art of loading and firing a musket, with no armour, nor anything more than a bayonet for close-quarters combat. If we were to cut off their weapons supply, they would become nothing more than a poorly equipped, untrained militia. Another key advantage that cannot be overlooked . . .'

His words drew cheers from some of the dwarves and soon they began chanting his name. 'Hakon! Hakon!'

But many dwarves remained silent, staring up at him with their arms crossed. Clearly, the crowd was divided.

'Another advantage, perhaps our greatest of all, is ammunition. The Pasha mines are controlled by our allies and worked by dwarven miners. It is dwarves who manufacture the gunpowder and the lead bullets. Without these two resources, the muskets that Hominum already have will be useless. Once they run out of their ammunition stockpiles . . . we will win this war!'

More cheers followed, but this time there were boos as well. A dwarf leaped from his seat and rushed on to the stage. He shook Hakon's hand and whispered in his ear.

'It's Othello!' Sylva gasped.

Fletcher shook his head.

'No, it's not, I can tell from the way his hair has been braided. Othello has a twin, remember? His name is Atilla and he hates humanity with a passion.'

'Traitors and cowards!' Atilla bellowed as Fletcher tuned in again. 'Are you true dwarves . . . or half-men?'

Several dwarves leaped up in anger, shouting so loudly that Fletcher could almost hear the echoes from the cave below where he and Sylva sat.

'Have you not felt the batons of the Pinkertons? How many of you have had your hard earned money extorted from you? Who here has not had a son or brother thrown in jail by a dwarf-hating judge? Do you like having to go crawling to the King if you want more than one child?'

The yelling almost doubled in volume as dwarves leaped to their feet and bellowed in anger.

Suddenly, a guttural roar thundered through the cave, silencing the noise.

'Enough!' a familiar voice shouted. Othello pushed his way through the crowd and mounted the stairs two at a time. Solomon, the source of the roar, followed him.

'I am Othello Thorsager, first dwarven officer in Hominum and the first summoner of our kind. I claim the right to speak.'

'Get on with it then, human lover,' Atilla shouted.

'We cannot go to war with Hominum,' Othello said in a loud, clear voice. 'King Harold is giving us a chance for equality, don't you see? If we go to war we will lose, without a shadow of a doubt. Hominum's army alone outnumbers the dwarven population by ten to one. Most dwarves of fighting age are on their way to be trained on the elven front, surrounded by veteran soldiers and as far from Corcillum as is possible. Do you think you can storm the palace with the hundred or so dwarven men left?'

'If we must!' shouted Hakon, spurring on shouts of agreement from his supporters.

'What happens then? The news of our assault will reach the generals in the north in a matter of days, carried by flying demons. The northern generals will slaughter our young warriors without hesitation. Even if we planned it with them, what then? Will a thousand untrained dwarves try and take over the entire northern front? Even without muskets, the battlemages would tear our warriors apart in minutes. The King himself is one of the most powerful summoners to have ever walked the earth, yet you presume to take him hostage! We wouldn't stand a chance.'

'So what? I'd rather die fighting against them than alongside them. I bet they think you're a joke, wandering around with that little demon of yours,' Atilla said.

'That is what I thought too, when I first arrived at Vocans. But I was wrong. There are good people there. Hell, the first day I arrived one of them showed me an Anvil card,' Othello replied.

'The Anvils? They are just humans who pity us, nothing more. It is but a hobby to them. The elders didn't trust them enough to even bring them to this meeting,' Atilla retorted.

'Neither would I, not if we are going to discuss open war against their people. We are slowly gaining allies; first the Pashas and now the Anvils are starting a movement in our support. Even the King has said he is willing to revisit the laws and rein in the Pinkertons, once we prove that we can be trusted. But what do we do? We do the very thing that would prevent him from ever supporting us – discuss rebellion.' Othello spat on Atilla's boots in fury.

'You are no true dwarf! You don't deserve the dwarven sigil that is stamped upon your back. I am ashamed to call you brother!' Atilla shouted.

He tore Othello's shirt away, to reveal the tattoo on his back. With a roar, Othello grabbed Atilla by the throat and they spun around the stage, throttling one another. Solomon moved to help, but then stopped, as if Othello had commanded him to freeze.

Uhtred burst on to the platform, ripping the brawling twins apart. Behind him, a procession of white-haired dwarves mounted the stage. They were old and venerable, with long, chalky beards that were tucked into their belts.

'They must be the Dwarven Council,' Sylva breathed in Fletcher's ear. Fletcher nodded and urged Ignatius to listen closely, for these dwarves did not seem like the type to shout and scream.

The room was in a deep, respectful silence. Even Atilla had calmed himself, bowing his head in reverence. The oldest of the elders stepped forward and opened his arms wide.

'Do we not all want freedom for our children? If we cannot stand united in the face of adversity, then we have already lost.'

The dwarves began to seat themselves, many looking at their feet in shame.

'We have heard all we need to hear. There are many hot heads here tonight, but the decision we are about to make will not be taken lightly. I ask you this . . . what good will it do, to die bravely in pursuit of freedom? Fourteen times the dwarves have rebelled, and fourteen times we have been brought to the brink of extinction. You young dwarves do not remember the slaughter we faced in the last uprising. Every time we lose, more freedoms are taken from us, more dwarven blood is shed.'

There were nods of agreement from the crowd.

'I see two paths before us. One is well trodden, yet every time we have taken it, we end up back where we started: defeated and bloodied. But there is a second path. I do not know where it leads, or what dangers there are along the way, but I know in my heart that it is better to take the path of uncertain fate, than the one of glorious, yet certain defeat. There will be no war, my friends. We will honour our agreement with the King.'

Fletcher was flooded with relief. Othello had snuck out to argue against rebellion, not support it. Not only that, but he had managed to win over the elders. He did not want to think what Othello would have done if the decision had gone the other way, but it was not worth thinking about. Everything was going to be OK.

'Fletcher, what was that?' Sylva gasped, jerking Fletcher's arm.

There were torches ahead of them, moving through the trees

at speed. They ducked behind the cliff and watched, their hearts in their mouths.

There were ten men, each one armed with a musket and a sword. Their leader was wheezing with effort; even in the darkness, Fletcher could tell that he was an abnormally fat man.

'Are you certain this is the right cave?' one of the men asked, holding his torch high to illuminate the area. Fletcher was hit by a wash of cold as the light revealed their faces.

'I'm dead certain,' Grindle said.

43

'Those are the men that kidnapped me,' Sylva hissed, pointing at the armoured soldiers below.

'I know. I would recognise the fat bald one anywhere,' Fletcher replied, gripping the hilt of his khopesh. 'His name is Grindle – he's the one who was going to perform the execution. I thought you killed him. Guess he must have a thick skull.'

'There're too many of them,' Sylva muttered, but Fletcher could see her tensing, as if she were preparing to jump into the fray. Behind them, Fletcher could hear a low growl as Sariel sensed the elf's agitation.

'Try to stay calm. We need to find out why they're here,' Fletcher forced his own anger away and leaned over the shadowed parapet to listen.

'I don't understand why we don't just wait out here and ambush them when they come out,' one of the men was complaining.

'Because this is just one of five exits,' Grindle replied, sitting down on a boulder. 'Not to mention that three of them lead back to the tunnels under the Dwarven Quarter.'

As the other men gathered around, the light from their torches showed Grindle's bandaged shoulder, still injured from Ignatius's fireball.

'I should have made sure he was dead,' Sylva whispered through gritted teeth. Fletcher laid a calming hand on her shoulder. If it came down to a fight, he didn't feel confident about their chances.

There were ten men, each clad in boiled leather armour. It would allow them fast movement whilst still protecting them from light sword strokes.

Fletcher eyed their muskets. His feeble shield spell wasn't going to help him tonight.

'What are we waiting for then?' another man asked, peering into the dark depths of the cave.

'Did you not pay any attention in the briefing?' Grindle growled, reaching up and gripping the speaker by the front of his breastplate. He dragged the man down to his level.

'There are several hundred of Lord Forsyth's troops gathering at the other accessible exit,' Grindle spat, spraying the speaker's face with saliva. 'We go in when they do, which will be when the horn sounds, around five minutes from now. Or did you think ten men against a hundred dwarves was the plan all along?'

Fletcher's heart froze. This was what he had overheard Tarquin and Isadora talking about. It was not Seraph's family that was in danger, but the dwarves!

'Five minutes,' Sylva breathed. 'We have to do something.'

Fletcher assessed the options, his eyes darting from the men to the cave entrance. There was not enough time. Fighting

Grindle's soldiers would take too long. If they tried to get past, they would barely make it into the cave mouth before a musket ball burst through their shoulder blades. Even if by some miracle they made it, they would still need to convince the dwarven guards of what was happening.

'If only Ignatius could talk,' Sylva muttered, watching the dwarves on the scrying crystal. They were still there, milling around and discussing the decision amongst themselves.

'He doesn't have to,' Fletcher said with sudden realisation. He needed the dwarves to know that they were under attack. So why not attack them?

He sent his orders to Ignatius and felt a flash of confusion and fear from the demon. As his intentions became clear, the fear was replaced with steely resolve.

'Watch,' he whispered to Sylva.

Ignatius crawled down the stalactite, wrapping his tail around the tip and digging the spiked tip into the soft stone. He hung there like a bat, stretching his neck to get as close to the dwarves as possible.

'Now, Ignatius,' Fletcher murmured, feeling his vision intensify as the mana flared inside them.

Ignatius unleashed a thick plume of fire, a roiling wave of orange flame that billowed just short of the elderly dwarves below. It singed their heads, filling the room with the acrid stench of burning hair. Then, with a chirr of excitement, Ignatius was back on the ceiling and scampering back to Fletcher.

'We're under attack!' Hakon roared, as the room descended into panic. 'Retreat to the caves! Protect the elders!'

The boar riders returned from their posts at the exits,

herding the milling crowd of dwarves to a tunnel that led down into the earth.

'It worked,' Sylva whispered. 'Fletcher, you genius!'

Suddenly, a hurlbat axe came flying from the crowd, embedding itself just a few inches from Ignatius.

'A demon from Vocans! Treachery!' It was Atilla, still standing on the podium with Othello. 'Who did you tell about this meeting?'

'Nobody, I swear it,' Othello shouted back, his face filled with confusion as he recognised Ignatius. 'I know this demon. Its owner is a friend to the dwarves!'

'Then he won't mind me killing it for him!' Atilla howled, snatching another throwing-axe from his belt.

He jumped from the podium and began to sprint towards Ignatius, who had frozen in fear.

'No, Atilla, stay with the others!' Othello shouted, running after him.

Ignatius screeched and scrambled down the tunnel, narrowly avoiding Atilla's next throw.

'Stop him, Fletcher – you'll lead them to Grindle,' Sylva whispered, tugging on his sleeve.

But it was too late. The dwarf twins were running directly beneath Ignatius now.

'Get ready,' Fletcher whispered. 'We're going to have to fight.'

Sylva nodded, drawing her stiletto from a scabbard at her thigh. Sariel sensed her mood and crouched, ready to leap on the men below. They waited with baited breath as the seconds ticked by.

'Footsteps!' Grindle said hoarsely, pointing at the tunnel entrance. Fletcher could hear them now too, echoing down the cave as Atilla and Othello ran on.

'Two rows; front rank kneeling, second rank standing. Fire on my command!' Grindle ordered, drawing his sword and lifting it high above his head.

The steps were getting closer now. Fletcher could hear the clatter of another axe as it missed Ignatius once again.

'I'll shield the entrance. You flash them with wyrdlight to throw off their aim; I don't know if my shield will be strong enough,' Sylva said. She was already drawing the shield symbol in the air. Moments later and she was flowing opaque light on to the ground in front of her, pooling it as if it were molten amber.

'Ready,' Grindle growled.

The men raised their muskets, pointing them down the cave. Fletcher pulled mana from Ignatius. It was harder with the distance between them, but soon his body buzzed with power. In his mana-filled vision, the torchlight glowed a deep orange.

'Aim,' Grindle uttered, lowering his sword by a foot.

The footsteps no longer echoed, they were that close. Any second now and the two dwarves would come into view. Grindle's sword fell.

'Fi—'

'Now!' Sylva shouted, sending a glistening square of white shield below.

Fletcher fired a blast of blue light into the gunmen's eyes, blinding them as the muskets crackled, belching black smoke into a haze in front of them.

Then Sariel burst through the ranks, scattering them like ninepins. She leaped on to the nearest man's chest and began to savage his throat.

Fletcher jumped from the cliff with a yell, stabbing down with his khopesh. It took a fallen man through the stomach, then it was on to the next dazed opponent, cutting him down at the neck. He could hear Sylva screaming behind him, then the gurgle of a man with his throat cut.

Ignatius dropped on to Fletcher's shoulder from above and blew flames at a man who was charging at him, sword raised.

'My eyes!' the man screamed, falling to his knees. Sylva darted past and stabbed him through the skull.

Sariel bounded back to them, the fur around her snout a grisly mess of blood and pulp. Sylva grabbed her by the neck fur and dragged her back to the cave mouth to stand beside Fletcher. There were five men left, including Grindle. They had regrouped, spreading in a wide fan that kept their enemies trapped in the cave.

Othello and Atilla arrived, gasping as they tried to catch their breath. The shield must have worked.

'It's an ambush, Atilla. Fletcher and Sylva are on our team,' Othello muttered. Solomon rumbled in agreement.

'I'd rather kill five men than one boy.' Atilla grasped a sword from one of the fallen men. 'I'll fight beside you . . . for now.'

He handed Othello a tomahawk from his waist.

'You were always better with it than me. Show these humans what a true dwarf can do.'

Then Grindle threw a torch into the cave, illuminating their faces. He spat in disgust.

'Elf filth. I should have killed you as soon as I had the chance. If Lord Forsyth hadn't made us do it publicly, you'd be rotting in the ground right now.'

Fletcher froze at the mention of the Forsyth name, realising who had been behind Sylva's kidnapping. It was no coincidence that the Forsyth twins were with her when she was taken. He shook the revelation from his thoughts, focussing on the task at hand.

'I'm going to disembowel you,' Grindle snarled, jabbing his sword at her stomach. 'I always wondered if elves have the same insides.'

'That shoulder looks painful,' Fletcher jeered. 'How would you like it today? Medium rare, or well done?'

Grindle ignored his comment and smirked.

'Reload your muskets, boys. It'll be like shooting rats in a barrel.'

'Not so fast!' Atilla said. 'First one to reach for their musket gets an axe through their face.'

He took the last hurlbat axe from his belt and twirled it in his fingers. The remaining men looked from Grindle to their muskets on the ground. They didn't move.

'It's seven of us against five of you; and three of ours are demons. Do yourself a favour and go back to whatever hole you crawled out of.'

Grindle smirked and pointed his sword at the cave behind them. In the distance, Fletcher could hear the sound of a horn, the sign for Forsyth's men to attack.

'If I keep you here long enough, reinforcements are going to arrive. They'll cut you down like dogs.'

'If . . .' Fletcher said, taking a step forward. But he realised Grindle had a point. The distant shouts from Forsyth's soldiers echoed in the tunnel behind him. When Grindle didn't charge in with them, they would come and investigate. Fletcher needed to get out of there right now. Fighting could take far too long.

Fletcher flared a ball of wyrdlight into existence, feeding it mana until it was the size of a man's head. It throbbed with a dull pulse, glaring in the gloom of the cave's entrance. He propelled it at Grindle, who edged away from it.

'Have you ever seen what a mana burn looks like, Grindle? You think real fire was bad . . . wait until you feel your flesh peel from your bones when the raw mana touches your skin. I hear the pain is unimaginable,' Fletcher bluffed. He knew full well that a wyrdlight would dissipate as soon as it touched anything solid, with no ill effects. Grindle didn't know that though.

Sylva and Othello followed suit, sending smaller balls of wyrdlight zooming around Grindle's head. He ducked, batting at them with his sword.

'Run home, Grindle,' Fletcher laughed. 'You're out of your league. Count yourself lucky that we let you live.'

Grindle howled his frustration, bawling at the sky. Finally, he stepped aside, then motioned for his men to do the same.

Fletcher bowed low with exaggerated theatricality, then led the others past them. He kept his wyrdlight floating above Grindle's head. It was important to keep up the appearance of being in confident control.

'Well done, Fletcher,' Othello whispered. 'That was great acting.'

'I learned from the best,' Fletcher whispered back, remembering their encounter with the Pinkertons.

They walked as quickly as possible, aware of Grindle's malevolent stare boring into their backs.

'What's all that racket, Grindle? The men said they heard gunshots!' a booming voice shouted from the cave. The entrance was lit with torches as armoured figures streamed out of it.

'Run!' Fletcher shouted.

A musket ball plucked at his sleeve and shattered on a boulder ahead of them. More shots followed, buzzing overhead like angry wasps.

It was impossible to see more than a few feet ahead. All Fletcher could hear was their ragged breathing as they stumbled in the darkness. Wyrdlights were out of the question. The cover of night was all that protected them from the volleys of fire that crashed in the distance behind them.

A bullet whistled close by and then there was a thud as a body fell in front of him. Fletcher tripped in a tangle of limbs, sprawling in the mud with whoever had fallen.

'It's my leg,' Atilla groaned. 'I've been hit!'

They were alone. Sylva and Othello must have lost them in the mad rush to escape.

'Leave me. I will cover your retreat,' Atilla choked, pushing Fletcher away from him.

'Not a chance. I'm going to get you out of here, even if I have to carry you,' Fletcher replied stubbornly, trying to pull Atilla to his feet.

'I said leave me! I will die fighting, like a true dwarf.' Atilla growled, shaking Fletcher off.

'Is that how a true dwarf dies? Shot in the mud like a dog? I thought you dwarves were tougher than that,' Fletcher said, layering his voice with contempt. Anger seemed to be what drove this dwarf, and he would use that to his advantage.

'You little prig. Let me die in peace!' Atilla roared, shoving Fletcher back into the mud.

'If you want to die, then fine! But not tonight. If they capture you, they can use you as proof of a secret meeting here. Don't do this to your people. Don't give the Forsyths the satisfaction.'

Atilla snarled with frustration, then took a deep breath.

'We'll do it your way. But if they catch up with us, there will be no surrender. We fight to the death.'

'I wouldn't have it any other way,' Fletcher replied, hauling the dwarf to his feet.

It was hard going, as their height difference didn't allow Fletcher to put the dwarf's arm around his shoulders. Worse still, the shouts of their pursuers were getting louder and louder. Unlike Fletcher and Atilla, they had torches to light their way.

They carried on for what seemed like hours, then Atilla stumbled and fell to the ground.

'You're just going to have to carry me. It will be faster that way,' Atilla gasped. The injury was taking its toll, and Fletcher could feel that the dwarf's britches were soaking wet with blood. He knew that the dwarf would have had to swallow a lot of pride to make such a request.

'Come on. Jump up on my back,' Fletcher murmured. He grunted as Atilla's weight settled, then trudged on, breathing through gritted teeth. Ignatius chittered encouragement at his new riding companion, lapping at the dwarf's face.

Without warning, the area was lit by a glow of dim blue light. A globe of wyrdlight had appeared in the sky, hundreds of feet above. It hung there like a second moon, spinning above the clouds.

'Was that you?' Atilla asked.

'No. It wouldn't be Othello or Sylva either. The Forsyth men must have a battlemage with them. I wouldn't be surprised if it was Zacharias himself; that wyrdlight is huge!' Fletcher replied.

He looked around them and his heart dropped. The surrounding landscape looked almost identical, and he realised that he was hopelessly lost. But if he didn't make it back to safety soon, Atilla would not last the night.

The shouts were in the distance now, but they were by no means safe. If the enemy battlemage had a flying demon, it might spot them.

'Stop right there!' a voice shouted. A man stepped out from the shadows, pointing a musket at them. Again, Fletcher cursed his inability to perform a shield spell.

'No surrender . . .' Atilla muttered in his ear. But the dwarf's voice was slurred and faint. Fletcher doubted Atilla could take more than a few steps before collapsing.

Ignatius jumped from Fletcher's neck and hissed. The man ignored him and continued to point the musket directly at Fletcher's face.

'Keep that thing away from me, or I fire,' he said, jerking the muzzle threateningly.

Fletcher lifted his hand and flared a ball of wyrdlight into existence.

'I can whip this into your skull faster than any bullet. Drop the weapon and there will be no trouble.'

'I'm a soldier, you idiot. I know what a wyrdlight is. Drop the dwarf on the ground and— agh!' The man yelped and clapped his free hand to his neck.

A dull brown Mite buzzed above him and then flew in a circle around Fletcher's head.

'Valens,' Fletcher breathed. Somehow, the little demon had found them. The man fell over sideways, his musket still raised. It was as if he had been frozen.

'Major Goodwin wasn't kidding about a Scarab's sting,' Fletcher marvelled. Valens emitted a loud buzz and then flew back and forth in the air.

Fletcher watched him for a moment, then realised that the little demon wanted him to follow.

'Just a little longer, Atilla,' Fletcher murmured. 'We're going to make it.'

44

Atilla was unconscious by the time they arrived at Vocans, but he was still breathing. The dwarf's leg was stiff with clotted blood, but in the darkness Fletcher could not see the extent of the damage. He wrapped the wound as tightly as he could with a strip of cloth from Atilla's shirt, then followed Valens over the drawbridge.

'Where do we go now?' Fletcher whispered to the hovering demon above him.

The Mite buzzed encouragingly and stopped halfway up the eastern staircase. Fletcher eyed the steep steps with apprehension.

'I don't know if I can do it!' he groaned, hefting Atilla's body. Sensing Fletcher's mood, Ignatius leaped to the ground.

'Thanks, buddy, that's much lighter,' Fletcher murmured half-heartedly, rubbing the demon under its chin.

Valens led him up the stairs, the thrum of his wings guiding Fletcher in the darkness. He did not risk a wyrdlight. If Rook caught him with Atilla, it would be reported to old King Alfric.

They stopped on the top floor, then continued up to the

northeastern tower. By this time, Fletcher's knees were close to buckling, but he continued on doggedly. Somehow, Valens had a plan.

Finally, they reached a set of heavy wooden doors at the very top of the tower, and Fletcher realised they were at the infirmary. Before he had a chance to knock, the doors swung open and a frantic Sylva appeared.

'You're OK! We thought you had died,' Sylva sobbed, burying her face in Fletcher's chest. Othello stared at him, his face pale and streaked with tears. The dwarf rushed to Fletcher's side and took Atilla into his arms.

Fletcher patted Sylva's head awkwardly and looked around the room. There were several rows of beds, their frames rusting and covered in dust. Three newer beds lay close by the door, with Sariel resting beneath them. As Othello laid Atilla on one of them, Fletcher noticed that they were not all empty.

Lovett lay motionless on the nearest bed. She was so still that she might have been a corpse, were it not for the almost imperceptible rise and fall of her chest. She was dressed in a nightgown, with her long black hair falling about her head like a halo. The others had lit the torches and candles on either side of her bed, which cast the room in a dull, orange light.

'Valens led you here too?' Fletcher asked, as the Mite landed on Lovett's chest.

'He found us about an hour ago, then flew straight out of the window as soon as we got to this room,' Sylva said, wiping a tear from her eye. 'He must have sensed you were in trouble.'

'I don't think it's just Valens we need to thank,' Fletcher said, stroking the beetle demon's carapace.

'What do you mean?' Sylva asked.

'Arcturus told me that some summoners can learn how to see and hear through their demon, effectively using their own mind as a scrying stone. I doubt a Mite could have done what Valens did tonight without someone guiding him. Were you with him, Captain Lovett?' Fletcher looked at her immobile face.

The demon buzzed and spun in a circle.

'Not possible!' Sylva gasped.

'How did she know?' Fletcher asked, his eyes widening in wonder.

'She must have been watching out for us. Probably since Rook showed up,' Sylva said, smoothing Lovett's hair out on the pillow. 'We're lucky. We could be dead if it wasn't for her.'

'If you're all done being amazed, I need help over here,' Othello said in a cracked voice. Fletcher's eyes widened when he saw Atilla's leg.

Othello had cut through the cloth around it to reveal a jagged hole that streamed with blood. Fletcher had never seen a bullet wound before, and the damage looked far worse than the tiny puncture he had imagined.

'We are lucky, the bullet didn't hit any major arteries. The bone is definitely broken though, so we can't attempt a healing spell. Last time I saw a wound like this, a Pinkerton had shot a young dwarf for not paying them protection,' Othello said, cutting a long strip from the bed sheet using Atilla's tomahawk. 'The best we can do is dress the wound to stop the bleeding. Lift his leg for me.'

They helped Othello wrap the wound, until Atilla's leg was swathed in a thick band of white bandage. Tenderly,

Othello wiped the crusted blood away.

'I know Atilla seems as racist to humans as many humans are to the dwarves, but he has a good heart. He just has a hot head to match,' Othello murmured, propping a pillow under the sleeping dwarf's head.

They stood in silence whilst Othello dabbed at his brother's forehead.

'I think we need to discuss what happened tonight,' Sylva spoke up.

'I agree,' Fletcher said. 'But we need to get Seraph first. He deserves to know what kind of danger his family might be in.'

'I'll go,' Othello said. 'I need to get a spare uniform from my room anyway. We will need it if we are to sneak Atilla out tomorrow.'

He stomped away, followed by a dejected looking Solomon. Fletcher knew that Othello was probably holding the whole world on his shoulders at that moment.

He sat on the side of Lovett's bed, groaning with satisfaction as he relieved his tired feet. He stroked Sariel's head absentmindedly and she responded with a rumble of appreciation. Grinning, he scratched her beneath the chin the way Ignatius liked. She rubbed back and yipped with pleasure.

'Um, Fletcher,' Sylva stuttered.

Fletcher looked up and saw that she was blushing, her face and neck flushing with scarlet.

'Sorry . . . didn't think,' he blurted, pulling his hand away.

She stood for a moment, then sighed and sat down on the bed next to him.

'I never thanked you,' she muttered, twisting her hands together.

'For what?' Fletcher asked, confused.

'For following me. If you hadn't . . . Grindle might have caught me again.'

'I don't know; I think Grindle might have been in for a bit of a surprise. You said Sariel was worth ten men, that makes it an even fight. If it hadn't been for you, we could be in the middle of a civil war right now. You made the right call.'

Valens buzzed excitedly and nudged Fletcher's hand.

'I think Captain Lovett wants to know what's going on. Tell her what happened in Valentius Square and I'll let her know what went down tonight.'

The story took some telling; Othello and Seraph arrived by the time they had finished it. Seraph was still in his pyjamas and squinted in the light.

'Othello filled me in on the way,' Seraph said, staring at Atilla and Lovett's unconscious bodies. 'I just have one question. Why would the Forsyths hire Grindle to kill you that night in Corcillum, but also want to be your friend?'

Sylva stood and chewed on her lip.

'I always thought they wanted my friendship so that they could supply the elves with weapons should an alliance be on the cards,' she said, pacing around the room. 'But what makes me their enemy? Why would they want me dead?'

'I think the real question is, why would they want you executed publicly,' Othello said matter of factly. 'They could have killed you at any time. Why make such a statement?'

'To incite a war between the elves and Hominum,' Seraph suggested. 'A real one. That would increase the demand for weapons and keep their business afloat, even with the dwarves competing with them.'

Fletcher felt a wave of disgust. Starting a war, for profit?

'So they want the best of both worlds . . .' he muttered. 'If the elves ally with Hominum, the Forsyths plan to secure a weapons contract through their fake friendship with Sylva. But they would prefer a war because it would make them more money. They didn't abandon you at the market, Sylva, they led you right into Grindle's arms!'

'Don't say I told you so . . .' Sylva stared at her feet.

The room went silent, only broken by Valens's angry buzzing as he flitted to and fro.

'Those evil little prigs!' Seraph growled. 'I knew they were up to something but this . . . this is treason!'

'We can't prove anything!' Fletcher cursed, clenching his fists together. 'In fact, if we tell the King the whole story, he is more likely to think it was the dwarves committing treason, what with the war council and all.'

'It doesn't matter,' Sylva announced. 'Their plan is ruined now. I will write to my father tonight and tell him that the Forsyths are not to be trusted. The plot to start a civil war with the dwarves has been foiled and I am relatively safe at Vocans. There is nothing they can do to harm us now.'

'Yes, there is,' Seraph cautioned. 'The tournament. If one of the Forsyths wins, they will become high-ranking officers and gain a seat on the King's council. That's an extra vote for Zacharias and another voice speaking out against my family, not to mention the elves and the dwarves.'

Othello nodded, then scratched his beard contemplatively. 'Let's not forget that the most powerful people in Hominum will be watching it; the nobles and the generals,' he said, pacing back and forth. 'They will be deciding if the elves and the dwarves are worthy allies, then reporting back to the King. We can be sure the Forsyths will be doing everything they can to discredit and embarrass us during the tournament too.'

'Then we beat them!' Fletcher jumped to his feet. 'Who says we can't win the tournament ourselves? We have a Golem, a Barkling, a Canid and a Salamander!'

Seraph shook his head.

'We aren't as powerful as them. Even the second year commoners will have an advantage over us. How are we supposed to win?'

Fletcher took a deep breath and looked him right in the eye.

'We train.'

45

A heavy mist hung around the castle, fading the horizon into a shadowed whiteness. It gave Fletcher and Atilla the cover they needed as they hobbled down the road outside.

'I hope Uhtred makes it in time,' Fletcher said. 'Rook will be suspicious if I don't turn up for his lesson.'

'He'll be here. You said Valens delivered the pick-up instructions just fine,' Atilla replied. He was ashen faced, but had recovered enough to walk, even if with a pronounced limp.

They had managed to sneak out of the castle with barely any trouble. Tarquin had made a snide comment as they passed on the stairs, asking if the dwarf was limping because someone had stepped on him that morning. Fortunately, with Othello's spare uniform and some quick braiding of Atilla's beard, the twin dwarves were indistinguishable.

Fletcher's heart leaped in his chest as a shadow darkened the mist in front of them.

'It's OK. That's my father,' Atilla grunted.

A boar emerged from the fog, pulling a chariot behind it. The rider wore a hood, but Uhtred's bulky figure was unmistakeable.

'Get on, quickly. It is not safe out here,' Uhtred said, pulling the chariot to a halt beside them. Fletcher helped Atilla sprawl at his father's feet.

'The dwarves are in your debt. If you need anything, anything at all, just ask,' Uhtred rumbled, flicking the boar's reins and turning them around.

'Wait! I have something to say,' Atilla announced.

Fletcher turned back, wary of being late for Rook's lesson that would be starting any minute.

'Thank you. I owe you my life. Tell Othello . . . I was wrong.'

With those parting words, they disappeared into the mist, until all Fletcher could hear was the echoing clop of the boar's hooves.

Fletcher was late. When he arrived in the summoning room, both Rook and Arcturus were there waiting for him, with the rest of the students standing in silence before them. Fletcher noticed that Arcturus was wearing an eye patch. Fletcher couldn't help but smile. With his tricorn hat, Arcturus looked like a pirate captain.

'Wipe that grin from your face, boy. Do you think your time is more valuable than our own?' Rook snapped, waving him over to the other noviciates.

'I'm sorry, sir,' Fletcher said, standing with the others.

'I will deal with him later, Rook,' Arcturus said. 'But perhaps we should get on with the lesson.'

'Yes, perhaps we should,' Rook said dryly, stepping forward. 'With the tournament coming up, we think it is time to demonstrate how a duel works. Now, Arcturus here believes that learning to duel another battlemage is a useless practice—'

'The orc shamans rarely duel,' Arcturus cut Rook off. 'It is unlikely that you will ever go toe-to-toe with one. They prefer to hide in the shadows and send their demons to do the fighting for them.'

'A strategy that has served them well in the past. I suspect our battlemage attrition rate is several times what theirs is, but the fact that we fight on the front lines and put ourselves in harm's way is why we are winning this war,' Rook countered.

'But that is not duelling, Inquisitor. That is using our abilities to protect and support the soldiers,' Arcturus retorted.

'Yet we use the same skills, do we not?' Rook mused, rubbing his chin in mock pensiveness.

Fletcher was surprised that the two teachers could argue like this in front of their students. If there was any doubt before, this confirmed it; there was no love lost between the two men.

Arcturus sighed and turned to the students.

'Regardless of my opinions on the tournament, it has been a tradition since the battlemage school was founded, two thousand years ago. Usually it would take four years of training before you were allowed to compete in the tournament. Last year, it was reduced to two. Now, it is one. We are lucky, in that all of you have been very fast learners. For most novices it takes two years to learn how to perform a basic shield spell. Even you, Fletcher, are ahead of the game. There are plenty of second years who will be unable to form a decent shield.'

Fletcher blushed at being singled out, but felt better. At least he wasn't going to come last in the tournament.

'Now, watch closely,' Arcturus said, etching the shield symbol in the air and fixing it in place above his index finger. He blasted wyrdlight through it and formed a thick, opaque oval shield in front of him.

'A shield is always stronger when you brace against the impact of whatever is coming your way,' he lectured, crouching slightly and crossing his forearms in the shape of an X. 'When defending against an attack spell, the blow has a . . . violent effect.'

'Are you ready?' Rook asked lazily, holding up a glowing finger.

'I a—'

Light flared in the room as Rook whipped a lightning spell at Arcturus, crackling the air with forks of electric rays. He had been so fast, Fletcher barely saw his finger move.

The shield cracked like ice on a lake, emitting loud, sharp snaps with every fracture. Arcturus's face contorted with effort as he fed more mana to the shield, opaque threads flowing like silk to cover the damage. The force of Rook's blast pushed Arcturus back, his feet sliding over the leather.

Arcturus extended a finger from his other hand and stirred the air, then with a roar he uncrossed his arms and fired a kinetic blast around the side of the shield.

Rook was sent flying back, slamming into the wall and sliding to the ground.

'That is why a shield spell is the first thing you should do when entering a duel. You may get them on the back foot by attacking first. But if you don't beat them with that first shot, they just need to get one attack spell off whilst you're distracted and it's over. To attack without a shield is an all-or-nothing

335

move.' Arcturus smiled and the shield dissipated. The light was sucked back into his finger with a soft swish.

'It's best to recover the mana from your shield where possible, especially for those of you with low-level demons. You will need all the mana you can get if you want to last the tournament.'

Fletcher heard Rory curse under his breath behind him.

'That was a cheap shot!' Rook snarled, brushing himself off.

'You have been away from the front lines for far too long, Rook,' Arcturus laughed, twirling his moustache. 'Even a second lieutenant knows that you need to put a shield up if your first attack doesn't work. It is bullheaded to think otherwise, if you'll pardon the pun.'

'We'll see what you think of bullheadedness when my Minotaur has its claws around your Canid's throat,' Rook snarled, taking a step towards Arcturus.

The two men glared at each other, their hate unmistakable. They reminded Fletcher of rival hunting dogs, straining at their leashes to attack one another. If the noviciates had not been in the room, Fletcher was sure there would have been an illegal duel taking place there and then.

'Class dismissed!' Rook snapped, striding from the room. 'It's not like any of you will catch anything before the tournament anyway. Useless, the lot of you!'

Fletcher caught Rory grinning. Despite Rook's best efforts, the nobles were yet to come close to capturing new demons. Even with the charging stone, their scrying ability was too poor to control their demons effectively. On the other hand, the commoners could now handle their demons with ease, sending them running and leaping over the obstacle course they had set up in the corner of the summoning room. Fletcher was good, but his small scrying crystal hampered him. He pulled it from his pocket and scrutinised it.

'You heard him; out, everyone!' Arcturus growled. 'Not you, Fletcher. Come here.'

Fletcher slowly walked up to him, waiting to be berated for being late. Instead, Arcturus laid a hand on his shoulder.

'Let me see that scrying stone.'

Fletcher handed it to him without a word.

'You won't win the tournament with this. There are challenges, Fletcher, which will require extensive scrying. I can't lend you my stone; I'm not allowed to show you any favour and even if I wanted to, Rook is watching me too closely. Sort it out.'

Arcturus dropped the crystal back into Fletcher's hand and looked him in the eye.

'That's the difference between a good warrior and a great one. Rook fought hard, but he lost that battle. Don't fight hard. Fight smart.'

46

The blow came thrumming through the air, slipping past Fletcher's guard and slamming into his collarbone with a painful crunch.

'Again!' Sir Caulder growled, kicking out at Fletcher's shin with his peg leg before swinging another blow at his head. This time, Fletcher caught the blow with his wooden sword, heaving it aside and kneeing Sir Caulder in the stomach.

The old man collapsed, wheezing on the sand of the arena.

'Fletcher!' Sylva shouted from the sidelines. 'Be careful.'

Sir Caulder held up his hand and slowly got to his feet.

'It's all right, Sylva,' he wheezed, rubbing his stomach. 'A warrior should never hesitate at an opening. Heaven knows the enemy won't.'

'Didn't you hit Sir Caulder in the face just ten minutes ago?' Fletcher teased.

'That was different . . .' Sylva replied with a rueful smile.

A yell came from behind them. Fletcher turned to see Othello on top of Seraph, their weapons forgotten on the ground.

'No no no; you need to learn finesse!' Sir Caulder groaned at them. 'You can't just lay into each other until one of you has had enough.'

The two boys got to their feet, grinning sheepishly. A yellow bruise was blossoming on Seraph's face and Othello's lip was swollen like a ripe plum.

'If you went to the trouble of having Uhtred carve us wooden weapons for practice, you should probably use them,' Fletcher laughed, eyeing the discarded wooden battle-axe and broadsword.

'We just got a bit overexcited,' Othello admitted, picking up his axe and brushing the sand off.

He swung it with practised ease, spinning it in the air before slamming it into the sand beside him.

'Well, you've improved a lot since we started training, I'll give you that,' Sir Caulder conceded. 'But Sylva and Fletcher have already advanced to an exceptional level of swordsmanship. I expect you two might be a match for some of the nobles by now, but it will take a lot more work to surpass them. Good is not good enough.'

Sir Caulder glared at the pair for a while longer, then stomped off towards the arena exit.

'Sparring lessons are done for today. You can practise your spellcraft down here if you like, I won't stop you.'

The clack of his peg leg against stone faded until he had left the arena.

'Well, that's the most praise I've heard out of him,' Seraph observed, picking his broadsword up from the ground. 'Still, plenty of time to improve; we have a couple of months yet. I'm more worried about next week's demonology exam. With all this training, I fall asleep as soon as I open my books!'

'We'll be fine,' Othello insisted. 'I'm yet to see a noble set foot in the library and even Rory, Genevieve and Atlas spend most of their time in Corcillum. If we fail, everyone else will too.'

'So, shall we practise some spellcraft?' Sylva said, stepping on to the sand and flaring a ball of wyrdlight. 'Why don't you try a fireball this time, Fletcher. I'll throw up a shield over there and you can use it as target practice.'

Fletcher felt his cheeks flush red, embarrassed at his inability to produce even the most basic of shields. He could blast out a wave of fire, telekinesis or even lightning, which was effective, but wasted a lot of mana. To his chagrin, he still struggled to shape them into a beam or even a ball. Powering a glyph and the spell itself at the same time was too much to hold in his head at once. That being said, he was slowly improving, if not at the rate he had hoped for.

'You guys go ahead, you're far more advanced than me. I'll just practise on the sidelines where I won't get in the way . . .'

'OK, if that's what you want,' Sylva said with disappointment. 'Boys, why don't you try and hit a moving target?'

She hurled a large ball of wyrdlight into the air, sending it zigzagging around the room in a random pattern. Othello laughed and etched the fire symbol, unleashing a tongue of flame that he shaped into a fireball and sent speeding after the blue light. Seraph was not far behind.

Fletcher sat dejectedly on the steps, etching the fire symbol over and over again in the air. He had shaved off some time with his etching, able to form a glyph quicker than any of the others. But that was where it ended. He trickled through some mana and watched as a fan of flame roiled out. With a colossal effort, he compacted it into a rough ball. He looked at it in surprise, then hurled it at the wyrdlight before his concentration broke.

It shot past the spinning blue sphere, grazing the edge and snuffing it out of existence.

'Yeah!' Fletcher yelled, punching the air.

Behind him, a slow clap echoed from the arena entrance.

'Well done, Fletcher, you managed a spell,' Isadora taunted. 'Why, you actually performed one of the most basic of abilities required of a battlemage. Your parents must be so proud. Oh . . . wait.'

Fletcher turned, his elation immediately replaced with outrage. Isadora gave him a dainty wave, skipping down the arena steps. Fletcher was surprised to see the seven other first years, trailing behind her into the arena.

'So as you can see, we were right.' Tarquin pointed an accusatory finger at Sylva, Othello, Fletcher and Seraph. 'They are training here, in secret!'

'That's why you're never in the common room,' Genevieve exclaimed, tossing her hair with surprise. 'You always say you're in the library.'

'We are,' Fletcher tried to placate her. 'We just come here afterwards, to practise our swordplay with Sir Caulder. Remember, he offered private tuition to all of us in our first lesson.'

'That didn't look like sword practice to me,' Atlas said, pointing at the empty space above the arena where Fletcher's fireball had snuffed out Sylva's wyrdlight. 'Sir Caulder isn't even here.'

'Why didn't you tell us?' Rory stammered. 'You never give me a straight answer when I ask what you've been up to.'

Fletcher had no answer for that. It had felt wrong to not include the others. But it would have been too hard to explain, too high a risk of Tarquin and Isadora finding out about what they were doing. Not that it had helped in the end.

'Why would they hide it from you?' Tarquin pondered aloud with a theatrical air. 'Perhaps because . . . no, they wouldn't. Would they?'

'What do you mean?' asked Genevieve, her bottom lip trembling.

'Well, I'm sorry to say, but it looks as if the other commoners are training in secret to beat you,' Tarquin theorised, shaking his head with mock disgust. 'I mean, they haven't a hope of beating us nobles, let's be reasonable here. But, if they can embarrass you three in the arena, it might just snag them a commission.'

'That's a goddamn lie!' Fletcher yelled, leaping to his feet and rounding on Tarquin. 'And if you think we can't beat you, you're more arrogant than I thought.'

'Why don't we do it right now?' Tarquin brought his face an inch from Fletcher's. 'We're in the arena. Plenty of spectators. What do you say?'

Fletcher seethed, his hands itching with violent intent.

'Plenty of *witnesses*, more like,' Sylva interrupted, pulling Fletcher back from the brink. 'So that everyone can say they saw Fletcher duel and he can get expelled. Don't you care about your own career?'

'Scipio would never expel me,' Tarquin snapped at her, venom dripping from his words. 'It's an empty threat. My father is the King's best friend; it would never get that far. As for a common bastard like Fletcher . . .'

But Fletcher was on to his game now. He wouldn't give Tarquin the satisfaction.

'You'll get your duel, in good time. When I can beat you with everyone watching. We'll see who's the better summoner then.'

Tarquin smiled and leaned in, until Fletcher could feel the noble's breath in his ear.

'I look forward to it.'

Tarquin swept out of the room, followed by the rest of the nobility. For a moment Rory hesitated, his face filled with indecision. Atlas lay a hand on his shoulder.

'They were caught in the act, Rory. We should have known not to trust the likes of them. A wannabe noble, a bastard, an elf and a half-man. You don't need friends like them.'

Fletcher bristled at the jibe, then realised that by calling Seraph a 'wannabe noble', Atlas must have overheard Seraph and him talking in the common room.

'You've been eavesdropping, Atlas,' Fletcher said. 'That was a private conversation.'

'Oh yes, I've heard a lot of things these past few weeks. Who do you think told Tarquin and Isadora about your extracurricular activities?'

'Sneak,' Seraph spat, kicking the sand in anger. 'What did he promise you?'

'A commission in the Forsyth Furies, if I play my cards right. You two should do the same,' he said, turning to Rory and Genevieve.

'You would trust those two snakes?' Fletcher cried. 'They're

343

lying to you and they'll do the same to Rory and Genevieve. Don't do this, please!'

But it was too late, their minds were made up. One by one, they turned their backs on him and walked away. Until the four were alone once again.

47

Sweat dripped from Fletcher's brow as he etched the shield symbol in the air in front of him. He fixed it in place, twirling his finger and watching as it followed his every movement.

'Good. Now the hard part,' Sylva instructed, her voice echoing in the empty space of the arena. Seraph watched him from the sidelines, having finished his training for the day.

His mind felt like it would split in two as he tried to regulate a flow of mana both to and through the symbol at once. He was rewarded by a thin stream of white light that hung in the air before him.

'That's enough for now, Fletcher. Shape it.'

It was easy to pull the fluid into an opaque disk, countless hours of wyrdlight practice finally paying off. It was thinly spread and would shatter after a few sword blows, but it was enough for now.

Fletcher sucked the shield back through his finger and felt his body suffuse with mana once again. With the tournament just hours away, it would not do to waste any of his mana reserves.

'Well done, Fletcher! You can do it on almost every try. You'll be better than some of the second years by now,' Sylva encouraged.

'I don't care about where I come in the tournament,' Fletcher moaned. 'I only care about beating Isadora and Tarquin. They can flash up a shield in a few seconds and theirs are twice as thick as mine. It's the same with all the attack spells as well. Consistency, speed and power, that's what Arcturus said matters. They beat me at all three.'

Sylva gave him a sympathetic smile and squeezed his shoulder.

'If you come up against them, they will need to use more mana to beat you, which gives us a better chance. Seraph, Othello and I have caught up with them after all this training. We would never have been able to do that without your help, especially the sword practice. Even Malik says that you're a good swordsman, and the Saladins are reputed to be the best fencers in the land!'

Fletcher gave her a weak smile and went to sit beside Seraph. It was almost midnight, but Othello had asked them to wait for him in the arena. He had disappeared just a few hours before, on mysterious business in Corcillum.

The past few months had been gruelling, filled with constant practice and study. Their demonology exam had come and gone, which all of them had passed with flying colours. Fletcher wasn't sure what had hurt his wrist more, the incessant sword training or the endless hours of scribbling essays during their daylong exams.

He could have borne the past few months with relative ease, were it not for the coldness that he, Sylva, Seraph and Othello had received from their former friends. Despite their attempts to make peace with them, Rory, Genevieve and Atlas were still upset, eating separately at breakfast and avoiding them wherever possible.

'Ah, they're still here,' Othello's voice came from behind them. 'We have company, everyone. Step lively now and welcome some old friends.'

Fletcher turned to see Othello, Athol and Atilla standing behind them. He leaped to his feet and was immediately wrapped in a bear hug, Athol's strong arms picking him up as if he were no heavier than a child.

'I thought Othello said he was going to pick up my order tomorrow!' Fletcher laughed. Atilla smiled awkwardly from a few feet away and gave him a respectful nod.

'True friends of the dwarves get personal delivery,' Athol boomed, releasing him. 'Atilla has been working day and night on your request. Now that his leg has healed, he thought he would come along as well.'

'Aye, it was delicate work, but a joy to make,' Atilla said, holding his handiwork up to the light.

Fletcher had first thought of it after his talk with Arcturus. The scrying stone he'd been given was only useful when Fletcher held it close to his eye. Arcturus's eye patch had given him the idea of fixing it in place there, leaving his hands free.

'I realised your idea for a monocle wouldn't work as soon as I started, Fletcher. It would become dislodged if you ever had to fight whilst wearing it. But you said your idea came from a teacher's eye patch. So I filed your crystal down until it was transparent, mounted it in silver and attached a strap to it instead. Try it for yourself.'

The leather strap of the eyeglass fitted snugly around Fletcher's head, with the scrying stone sitting just in front of his left eye. He could see through it almost perfectly, although the left side of his vision now had a slight purple tinge.

'It's perfect! Thank you so much!' Fletcher cried, marvelling at the clarity. If he were to scry, he would literally be able to see things from Ignatius's point of view, at the same time being free to act as he chose.

'Can I get one of those?' Seraph asked with a hint of jealousy. 'I would never have thought of that.'

'Too late now,' Atilla replied, pulling his beard at the compliment. 'But if you have the coin and the crystal, I would be happy to start right away.'

'Hmmm, I need my stone for tomorrow. But I may take you up on that soon.' Seraph pulled out his own shard of crystal and looked at it with disappointment.

'Very impressive,' Sylva said, yawning as she walked up the stairs. 'But the tournament is in the morning and I need a good night's sleep. Are you coming, Seraph?'

'Yeah, I need my beauty sleep if I'm going to win Isadora's heart tomorrow,' Seraph joked, giving Fletcher a parting wink as he followed her. 'Goodnight all!'

After their footsteps had faded down the corridor, Athol cleared his throat and gave Othello an apprehensive look.

'Right, there is one more item of business to discuss, Othello. Atilla has a new tattoo, to cover the scar on his leg. I know you hate doing this, but I've brought the tattooing kit in case you want the same. After the failed attack, the Pinkertons are more aggressive than ever.'

Othello groaned as Athol pulled out several thick needles and a pot of black ink from his pack.

'No! Not this time. I have come to realise that taking the blame for Atilla has only served to make him live a life without consequences. If anything, his near-death experience probably taught him more life lessons in one night than he has had in his entire fifteen years of existence. Is that not so, Atilla?' Othello observed, nodding pointedly at Fletcher.

'I was wrong about humans,' Atilla mumbled, looking at his feet. 'But that does not change the many atrocities we have suffered at their hands. I have realised it is not their race that I hate, but the system that we live in.'

'And if we are to change that system, we must do so from within.' Othello gripped Atilla by the shoulder. 'Will you enlist in Vocans next year? I cannot do this alone, brother.'

Atilla looked up, his eyes burning with determination.

'I will.'

Othello laughed with joy and slapped Atilla on the back.

'Excellent! Let me show you my room. Can your leg manage the stairs?'

The twins left arm in arm, Othello helping Atilla limp up past the steps and out of the arena. Their cheerful voices echoed down the corridor, leaving Fletcher alone with Athol.

'How things change,' Fletcher murmured.

'Aye. It does my heart good to see them back as friends,' Athol said, wiping a tear from his eye. 'They were inseparable as youngsters, always getting into mischief.'

'Atilla's heart is in the right place,' Fletcher said, thinking of his own hate for the Forsyths. 'I do not know if I would be so forgiving.'

'It is not in a dwarf's nature to forgive,' Athol sighed, sitting down and lifting one of the tattooing needles to the light. 'We can be as stubborn as mules, myself included. Not Othello, though. I remember back when Othello volunteered to be tested by the Inquisition, and I told him that he was joining the enemy. Do you know what he replied?'

'No, what did he say?' Fletcher asked.

'He said that a warrior's greatest enemy can also be his greatest teacher. That young dwarf has wisdom beyond his years.'

Fletcher contemplated those words, once again feeling a deep admiration for Othello. Dame Fairhaven had said something similar: *know thy enemy*. But what could he learn from the Forsyths, or Didric? Perhaps if he had access to James Baker's book, he could learn something from the orcs. Annoyingly, it was yet to return from the printers, who were having trouble carving wooden presses for the intricate diagrams that adorned each page. Though it mostly concerned the anatomy of demons that lived in the orc side of the ether, it was impossible to know what other useful observations Baker had inscribed in those pages.

'You don't want a tattoo, do you? I did Othello and Atilla's, so I know what I'm doing,' Athol half joked.

'No, it's not my style,' Fletcher said, laughing. 'No offence, but I think they look quite brutish. I've even seen an orc . . .'

He froze. In his mind's eye, he saw the albino orc raising his hand, the pentacle flashing violet on his palm. Could it really be that simple?

'You saw an orc with tattoos?' Athol said slowly, confused by Fletcher's abrupt silence.

'It was a dream . . .' Fletcher murmured, tracing his finger over the palm of his left hand.

Fletcher drew his khopesh and began to sketch the outline of a hand in the arena's sand. His heart beat madly in his chest at the thought of what he was about to do.

'I hope you're as good as you say you are, Athol,' Fletcher voiced. 'I need this tattoo to be perfect.'

48

It was blazing hot in the arena, made more so by the dozens of torches that Sir Caulder had ensconced in the walls. The sand the noviciates stood on seemed to stir and shift in the flickering light.

'Are there really only twenty-four of us? I thought there would be more,' Seraph whispered in Fletcher's ear.

'No, that's it. Twelve first years and twelve second years, with an equal number of commoners and nobles,' Fletcher replied, in a terse voice.

He did not feel like talking. Each beat of his heart made his left hand throb with pain. It had not been a pleasant experience with Athol the night before, and he had not been able to test his theory yet. The dwarf had told him to let his hand heal as much as possible before he tried anything.

'Eyes front!' Sir Caulder barked from behind them, making the students jump. 'Show your respect for Hominum's Generals.'

Fletcher stood a little straighter as the corridor into the arena darkened. First came the generals, resplendent in smart uniforms of blue velvet, edged with gold thread that ran from their sleeves up to their epaulettes. Their chests were adorned with a plethora of medals and tassels and they clutched their bicorn hats tightly to their sides as they walked stiff-legged down the steps. These were hard men, with faces that spoke of weary experience. They did not speak, but instead raked their eyes over the cadets as if they were horses at auction.

'If they're impressed, they commission us directly after the tournament to fight in the King's army,' Seraph murmured out of the corner of his mouth. 'The pay's not as good, but they promote faster than the noble battalions do, because of the higher attrition rate. Filling dead men's shoes and all that.'

'Silence in the ranks!' Sir Caulder snapped, limping to the front and daring them to break silence. 'Stand to attention. If I see you move an inch I'll make you wish you hadn't!'

But Fletcher was not listening. A man had ducked into the arena and was staring at him. The family resemblance was unmistakeable. Zacharias Forsyth.

Zacharias was not as Fletcher had imagined. He had pictured a man with cold, serpentine features. Instead, Zacharias was tall and brawny, with half his ear missing and a confident grin. He flicked his eyes away from Fletcher and on to his children, who were standing side by side.

'Come now, Sir Caulder, let the cadets relax. There will be plenty of time for all that ceremony later,' Zacharias said in a deep, cheerful voice. He stepped on to the sand and embraced his two children, mussing up Tarquin's hair and giving Isadora a kiss on the cheek.

For some reason, it confused Fletcher to see this. It seemed strange to think that anyone could adore Tarquin and Isadora, even if he was their father.

'And who's this strapping young lad?' Zacharias boomed, stepping in front of Fletcher and looking him up and down, noting his shaggy black hair and the khopesh at Fletcher's side.

'It's the bastard, Father; the one with the Salamander,' Tarquin drawled, looking at Fletcher with disdain.

'Indeed?' Zacharias said, staring deeply into Fletcher's eyes. The smile remained fixed on Zacharias's face, but Fletcher saw something stir behind the man's eyes. Something dark and ugly that made him want to shudder.

'It will be interesting to see what your demon can do. Why, I bet it could burn a man's shoulder to the bone, if it were so inclined.' The smiling mask remained, but Fletcher would not let himself be intimidated by the brute of a man.

'It can, and it has,' Fletcher replied, setting his jaw. 'Perhaps I could give you a demonstration some time.'

Zacharias's smile wavered, then he laid a hand on Fletcher's shoulder and pointed at the arena steps, which were filling with more nobles, all in varying uniforms and colours, representative of their personal battalions. Others had joined Zacharias on the sand, hugging their children and talking loudly, much to Sir Caulder's annoyance.

'It will be nice for you to have your family here to support you. Why don't you wave hello to your father?'

Fletcher froze. Was Berdon here? It couldn't be! But no, Zacharias was pointing to a grey-haired man and woman, who were staring at Fletcher with a look of pure hatred.

'I took the liberty of informing the Favershams about your

claims,' Zacharias said, his eyes filled with malice. 'Even the King has taken a special interest in your case. After all, you have accused Lord Faversham of being unfaithful to the King's cousin once again, so many years after all the troubles with Arcturus and the other bastards.'

'I claimed no such thing!' Fletcher fumed. 'I would never—'

'I invited them to join me and see you for themselves, I hope you don't mind. Arcturus has been sent away so he doesn't run into his father and stepmother, part of the terms of his agreement with the old King. That leaves Rook in charge of the tournament. An old family friend, don't you know. I'm sure he will take great pains to make sure everything is as fair as possible.'

Zacharias winked at Fletcher, then left the pit to take a seat with the other nobles, but not before flashing a shark-like grin at Sylva and Othello. Fletcher shook with rage, balling his hands into fists despite the pain that throbbed through his left hand.

'Don't let him faze you, Fletcher,' Seraph whispered. 'We're going to wipe the floor with the Forsyths.'

'Sit down, sit down, everyone!' Scipio bellowed, ducking out of the corridor and walking down the steps of the arena, followed by a smirking Rook. He nodded and waved to generals and nobles alike. As the spectators took their seats, a hush fell on the arena.

'So: another year, another fresh crop of cadets, ready to test their mettle in the arena,' Scipio said, throwing his arms wide and beaming at the students. 'This year is a rather unusual affair. Traditionally, there would only be a dozen or so candidates, with duels by knockout to determine a winner. But this year, we have extended the opportunity to both first and second years, leaving us with twenty-four candidates to sort through. I will leave you in the capable hands of Inquisitor Rook to explain the new rules of the tournament for you all.'

Scipio stepped away and took a seat at the very front of the arena steps, his job done.

'Thank you, Provost. I would like to take this opportunity to thank you all for coming; I know your time is precious. Every minute away from the front lines is a minute your soldiers are without your fine leadership. To speed things up, I have decided that there shall be a three-way battle in the first round, where only one candidate will proceed to the next. It will not be a traditional duel; but more shall be revealed later.'

There were murmurs of curiosity from the watching crowd, but there was no disagreement. Rook allowed the noise to die down, then continued.

'The following round will be the traditional knockout between two cadets, but with no spellcraft or demons allowed. Historically, the combatants in the tournament rarely come to blows, preferring to hurl spells at each other or let their demons do the fighting for them. It seems a shame to waste the years of sword training your children have had, even before coming to the academy. The second round will showcase this important skill.'

This time, there were nods of agreement from the nobles in the stands, but the generals seemed less happy with the arrangement, pursing their lips and shaking their heads at each other.

'I must object. This gives an unfair advantage to the noble children, who will have all had private tuition in swordplay,' one of the generals said, addressing Scipio directly. 'We would prefer a fair assessment of the cadets' abilities.'

'Perhaps you would prefer us to handicap the nobles, simply because they are better prepared?' Rook replied with a hint of sarcasm. 'Have they not also had some training in spellcraft before arriving at Vocans too? Maybe we should limit the tests to the demonology exam?'

Scipio stood and turned to the general who had spoken.

'I'm afraid I must agree with Inquisitor Rook. I too took issue with this change at first, but I soon remembered one thing. War is unfair – the weak fail and the strong survive. If the tournament is unbalanced, does it not provide a more accurate representation of true battle?'

'I have also put a measure in place that will allow an equal number of nobles and commoners to make it to the second round,' Rook announced. 'Commoners and nobles will not compete with each other in the three-way battle, as the groups will not be mixed. Does that satisfy you?'

'It does, Inquisitor. Thank you.' The general took his seat once again, although his brow remained furrowed.

'Good. Rounds three and four shall be traditional duels, so I assume there will be no disagreement there. Now, the arena must be prepared for the first round,' Rook said, rubbing his hands together. 'Sir Caulder! Take the cadets to their cells!'

49

Fletcher sat in the darkness of the prison cell, his heart fluttering beneath his ribs like a caged bird. He had hoped that he would be able to watch the tournament, but the rules stated that all combatants were to be kept separate. It felt like hours had passed, and the anticipation was torture.

He stared at his hand, tracing the deep black lines that Athol had drawn. In the centre of his palm lay a pentacle, the five-pointed star within a circle. If this worked as he had planned, he would be able to summon and infuse Ignatius simply by pointing his hand, rather than positioning the demon above a summoning leather. He wasn't too sure how much that would help him in a battle though.

He had left his index finger blank, so that he would be able to etch with it as normal, in case he needed to use another spell. The other fingertips had been tattooed with the four battle symbols of telekinesis, fire, lightning and shield. With any luck, he could shoot mana through each finger without ever having to etch a symbol in the air.

A sudden buzz startled him and Valens hovered into view, gliding through the cage bars and settling on his lap.

'Come to watch, Captain Lovett?' Fletcher asked, stroking the beetle's smooth shell.

Valens waggled his antennae and buzzed cheerfully. Somehow, it made Fletcher feel better.

'I hope you do watch. It will be nice to have someone cheering for me. Or buzzing.'

Footsteps rang out in the corridor and the beetle shot away, secreting himself in a dark corner of the room.

'Fletcher.'

It was Sir Caulder, staring at him through the bars of his cell. 'You're up.'

Fletcher stood on a wooden platform on the edge of the arena, with his back to the spectators. A large summoning leather was spread in front of him. Both Rory and a second year commoner named Amber stood on their own platforms, at equal distances on either side of him. He could feel the Favershams' eyes on him, prickling the hairs on the back of his neck. Rory's gaze was also laden with malice, as if their return to the arena had reminded him of Fletcher's apparent betrayal. With a shake of his head, Fletcher forced himself to ignore them and turned back to the task at hand.

The battleground had been filled with large, jagged rocks, as if an enormous red boulder had been shattered and scattered across the sand. In the very centre, a giant clay pillar stood, at around thirty feet high. A spiral pathway from the base to the top was wrapped around it like a snake, wide enough to accommodate a horse.

He heard an almost imperceptible hum above his head and looked up. Valens had just flown by, circling around the arena before settling on the concave ceiling, blending into its shadows. Fletcher smiled. Lovett had the best view in the house.

'The rules of this challenge are simple,' Rook declared from the sidelines. 'The first demon to reach the top of the pillar and remain there for ten seconds will win. You will only use the telekinesis spell. You cannot attack your fellow cadets. You cannot leave your platform. If you do, it means instant elimination. Begin!'

Fletcher dropped to his knees and laid his hand on the leather, summoning Ignatius with a blast of mana. He swiped the demon's back with his scrying stone. The imp gave a chirrup of excitement and then leaped into the arena without a moment's hesitation.

Across from him, Amber had summoned a Shrike and Malachi was already zipping towards the pillar. Rook had chosen Fletcher's opponents well – flying demons, one small and hard to target; the other large but hard to knock down. This was not going to be easy.

Fletcher lifted his hand and pointed at Malachi with a tattooed finger.

'I hope this works,' he whispered to himself, flooding his body with mana.

The air shivered in a long thin streak, then Malachi was knocked out of the air, tumbling into the rocks below. It had worked!

'Go, Ignatius, now!'

The Salamander galloped through the rocks, cutting this way

and that as Rory and Amber fired at him frantically. The sand erupted around Ignatius. Rocks shattered, sending razor sharp shards exploding like shrapnel. As the demon took a flying leap for the pathway, a kinetic blast from Rory hit him hard and sent him tumbling behind a rocky outcrop near the pillar's base. Fletcher felt a dull throb of pain, but knew that Ignatius was not too badly injured.

The Shrike had already hopped to the ground, preferring to hide in the rocks than be knocked out of the sky. Fletcher took the opportunity to put on his eyeglass, before Malachi made another break for it.

He could see Ignatius was hidden beneath a concave rock, and that the pathway was close by. But if the Salamander were to run up, he would be too exposed to make it very far. Even if he made it to the top, it was unlikely he would be able to stay there for more than a few seconds.

'We need to hunt down the other demons, take them out before they get a chance to fly up there,' Fletcher murmured, sending his intentions to Ignatius. The Salamander growled in agreement, then darted to the next rock, searching from below whilst Fletcher watched from above.

Rory and Amber were also peering at their scrying stones, their eyes switching back and forth between the crystal and the sand like an angry cat's tail. Fletcher grinned, amazed at how well the eyeglass was working. He could still see with both eyes, with a ghostly, purple-tinged image overlaying his view on the left side of his vision.

Ignatius froze. The Shrike was ahead of him, crouched silently under the overhang of a large rock. It was a small Shrike, around the size of an overgrown eagle, but powerfully built, with shining plumage and fierce talons. Ignatius could take him.

'Flame,' Fletcher breathed, feeling the mana roil in his veins.

The Shrike was caught in a whirlwind of fire, crashing against the face of a rock. It cawed and fluttered its wings, but Fletcher blasted it back to the ground before it made it a few feet into the air.

'That's one cooked turkey!' Scipio shouted, as the spectators cheered and booed.

Ignatius leaped on to the smoking Shrike, clawing at it in a frenzy and stabbing with his tail like a scorpion. The Shrike raked back with a talon, gouging Ignatius's side. Ignatius screeched with pain, then reared back, ready to blast the Shrike with flame.

'No!' Amber yelled, leaping from the platform. Ignatius paused, startled by the noise.

'Don't hurt him, don't hurt him,' she cried, throwing herself over the Shrike's head.

'That's enough, Ignatius. They're out of the tournament!' Fletcher shouted.

But Fletcher was not the only one shouting. The crowd behind were roaring, and Fletcher saw that Malachi was on the top of the pillar, peeking over the far ledge.

Ignatius was already racing towards the pillar, but he wasn't going to make it in time. Fletcher fired a shot, but all it did was knock dust from the top of the pillar. The angle wasn't right. It would be a miracle if he even managed to graze Malachi.

'Ten, nine, eight . . .' Rook shouted.

Fletcher needed to do something drastic. He let the next ball of kinetic energy grow to the size of a grapefruit, gritting his teeth as he pumped it full of mana.

'. . . Seven, six, five . . .' Rook continued, barely disguising his glee.

Fletcher howled, holding the expanding ball over his head. He could feel the air above him distorting and shaking. He hesitated, his eyes fixed on Malachi's fragile frame.

'. . . Four, three, two . . .' The pace had quickened now; Rook knew what he was about to do.

Fletcher hurled the ball across the arena with all his might. The pillar's top shattered like porcelain, blasting Malachi away in a roaring maelstrom of dust and splinters of stone.

'Nooooo!' Rory yelled, jumping down and kneeling in the sand. He scooped up the broken body of Malachi from where it lay. The Mite twitched and shuddered, his six legs spasming in the air. Rory sobbed, desperately trying to etch a healing spell in the air.

'Dame Fairhaven will take care of him,' Scipio announced, as the crowd began to murmur with sympathy. Dame Fairhaven rushed over and kneeled beside Rory. She etched the heart symbol in the air and began streaming white light over the stricken demon.

'You're a monster!' Rory shouted at Fletcher. 'He's dying!'

Fletcher felt his stomach lurch as he saw a patch of dark blood where the Mite had landed in the sand.

'Come on,' Sir Caulder said, gripping him by the arm. 'There's nothing you can do for him now.'

'Let me go!' Fletcher shouted, as Sir Caulder dragged him away. 'Malachi!'

50

This time, Fletcher was left in a larger cell. It was just as dark and miserable, but he was pleased to find Othello and Sylva in the barred cells on either side. Ignatius chirruped with joy when he set sight on them.

'You made it!' Sylva cried, jumping up and grinning at him.

'Rory almost beat me to it. It was as if that challenge was designed for Mites.' Fletcher stared at the ground. He still felt guilty, and his mind lingered on Rory and Malachi. The image of the bloodstained sand flashed in his mind, and he felt a wave of nausea rush through him.

'It *was* designed for Mites. Don't you see what Rook did?' Othello growled, clutching the bars between them. 'He wanted to knock out all the powerful commoners early, by making it easier for the weak ones to beat us. If his plan had worked, the nobles would be fighting Rory, Genevieve and some of the second-year commoners with Mites in the next round. He didn't separate the commoners and nobles in the first round to be fair. He did it to make it unfair on us!'

'Well, it's a good thing he underestimated us,' Sylva replied, a look of grim determination on her face. 'I hope Seraph makes it. I saw that he was up against Atlas and a second year, when they walked past my cell.'

'More like let's hope Tarquin and Isadora *don't* make it. With Rook deciding who they fight against, somehow I doubt it,' Othello muttered darkly.

'So what's next?' Fletcher asked, watching Ignatius lick the wound in his side and wondering whether he should attempt the healing spell. 'He said something about a sword fight. Athol did me the favour of sharpening my blade last night. But what are we going to do, slice at each other until one gives up?'

'No; I asked Scipio about that last week,' Othello explained. 'The barrier spell protects the skin from being cut. It's like a very flexible shield that sheathes around your body. It will still hurt like hell, but it blunts the cut, as if a bar of metal is hitting you. Once Rook judges that you have struck a killing or maiming blow, you win.'

'Rook again. Well, at least he can't be too unfair with everyone watching,' Fletcher grumbled, scratching Ignatius under the chin.

'Hang on, I've never heard of this spell. Why haven't we learned how to use it? I know orcs tend to use blunt weapons anyway, but surely it's a game changer!' Sylva exclaimed.

'Because you need at least four powerful summoners to provide a strong enough barrier,' Othello explained. 'Some of the nobility will have to merge their mana and provide a constant stream to you throughout the battle. Other than in a tournament, the spell is almost never used. Except for when the King is on the battlefield, of course.'

'I see. Well, let's hope it works; I don't fancy getting my head cut off tonight,' Fletcher said, beckoning Ignatius to jump on to his lap.

'Here, let me heal Ignatius,' Sylva murmured, noticing Fletcher's mood.

'Don't. You need all your mana to beat the Forsyths in rounds three and four. He'll be all right,' Fletcher said, wishing he could perform one himself. Unfortunately, the healing spell glyph was usually very unstable, and Fletcher was a long way from mastering it.

'Let me have a look at it.' Fletcher lifted Ignatius closer to his face.

The scratch was shallow, far shallower than Fletcher had expected. In fact, the scratch seemed to be shrinking before his very eyes. He sat and watched with growing amazement as the cut gradually began to seal itself.

'Bloody hell,' Fletcher murmured. 'You are full of surprises.'

Ignatius purred as Fletcher traced the fresh skin with his finger.

'Someone's coming,' Othello said, shrinking back into his cell.

Sir Caulder came into view, leading a happy looking Seraph behind him.

'I still don't understand why they keep you in these cells like goddamned criminals,' Sir Caulder grumbled, unlocking the cell opposite Fletcher for Seraph. 'The least I can do is give you all some company.'

'Do you know who's fighting next?' Fletcher asked.

'Aye. It looks like none of the second years have made it to the next round. The pairs are Seraph and Tarquin, Sylva and Isadora, Othello and Rufus, Fletcher and Malik. You're going to be hard pressed to win, all of ye. Especially you, Fletcher; you're the first to fight, and Malik was trained by his father. I'll come and get you in a bit, they're just organising volunteers for Malik's barrier spell.'

He limped off, still grumbling, the clack of his peg leg echoing down the corridor.

'I'll tell you what, if we hate these cells, imagine how those prissy nobles feel,' Seraph said cheerfully.

'I take it you won then?' Fletcher asked.

'Of course. Sliver took out Barbarous with a few poison spikes from his back. Atlas was not happy! The second year's Mite just hid under a rock until it was all over. Whoever was in that last battle really did a number on that pillar! Half the thing was blown off by the time I got to it, not to mention the state of Rory's Mite! Scared the hell out of that second year!'

'Is Rory OK?' Fletcher asked, feeling another pang of guilt.

'He looked pretty miserable. Malachi was still being treated last I saw him. The losers get to sit with the rest of the spectators, so you'll see for yourself in a bit. We'll have a bit of an audience for the next round, that's for sure,' Seraph said, still grinning.

'You need to beat Isadora and Tarquin. That's what we're here for. That's why I almost killed Malachi. Get your game face on,' Fletcher snapped, rounding on Seraph.

'I'm sorry,' Seraph said. 'I didn't mean . . .'

The echo of Sir Caulder's footsteps returned, sending them all into nervous silence.

'Come on, Fletcher. You're first up,' Sir Caulder said in a gruff voice.

He unlocked the cell and, with one last look at the

others, Fletcher followed.

'Remember what I told you, Fletcher. This isn't a race, this isn't emotional. Your career is war, and this is just business. Malik knows you are impatient, that your emotions can get the better of you. Good, let him think that's how you're going to behave. Use it.'

With those parting words, Sir Caulder pushed him into the arena.

'Ah, Fletcher. Can I say, we were all very impressed with your performance in that last battle; it surprised us all!' Scipio placed his hand on Fletcher's back and propelled him on to the rock-strewn arena. 'Unusually fast etching, I didn't see your finger move at all. As for your Salamander, what a show! I'm sure a first-lieutenancy is on the cards, if one of the generals sees the same potential I do!'

Fletcher barely heard his words, instead staring at Rory's tear-streaked face as he held Malachi to his chest. The demon was flapping his wings weakly, but he appeared to be alive. Relief flooded through Fletcher like a drug.

'Rory, is he OK?' Fletcher yelled from across the arena.

'No thanks to you,' Rory yelled back. The pain in his voice was obvious, but there was no real anger there, only the remnants of fear.

'I'm sorry, Rory,' Fletcher implored, but Rory turned away, fussing over his injured demon.

Despite this, Fletcher felt a lot better. Malachi was going to be fine, and that was what mattered. Rory would come around.

It was only when he saw Malik, scimitar in hand, that he came crashing back down to reality.

'I need volunteers, to produce the barrier spell for Cadet Wulf!' Scipio declared to the crowd.

'My pleasure,' Zacharias Forsyth shouted. 'And I believe that the Favershams are also eager to help. Inquisitor Rook, would you join us?'

Fletcher blanched as the Favershams and Zacharias walked down to the edge of the arena. The couple did not bother hiding the hatred in their eyes. Was Scipio really going to allow them to be responsible for his life?

Scipio harrumphed and looked at them suspiciously.

'While I do respect your willingness to overlook the . . . complexities you have with Fletcher, Lord and Lady Faversham, I must insist that Rook remain focused on judging the tournament. No, I shall take that responsibility.'

'But my lord,' Zacharias stuttered. 'You are . . . retired, are you not?'

'The King was kind enough to send me a summoning scroll last night.' Scipio flared a wyrdlight into existence before snuffing it out with his fist. 'He feels that I will be needed on the orc front soon, and that I have been grieving for far too long. I am inclined to agree with him. I must put the death of my first demon, so many years ago now, behind me and move on. My new Felid kit is still growing, but I am sure with a powerful summoner such as yourself, we will do just fine. Now, pay us no mind, Fletcher. You will feel a slight tingling on your skin, but that is all. We shall take care of everything else.'

The four battlemages joined hands and Scipio began to sketch a complex glyph in the air.

'Go on, Fletcher,' Scipio said. 'Malik is waiting.'

51

The khopesh was slippery in Fletcher's palm. He tried not to think of what might happen if Zacharias or the Favershams decided to cut the mana off at the wrong moment. A tragic accident – that is what they would claim.

'Come on, Fletcher, we haven't got all day,' Rook sneered, walking into the centre of the arena. 'There are three more battles to get through this round.'

Fletcher ignored him and instructed Ignatius to go and sit on the steps, away from the battle. If the demon interfered, they would be disqualified.

'Begin!' Rook uttered, giving the contestants an exaggerated bow.

Fletcher took a few steps forward, trying to acclimatise to the new landscape. Whereas before they had trained on flat sand, now the place was strewn with jagged rocks and debris from the first round.

As Fletcher circled, Malik stood like a statue, watching him. The young noble had chosen his place well, an area surrounded by loose rocks where an attacker might lose his footing. Fletcher decided he would not allow him to choose their combat ground.

Instead, he looked to the tower, with its spiral pathway to the top. He remembered what Othello had said, about how the dwarves built their stairs in an anticlockwise spiral, so that the attacker's sword arm would be encumbered by the pillar when fighting downwards. By that same logic, an attacker would be equally encumbered in a clockwise pathway on their way up!

Fletcher darted to the pillar and clambered up on to the pathway. Keeping an eye on Malik, he manoeuvred himself around until he stood just below the broken stump that he had blasted a few minutes before.

'Come at me, if you dare!' Fletcher shouted, for the benefit of the spectators.

'I will not fight you on the pillar, Fletcher,' Malik's voice was calm and considered. 'Why not come down and meet me in the middle, on neutral ground?'

If impatience was supposed to be Fletcher's weakness, he would wait Malik out. He did not give a damn what the generals or nobles thought of him. But Malik did. If they were to stand at this impasse for too long, it would ruin both their reputations in the eyes of their audience. And if it was reputation that Malik cared about, Fletcher would use it to his advantage.

'So, the son of the great Baybars refuses to fight! Perhaps the apple falls far from the tree in the Saladin family.'

Malik bristled at Fletcher's words, taking an angry step forward.

'A Saladin will fight anytime, anywhere. We have fought from the desert to the trenches, into the deepest jungles of orcdom itself. I doubt you could say the same of your family.'

'So prove it! Come show me what a Saladin can do,' Fletcher goaded, twirling his khopesh in mock confidence.

Malik needed no more provocation. He raised his curved scimitar high and mounted the pathway, taking long, measured strides. Even in his anger, the boy was a natural swordsman. Fletcher hoped that the pillar would give him enough of an advantage.

The first blow came whistling around the corner, chopping at his legs. Fletcher caught it in the curve of his khopesh and turned it aside, before cutting at Malik's head. The noble ducked, leaving the blow to crunch into the pillar.

Malik stepped further out and came at him head on, feinting a crooked slice around the pillar at Fletcher's head, then sweeping again for the legs. Fletcher leaped, letting the scimitar whistle under his feet. Landing in a crouch, he punched out and caught Malik on the cheek, knocking the noble back a few paces.

They glared at each other, panting. Fletcher had felt the silky smoothness of the barrier in the punch. He ran his palm along his own hand and felt the same, but barely. It was probably only Scipio who was channelling mana correctly to it. He put it to the back of his mind. There was nothing he could do about it now.

The scimitar swung back and forth, held lightly in Malik's hand. It was not unlike a khopesh, with a curved blade and sharp point. With a flick, Malik tossed it from his right hand to his left.

'My father taught me to fight left-handed. Did Sir Caulder ever teach you that?' Malik snarled.

Fletcher ignored him, but a cold sweat trickled down his

back. With the scimitar in Malik's left hand, the pillar was no longer a barrier between them. Still, at least Fletcher had the high ground.

Malik stabbed at Fletcher's stomach, but Fletcher caught it in the curve and forced it into the ground. They struggled, chest to chest, the wooden pathway creaking under their feet.

Fletcher could feel Malik's hot breath on his face as the noble used his height and strength to lever the blade towards Fletcher's crotch. He heaved, but the sword scarcely wavered as it slowly inched upwards.

He felt the point scrape along the inside of his thigh. Was that blood he felt trickling down his leg? The blade was just an inch away now. In a few seconds, it would be buried in his flesh.

Fletcher saw his life flashing before his eyes, images of Berdon, Didric, Rotherham. His first fight. Rotherham head-butting Jakov, a man twice his size.

It clicked. Fletcher looked up to the ceiling, then whipped his head forward, smashing Malik on the bridge of the nose with his forehead. The boy stumbled, and then fell, flailing, over the side.

Malik bounced off a jagged rock, which hit him squarely in the stomach. He lay in the sand, gasping like a beached fish.

'A killing blow! The rock would have impaled him,' Fletcher shouted.

'Not in my opinion,' Rook replied with a sneer. 'It doesn't look so sharp to me. See, he's getting up already!'

Malik was indeed getting up. He glared up at Fletcher, taking deep, rattling breaths.

'Give up! You're injured, and I have the high ground!' Fletcher implored.

But Malik would not. Fletcher had pushed him too far, hurt his pride too much. The young noble raised the scimitar with a roar and sliced it into the pillar. It clattered loudly, but Fletcher saw flecks of clay come spraying off.

Malik swung again, this time with greater success. Great chunks of red clay crumbled and the platform shook under Fletcher's feet.

'*You* give up!' Malik shouted.

But there was no time for Fletcher to even reply. With a crack, the pillar began to collapse in on itself, hairline fractures spreading up the column like forked lightning.

With seconds to spare, Fletcher leaped from the top, praying for a soft landing. As he rolled into a crouch on the sand, the pillar crashed beside him, sending a maelstrom of ceramic dust into the air.

He could see nothing, the red powder coating his lips and tongue. It was hard to breath. A shadow went by on his left, then his right. Was it Rook? Or Malik?

Suddenly, Malik burst from out of the red haze, screaming in fury. He swung down hard, but Fletcher dodged aside, feeling the blade graze his forearm. Malik disappeared again, blending into the rusty gloom.

Fletcher looked at his arm. Blood welled, but it was just a scratch. He knew one thing now. This was for real – the barrier was useless. Just one lapse in concentration, and he was a dead man.

He spun around, looking for the shadow once more. A figure

moved, just out of sight. He squinted, watching, as the dull figure raised its arm. A rock came flying out of the fog, cracking him on the forehead. Stars burst across his vision, and he was on his back, staring into the billowing dust.

Fletcher swam in and out of consciousness, the edges of his vision bruising. It would be so easy to just let it all go.

A searing pain flared in the palm of his hand, bringing him back from the abyss of unconsciousness. His head lolled to the side and he saw Valens, biting into his flesh with his mandibles. Fletcher coughed and shook his hand, trying to dislodge him. The beetle gave him once last nip, than shot off into the dust, his job done.

Fletcher began to stand, but the khopesh was kicked from his hand and a foot was pressed down on his throat.

'I'm going to knock you out cold, Fletcher. Nobody disrespects the Saladins.' Malik's voice was faint, as if Fletcher was hearing it from a great distance. He needed help. Ignatius? No, he was too far away.

His hand scrabbled for a rock, anything, but all he could feel was sand. Malik raised his sword, his teeth stark white against the red dust that coated his skin. As the dust began to settle, he could see the watching crowd through the haze. Their cries of excitement reached a fever pitch.

'Good night, Fletcher.'

Fletcher hurled a handful of sand at Malik's face. The noble screamed and span away, blinded. Fletcher got to his feet unsteadily, then, with his last ounce of strength, tackled Malik to the ground. There was a thud as the noble's head slammed against a rock, then silence.

They lay there for a while, the dust settling around them like a warm cloak. It was peaceful, lying in the dirt. He barely felt the hands that lifted him to his feet, or the glass of water that was pressed to his lips. But he did hear the words that Scipio was shouting.

'Fletcher wins!'

52

'I can't do it, Fletcher. It has to be you,' Othello implored through the bars of the next cell.

The dwarf was determined. Sir Caulder had just told them they would face each other in the semi-final, and Othello was refusing to fight.

'No, Othello. I used up too much mana in the first round. I won't be able to win,' Fletcher replied.

'Well, neither will I; Rufus broke my damned leg! I was lucky to beat him at all,' Othello said, pointing at his heavily splinted shin. 'In the next round, I'm going to tap out and let you go to the final. If it came to a fight between us, you would probably beat me at this point anyway. If I disqualify myself, you don't need to use any mana in round three at all.'

'Why don't you just get Dame Fairhaven to heal it?' Fletcher asked.

'The healing spell only works for flesh wounds, remember? If you start messing about with healing bones, they fix crooked. Trust me, I've asked. I want a crack at Tarquin as much as you do, maybe even more so. But I know that I wouldn't stand a chance.'

'Look, it might not matter anyway,' Fletcher argued, pointing down the corridor. 'Tarquin may have beaten Seraph, but Sylva beat Isadora. Sylva and Tarquin are fighting right now to see who goes to the final. If she wins, I'm going to tap out. The dwarves need one of their own to make it as a finalist; it will impress the generals more. I can say I have concussion. That's half true anyway.'

He rubbed the cut on his head, where the stone had struck. The injury had almost been a blessing in a way. When Scipio saw the broken skin, he immediately realised that there had been foul play. The Provost had suggested that Zacharias and the Favershams take a break and had replaced them with more impartial nobles, who would shield Fletcher properly for the next fight.

There was a rumbling noise from Othello's cell. Solomon was groaning in distress. He paced around the cell, before stopping to stroke the splint on Othello's leg. Ignatius chirred sympathetically, lapping Fletcher's face with a wet tongue.

'I'll be fine, Ignatius. Tarquin doesn't know about the tattoos. He's going to underestimate us,' Fletcher whispered.

Sir Caulder rapped on the cage bars with his staff, making Fletcher jump.

'Come on, you two. Battle's over.'

'Did Sylva win?' Fletcher asked as Sir Caulder unlocked the cells.

'See for yourself,' the old soldier said grimly.

Dame Fairhaven and Scipio were carrying Sylva out on

a stretcher. Her arms, legs and face were black and blue, with a terrible lump on the side of her head. Sariel staggered behind them, her tail between her legs. The Canid's fur was matted with blood, and there was a nasty scratch along her side that ran from snout to tail.

'He hit Sylva with a kinetic blast,' Scipio said, glancing at their worried faces. 'She landed badly. We don't know the extent of the damage yet.'

'Poor girl, she had to fight both twins, one after the other,' Dame Fairhaven said, shaking her head. 'She used most of her mana in the first round, and then it took all her physical strength to beat Isadora, so she was exhausted when she went up against Tarquin. She put up a hell of a fight though. Nobody will go away thinking that the elves are weak,' Dame Fairhaven said, her voice laced with sympathy.

'With a head injury like this, it's not safe to heal her, especially if her skull is damaged. We're going to let her rest in the infirmary. If she wakes up, we will let you know.'

Fletcher clenched his fists, looking at the broken body on the stretcher.

'Let's go.'

Fletcher helped the dwarf limp into the arena. He remembered helping Atilla the same way; remembered the blood that trickled down his back as he carried him. The tears on Othello's face when he saw they were alive. The Forsyths were the centre of it all, like a fat spider in the centre of a web of deceit. Fletcher was going to make them pay for what they had done.

Othello could barely stand when they finally reached the sand. His face was tinged green, with beads of sweat dotting his forehead. The dwarf was right; he wouldn't last two seconds in a battle with Tarquin. Fletcher was their only hope now.

'The rules are simple,' Rook stated, striding between the two cadets. 'Demons cannot attack summoners, since the barrier spell is ineffective against demonic attack. My Minotaur will be helping to keep your demons away from your opponents, in case they get overzealous.'

It was then that Fletcher noticed the bullheaded demon, lurking behind the fallen pillar. It stood at seven feet tall, with sharp, curved horns and shaggy hair as black as his own. Its cloven hooves left round imprints in the sand as it paced back and forth, as if it couldn't keep its rage in check. Its hands would have been identical to a man's, were it not for the thick, black claws that jutted from its fingers. A pair of red-rimmed eyes stared at him balefully, then the Minotaur turned away, misting the air with a snort of disdain.

'Yes, he is quite the specimen isn't he?' Rook noticed Fletcher staring. 'Caliban has a fulfilment level of eleven, so he should be able to handle any unruly demons with ease. You have been warned.'

The Inquisitor continued on, walking around the arena, his hands clasped behind his back.

'If you step out of the arena, you lose. If your demon is knocked unconscious or leaves the arena, you will lose. If you kill the demon of your opponent, you will be disqualified and also expelled. We do not fight to the death here, and demons are a precious commodity. So, warn them to be cautious. They may injure, but not maim. They may hurt, but not kill.'

'What about us, can we kill?' Tarquin sneered from the

sidelines. He was seated on one of the dismantled platforms, stroking one of Trebius's heads.

'No, the same rules apply as they did in your last match, Master Tarquin,' Rook said, smiling at the young noble. 'If you land a spell or a sword cut powerful enough to be deemed a killing blow, you win. The barrier spell will prevent you from being shocked, burned or cut, although it will hurt like hell if you're hit. As I'm sure you are aware, Tarquin, after you finished with the elf.'

'She did seem to be in an awful lot of pain,' Tarquin smirked. 'But I soon put her out of her misery. I'm sympathetic that way.'

'Come on, let's get this over with,' Fletcher growled through gritted teeth. Othello was already limping to the side of the arena.

'Begin!' Rook shrieked.

Fletcher gave Rook a cool smile and watched as Othello clambered out of the arena and dropped on the floor.

'Oh, no,' Tarquin shouted with exaggerated dramatics. 'I was *so* hoping to fight with the half-man. Defeating two subhumans in one day; wouldn't that have been a treat.'

'Shut your filthy mouth and come and fight me, Tarquin. Let's get the final started, right now.'

Tarquin rolled his eyes and strode into the arena.

'Oh, very well. Let's get on with it.'

'Are the barriers up?' Scipio asked, holding up his hand.

'They are, Provost,' said a noble from the crowd.

'In that ca—'

'Begin!' Rook screamed.

Tarquin was already hurling fireballs before Fletcher even heard Rook's voice. He ducked behind a rock just in time, feeling the heat as one singed his hair.

'Ignatius, hide!' Fletcher whispered, sending the Salamander darting off into the jumble of rocks. Trebius was a powerful demon, but a well-placed fireball from Ignatius could end the battle there and then. Ignatius just needed to avoid his serpentine heads.

A kinetic ball slammed into the rock, crumbling the other side.

'Come out, Fletcher, I want to play,' Tarquin yelled.

'I'm just getting warmed up,' Fletcher yelled back, firing up an oval shield with a blast of mana. He could feel his reserves draining out of him. He knew from his studies that Hydras had very high mana levels. If he and Tarquin matched blow for blow, it would not end well.

He rolled out from behind the rock, sprinting for the cover of the fallen pillar. His shield crackled as a fireball slammed into it, but it was a small one, not nearly enough to knock him off his feet.

'Try this one for size,' Tarquin shouted, flinging a second from behind his back.

The fireball hit the shield like a battering ram, knocking Fletcher flying. As he scrambled to get up, Tarquin whipped another into the shield, blasting him back into the dirt.

'Come on; I thought you were going to make it interesting,' Tarquin laughed, as Fletcher huddled behind a rock. 'At least drag it out a bit. Trebius, find the Salamander. I want to *injure*!'

Fletcher took the opportunity to strap on his eyeglass. Ignatius was on the other side of the arena, trying to sneak up behind Trebius. The task was near impossible, with the three heads covering all angles.

'Go for it, Ignatius,' Fletcher whispered. 'You can take him.'

The Salamander darted out, haring towards the Hydra. He leaped from rock to rock, avoiding the heads as they snapped at him with vicious intent. With one last lunge, Ignatius skidded below Trebius, unleashing a tornado of flame against his unprotected underside.

Trebius roared as the fire scorched his flesh. He spun and stamped, but Ignatius was tenacious, weaving through the dancing claws and lashing the demon with tongues of flame.

'Enough!' Tarquin roared, pointing his finger at the milling demons. A kinetic ball flew under Trebius, knocking Ignatius head over tail into the centre of the arena. The demon lay there, like a broken toy on a nursery floor.

'I believe this match is finished,' Rook laughed, as the Minotaur shambled over and gave Ignatius a tentative prod with his hoof.

'Hear hear,' Zacharias shouted from the crowd.

Trebius hissed, stomping towards the fallen demon. He stopped a few feet away, lowering his three heads and flicking forked tongues over the prone figure.

But Fletcher felt no sorrow, no disappointment. He could sense Ignatius's mind, his intentions.

'That's right, Ignatius,' Fletcher breathed. 'Fight dirty. Gentlemen's fighting is for gentlemen.'

Fletcher absorbed the shield back into his body. With the manoeuvre he was about to do, he was only going to have one shot at this. It flew in the face of everything Arcturus had taught them about duelling. But it was a risk well worth taking.

'All right, Tarquin. Let's see how you like being hit by all three barrels at once,' Fletcher muttered, powering up his three

383

attack-spell fingers. 'I hope you're ready, Ignatius.'

Fletcher leaped to his feet and sprinted full tilt across the arena. Ignatius burst into life with a screech, blasting upwards with a wave of roaring flame.

The Hydra bellowed and reared on its back legs, then came crashing down at Ignatius with deadly force. A split second before he was crushed, Ignatius dissipated into white light, infused through the pentacle on Fletcher's palm.

Realising what Fletcher had done, Tarquin threw up a hasty shield. It was just in time, as Fletcher fired a spiral of lightning, fire and kinetic energy that sent Tarquin skidding back to the very edge of the arena, his feet leaving deep furrows in the earth.

The shield cracked and buckled, but Tarquin was just managing to hold on, feeding thick ribbons of white light to repair the damage. Fletcher doubled the power of the attack, flooding his body with mana and pushing it into the twisting corkscrew of energy that held Tarquin at bay. His fingers seared with pain and the air around the beam distorted and hummed with intensity, forks of lightning shattering rocks into glittering fragments. The sand below turned into a channel of molten glass, bubbling like lava.

Ignatius was with him now, sending every last ounce of energy and encouragement. Fletcher roared, putting everything he had into one final burst of mana, draining every last drop from their reserves. A shockwave flipped the world on its head as the shield exploded.

He spun and tumbled in the air, buffeted by a spray of dust and rock. Then he was on his back, staring at the ceiling. Darkness overwhelmed him.

53

'Fletcher. Wake up,' Othello's voice seemed to be far away. Someone tapped his face.

'You did it, Fletcher,' Othello whispered. 'You beat him.'

'I won?' Fletcher asked blearily. He opened his eyes.

Othello's face stared down at him, his green eyes sparkling with joy.

'You put us all to shame. Tarquin hit the ceiling when his shield broke, literally. If Zacharias hadn't caught him with a kinetic cushion, he would probably be up here with us now.'

Fletcher sat up and saw they were in the infirmary. Lovett and Sylva lay in the beds next to him, both still and silent. Sariel was curled up beneath Sylva's bed, snoring softly. Valens had settled in the soft fur on the Canid's back, equally oblivious to the world.

'How is she?' Fletcher asked, reaching across the bed and brushing an errant thread of pale hair from the elf's cheek.

'Dame Fairhaven said she is going to be fine. She's going to have to heal on her own though, just like me. Her arm is broken in two places.'

Othello gazed at her with complex emotion in his face, then clutched her hand.

'We couldn't have done it without her, you know. She beat Isadora and weakened Tarquin, at great risk to herself. She could have tapped out, like I did. Instead, she chose to fight, even though she knew she couldn't win,' he murmured.

'She's twice the warrior I am,' Fletcher replied, watching her chest rise and fall.

'It was you two who did it in the end,' Othello said, with a hint of disappointment. 'I wish I could tell my father it was me. I wanted the Forsyths to know it was the dwarves who cost them their victory.'

'Othello, the dwarves gave me the tools I needed to win and if it wasn't for you, I would have used up all my mana fighting Rufus in the semi-final,' Fletcher said, looking the dwarf directly in the eye. 'This was all three of us. Even Seraph played his part; I bet he was no pushover when it came to his fight with Tarquin. I just wish Sylva was awake to celebrate our victory.'

'She will be,' Othello said, rubbing the tiredness from his eyes. 'It's the first thing I'm going to tell her. Hell, she'll probably be offered a commission as soon as she wakes up.'

'I'm sure you will too, Othello. The dwarven recruits are going to need leaders. By reaching the semi-final, I think you proved yourself. Just remember why you came here: to show the world that the dwarves are worthy allies,' Fletcher said.

'That's true,' Othello replied with a grin. 'I didn't think about that. Scipio will definitely let Atilla join Vocans now; he is my twin, after all. The first thing I'm going to do after this is learn how the Inquisition tests for adepts. We will need battlemages in the dwarven battalions.'

'You can count on it. I will bring the subject up at the council meeting straight away, if I can,' Fletcher replied.

He felt a flash of anxiety as he pictured a long table in a dark room, surrounded by the most powerful men in the land. Zacharias would be there, trying to discredit him at every turn. Even with the Forsyth twins beaten, he would still have their father to contend with.

Footsteps echoed in the stairwell, until Seraph's excited face appeared in the doorway.

'Guys, Dame Fairhaven said it was OK for me to come and get you, if you're able. They're going to start handing out commissions soon. Come on!' He disappeared from sight and they could soon hear him running down the stairs.

'Someone fancies his chances,' Othello laughed. 'Help me down, would you? I can't put any weight on my damned leg.'

'I swear, half my life seems to be spent as a crutch for an injured dwarf,' Fletcher joked.

He swung his legs over the bed and stood. There was a rush of dizziness for a moment, but it soon passed after a few deep breaths.

'We must look like a right pair,' Fletcher said, putting his arm around Othello's shoulders. 'I think I'm going to need your help as much as you need mine.'

He winced as he took Othello's weight, his aching body complaining at the effort.

They hobbled down the steps and corridors, stopping to rest every few skips.

'Come on, you can't miss getting made a captain,' Othello said.

At the reminder of his captaincy, the war trophies and weapons that lined the corridors took on a sudden new meaning for Fletcher. Sooner or later, an orc might be swinging one of those fearsome weapons at his head.

The atrium was milling with nobles and generals when they arrived, all of them staring at the pair as they staggered in. Some even had fear in their eyes.

'Pure, unadulterated genius,' Scipio shouted, striding over. 'Tattooing yourself to skip etching altogether; using a scrying stone as an eyeglass. Huge jumps forward in battlemage technology – how on earth did we not think of them before?'

Behind him, Fletcher could see Tarquin being berated by his father, hanging his head in shame. The other noviciates were seated on the low benches brought in from the dining hall, waiting for the commissioning ceremony in silence.

'Rest assured, I will be asking you all about this tattooing business later. Now, General Kavanagh, if you would bring over the papers so we can get Fletcher all signed up. When is the King's council, next month? We will need to get a tutor in to teach him about Hominum's politics before then; as a commoner he won't know a thing.' Scipio fussed about Fletcher like an overprotective mother, brushing the dust from his shoulders.

Fletcher stood up straight and surveyed the room, meeting the eyes of the generals and nobility with a steady gaze. With pride, he considered what he and his friends had achieved.

Sylva and Othello had proved to the upper echelons of Hominum that their peoples were a force to be reckoned with. Seraph's elevation to the nobility would be a smooth one, now that he had demonstrated his tenacity in the arena. As for Fletcher, he was just glad to have kept the council seat from the Forsyths and secured himself a bright future. He only wished Berdon was there to see it.

He squeezed Othello's shoulder and nudged him, pointing at the generals and nobles.

'One of those men is going to give you a commission today. Do you have any preference?'

'As long as it's not Zacharias or the Favershams,' Othello chuckled back. 'You should have seen the look on their faces when I beat Rufus.'

The main doors slammed open, sending a gust of wind rushing through the atrium. Three figures stood silhouetted against the light outside, before the oak doors were slammed shut again.

As Fletcher's eyes adjusted to the darkness, he was alarmed to see that the three men were Rook, Sergeant Turner and Sergeant Murphy. The Inquisitor smirked as he walked towards them.

Fletcher's heart dropped when he saw Turner was clutching a pair of manacles in his hand.

'Othello!' Fletcher gasped. 'The Pinkertons!'

'What is the meaning of this?' Scipio blustered, as the Pinkertons pushed their way through the surrounding nobles. 'This is a private event.'

'We're here for him,' Murphy said, nodding towards Fletcher and Othello. 'We have an urgent warrant for his arrest.'

Fletcher stepped in front of the dwarf, swaying on his feet.

'If you want him, you'll have to go through me first.'

Murphy stepped forward and smiled maliciously.

'Fletcher Wulf,' he announced, snapping the manacles on to Fletcher's wrists. 'You are under arrest for the attempted murder of Didric Cavell.'

Fletcher froze, as the meaning of the words sunk in.

'Get your hands off him,' Othello shouted, trying to put himself between them. 'This is a mistake!'

Turner gave Othello an open-handed slap, knocking him to the ground.

'Watch yourself, dwarf, or we'll have you on obstruction of justice,' he spat, prodding Othello with his foot. Rook stepped over the fallen dwarf and gripped Fletcher's collar, bringing him in close.

'This little jaunt is over, Fletcher,' Rook snarled, his breath hot in Fletcher's ear. 'You're going back to Pelt.'

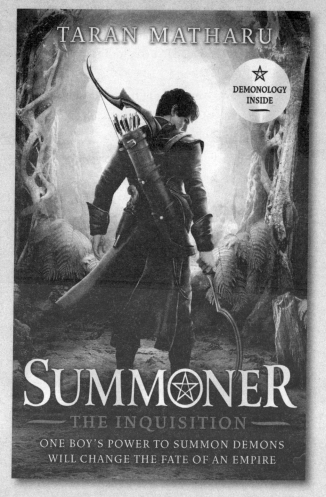

1

Fletcher opened his eyes, but all he saw was darkness. He groaned and nudged Ignatius, whose claw was splayed across his chin. The demon complained with a sleepy mewl, before tumbling on to the cold stone beneath them.

'Good morning. Or whatever time it is,' Fletcher mumbled, flaring a wyrdlight into existence. It hung in the air like a miniature sun, spinning gently.

The room was bathed in cold, blue light, revealing the cramped, windowless cell that was paved with smooth flagstones. In the corner lay a latrine, a simple hole in the ground that was covered by a jagged piece of slate. Fletcher stared at the large iron door embedded in the wall opposite him.

As if on cue, there was a rattle as the small flap at the bottom of the door eased back and a mailed hand pushed through the gap. It groped around for the empty bucket that sat beside the door. The sound of gurgling followed and the bucket was replaced, sloshing with water. Fletcher watched the flap expectantly, then groaned as he heard the echo of footsteps walking away.

'No food again, buddy,' Fletcher said, rubbing a crestfallen Ignatius under his chin.

It wasn't unusual; sometimes the gaoler just didn't bother bringing food. Fletcher's stomach growled, but he ignored it and reached for the loose stone he kept beside his bed to scratch another notch in the wall. Though it was hard to tell the time with no natural light, he assumed that he received food and water – or sometimes, like today, just water – once a day. He didn't need to count the hundreds of notches on the wall to know how long he had been imprisoned – he knew them by heart now.

'One year,' Fletcher sighed, settling back into the straw. 'Happy anniversary.'

He lay there contemplating the reason for his imprisonment. It had all started that one night, when his childhood nemesis, Didric, had cornered him in a crypt and tried to murder him, gloating about his father's plans to turn the entire village of Pelt into a prison.

And then came Ignatius, from out of nowhere, burning Didric as he advanced, giving Fletcher time to escape. The little demon had risked his own life to save Fletcher's, even in the first moments of their bond. In the aftermath, Fletcher had become a fugitive, for he knew Didric's family would lie through their teeth to frame him for attempted murder. His only consolation was that if it hadn't happened, he might never have made it to Vocans Academy.

Had it really been two whole years since Ignatius entered his life, and he first set foot in that ancient castle? He could remember his last moments there so clearly. His best friend

Othello had earned the respect of the generals and convinced his fellow dwarves not to rebel against the Hominum Empire. Sylva had cemented the peace between their races and had proven herself and the other elves worthy allies. Even Seraph, the first commoner to be elevated to nobility in over a thousand years, had impressed his fellow nobles during the Tournament. Perhaps most satisfying of all, the Forsyth plot to create a new war with the elves and dwarves, in order to profit their weapons business, had been foiled completely. It had all been so perfect.

Until Fletcher's past came back to haunt him.

Ignatius gave Fletcher an owlish blink from his amber eyes, sensing his master's despondency. He nudged Fletcher's hand with the end of his snout. Fletcher gave him a halfhearted swipe, but the demon dodged out of the way and nipped the tip of his finger.

'All right, all right.' Fletcher grinned at the boisterous demon, the pain distracting him from his misery. 'Let's get back to training. I wonder what spell we should practise today?'

He reached under the pile of straw that was his bedding and removed the two books that had kept him sane over the past year. He didn't know who had hidden them there for him, only that they had taken a great risk in doing so. Fletcher was eternally grateful to his mysterious benefactor; without the books he would have been driven mad with boredom. There were only so many games that he and Ignatius could play in the tight confines of the cell.

The first was the standard book of spellcraft, the same one they had all used in Arcturus's lessons. It was slim, for it contained only a few hundred symbols and the proper techniques for etching them. Before, Fletcher had only been vaguely familiar with them, so he could pass his exams – preferring to focus on perfecting the four main battle-spells. Now, he was able to picture every single symbol from memory, and could etch them in his sleep.

The second book was thick, so much so that whoever had hidden it had removed the leather cover to make it more easily concealable in the straw. It was James Baker's journal, the book that had started Fletcher on his path to becoming a trained battlemage. Within its pages, Fletcher had found a dozen new spells, diligently copied by the late summoner from the walls of ancient orcish ruins. Moreover, Baker had studied scores of orcish demons, detailing their relative power, abilities and statistics. Now Fletcher was an expert too. Perhaps most fascinating of all, Baker had compiled all of his knowledge of orcish culture, including their strategies and their weapons, in the journal. It was a veritable treasure trove of knowledge, which Fletcher had devoured in a few days, only to immediately begin again and hunt for details he might have missed.

These two volumes were all that distracted him from the deafening silence of the outside world. Every night, he dreamed of his friends, wondering where they might be. Did they battle on the front lines while he rotted in the bowels of the earth? Had they been killed by an orcish javelin or a Forsyth dagger?

But the most torturous thought of all was knowing that his adoptive father Berdon was close by, in the village above him. He remembered when the prison transport had brought him back to Pelt in the dead of night. He had peered through the cracks in the armoured wagon, desperate to catch a glimpse of his childhood home. But before he could get a proper look, the gaolers threw a sack over his head and dragged him away.

As Fletcher lapsed into miserable silence once more, Ignatius growled restlessly before snorting a tongue of flame that singed the straw beneath them.

'Wow, we are impatient today!' Fletcher exclaimed, powering up a tattooed finger with a blast of mana. 'OK, you asked for it. Let's see how you like the telekinesis spell.'

He allowed a thin stream of mana through his fingertip, the spiral symbol glowing violet until a strip of air shimmered above it. Ignatius began to back away, but Fletcher whipped his hand at the mischievous demon, curling the ribbon of energy around his belly and flinging him upwards. The demon splayed his claws and dug them into the ceiling, showering Fletcher with a trickle of dust. Before Fletcher had time to react, Ignatius hurled himself down, twisting in midair like a cat with his claws and tailspike pointed at Fletcher's face. It was only through a desperate roll that Fletcher avoided it, then spun on his heels to find the room cast in darkness. Ignatius had slashed the wyrdlight during his attack, snuffing it out like a candle.

'So, that's how you want to play it,' Fletcher said, powering up his index finger, the one without a tattoo. This time, he etched in the air, using one of the rarer symbols he had learned from Baker's journal. He twisted his finger so it was pointed directly at his face.

The cat's-eye symbol looked almost exactly like its namesake, a thin oval within a circle. Through trial and error, Fletcher had learned the spell had no effect until its light was shined into his retinas.

The glowing symbol gave away his position, as did the flash of yellow that soon followed, but Fletcher rolled to the side so Ignatius would lose him in the darkness. He could feel his eyes slowly changing, his pupils elongating into feline slits. It was not long before Fletcher's vision brightened and he could make out Ignatius's figure, crawling towards his previous position like a lion stalking a gazelle. Though Ignatius had far better night-vision than Fletcher did, in the pitch black of the cell even the demon was struggling to navigate.

'Gotcha!' Fletcher yelled, diving across the room and bundling the demon into his arms. They tumbled back into the straw, and Fletcher laughed uproariously at the demon's barks of protest.

The door burst open and the room filled with light, blinding Fletcher's sensitive eyes. He scrabbled to hide the books beneath the straw, but a boot kicked out, slamming into the side of his head and throwing him against the wall.

'Not so fast,' a voice rasped.

There was the tell-tale click of a flintlock being pulled back and Fletcher felt the cold metal of the weapon's barrel pushed against his forehead. As the effects of the spell faded, he could make out a hazy, hooded figure crouched beside him, holding an elegant pistol.

'One twitch from you, and I blast you into oblivion,' said the voice. It was hoarse, like a man dying of thirst.

'OK,' Fletcher said, slowly raising his hands.

'Ah-ah,' the figure tutted, pressing the muzzle harder against his temple. 'Are you deaf? I've heard of what you can do with those tattooed fingers. Keep your hands by your side.'

Fletcher hesitated, aware that this would probably be his best chance of escape. The gunman gave Fletcher a husky sigh of exasperation.

'Rubens, give him a little taste of your sting.'

Fletcher caught a flutter from the depths of the man's hood, then a bright red Mite buzzed out and alighted on his neck. He felt a sharp pain, then a cold sensation spreading through his body.

'Now I know you won't be playing any tricks,' the figure croaked, standing up so he was silhouetted against the torchlight from the open doorway. 'Speaking of which, where is that Salamander of yours?'

Fletcher tried to twist his head, but it seemed locked in place. At the mention of the word Salamander, Ignatius stirred from beneath him, and Fletcher knew that the demon was preparing to attack. He quelled Ignatius's intentions with a stern pulse through their mental link. Even if they managed to overpower the man, Fletcher wouldn't be able to crawl out of the cell door, let alone pull off an escape.

'Ah, he's in the straw there. Well, keep him quiet, if you want to keep your brains inside your skull. It would be such a shame to kill you, after all the preparations we have made.'

'Pr-pr-preparations?' Fletcher managed to stutter, his tongue clumsy and numb from the Mite's venom.

'For your trial,' the figure replied, holding out a hand for Rubens to perch on. 'We delayed it as long as we could, but it seems your friends have been very persistent in their petitions to the king. A shame.'

The figure stowed the Mite within the confines of his hood once more, as if he could not bear to be apart from him. The skin of his hand was smooth, almost feminine, with carefully manicured fingernails. The man's boots were made from hand-stitched calfskin, with fashionable, figure-hugging trousers above them. Even the hooded jacket was made from black leather of the finest quality. Fletcher could tell the stranger was a wealthy young man, most likely the firstborn son of a noble.

'I will allow you one more question, then I must take you to the courtroom. Take your time, so the paralysis can wear off. I don't want to have to carry you there.'

Fletcher's mind flashed to his friends, to Berdon, and to the state of the war. But he had no way of knowing if the stranger would have the answers he sought. Did they know each other? He pictured the other summoners that he had met at Vocans, but none of them had a hoarse voice. Could it be Tarquin, playing a cruel trick on him? One thing was for sure: his opponent would keep the upper hand as long as he remained anonymous.

'Who. Are. You?' Fletcher asked, forcing each word out through numbed lips.

The fact that he could speak at all meant that Rubens had pricked him with only a low dose of venom. He still had a fighting chance.

'Haven't you worked it out yet?' the stranger rasped. 'That *is* disappointing. I thought you would have guessed by now. Still, I do look quite different than when we last spoke, so you are hardly to blame.'

The figure crouched again, leaning forward until Fletcher's vision was filled with the dark confines of his hood. Slowly, the man pulled it back, revealing his face.

'Recognise me now, Fletcher?' Didric hissed.

DON'T MISS THE REST OF THE AMAZING SUMMONER SERIES...

THE ULTIMATE BATTLE FOR
SURVIVAL IS ABOUT TO BEGIN ...

CONTENDER

THE CHOSEN

TARAN MATHARU

DON'T MISS THE EPIC NEW TRILOGY FROM
BESTSELLING AUTHOR, TARAN MATHARU

DEMON⛧LOGY

MITE

Mites are the most common demon in Hominum's part of the ether and are the food source of many demonic species. Though there are several species of smaller insect-like Mites, Scarab Mites are the most powerful of the Mite genus. These demons appear as large, flying beetles and vary from dull brown to brightly coloured. When full grown, a Scarab develops a weapon to complement their powerful mandibles: a nasty stinger, which can temporarily paralyse their enemy. Many summoners use Mites as scouts to explore the ether before sending a more powerful demon in to hunt.

SUMMONER MASTERS:
Rory, Genevieve, Lovett

CLASSIFICATION: Arthropidae
SUMMONING LEVEL: 1
BASE MANA LEVEL: 7
MANA ABILITIES: None
NATURAL SKILLS: Flying
RARITY: Very common
DIET: Omnivore
HABITAT: Most land & freshwater habitats
TEMPERAMENT: Varied
ATTACK/DEFENCE 1: Paralytic sting **2:** Mandibles

LUTRA

This dog-sized demon appears very similar to an overgrown otter, with a tail spiked like a morning star and two large incisors. They are often found in the lakes and rivers of the ether, as they are especially fond of swimming.

SUMMONER MASTERS:
Rufus, Atlas

CLASSIFICATION: Rodentia

SUMMONING LEVEL: 4

BASE MANA LEVEL: 24

MANA ABILITIES: None

NATURAL SKILLS: Swimming

RARITY: Common

DIET: Omnivore

HABITAT: Fresh water & nearby land

TEMPERAMENT: Playful

ATTACK/DEFENCE 1: Spiked tail

2: Buck teeth

SHRIKE

These bird-like demons migrate annually across Hominum's part of the ether, making entry extremely dangerous for one week of the year. Well known for their long black feathers, their wingspan is as wide as a man is tall, with each wing's endmost feathers tipped with bleached white. A Shrike's beak is hooked, with a bright red wattle underneath its neck and a red ridge along the top of its head like that of a rooster.

SUMMONER MASTERS: Amber

CLASSIFICATION: Aves
SUMMONING LEVEL: 4
BASE MANA LEVEL: 25
MANA ABILITIES: None
NATURAL SKILLS: Flying
RARITY: Migratory
DIET: Carnivore
HABITAT: Varied
TEMPERAMENT: Vicious
ATTACK/DEFENCE 1: Talons 2: Beak

SALAMANDER

Salamanders are extremely rare and do not exist in Hominum's part of the ether. Not much is known about their habitat or history, though there is evidence that Orcs have captured them in the past. They are the size of a ferret, with a similarly lithe body and limbs long enough to lope rather than scuttle like a lizard. Their skin is the colour of dark burgundy, with eyes that are large, amber and round like those of an owl. Salamanders have no teeth to speak of, but their snout ends sharply, almost like a river turtle's beak.

SUMMONER MASTERS: *Fletcher*

CLASSIFICATION: *Reptilia*
SUMMONING LEVEL: 5
BASE MANA LEVEL: 45
MANA ABILITIES: *Fire breathing, Healing*
NATURAL SKILLS: *Agility, Climbing, Fire Proof*

RARITY: *Endangered*
DIET: *Carnivore*
HABITAT: *Unknown*
TEMPERAMENT: *Protective*
ATTACK/DEFENCE 1: *Fire breath*
2: *Tail spike* 3: *Claws* 4: *Bite*

SHRIKE MATRIARCH

The Shrike Matriarch is the maternal leader of a Shrike flock. Almost twice as large as the average shrike, these demons are not to be underestimated. It is not unknown for a Matriarch to carry off juvenile Canids, should the opportunity present itself.

CLASSIFICATION: *Aves*
SUMMONING LEVEL: 6
BASE MANA LEVEL: 38
MANA ABILITIES: None
NATURAL SKILLS: Flying
RARITY: Migratory
DIET: Carnivore
HABITAT: Varied
TEMPERAMENT: Vicious
ATTACK/DEFENCE
1: Talons 2: Beak

BARKLING

This badger-shaped demon has tough skin almost indistinguishable from bark, which it uses to camouflage itself in the jungles of the ether. Although relatively common, their tendency to hide at the top of tree trunks, and the ridge of poisonous spines they can shoot from their backs, make them difficult to capture. Their diet consists solely of vegetation, which they crush in their ridge-filled mouths.

SUMMONER MASTERS: *Seraph*

CLASSIFICATION: *Viridae*

SUMMONING LEVEL: *6*

BASE MANA LEVEL: *45*

MANA ABILITIES: *None*

NATURAL SKILLS: *Camouflage, Spines*

RARITY: *Average*

DIET: *Herbivore*

HABITAT: *Forest*

TEMPERAMENT: *Calm*

ATTACK/DEFENCE

1: Paralytic spine attack 2: Tough skin

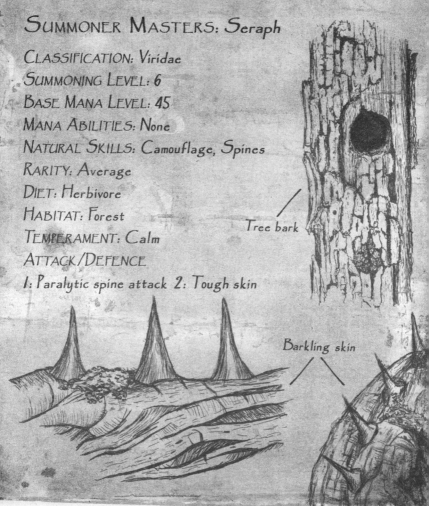

Tree bark

Barkling skin

VULPID

A close cousin to the Canid, this slightly smaller, fox-like
demon has three tails and is known for its agility and speed.

SUMMONER MASTERS: Penelope

CLASSIFICATION: Canidae
SUMMONING LEVEL: 6
BASE MANA LEVEL: 42
MANA ABILITIES: None
NATURAL SKILLS: Acute sense of
smell, Heightened hearing, Agility
RARITY: Uncommon
DIET: Carnivore
HABITAT: Most land habitats
TEMPERAMENT: Loyal
ATTACK/DEFENCE 1: Bite
2: Claws

CANID

A dog-like demon with four eyes, lethal claws, a fox-like tail and a thick ridge of fur down its spine. These demons range in size from that of a large dog to a small pony, depending on the breed.

SUMMONER MASTERS: *Arcturus, Sylva*

CLASSIFICATION: *Canidae*
SUMMONING LEVEL: *7*
BASE MANA LEVEL: *48*
MANA ABILITIES: *None*
NATURAL SKILLS: *Acute sense of smell, Heightened hearing*
RARITY: *Common*
DIET: *Carnivore*
HABITAT: *Most land habitats*
TEMPERAMENT: *Loyal*
ATTACK/DEFENCE 1: *Bite* 2: *Claws*

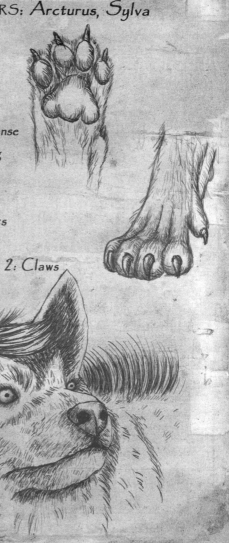

FELID

This bipedal cat demon has four eyes and the stature and intelligence of a jungle chimpanzee. Their breeds vary from leonine, tigrine and leopine, bearing resemblances to lions, tigers and leopards respectively.

SUMMONER MASTERS: *Scipio*, Isadora*
*Scipio's first Felid died. He has recently been gifted a new Felid kit.

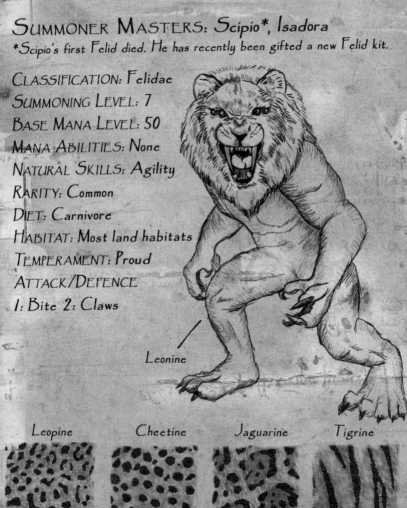

CLASSIFICATION: Felidae
SUMMONING LEVEL: 7
BASE MANA LEVEL: 50
MANA ABILITIES: None
NATURAL SKILLS: Agility
RARITY: Common
DIET: Carnivore
HABITAT: Most land habitats
TEMPERAMENT: Proud
ATTACK/DEFENCE
1: Bite 2: Claws

Leonine

| Leopine | Cheetine | Jaguarine | Tigrine |

ANUBID

This rare demon stands on two legs and has the head of a jackal. Though their bodies are rangy and gaunt, they are known for their agility and speed. Unusually for demons related to the common Canid, this demon has only two eyes.

SUMMONER MASTERS:
Malik and his father, Baybars

CLASSIFICATION: Canidae
SUMMONING LEVEL: 8
BASE MANA LEVEL: 53
MANA ABILITIES: None
NATURAL SKILLS: Agility,
Acute sense of smell,
Heightened hearing
RARITY: Very rare
DIET: Carnivore

HABITAT: Arid, desert habitats
TEMPERAMENT: Proud
ATTACK/DEFENCE 1: Bite
2: Claws

Lycan

Another distant cousin to the Canid, the Lycan appears much like an Anubid, with a thicker, bulkier body and the head of a wolf. Though stronger than their cousins, they are less intelligent and difficult to control.

Summoner Masters: Major Goodwin

CLASSIFICATION: Canidae
SUMMONING LEVEL: 8
BASE MANA LEVEL: 49
MANA ABILITIES: None
NATURAL SKILLS: Acute sense of smell
RARITY: Very rare
DIET: Carnivore
HABITAT: Most land habitats
TEMPERAMENT: Savage
ATTACK/DEFENCE
1: Bite 2: Claws

GOLEM

This rare, elemental-class demon can be made from many different types of minerals including clay, mud and sand, the most powerful of which is stone. Juvenile Golems begin at only a few feet tall, but over time can grow to over ten feet. They appear roughly humanoid, though they only have one large digit and an opposable thumb.

SUMMONER MASTERS: *Othello*

CLASSIFICATION: *Elemental*
SUMMONING LEVEL: *8*
BASE MANA LEVEL: *60*
MANA ABILITIES: *None*
NATURAL SKILLS: *Strength, tough skin*
RARITY: *Endangered*
DIET: *Herbivore*
HABITAT: *Mountainous regions*
TEMPERAMENT: *Protective*
ATTACK/DEFENCE 1: *Fists*
2: *Kick* 3: *Tough skin*

HYDRA

A Hydra is a large demon with three snake-like heads on long, flexible necks. Its body is similar to that of a monitor lizard, at around the same size of a large Canid. These demons were once more common in Hominum's part of the ether, but are now extremely rare.

SUMMONER MASTERS: *Tarquin*

CLASSIFICATION: *Reptilia*
SUMMONING LEVEL: *8*
BASE MANA LEVEL: *55*
MANA ABILITIES: *None*
NATURAL SKILLS: *Three-way attack*
RARITY: *Endangered*
DIET: *Carnivore*
HABITAT: *Most land habitats*
TEMPERAMENT: *Cruel*
ATTACK/DEFENCE 1: *Bite* **2:** *Claws*

GRIFFIN

This rare demon will occasionally stray into Hominum's part of the ether. Horse-sized, it has the body, tail and back legs of a lion and the head, wings and talons of an eagle.

SUMMONER MASTES: *Lovett*

CLASSIFICATION: *Aves*
SUMMONING LEVEL: *10*
BASE MANA LEVEL: *65*
MANA ABILITIES: *None*
NATURAL SKILLS: *Flying*
RARITY: *Migratory*
DIET: *Omnivore*
HABITAT: *Varied*
TEMPERAMENT: *Honourable*
ATTACK/DEFENCE 1: *Talons* 2: *Beak*

MINOTAUR

These humanoid demons are tall, hairy and muscular. They have the head of a bull and cloven hooves for feet. Unlike the Golem, they have clawed hands, which are capable of manipulating weapons, though teaching one to use them is a difficult task. It is very rare to see one of these in Hominum's part of the ether.

SUMMONER MASTERS: Rook

CLASSIFICATION: Caprid
SUMMONING LEVEL: 11
BASE MANA LEVEL: 72
MANA ABILITIES: None
NATURAL SKILLS: Strength
RARITY: Very rare
DIET: Herbivore

HABITAT: Most land habitats
TEMPERAMENT: Savage
ATTACK/DEFENCE 1: Horns 2: Claws 3: Fists

TARAN MATHARU

was born in London in 1990 and found a passion for reading at a very early age. His love for stories developed into a desire to create his own, writing his first book at nine years old. At twenty-two, while taking time off to travel, Taran began to write *Summoner*, which became an online sensation, reaching over three million reads in less than six months. Taran is now a full-time author, and spends his time travelling the world and writing. The Summoner series has been translated into 15 languages and is a *New York Times* Bestseller.

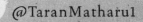 @TaranMatharu1